The Colour of Love

❧ Signature Edition ❧

Anne Hemingway

Printed in Victoria, Canada

National Library of Canada Cataloguing in Publication

Hemingway, Anne
The colour of love / Anne Hemingway.
ISBN 1-4120-0656-2
I. Title.
PS3608.E45C69 2003   813'.6   C2003-903893-9

TRAFFORD

This book was published *on-demand* in cooperation with Trafford Publishing. On-demand publishing is a unique process and service of making a book available for retail sale to the public taking advantage of on-demand manufacturing and Internet marketing. **On-demand publishing** includes promotions, retail sales, manufacturing, order fulfilment, accounting and collecting royalties on behalf of the author.

Suite 6E, 2333 Government St., Victoria, B.C. V8T 4P4, CANADA
Phone   250-383-6864   Toll-free 1-888-232-4444 (Canada & US)
Fax   250-383-6804   E-mail   sales@trafford.com
Web site www.trafford.com TRAFFORD PUBLISHING IS A DIVISION OF TRAFFORD HOLDINGS LTD.
Trafford Catalogue #03-1026   www.trafford.com/robots/03-1026.html

10   9   8   7   6   5   4   3   2   1

I know what I had Agreed to when I in simple childlike trust and faith said to you. *"I will write Your story Father, but if Your Holy Spirit isn't in it to help me, I will not do it."* It's almost as if I could see you smiling down on me saying. *"Child, I wouldn't have it any other way."* All I can say is this. I wouldn't trade what I have gone through in my journey through this project for anything in the world! Thank you Father for letting me express myself in Sarah, who is my past, my sunset, and in Lisa, my present, my sunrise. I love You with all that I am. I have been broken, emptied, only to have Your Gentle Hands remold and reshape my life Anew again. You told me that I would not recognize myself when You finished with me. And as always
Father.... You were right! To You be All the Glory, Honor, and all the Praise, and Thanksgiving forever Amen.   *Love, Your Handmaiden. Anne.*

To Mrs. Jarry Turner. What can I say about you my fellow maidservant! No one would've been there for me like you have been. I remember your excitement when I first told you about my project. Your sweet face lit up like the fourth of July. You opened up to me your home, shared your children with me. Took care of me after my surgery in February of 2001. I'll never forget the look on your face when I handed You your first copy of my book. That expression was etched in my heart forever. Thank you dear sister. I can hardly hold back the tears as I give you what's due you. I Love you.

To Ms. Alyce Marshall. You are about the most down to earth person that I've ever had the pleasure in knowing. You too opened up your home to me while the second phase of this project was underway. The play would not have been the same without your prayers, and encouragement That kept me going, when I felt that I was running out of steam! Love you much girl!

To Ms. Linda Walls. Hey Ms. Thang! What a hip little one you are! You were the blessing that God brought my way. My little Internet buddy! Thanks sweetheart for all the research information that you Supplied for me. Your time and patience is invaluable to me! Love you dearly. I'll see what I can do about that Oscar thing ok?

To My Pastors Dan and Lois Martineau and the Entire Congregation of Glad Tidings Assembly Church Of Battle Creek, Michigan. My Spiritual Mom and Dad. So much I've learned from you. It was your 1997 Sermon on "Enlarging your Capacity." That struck a very raw nerve in my spirit. I saw through your teachings, that there is nothing too big that I can ask God for that He is not already more willing to give me, than I am to receive it. Do you even remember that sermon? I can see you now, you had that look on your face again. (smile). Thank you for mentoring me in the Gospel. I love you both. Thank you for your example of Determination, and unwavering faith. Nothing is impossible to me!

To Mrs. Barbara Boyd. You too along with my friends Jarry, and Alyce also opened up
Your home to me and allowed me to talk your ears off about my dreams. I have some more glue if they fall off again! (smile). Thank you for the many winter nights that we shared laughing and just being plain silly! Wow! That felt real good to me. We should do that more often. I had fun! Whooo!

To Mrs. Valerie Partridge of Professional Skin Therapy. How could I forget my buddy. You many times Than you know were the highlight of all my weeks that I had a session with you. Do you remember those Cherishable Oprah moments? God Lady! I have learned so much from you in those times. And you do Good skin too! When's my next appointment girl! I love you dearly.

And to all of my many other readers, thank you for understanding me, and encouraging me through all of this. For it has not been an easy road for me to travel. And I still have a long way to go. But along the way. God will bring a host of new travelers that will make my journey bitter as well as sweet. But such is life. I would say that as I have been writing both my book and my play, my mind has been pulled in several different directions, all with memories that have been hurtful reliving such an awful past, that only the hand of God could have brought me from. As well as memories that He gave me with all of you. Which made the journey well worth it. I have grown much now, and am still growing. My relationshipWith God has deepened much since He

4

took me by the hand May 21, 2000 and lead me on my way down
The path of Love. I experienced much hurt, devastation,
confusion. And a myriad of other things. The joy,
The sorrow, sadness. Faith like I've never known before. What a
time this has been for me. And to think I haven't even scratched
the surface yet! All I can say in closing is that all of my future
readers have their Minds, as well as their hearts and lives
touched, and transformed by this simple message of love. And
see the devastating effects of racisim, and that with God's help.
May we all conform to His will in our Churches, Schools, homes.
And our Communities. May we realize that if we truly claim to
love our Fellowman, and Brother and Sister in Christ. Then we
should behave like this is so. If God shows no partiality, then
why do we? The wall of Racial predjudice MUST be Destroyed! If
you believe that. Then repeat the story's motto with me......

TRUE LOVE SEES NO COLOUR, NO COLOUR AT ALL......

In His Love and mine.

Anne Hemingway.

And Last but certainly not least. I want to extend a special thank
you to Mrs. Coretta Scott King. My dearest Lady, it is with much
humility that I write these words to you. What is it that the Bible
Says about the Soul Winners Crown? That it is the most
beautiful of God's rewards to those who have withstood the
persecution, stood against terrible opposition even unto the point
of death itself to see those who would've never been birthed into
God's Kingdom if it were not for them. You and Dr, King are

among those who I believe will wear such a Crown. What a Living Testamony you are to this day for what you have survived. You remind me of a woman whom God has given a spirit of Deborah of the Old Testament. A woman of great strength, a woman of great courage, yet a woman with a meek and gentle Spirit which in the sight of God is of a great price. Without even knowing me you have birthed in me A wisdom, a strength, and a burning desire to see God's Dream for Mankind come to pass in this time Before His Son Jesus calls us from this Earth. Thank you Mrs. King for helping me to see that this Journey that God has chosen me for is not just for me, but for the many souls waiting to hear a soft gentle Word, and touch of His Hand, transform their lives in a way that will be unforgettable to them. In closing, I would like to extend a deeper thanks for the way that you showed me how to trust and lean totally on God no matter what I face in life. And Ma'mam, I have suffered much. But yet I held fast to the Promises of God's Word. I failed Him many times in my learning to Know Him. But He has never failed me in allowing me to get to know Him. I pray that one day that I may get to meet you and just sit in your presence and learn more, as I am still developing as a woman. I have not arrived at the totality of complete Womanhood yet. May I learn from the deep richness of your wisdom, and your incredible life experiences. I am sure that even one passage from your life would change my life forever! I need that! It is with that I say with much Respect, adoration, and sincerest humility. May I echo your Husband's words in saying That because of what God has done through him, I can now say. *"Free at last! Free at last. Thank God Almighty, I'm Free at last!"*

Shalom, Anne.

The Colour Of Love
Anne Hemingway
Chap 1
1946.

Laura Nooooooo! Screamed little Jacob as his Mother and sister are taken away from him and his Father. The squad came for them to take them out and kill them all because of overcrowding. Word then came that There was room for two more men in hut twelve, but no room for the women. The squad of three came over to take Laura and her mother Elena from Jacob and his father Caleb. They smiled sadistically as they snatched the mother and daughter away. The officers pushed them out of the tiny hut into the front Yard. Then another officer walked over to Jacob and Caleb ordering them outside as well. He held them Both at gunpoint to watch what would happen next. It was cold, wet and misty out that day. But the chill In the air did not compare to the coldness in the hearts and faces of the Squad members as they prepared to Brutilize Laura and her mother before killing them. "Come here!" shouted the first officer in his language.

He was a man of medium height and build. His voice loud and strong. His expression was cold and demonic. Laura could not move, For terror had seized her entire being. She grips her mother tighter. She could not even speak, fear had snatched her words from her. His anger getting the best of him, he walks over to them and starts to pull Laura by her long brown hair away from her mother. "No! No! Cried Elena. Mommieeee!Mommieeee! Screams Laura, as she struggles to stay within her mother's Arms. No! No! Please No! begged Elena. Laura grabs her mother around her neck pulling from Beneath her clothing a silver necklace with the Star of David hanging from it. The Squad member Becomes even angrier at the girl, her mother tightens her hold on Laura more. They struggle more, and more as both mother and daughter fight to stay together, but the member fights to tear them apart. Just then, the officer holding Jacob and his Father at gunpoint shouted an order to him. Ja! He shouts back.

He then pushes Elena away with his booted foot, while snatching Laura from her mother's grasp. Mommieeee! Papa!, Papa! She screams. The officer flings Laura over to another officer who was standing there waiting for instructions. He seemed to be enjoying himself watching the struggle between Them all. He catches Laura in his arms, then throws her to the ground in the mud. He stood over her, his Face was harden, his chisled features made him look like a creature out of a horror novel. Evil filled his Expression. The member who flung Laura to him now looks at Elena. Just then another officer walked Over to them, he had more ranking than them all. He was their leader. He knew about the situation, and Decided that he would give the orders as to what they would do next. Laura stood there cold and shivering She was hungry earlier, but hunger had long since left her now. Somehow she knew that she her family would never live to see another day much less another meal.   They all felt that connection at that moment. Just then Elena spoke to the officer who was staring at her. "Please, sir please. Not our children! Kill me But save them alive! They are all we have! Please! He just laughed at her cries for mercy for their children. But it was useless. This only hardened his heart more towards them. He looked down at her

On her knees in the mud, her body frail from hunger. Her clothes tattered and hanging, for they were all that she owned. He spoke to her in his language. "Where is your Jew Jesus?" "Let Him save them and you." "Sir please!" she pleaded. "Silence!" He backhands her face. She falls into the mud. All the Squad members laugh out loud. "She's a good pig eh?" He said to his cohorts. He looks up into the Sky the clouds were dark and dreary out that morning. A light drizzle was sprinkling forth from them.

"Where is He?" he grunts at her. "Hey, said one of the officers. A short stout sort've a man, his voice loud and strong. "If He cannot save you, then my friend must kill you." They all laugh again. He slaps Elena, harder this time leaving his handprint on her face. "Elena!" shouted her husband, he bowed his Head and sobbed painfully as he stood there helpless to do anything to help her. The one officer who was holding him and Jacob at gunpoint, takes the butt of his rifle and hits him in the stomach hard, knocking the wind out of him. He falls to the ground gasping for air.   PAPA! Shouted their children. Jacob trying to help his father back to his feet again. Caleb! Shouted Elena. She tries to crawl over to him, but the officer standing next to her, grabs her by her long braid pulling her back over to him. She falls back into the mud Sloshing it all over his uniform. He utters an obscenity at her in his language. He becomes enraged at her, And positions her back on her knees taking three steps back from her. Elena tired, from her torture, hangs Her head down. She begins to mutter something under her breath. The officers were bewildered at what she Was doing. But her family knew that she was praying. He snatched her head up looking at her. She said nothing to him, there was a calm about her. Serenity had overtaken her. A peaceful look filled her expression. He pushes her, she faltered off balance a little. She held her head up to him and laughed in his Face. All the other members including the Leader member himself looked at each other unable to comprehend Elena's actions. She did not behave like a Jew who was about to die. She behaved like Someone who was excited about something. Something that they did not understand at all. She no longer pleaded for her life. But she welcomed her death. She looks over at Laura who was still being held by the officer. "I Love you!" she mouthed to her. Laura mouthing the same back to her. Tears streaming down both their faces. She then looks over at Caleb and Jacob mouthing the same to them too. It would be the last time that she ever told them that. And they knew it as well.

She looks back at the officer who was now standing in front of her. He had cocked his rifle. Elena Lifted her head towards Heaven with her hands folded down in front of her. She closed her eyes. The officer steadied his aim, cracking a sinister grin. Cackling as he slowly pulled the trigger. Elena cries Out her last words, in her Hebrew tongue... *"Adonai Yeshua!"* Lord Jesus! She smiles. The officer then Lets out an ear piercing shriek as he fires two shots into her body. Both hitting her in the chest. "ELENAAAA!" Shouted her husband. Mommieeee!!! Shouted Laura and Jacob. Her body falls forward into the mud. The other officer holding Laura, chuckled out loud. The Leader Officer walked over to Elena, he noticed that she was still breathing, and moving slightly. He reaches into his holster and takes out a small pistol. He fires one last shot into the back of her head. Her body jerked violently. She lay there still, and lifeless. Caleb shuts his eyes tight looking away from her. Laura shakes her head in unbelief. No! no! she cries. Mommy, breathed little Jacob, his eyes unable to take in the horror that Was just displayed before him. Laura stood there in shock staring at Elena as she bled into

9

the mud. The sight of her lying dead in a pool of blood made her sick to her stomach. She grabs her belly and Vomits all over the officer's uniform. He utters an obscenity at her pushing her away from him.

He looks in disgust as he watches the steam rising off the substance that was just spewed all over him. The gruel that she ate for breakfast that morning, now made it's way back to the animal that fed it to her. Her belly was empty now. But it's emptiness did not compare to the emptiness of her heart. Laura looked over at her mother, blood pouring from her mouth. She screams. Mommaahhh! Her father stood there silent holding little Jacob's hand. She tries to crawl over to her, but the Leader member flings her back over to the officer she had just heaved on. He takes her and slaps her to the ground. Laura lies there in the mud not moving a muscle. The officer then takes his rifle and sets it up against the hut. He turns to look at her.

He unzips his pants, a hot stream of fluid is sprayed all over Laura as he urinates on her. All the other members laugh hysterically. Now steam was rising from her muddy clothes. As he finishes relieving himself, he starts to zip up his pants. He stops and notices her soft young thighs. Now he wanted relief Of a different kind this time. His eyes tighten, as he grips the same member that he just finished emptying All over Laura with. He calls to another officer to come and see. "Not bad eh?" He said to him. No. The other member said. Laura then knew what they were about to do when they both looked at her. An expression of savage hunger filled them. They begin to walk towards her. "Oh my dear Lord Jeshua no! Not my daughter! Lauraaahh!" Her father screamed. The leader tired of his screaming decided to silence him once and for all. A single shot was fired, hitting him in the middle of his forehead. Jacob feels his father's hand loosing it's grip on his little hand. Laura turned around to see her father's body falling silently to the ground. With his arms outstretched, he resembled a human crucifix as he fell slowly backwards to the earth. Then there was a heavy thud in the mud. Jacob never turned around to see his father lying dead behind him. He just stood there in silence The leader member then nodded for the other members to finish their business with the young girl. What Jacob saw next horrified him beyond all his ten Year old imagination. With his eyes wide and staring, he watched all the members of the squad, even the Leader member

10

swarm on his sister like flies on carrion. All like savage animals taking their turn with her. He watched in horror as his thirteen year old sister is brutally raped right before his eyes. He listened to her blood curdling screams, his heart breaking for her. With his mother lying dead before him, and his father behind him. He stands in silence as the squad brutilize his sister. He could only find enough strength to say one word. *"Laurie."* His nickname for her. Then all was silent again. They each emerge from off her. Zipping their pants, and fixing their uniforms. Jacob looked up to see the men dispersing in different Directions. Laura was still lying there on the ground. Then he hears a soft moaning sound. It was Laura

She was still alive. But just barely. One of the officers came over to her, and snatched her up from the ground. She stands there momentarily trying to find some reserve of strength to even stand at all. Her hair was matted to her head, her clothes ragged and hanging from her body that was shivering from the cold. Beads of sweat had formed on her face from the excruciating pain caused by her brutal rape. She feels something trickling down her thigh. A stream of blood was making its way down from under her dress. She wipes it with her hand. She stares at the bloodstained hand for a moment, she then falls to her knees The member that she had spewed on, went back over to the hut and picked up his rifle. He walks back over to her. She looks over at her baby brother for the last time. And like her mother, mouths the words. *"I Love you."* To him. She looks toward Heaven, and utters one last word. The officer was already standing in front of her, with his rifle aimed at her. *"Yeshuaaaa!"* She screamed with her last breath. All of the members again screamed in agony at the sound of the Name. The member fires two shots into her body Both hitting her in the chest. She dies instantly. She falls face forward into the mud. Her eyes fixed in place. She is dead. The officer who had just killed her, noticed something shiny wrapped around her wrist. He bends down and picks it up from the dead girl's hand. It was her mother's necklace, it had snapped from her neck when she was forced from her arms. He looks at it in disgust, and flings it over to Jacob.
The little boy bends down and picks it up. It was all that remained of his family. He looks at it smiling somewhat. A cool crisp wind blows spinning the star around to the other side. Jacob's smiling Stopped abruptly when he saw that it was splattered with Laura's blood. He froze at the sight of it. He looks

over at her lying dead, then back at the star. It seemed to mesmerize him, he never took his eyes off of it. The Leader looked at the young lad and shook his head he looked at the other members Who were talking amongst themselves, he then looked back at the young child. He for a brief moment Felt something well up inside of him. It was unmistakable, there was no denying that he felt something that he's never felt for any Jew. No matter how young or old. But this time, he did. He felt Pity! His face hardened up even more as anger surfaced. Pushing his brief encounter with pity from his expression.

He then blew his whistle, and five other members came from all directions. They saluted him. He gave instructions for them to dispose of the bodies. One of the officers informed him that the pit was already full and being covered over. Take them to the chambers! He shouted. Ja! They said, as they prepared to remove the corpses from their execution places. The members began to pick up the bodies of Jacobs family. One by one they carried them over to an area where the large gas ovens were. Smoke fumed out the chiminey's rising high into the sky, it looked as though the souls of all who had died in there were rising from within it. One of the operators opened the door. A huge cloud of smoke billowed out in front of them. The stench of death was unbearable! The officers took their hankerchiefs and covered their mouths and noses. Even with all their hardness, they were no match for the foulness of death, as nausea Overwhelmed them nearly to the point of vomiting. Jacob looked up to see them carrying the bodies of his Father and Mother to the oven. They were thrown in first onto a heap of the charred remains of those who had died before them. Next he saw them carry the lifeless body of his sister to be disposed of last. Her body limp like a rag doll. They throw her inside onto the body of her Mother. Her eyes still opened, they seemed to be staring right at him. A single tear makes its way down his mud smeared cheek. He never flinched, he just stood there like a small pale statue. It's though all life had been drained out of him in a matter of moments. He tried to speak, but he could not. His voice had abandoned him. The leader member Came over to see that all had been done and gave the order to close the door. Jacob listened to the eerie sound that the door made. It's creaking sounded like an old coffin closing. It echoed in his ears. Just then the officer who was closing the door. Looked over at him, he smiled an evil smile at him. He saw the hatred in the young child's eyes. But he had no compassion for a ten year old boy who had just witnessed his entire family brutally murdered right before his eyes. To him Jews were like pests that should be done away with. And he was all too willing to help in their extermination. He chuckled as he slowly began to close the door. Jacob closed his eyes, his tears falling into the mud like small raindrops. As he heard the clanging sound that the door made. Sealing inside all his beloved family. All that he had ever known and loved in the darkness of the chamber along with others of God's chosen people. Rabbi Yacov Epstien opens his eyes in the quietness of his study. He is seated at his desk, sweat beads had formed on his brow as another episode of Holocaust memories flood his tortured mind. He cries out his sister's name and lays his head down on his desk and weeps painfully.

The Colour Of Love

Anne Hemingway.

Chap 2
Tue. 2000

The phone rings loud. Hello, Anderson Residence. Said the deep baritone voice. Hey big brother. It was his younger sister. Mamie? Yes, its me. She said in a sassy tone. How are you doing sister? He was glad to hear from her. I'm doing well I suppose. How are you and Debbie? We're fine up this way What about my angel, how's Lisa? There was a pause on the line. Mamie? I'm here Ben, I'm here. You didn't answer me, How's Lisa? Hesitation filled her answer. She's ok. There was another pause. Well may I speak to her? I haven't heard from her in about two weeks. Her mother and I were concerned for her. There was silence again. Rev. Anderson begins to feel frustration rising . Is everything alright down there?

Uh, I. She stammered. Mamie, whenever you do this I know something's wrong. Now what has happened? Talk to me! Now don't go jumpin the gun Ben, like I told you everything 's alright. Then where is my daughter? I'd like to speak with her. Mamie was getting nervous, and stalling him. Well......She said dragging the word out trying to think of something to say. Where is LISA!

He shouted, shaking his fist. Oh, God! Whispered mamie clutching her chest. What! He said to her. She's at work, ok she's at work. Rev. Anderson's eyes became wide, nearly bugging out of his head. Work! When did she get a job? Since uh..... She said stalling him again. Mamie? Since about four months ago. She said in a childish tone. What! He said anger surfacing slowly. Why would she have to work? I send her a nice little check every month. Why would she need a job? Well she had to help me make ends meet some kinda way. Help you make ends meet? Why is that? He said. Bertie left you plenty to keep you comfortable for the rest of your life. Why is my child working to help you now? Well..... she said in a childish tone. I was a little low on funds, and she was helping me out that's all. Low on funds? He knew from her answer that there was only one reason for her to be low on funds, and that was because she had been gambling again. While mamie struggled to find the words to answer him. He just answered for her.

How much did you loose this time? His voice saddened. He knew how hard it was for her to give up the habit. I,I. She stuttered. Don't I,I me, how much mamie? She was quiet for a moment, then she spoke. All of it Ben. He gasped at her news. I lost it all, nearly every penny that Bertie left me. Rev. Anderson closes his eyes tightly nearly in tears for her. Say what? I lost nearly all of it Ben, I'm broke. All I have is $1,500 left, and Lisa gave me the $500.00 out of her savings to help me with my Doctor bills. You know I aint been well since my husband passed. I'm old and sickly and I have conditions. I need help. She said sounding more like a spoiled fourteen year old instead of a fifty-four year old woman. Well at least you got that last part right, you do need help. He said sarcastically. His anger surfacing instead of pity.

You mean to tell me that you used all of Lisa's money, money that she had left over from college? I didn't use all of it Ben. She still has some money left over. Mamie Lisa was gonna use that money that we gave her for when she gets married. Now look what has happened. How could you do this? I thought that you were getting help for your problem, what happened with that huh? I was going to GA, but one of the members bet me he could beat me at pitty-patt. Rev. Anderson's expression changed, it used to be his favorite card game. How much a point? He said clearing his throat. Penny a point. She said. You know that skunk beat

14

me out of five dollars? What! Mamie! His anger returning to him again Well how was I supposed to know that he used to work the tables at one of them casino places? Oh, God! He sighed at her.

What am I gonna do with you? He takes a deep breath. Did you tell the Support Leader? It was the Support Leader. She said. Rev. Anderson takes a deep breath attempting to say something else to her.   But instead, he accidently hits himself in the forehead with his rolled up newspaper. He threw it down on the floor in frustration. I don't know why I put up with you!

I'm sorry Ben, I can't help it, I just can't help it! It's hard for me to stop, I tried but I just can't do it. Shoot! I wish Bertie was here. Ohh! How could he go off and leave me like this! He knew that I couldn't live on my own. I swear Ben, if that man were alive, I'd kill him! Once a baby always a baby. Oh for once in your life woman grow up! Sounding more like her father, than her older brother. Don't start lunching on me ok? Cause I ain't hungry for no mess! She said in a home girl attitude.   That's enough! He thundered at her. I'm tired of hearing about how you can't do better with your life, and all your lame excuses Mamie. Then to blame Bertie for all your troubles and irresponsiblitities. Look Albert Simpson Was a good man, who loved and took darn good care of you. You wanted for nothing. Now look at what you've done. This is strictly all your own doing mamie and you are the one who must take the responsibility for being so darn irresponsible. And to top it all off. To take money from my child forcing her to work to take care of you, and pay for all your habits and troubles. I'm trying hard to understand this mamie but I just can't. His voice booming all through out the house. There was another pause on the line. Mamie was quiet listening to him. She knew that he was right about everything that she had done. When Are you going to learn that the love of money is the root of all evil. Not money itself mamie but the love of it. Look at what you have done to yourself as a result of that. Wiped out both you and my daughter. Now what do you have to show for it all? Can you tell me that sis? What! Don't start preachin at me Ben, cause I ain't one of your Church members! She said to him in a sassy tone.   There was silence between them again. Rev. Anderson calms himself before he spoke further to her. Look sis, lets just take a moment to calm down ok? That's right calm down. Mamie was nearly in tears, her breathing was heavy.

Alright now? He asked her, his voice comforting. Yeah, I'm
alright, but if you holler at me like that again Ben,the next sound
you hear will be the clickety-click-click of the dial tone in your
ear! He clears his throat. I'm sorry that I yelled at you like that.
But come on sis. To blow off all your savings for a hunch at the
track is a bit much don't you think? I mean isn't it? Yeah, yeah,
I guess so. You're right, you're right. Why didn't Lisa tell me you
were in trouble again? Now don't get mad at her Ben. It was my
fault, I made her promise not to say anything to you and Debbie
at least until I've had a chance to win some of my money back.
Oh, and just how were you going to do that? Huh? What
hairbrained scheme were you gonna come up with this time?
Three card monty? Dog track, cat track, horse track? Rat races,
tiddly winks for two cents a wink. Turtle racing, frog jumping
contest? What! His anger his frustration returning to him. You
lunchin again Ben, I told you, I ain't hungry this morning, so
knock it off! Remember the dial tone? Rev. Anderson takes a
deep breath calming himself again. Look, I have an idea of how to
help you and Lisa. Will you listen to me? Go ahead, I'm
listening. She said her tone calmer now. Is there a good Real
Estate Company down there in Springfield? I guess so, Lisa
works for a Insurance Company down here, I could ask her when
she gets home. She knows all about that stuff. She should know
he said proudly. She used to work for her old man. Talk to her,
and let me know what you find out. What do you have in mind
Ben? Her suspicions begin to rise. How do you feel about moving
back up here to Chicago with me and Deb? At least until you get
back on your feet, get your life back in order. You want me to sell
my house? Ben, it's the first house that Bertie and I ever owned,
I mean it's paid for. You want me to sell my house Ben? I want
you to do something responsible for once in your life. Do what
you have to do to get your life back in order. That's all. I don't
know if I want to do that or not Ben, I mean all that I have is
here. All my memories. I just don't know if I want to do that or
not. Rev. Anderson pauses slightly. All of what mamie? Does all
of your memories include all of your hurts, your cares, and
burdens. What about all of your hopes and dreams of a life that
you destroyed because of your gambling. What about the debts
that you now owe, and my daughter is caught right in the middle
of your mess. She is now paying for all of your past mistakes. So
what is it really that you have there that's so precious and dear
that you can't part with to make a better life for yourself Mamie?
And as far as your memories go. God will show you how to make
new ones. Mamie thought on her brother's words. She again

knew that he was right. She had made a shambles out of her life in the worst way this time. And she knew that she definitely needed a change. I understand Ben, but I've lived here for too many years to leave now. How much money did you say you Had left? He asked her. $1,500. She said. Uh, huh. And how much does Lisa have, now that hurricane mamie blew threw it and wiped her out? Not funny Ben, I know it's not funny, how much? That's her business. That maybe, but she's still my daughter, and my business how much? She paused. $2,000. left What! You mean to tell me you used nearly all my baby's money? He wipes his face with his hand. Ohhh You little..... Watch it Ben, I beat cha down once before, I ain't to old to do it again.   I don't care if you were drunk at the time. I still kicked your big....Never mind that! He interrupts her.   He takes another deep breath. Look sis, all I want to do is help you and my baby girl in anyway that I can. That baby girl As you call her is thirty-three years old, and still sweet if you know what I mean. Yes I know how old she is, and what you mean. He said smiling about his daughter's sexual purity. Lisa had vowed that she would only give her virginity to only one man. Her Husband, and not before. Well what do you say? Do you accept my offer, or do I come down there to retrieve my daughter so you and all your problems can be alone? Alright, alright! I'll do it! She said laughing a little. I thought you might. He said to her smiling himself. To tell you the truth Ben, that's the real reason that I called in the first place. To see if you and Debbie would let us move back there to Windy City with you until all this smoothes itself out, and like you said get my life back in order. It won't smooth itself out sis. You have to straighten it out for yourself. We'll help you as best as we can. You know that. Yes, I know that big brother. I know that.

There was a calmness to her voice now. To know that things were now looking up for her, and Lisa. My door is open to you. At least this way I can keep an eye on you and my daughter. Well when we move back, there is someone there who has enough eyes to keep on Lisa for us all. Rev. Anderson chuckles a little. Yosef. Yeah child. That boy calls her every other day. And on the days that he don't call her, she calls him. I mean they write all the time, he sends her things and she sends him things. I've never seen two people so much in love as they are.   Yeah, they really do love each other don't they? I mean their love is so pure, so untouched, unblemished by prejudiced.   They have loved each other that way every since they were kids.

17

I'm darn proud of them both. He's a successful Industrial Real Estate Executive, and Lisa a Successful Insurance Represenative. You and Debbie ought to be proud, you raised her well. And him too!

I'll tell Deb you said that sis. Well you did, he stayed at your house more than he did his own. There was a chuckle between them, then a slight pause. Ben, she said in a childish tone again. Yeah. I guess I was wrong for the way that I wasted away all my savings like I did. And for borrowing so much money from Lisa, she had to go back to work to help me. She seemed happy to be working again. But I can still tell that she was very hurt about me. She watched me all the time struggling to try to get this demon off my back. But I just can't seem to shake this thing off me. She whimpers a little. You know Ben I was in a bad way one night, I couldn't get to sleep. She must've heard me crying, she came in my room and sat down next to me. She never said anything to me, she just laid her hands on me. All of a sudden, I began to get so sleepy. I heard her say to me. *"Hush now mae, mae. I'm here .I love you."* That little sweet voice of hers. I tell you Ben that blessed me so. I never slept like that before. I don't know what I would've done without her . She's been such an angel to me. I'm so sorry for being so darn stupid and foolish. Gambler's A tried to help me. But I was too hardheaded to listen. Now I wish that I had. Can you and Debbie ever forgive me? She said sniffling. There is nothing to forgive dear, Now, now there sis. We all have shortcomings don't we? He said, His voice comforting, I guess so Ben. Sure we all do. Look do you remember how hard it was for me to give up booze and uh, being a ladies man? But God touched my life one day in Daddy's Old Camp meetings. I got saved and filled with God's Holy Spirit, and I haven't been the same since. Child, I know God had to touch your life for you to give up all that mess Ben

Because you had issues, You were something else! They both laugh hard. When I gave my life over to God to follow His calling on my life. I realized that, I didn't need all that other stuff, the women, the booze. All I needed was Him. And for Him to show me what He wanted me to do for Him. All the people that I ran with during that time, were all the wrong people for me, they were bringing me down because they had no direction for their lives. I was very close to them all, but I had to make a decision. And

because of that. God gave me a new life in Him. One beautiful woman, whom I will be with until the day that I die. Two great kids, and I've never looked back as though I'm missing something. I think about
All the gang from time to time. But those thoughts are very momentary. They are more thoughts that pass by quickly, not anything that lingers with me for any length of time. And you know what sis. I've never regretted that decision to this day. You know what I'm saying here sis. He changed my life, and He'll do the same thing for you too. It's your call sis. I know Ben, I know she said in a whispered tone. She pauses again. Look talk to my daughter for me will you? Tell her daddy wants her back home.

She'll be glad to hear that news Ben, cause child I tell you. Yosef is all that girl talks about. Well he's talked my ears off several times about her too. He'll be glad to hear that she'll be coming home for good this time. Talk to her for me. I will, Oh and Ben. Yes dear. Since I brought it up about beatin you up that night. I'm sorry that I hit cha in the head with that combat boot. She sniggled a little. Rev. Anderson laughs out loud. I know sis, I know. And I didn't mean to heave all over your backside either. I told you not to drink daddy's homebrew. And I told you to get outta the way, that the brew was coming back through!
They both laugh. Did you ever get the heel back on your boot? No, uh it was never quite the same after that. He said rubbing the back of his head. I'll see you both soon. Kiss my baby for me and her mother.
We love you both. Ok big brother. Bye now he said. They both hang up.

Mamie told Lisa the good news that they were moving back home for good. Lisa was overjoyed All she could think about was being back in her Beloved's arms. Hearing his soft voice, and holding him close to her again. She wanted her homecoming to be a secret, and asked everyone not to tell Yosef. She wanted it
To be a surprise. They sold nearly all of their belongings. The house   sold   quickly.
Quicker than they expected. The house was in lovely condition, and brought a hefty sum for mamie. She was able to pay off everything that she owed, and she owed plenty. She even paid Lisa back the money that she borrowed from her. Saturday came in kinda warm as it was nearing summer, it was Mid-Spring, and mamie   and   Lisa   were blessed with beautiful moving weather, a warm 70 degrees that day. Mamie rented a large moving van, and loaded up the remains of her and Lisa's life with the help of the movers, and moved back to Chicago. One week later on a beautiful and hot Friday afternoon Yosef and Johnathan were out on the Basketball court playing a game of one on one. Yosef went to shoot for a basket. It bounced off the rim.
He seemed distant and withdrawn. There was a list of things on his mind. And Lisa was at the very top of that list. "What's up with you man." Said Johnathan, he was concerned about him. He was still holding the ball bouncing it a little. I just have a lot on my mind that's all. I can see that. Like what? He said bouncing the ball again. Yosef takes a deep breath. Well for starters I'm trying to help my boss land this huge land deal with this bigwig Company in New York. They want to expand their Company, so we checked into some property for them out in California. If I help Mr. Dennis land this deal, it could mean a lot of money for our Company. That's all? Said Johnathan spinning the ball on his index finger. Well it could mean a promotion to Partnership for me. He said in a depressed tone.   Say what? Said Johnathan
Nearly dropping the ball. He looked at him. That's great man! I mean great!. Yosef, shrugged his shoulders. Still distant. So why the long face? Yosef never answered him. He was not interested in the land deal, Mr. Dennis, his possible promotion or anything at that moment. All he could think about was Lisa.

Johnathan looked at him. What else? Said Johnathan, still spinning that ball. What do you mean what else? I mean is that all that's bothering you? The Land deal thing, sounds very exciting jo, but look, I know you man. I've known you every since you were a snotnosed brat. Yosef laughed a little. You don't miss baskets like that unless something is really weighing your mind down. Yosef had gone over to sit

Down on one of the benches, he was tired, and hot from their game. He reaches into his sports bag, and pulls out a chilled bottle of water. You might as well talk to me man, cause I'm not gonna leave you alone until you do. His voice somewhat deep like his father's. Yosef puts a towel around his neck, and wipes his face.
He was a little out of breath, and sweaty from the heat. You know you usually can whip my butt at this game, but today I skunked you out there man. Yosef takes a drink of water. He still never answered him. Johnathan stops spinning the ball, he looks at him sitting there by himself looking like he had lost his best friend. He goes over to the bench and sits down next to him patting him on the back. Yosef smiled slightly. He had always looked up to Johnathan as his older brother since his older brother Michael was killed years ago. Yosef wipes his face with his towel again. He then looks down at his pinky ring that Lisa had given him a year ago before she left on his birthday. His loneliness for her overwhelmed him, he was thinking about all their good times together. His thoughts for her filled him with both joy for the love they shared, yet with sadness because of the time that they were apart from each other. He whispered her name

Out to himself. *Lisa*. Johnathan heard him, and smiled. His compassion for him flowed as though someone had turned on a faucet. It flowed like a steady stream. His love for his adopted brother overtook
Him. He couldn't hold back the news about Lisa from him any longer. He knew that he missed her terribly, and that depression was getting the best of him. You miss her don't you man? Yosef looked over at him.
Johnathan smiled. God yes I miss her! Everyday that I'm without her in my life feels like a slow death. I feel myself dying without her. Johnathan nods his head at Yosef's words. Well I

have some news that will bring life back into that broken heart of yours. It's gonna make your day man. And what is this news that

You have for me john? He said as he wiped his hair back on his head with his towel. It's gonna cost you Jo. Cost me? Cost me what? Ya know it's hot as hell out here! He said looking up at the Sun squinting. It was blazing down on them mercilessly I could sure use a drink of cold water. Yosef looked at his water bottle, the ice inside had begun to melt, It looked cold and refreshing. Is that all you want? Here. He hands him his bottle. Johnathan takes a drink, he even poured some on his bald head to cool him from the heat. Thanks man. You're welcome. Now what is this news that you have for me? Johnathan pauses a little. She's back jo. He said about to bust. She? She who? Johnathan shakes his head at him. He nods down at his pinky ring reciting this quote. *"As far as the eyes of God can see, not even the spirit of death can keep you from me."* Yosef looks down at his pinky ring, he lowers the bottle down from his mouth letting it slip from his fingertips. It fell slowly to the ground. He stood up dizzily from the bench, the sound of her name made him lightheaded for a moment. His expression one of unbelief. "Lisa"? He whispered. Johnathan nods his head smiling bigger than ever at him. She's back Jo. Yosef walks up to him. You're kidding! Johnathan shakes his head. I mean you're kidding me right man? No, I'm not kidding you . I wouldn't do that to you little brother. Are you serious? Serious as an execution. Yosef paused.

That's serious. He said. Yosef looks at him. When? Last Saturday, her and my aunt Mamie moved back to live with my parents until Mamie gets back on her feet again. And when she does? Asked Yosef. I guess she'll move back to Springfield. And Lisa? That's up to you man, that is if you still want her.
Want her. Said Yosef, walking around Johnathan. Want her! I want her more than I want my next breath!
His eyes filling up with tears. Yosef stands there and looks at Johnathan. Still unable to believe that Lisa had come home to him. The unbelief in his expression spoke to Johnathan. What? You don't believe me?
I wouldn't jerk you man! You know me better than that. Johnathan could tell that Yosef was still not too believing of him.

He walks over to Yosef, and takes his hand into his. They shake like Black men do when
They greet each other. The handshake symbolizing Truth, Brotherhood, and Friendship. He then looked in
Yosef's eyes. The sincerity in his expression was as deep as the sound of his voice when he spoke. She's back Jo-Jo. His nickname for him. Yosef then realizes that he was telling him the truth. He smiles big at Johnathan. His unbelief quickly gave way to his excitement. She's back John? I mean really back? He said nearly shaking Johnathan's hand off. Yes, she is little bro. He said laughing at the child likeness of Yosef's happiness. She can't wait to see you. Let's go! Said Johnathan. Anything you say man! Let's go! They pick up their sports bags and leave to go pick Lisa up from Dance class. Yosef still in shock

Walks in the opposite direction. Hey Jo! The car's this way man! He shouted to him. Pulling him by the arm. Oh, yeah. He said. They both laugh as they go together in Johnathan's car. They pull up in front of
Step by Step Dance Centre. Lisa had just finished up with her Aerobics class. She was receiving some last minute instructions from her Teacher. Lisa was dressed in white tights with a low v-necked white leotard with matching white dance skirt. Her hair was pulled back into a pony-tail that hung down her back. Ok Ladies, see you next Friday. Said the Instructor. Class dismissed. All the women and young girls began to walk in different directions, some into the dressing room. Lisa lingered for a while she felt an overwhelming sense of love for her Beloved well up inside of her. She put a CD in the player. The music was the same one that her and Yosef did their Tai Chi to. She could still see it her mind. His tall
Lean muscular body, guiding her every move with his strong gentle hands. Yosef and Johnathan walked inside the center. They sat down in the chairs that were lined up against the wall. Yosef watched her slender body move effortlessly across the dance floor "Whoa" he whispered. She looked like an angel that had swooped down from Heaven, and right into his heart. He clenched his chest trying to soothe the pounding of his heart, as his Beloved Lisa performed the routine with the precision and flexibility of an experienced Master of the Art. He even recognized the routine. He taught it to her two years ago before she left. He could see that time in his mind as well. He flowed to that moment with Lisa. Her soft slender

Body feeling like the finest of silk in his arms. They turn to look at each other. They then loose themselves in each others eyes. Their expressions told them what their minds were thinking. He takes her into his arms pulling her closer to him. They kiss deeply. He gently caresses her, enjoying the softness of her body. Oh, God Lisa! He breathed. His own voice snapping him back into the now. Yosef's eyes rested on Lisa's every move. Johanthan noticed that Yosef's leg was bouncing up and down. You alright man? He laughed. Huh? Said Yosef. Johnathan nods his head down at his leg. Just a little nervous I guess. It shows man, it shows. Said Johnathan. Well what do you expect? I haven't seen her in about a year. Just then, the music ended, and so did Lisa's routine. There was applauding from some of the classmates who stayed around to watch her. Yosef and Johnathan gave her a standing ovation. Lisa turned around to see who it was that was clapping behind her. Her eyes found her Beloved Yosef standing there

Smiling big at her. She froze at the sight of him. Standing there looking strong and even more handsome than he was when she left. It seemed as though all time had slowed around her. Her breathing became

More rapid than before, but not from the tiredness caused by her dancing. But because her Beloved was standing there longing for her as she had longed for him. "Lisa, Lisa" the voice spoke behind her. It was

Jessie. Lisa never answered her. How many of these do I do to tone and firm my abs? The heavyset woman asked her. She could not take her eyes off him! Lisa? Are you alright? Do as many as you want

Jessie. She answered her in a trance like tone. She thought that she would faint at the sight of him! Her desire for him was overwhelming! Yosef was experiencing the same thing as she. The intoxicating effects of their desire, their passion, their love. Their hunger for each other. She thirsted to drink the sweetness from his kisses again. His body ached in that all too familiar way to hold her close to him so tightly that you could not tell one from the other. She pulled the tie out of her hair letting it fall down her back. Yosef stood there motionless, wondering what to do next. Johanthan saw Lisa walking towards them.

He pushed Yosef a little. Go on man, get over there! Go get her! He said,excited for Him. They began to walk slowly towards each other. To Yosef, it was as though she was an eternity away from him.

She felt that too. Closer and closer. Until she walked passed Johnathan, right into her Beloved's arms.

His embrace swallowed her tiny frame. Johnathan, and a few other classmates watched the reunion of the two lovers. He gathered her up into his large arms. With their eyes closed tight, they kissed hard and long, and very deeply. His hands running up and down her body. She massaging his body close to hers. He runs his fingers through her hair, pushing her close into his mouth. Johnathan noticed some of the classmates looking at them in disgust. He breaks up the huddle of girls. One woman had come to pick her teenaged daughter up from class."The nerve of some people!" "I never!" she said in a stuffy tone. Ma'mam, it's obvious that you never. And we hope you never do! Now step on! He said to her pointing at the front door. "Come on Rachel!" she snatches her daughter by the arm leaving. "But mom, I want to see Lisa and her boyfriend love each other look!" she said, she was happy for the both of them. Her mother looks around to see that Yosef, and Lisa were still lost in their passion. Her disgust rose even more. Ohhh! You wait till I get you home you!.. She said shoving her to the door. Go Lisa! Yeahhh! She said as her mother

Shoves her out the door. Some of Lisa's friends cheer them as well. They leave the couple lost in their

Passion giving them privacy. Well, I'll just be out in the car if you need me. There was no answer. He clears his throat. Am I coming in loud and clear? They never acknowledged him. Yosef fans him away.

"Right!" he said. He then turns to leave the couple alone. Yosef and Lisa moaned to each other softly

Finally she spoke first. Oh Yosef. I have had moments where I dreamt of you everyday. And I

Pray that this moment is not one of them. She said to him, tears in her soft brown eyes. Oh God Lisa!

I've dreamt of you too. Please tell me you're real. And that I'm not dreaming again. It would be a nightmare for me to wake up and find that you are not real. Tell me Lisa! He said, tears streaming down his

Face.   Oh, my Beloved, my Beloved! How I've missed you! I've missed you so much Yosef. She said
Crying uncontrollably in his arms. Shhh, I'm here now baby, I'm here now. He kisses her into silence.

He stops kissing her for a moment just to stop and look at her. Still unable to believe that she was home.
I've missed you so much Lisa, I have no words to tell you how much I missed you. I can't believe it, I just can't believe it! Johnathan said that you were back, I didn't believe him at first, but here you are in my arms again. Where I want to stay forever. She interrupted. That won't be a problem at all. He kissed her again briefly. Ummmmm. He moaned. What was that ummmmm for? She said rubbing his chest. Your kisses are still just as sweet as I remember them from last year. He said to her stroking her cheek. Well no other lips have touched mine since I've been away. Really? Yes really. He embraces her again.   A thought came to her mind about their vow to each other. She begins to squirm in his arms.   He looks down on her, his expression was troubled. She was trying to break away from him. She pulls away slightly.   What's the matter? She looked up at him. She had wondered in all this time that she was away, if he had kept their vow. She had kept her promise to him, but she was concerned about his to her. Lisa what is it?
He was beginning to worry. Yosef, you know that I had to leave to go help my aunt, which just really messed up all of our plans. I understand that Lisa, but what's wrong now? He walks back up to her.

Baby please tell me what's wrong. He said, worry was beginning to speak to him. He walks back up to her. I was gone a long time Beloved, and if you've found someone else while I was away, I would understand, I promise. Yosef let out a sigh of relief. He was concerned that she had found someone too.
But relieved that she had not. Whoa! Stop right there. He interrupted her. Yosef, I kept my vow to you, but if you couldn't, I mean, if you've been with someone else, I won't be upset. She looks at the floor.
Well maybe a little. He lifts her chin up to him, smiling at her. She takes a deep breath. Ok, ok, a lot.
Come here. He said pulling her to him. Lisa I give you my word. I have not been with anyone else since you've been away. It was a

challenge for me at first. But it was your letters to me, and seeing you on weekends that kept me strong. Most of our friends thought that I was strange or something because I refused to let my guard down. It wasn't easy because I missed you so. But when I thought about how much God blessed my life with you, all the times that we've shared together. I knew then that I could never do anything to hurt you. I've committed my life to Serving Him, and Loving you. And now that I know that you've been just as faithful to Him as well as to me. I'm so glad that I didn't let those guys talk me into doing something that I would've only regretted for the rest of my life. I could never hurt you like that Lisa, never. They dogged me for that, but I don't care. His expression becoming serious. Most of them are working on their second and third marriages. But I said to them. When my girl comes home to me, and we're official. Then that time with her will be a special time in our lives. But until then I have to say, No way! My first time will be my one and only time. Because I will marry the only girl that I've ever loved. I Love you Lisa. He kissed her deeply. Oh Yosef! I can't tell you what this means to me! She said tears streaming down her face. She hugged him hard, jumping into his arms, wrapping her legs around him. He picks her up walking her towards the dressing room. We have a lot of catching up to do. She said to him rubbing his nose with hers. He puts her down. There's no one else in my life Lisa. There is only room in my heart for one woman. And that's the woman that I've always been in love with. And always will be in love with. And that's my Lisa. Can I get an Amen? He said smiling. Amen sweetheart. They embrace tenderly. Yosef? Hum? I have to get dressed now ok? Ok. He whispers. He held on to her

Hand for a moment, It was hard for him to let her go. Honey, Johnathan is waiting for us. She said. Smiling at him. Let him wait. I've been waiting for you longer than he's been waiting for us. So let him wait awhile. He laughs. I've got you back in my life Lisa, I'm never letting you go again. He said, his expression was intense. I'll be right back ok? Ok baby. He said softly. She turns to walk away. Lisa!
She pauses, she turns to look back at him, knowing what he was about to ask her. She answers him before he could even speak. No Beloved, I'll never leave you again. I promise. She winks at him smiling. He winks back at her smiling. Yosef was standing outside the dressing room waiting for her to return. It was only a

few moments, but to him, it seemed like forever. Finally she emerges from inside. She was wearing a pair of blue jeans, with a soft v-necked blouse with long sleeves. Whoa! He breathed. He looked at her slender frame, her large soft breast bounced with her every move. He pulled his coat over the front of his slacks, he didn't want her to see what was going on with him. You look beautiful! I do? She said looking herself over. Honey, it's just an old pair of jeans that I've had forever. Well, forever never looked so beautiful. He said. He took her hand, kissing her cheek. Yosef, remind me never to leave you again.
She laughed. Lisa, he said walking her to the front door. Yes, Beloved. Don't leave me again. I won't honey, I won't . I promise. They leave hand in hand.

Johnathan was out in the car, he looked at his watch, wondering what was keeping them. He turned the car radio up louder. Yosef walks out with Lisa, he hits the car on the hood, Snapping Johnathan out of his moment with his music. Yosef let's her in the car first, then himself. I thought I was gonna have to send the troops in after you two. He turns the music down softer so they could talk. I'm sorry John, but I had to get dressed didn't I? She said. Scooting closer to Yosef. He hugged her closer to him, caressing her gently.
He kissed her forehead. I guess so baby girl, I guess so. He said laughing. So tell me guys, what 's on the agenda tonight? As If I don't know. Well we haven't had chance to make any plans yet, but give me a few moments, I'm sure I can come up with something. He pauses looking deeply into Lisa's eyes. Romantic. He said, nearly choking up a little. He pulls her over onto his lap. Lisa now felt what he had been hiding from her earlier. He embraced her tenderly, they stared at each other for a moment still feeling the
Joy of their reunion. Well I'd like to make a suggestion if you don't mind. He said. I know this cute little Chinese restaurant in Chinatown. You remember? I took you there when you kicked my butt on the B'ball court last month. He laughs. You remember that Jo? There was no answer. The car was silent, but Yosef and Lisa's love spoke loud and clear. He looked up into the rearview mirror, and saw them lost in a passionate kiss. Okey-dokey. He said smiling. Welcome home baby girl. Welcome home.

The Colour Of Love.
Anne Hemingway

Chap 4.

Yacov! You're going to be late for your meeting if you don't hurry.
Rabbi Yacov Epstien lifts his head up from his desk. He had been
here for what felt like forever. His memories from his past had
crept up on him to haunt him again in a most merciless way. He
could still hear the screams and the pleas of his family begging
for each other's lives. He could still hear the gunshots, see the
images of his family in the Chamber. All had come back to rob
him of another piece of his life. Only leaving behind a trail of
bitterness, and pain to mock him. He takes his hankerchief ,
and wipes the sweat from his brow, and the tears from his eyes.
He looks down , his tears had stained his notes in his notebook.
He closes it abruptly as his wife Sarah walks toward the study.
She had not known of his episode, but she would find out soon
that it had come back to rend and tear at his heart once more.
Leaving him with the demon that
He would unleash on her in a fury. On her and their son Yosef.
Yacov! Come now, what keeps you?

I'm coming Sarah, give me a moment eh? She walks in to find
him searching frantically through a mess of papers, and books.
Where is it? He picks up a pile of folders, then lets them drop
back down to the desk. I know it's here somewhere. Where is it?
His frustration had risen to an all time high, but not entirely
because he couldn't find what he was looking for. But because
anger had come on him from his memories, and it was looking for
a victim. And Sarah was it's usual target. What are you looking
for Yacov? She said drying her hands on her apron. My prayer
book Sarah, have you seen my Siddur? No I haven't, but
I know where it is. She stands there in the doorway with her
arms folded. Rabbi stands there and looks at her waiting for her
to tell him. Well, where is it? He said to her, wanting to grab her
and shake her until every tooth in her head fell out her mouth.
It's where it is the last time that you misplaced it. He gives her a
cold stare. And where might that be my dear wife. Sounding

sarcastic. In the car! She said in a huffy tone. Oy! He said. It's underneath your briefcase and the books with the girls that wear the rabbit ears but nothing else. His expression changed. He was embarrassed that his wife had discovered them. They don't look like rabbits either. You know my dear husband, I thought that I would take a look see for myself what

Holds your interest so in these books of yours. I guess it's silly of me to think that since they dress like these creatures, they must also eat like them too. I saw what they were eating in there. And it didn't look like a carrot to me Yacov! He for the moment was torn between embarrassment, and anger. You ramble through my things Sarah! My things are no place for you, I've told you this before! Oy! You woman you!
You leave me now eh! Eh! She shouted back at him, walking away into the kitchen. He grabs his car keys out of his suit coat pocket, and goes out to the car. He fumbles the keys to find the right one letting him into the vehicle. He searches underneath his briefcase to find his prayer book right where Sarah said it would be on the passenger seat. That woman! He fumed in frustration. He leaves everything there, and goes back into the house to get his notebook. Sarah! Sarah! I'm leaving now! You tell that son of ours

That Rabbi Marcus missed him last Friday. He needs him to help with this years planning for Feast.
Sarah came out of the kitchen with a small note pad, she was making a grocery list. Yacov, Feast isn't until October. It's only March. No need to wait until the last minute Sarah. You tell him eh? Eh. She said. He nods his head. There was a pause between them. She holds her cheek up to him wanting him to kiss her goodbye. He looks away from her, and then walks away. I'll see you tonight for dinner Sarah. His voice hesitant, and void of any affection for her. Of course Yacov, of course. Disappointment filled her being. Rabbi could see it in her expression, and hear it in her voice. But he never said a word further to her. There had not been any intimacy between them, much less sex in five years. And she knew why. Things were never the same after she told him about her news. He walks out the front door onto the porch. He gets out to the car, he looks back at her standing there watching him. He saw her longing for him in her expression. I'll see you tonight! He waves at her. She waves back. She watches

him drive off to Temple for another meeting. They had become quite frequent, but always important according to him. Yet none of the other Rabbi's ever talked about having so many meetings. Suspicion began to speak to her. It spoke to her reminding her of the time that she broke the news to him. The news about her parents. Rabbi's behavior changed towards her after he learned the truth about them, and her. He had not loved her, touched her, or even said I love you to her in over five years. So now she waits, longing for the day when God would answer her prayers, and intervene in her marriage, to renew the love that has lain dormant for so many years. As she watches him leave, her mind flowing back in time to that moment that changed her life and marriage what seems like to her forever. A single tear makes it's way down her ashened face. Each tear trace, traced over by another. She had aged rapidly. Aged not so much because of time per se.

But because that which is void of Love, ages and withers quickly. And death comes slowly and painfully. As life is drained from her being. Sarah is slowly dying for her husband's love. Yes Yacov, I am your wife. But not so dear to you anymore. She shuts the front door, and turns to walk back into the kitchen.

Crying every step of the way. About half way there, she hears a car horn blowing out front. She goes back

Over to the front door pulling the small curtain back. It was Yosef. She brightened up quickly, she opened the door and steps out onto the porch. He goes over to the other side to let out his passenger. To her delight, it was Lisa. Her face lit up like a tree at Christmastime. She runs down the front steps Laughing uncontrollably. Lisa! Oh Lisa! My dear child! She runs up to Lisa embracing her so tight she nearly lifts her from the ground! Yosef stands there watching their reunion, smiling big at them. Hello Ms. Sarah.

Oh Lisa! You're home! You're home! When did you get back? Oh Yosef, look! She's home! She walks back over to her embracing her warmly. Sarah was so excited about her being home again, she could hardly speak. She walks back over to her son. Yosef, you naughty boy you. Why didn't you tell me she come back huh? I just found out myself this afternoon mom. His mother grabbing his face, kissing his cheek. As she pulls away from him. Yosef feels his cheek is wet from her tears. He could tell she had been crying. And he knew who was responsible for his mother's tears. Who is always responsible for them. His

Father. He looks over at the driveway, his father's car was gone. His anger was beginning to surface. Lisa could tell that he was upset about something. Lisa you're home to stay for good now eh?

Eh, for good Ms Sarah. It's so good to see you dear. Said Sarah. It's good to see you too ma'mam.

You're looking as beautiful as ever. Sarah looked at Lisa surprised that she complimented her so highly. She was blushing a little. Thank you dear one, thank you. Doesn't she Yosef? Lisa asked him.

But she too could tell that something was wrong. She saw the tear traces on Sarah's face. They looked like small serpentine rivers that had dried in the summer Sun. She then knew what upset Yosef. She saw him wiping his mother's tears from his face when she kissed him. She like Yosef knew who was the cause

Of her tears. Yosef was torn between his joy at Lisa's homecoming, and his disgust at his Father for hurting his mother again. Come children come. Let's get out of this hot sun before we all fry like fritters on a griddle eh? Eh. Said Yosef and Lisa. They all laugh as they walk towards the house. Yosef runs up the front steps and opens the door for his mother and Lisa. Oh dear child let me look at you. She takes Lisa by both of her hands. Isn't she beautiful mom? The sight of Lisa made him for the moment forget about his

Father's abuse towards his mother. He was still in shock over her being home. Just like your mother dear.

Oh, Ms Sarah, thank you. That is so sweet. Said Lisa hugging her again. Come we go into the kitchen

I've have just put on a fresh pot of coffee. No coffee for her mom, tea. Chamomile, he said looking into Lisa's eyes. He had remembered that it was her favorite. You remembered Yosef? I could never forget anything about you Lisa. Ahh, mush stuff, in here with you. Said Sarah laughing. He takes Lisa by the hand into the kitchen. He pulls a chair out from the table, and seats Lisa, then himself. My son the gentleman. Said Sarah. They all laugh. Oh, Ms. Sarah would you fix this for my Beloved. She hands her a small bag. Sarah opens it. It was a small can of English Toffee Cappuccino. Oh, Lisa! You remembered, it's my favorite. Yes, Beloved, I remembered. I could never forget anything about you.

Oy! Breathed Sarah, as she takes the little can over to the counter to prepare the beverages for the couple.
So tell me Lisa, how's your mother? Oh, she's fine, and at the hairdressers getting her hair done today.
And your Father? He's great too, he went to Church for a business meeting with the Elders. They're preparing for Pastor's day International coming up in June. This will be the biggest one yet. Churches
From all over the Country from every Denomination will be there. Dad says that all the Speakers will have
About ten minutes each to tell what God is doing in their Church, and share with everyone their faith, and Culture. Dad will bring the overall Message that day. Oh will he? Said Sarah, as the tea kettle whistles loud. What will he speak on this time. I loved his message last year. Our Oneness In Christ. Well this time he will speak on Unity through Love. Oh, that sounds wonderful! She gasped. I can't wait. Have they set a time yet? She said pouring the hot water in a small flowered cup giving it to her. Be careful dear. She sets the cup down in front of her. She walks back over to the Cappuccino machine and pours the beverage in a large white mug, it had a rainbow on the front of it. The caption read. *"Love comes in all Colours."* Oh, Ms. Sarah. Yosef and his band Daystar will also play for the program too. She looks at him smiling. And this is good news that you keep from me? I'm sorry mom. I was gonna tell you, but I got so caught up in my girl being back home, I forgot about it. Oy! She said laughing, she set his mug down in front of him. Both sample their beverages. Ummm, this is wonderful Ms. Sarah. Perfect mom.
Said Yosef. I brewed it extra strong the way you like it Lisa. It's great Ms. Sarah. And you too my handsome son. Musing his hair. Mom....? He said playfully. What? You give me mouth now? Lisa, all his life I do this to him, nothing. Now he speaks. And this I need eh? Yosef I need you to go to the market for me. There was no answer. His eyes were resting on Lisa again. Lisa takes his hand and squeezes it gently. He squirmed in his chair a little. Yosef? Sarah called to him, going over to the cupboard. Still no answer. She looks over at them, they were staring lovingly into each others eyes. She chuckles a bit. Lisa when my son wakes from his stupor, tell him I need him to go to the market for me.

Yosef? Yes baby. Your mom wants us to go to the market for her now ok? Ok. He said nodding his head at her. His gaze was still transfixed on her. Do you have a list Ms. Sarah? She said softly stroking his hand. Of course dear. She reaches into her apron pocket and pulls out a small sheet of paper with a list of items on it. The writing was somewhat scribbled. She stops a moment and hits Yosef on his shoulder playfully. Snapping him out of his moment. Yosef, it's impolite to stare. What are you trying to do to the poor girl? Stare her face off? She looks over at Lisa, who was just as guilty of staring as he was. Your father and mother will never forgive me if I send you back home to them with no face. They all laugh

Together. I can't help it mom, she's just so beautiful. Yes she is son, but if you stare her face off now, what will she have for you to look at when she is old? Now get going for me you two. I hope you can read my writing Lisa. I'll do my best ma'mam. She was looking at Yosef, he was sipping on his cappuccino.

Honey? Hum? Where are we going tonight? She asked him. Anywhere you want baby. You just say the word and we're there. How about your favorite place. Bernies? You remember that place Lisa? Of course I do, you took me there two years ago when all that stuff went down between us and what's-his-nose. Uh, Billy. She said laughing. What's- his-nose. Echoed Sarah laughing. She walked into the hall leaving them alone. Yosef's expression changed, he sets his cup down and looks away. He remembered that night. His anger rises slightly, a deep sorrow fills his expression. Yosef? He didn't answer her. Honey, what's wrong? His voice trembled, I never forgave myself for what happened to you that night Lisa. I've lived with that nightmare everyday of my life since it happened. What he did to you. I, I. He stumbled over his words. She gets up and walks over to him, he was still seated. He looks up at her. His expression spoke to her, telling her how sorry he was for leaving her that night. Her soft brown face melted

His heart Oh God! Lisa. Why did I ever do that! Shhh baby. Don't Yosef. Don't. But he. He interrupted
Yosef, it's all in the past now. Ok? Let it stay there. He whimpered in her arms. They felt strong, yet comforting to him. There was a pause between them. Do you remember the Scripture that says... *"As far as the east is from the west, so far*

has He placed our transgressions from us." Yes, it's in the Book of Psalms. He said. When God forgives us of our sins. He places them into the sea of forgetfulness, and He doesn't give us a license to go fishing there. He blots them out completely. He has no memory of them Yosef. Now if He can forget, so can you. Let it go baby. Ok? Let it go. As far as I'm concerned, you did nothing wrong. There's nothing more to forgive. She slides her hands around the back of his head pulling him close into her bosom. She lifts his face up to hers. Flashing a radiant smile at him. Whoa! He breathed. He could feel her heart beating faster. He stood up, and pulled her into his body. They kiss deeply. I never blamed you for what billy did that night. It wasn't your fault. Ok? Anything you say ma'mam. Anything you say. They embrace warmly. He looks at her smiling. I'm so blessed of God to have a treasure like you in my life. Thank you Lisa. Thank you for what honey? For putting up with me, for loving me. No matter what has ever happened in my life, you were always there for me, to make all my fears go away. I was able to face all my fears with faith, all my cares with confidence, and all my tomorrows with hope. As long as I have you to face them with me. He pauses a moment. I Love you Lisa. We better go now, your mom is waiting His mother had been waiting, but she was also listening

From the hallway. She wiped the tears from her eyes. They had returned to her. But for a different reason this time. Not from the abuse of her husband earlier, but because she was proud of her son, and the love that he and Lisa shared. They walk into the living room. Sarah hurries in the same direction so they would not know she had been evesdropping on them. Ms. Sarah, we're going now! So soon dear? she said sniffing. Well.....? said Lisa holding up the list to her. Of course dear I forgot. She walks up to Lisa, and kissed her on the cheek, and Yosef. Tell your mother I missed her at prayer group last night. I will. She said. Yosef and his mother look at each other. Mouthing the words I Love you. I'll be back soon mom.

Ok dear. Sarah watches them leave. She stood there reminiscing about the love that she and her husband once shared in their youth. But now all that she has left of that love is her memories of it. She shuts the door. In the silence of her sorrow, she walks back into the kitchen weeping painfully.

The Colour Of Love.
Anne Hemingway.
Chap 5.

Mamie stands looking out the window as Yosef and Lisa drive off. She is filled with fond memories of her youth with her husband *"Go Head Lisa."* She said in approval of their relationship. She was playing with a beautiful pearl necklace that Albert had given to her on their twentieth wedding anniversary. As she continued on in her reminiscing, Deborah walked out to her, she walked up to see the couple drive off.

She looked over at Mamie, she had a glow about her, the kind of glow that a husband and wife experience on their wedding night after they've made love for the first time. Watching Yosef and Lisa gave her that kind of feeling. Her memories seem to wash all over her bathing her in a sweet flow of ecstacy. Are you alright sissy? Deborah always called her that. Yes, I'm fine. She said in a soft tone, which was unusual for her, since she was a very outspoken woman. You look like cupid just shot you in the... Watch it girl said Mamie laughing. I'm ok, just memories that's all, just memories. Ok..... said Deborah dragging out her word. Nodding her head at her. Well, sorry to interrupt you and your moment. But I want to tell you something. If you see Lisa before I do, tell her that her old boss at the Insurance Company. Webber & Wright. Mamie interrupted. Yes, tell her that he wants her to start back to work on Monday. Ok, I will. She said floating through the house. I think I'll go back into the kitchen and get dinner started. Oh, I'll come with you, I'll help. Said mamie. The mention of dinner snapped Mamie out of her mood. She loved to cook, she just couldn't cook very well. No, no mamie! You remember what happened to us the last time you cooked supper. We were all sick for a week with that concoction that you fixed from the cookbook from hell. Said Deborah laughing. Honey that was good seafood casserole, what you talkin' about child? Mamie? Tuna and anchovie casserole, come on please! Child that stuff made the dog throw up. Said Deborah. It was horrible wasn't it? Said mamie. Sweetheart, if they ever need a new method of

Capitol punishment, that stuff would be the way. Talk about cruel and unusual punishment. They both bust up laughing. Come on, you can help me by not helping me. Ok? Said Deborah as they turn to walk into the kitchen. Deborah stops and looks at Mamie. Why do you look like that? You never looked like that before. Like what? Said Mamie. You know, goofy or something. Shut up girl, I'm just enjoying my moment that's all. What moment? Now that's between me and my memories ok? Well go head big girl.

They both laugh walking into the kitchen.

Yosef drops off his mother's groceries to her, and heads over to his bandmate Terry's garage for a quick rehearsal. He also wanted them to see that Lisa was back home too. Honey, you go on inside, I need to step to the inhouse. The what? The inhouse she repeated. What's that? He said looking puzzled at her. The bathroom silly. She said chuckling at him. Oh..... He said. He just shakes his head at her. Well think about it, when they were outside, they were call outhouses right? Yeah. Now that it's inside, it's called the bathroom, the little girls room, the little boys room, the powder room, the john. Take your pick, but you never hear them called inhouses do you? No baby I guess not. I never would've thought of that.

She thinks a moment. Well to be frank with you, I don't know why I just did. Strange how things change huh? I guess so. I'll see you inside ok, I just want to freshen up a little. You look fine to me just the way you are. You're sweet honey. She said brushing his cheek with her finger. See you in five. Ok. He said taking his bass out of the backseat and goes inside. Hey guys! He said, he was very excited about the up coming Pastors Day Conference coming up. It was to be in June. And they had to be prepared to Minster in song that day. Terry looks at him walking over to him with his head leaning to one side. Jo? Yo! Said Yosef hooking his bass into the amplifier. What are you smiling like that for? Like what? He said tuning it slightly. Like that! He said. Man you look like a neon sign in Las Vegas. What's up with you?

Hello guys. Said the soft voice coming from behind them. They all turn around to see Lisa. She had come in the garage from inside the house. She looked very beautiful! Whoa! Breathed Yosef. She's what's up with me. He said to Terry, adjusting his guitar strap. Lisa? Said Terry. Guys, its Lisa, she's back! Yosef stands there smiling at them all. Brad walks over to her to help her down the stairs. It is ok isn't it Jo?

They knew how protective he was over her. He didn't just let anyone around her. And they all respected that. He takes her hand, helping her walk down them. Wow! You look wonderful girl! Thanks Brad she said to him and you're still a knock out yourself! You look just great Brad! Gee thanks Lisa! He said unable to take his eyes off her. Yosef looked away smiling. What can I say Lise? Except, what he said pointing over to Brad. Thank you too Terry, and might I say that you still got it going on too. Man you could make Valentino jealous. Oh,oh. Get outta here. He said putting his hand on his chest. She walks over to Yosef, who was standing there waiting for her more than anything. She walks up to him and kisses him on his lips softly. He hit a sour note on his bass. The band chuckle a little. He clears his throat looking at her. Behave yourself girl. Ok? Anything you say Beloved, anything you say. There was a small stool

Behind her , he helps her sit down. He kissed her cheek, and walked over to Terry and Brad, to start the rehearsal. He looked around him. Hey, uh. Where's James? Drummer man is in Wisconsin looking at some sound equipment for us. He should be back tomorrow sometime. Yeah, he said he could get us some Great deals on some new equipment up there. Sounds like a plan to me. And uh, he stalls a minute looking over at Lisa. She was reading her Torah that he gave her for Christmas three years ago. He walks them farther away from her . Where's Billy? They all look over at Lisa, she was still deep into her reading, she never heard their conversation. He's not here either, he went over to Helen's. for what? Well he wanted to come back to the band, but we told him no way after what, well you know man. Said Brad. Every since the , incident, they've been kinda close. You know, she was there for him, he was there for her. Yeah, and they've been there every since. Said terry interrupting Brad. He went to go get her and his instrument and come back here. He really thinks that we'll let him back into the band, but that's never gonna happen, I get the feeling that they're not gonna show. Said Terry. I hope not. Said Yosef, looking over at Lisa,

I don't want her upset if you know what I mean, she still remembers that. We all remember that. Said Brad. That was one heck of a night, which I don't want to talk about anymore

guys. Ok? Said Yosef. He saw that Lisa was still reading. She's never been the same since that happened to her. I thought that I could never forgive myself for being such a butt head and leaving her like I did. If I hadn't left her, he never.. He said choking up some. Come on man don't even go there ok? Like you said Jo, let's not talk about it anymore. Besides, that was two years ago. Said Terry patting him on the shoulder. They all looked up to him, he was kinda like a Mentor to them, But they were that way with each other. They were more like brothers than bandmates. There was a cohesiveness between them, and that bond was forever cemented. They knew of the troubles that he had at home with his father, torn between his love and respect for him. But his hatred for him because of his abusiveness towards his mother, and his bigoted behavior towards Lisa. He was also abusive towards him as well, and he had no idea as to why. He never told him why he was so hard on him at times, then at other times, he was so distant and reclusive. He was a cold, and bitter man. That treated him more like an alien than a son. They all continued in their huddle, until Yosef felt something pushing underneath his arm. It was Lisa. I'm sorry baby, you must've thought
That I forgot about you. He said caressing her to him. Well, what are we gonna do? Are you guys gonna play, or talk all afternoon? You heard the lady. He said looking at his watch. It was 4:30 p.m. How about we do that number that you wrote for us, we've been rehearsing it for about three weeks now. Said Yosef.

How about it boys, he said. Let's do it said Terry. I'll get the tape said Brad. They all began to tune their instruments to play along with the tape. Lisa steps up to the microphone. Which one is this again? Said Brad, come on man you were just humming this song two days ago. Said terry. I know but Lisa writes all of our songs, I just want to make sure it's the right one. "In His Time". Said Yosef, laughing at them. Got it! Said Brad. He puts the tape in. The music starts. Ok boys, lets do it! She said as they started the chorus. Her voice rang out beautifully . The melodic sound filled the garage as they lifted their voices in harmony.

In His time, hold on. In His time, hold on.
How long I've waited for You, to do what You promised

To do. My Patience is at it's end, not knowing now, Lord
Or when. But there's hope in the Word I find. For now I
Know that its all...... In His time. Hold on, In His time hold
On.

You've given me Grace and Mercy, and Your Favor goes before me.
Oh hear the Righteous sing. Cause You withhold no good thing.
Lord
Cause Your Glory to shine. Help us remember its all......In His time
hold
On. (If you believe, you'll receive). In His time. Hold on.

Blessed is the man who trust in You. All your desires will all come
true.
Walk on in faith, and peace of mind. Rest in His Assurance its
all......
In His time. Hold on.... In His time hold on..... Give Him Praise
and Glory.

Yosef, and the rest of the band look at Lisa with tears in their eyes. Her sweet soprano voice had once again captured their hearts. Wow! Now that's a song! Said Brad. I love the bass run on that man.
Awesome, just awesome! Said Terry. I love the words to the song myself said Yosef. Lisa had stepped away from them and went back over to her stool. She sat there pondering the words to the song she just sang. It seemed to linger with her in an unusual way. She picked up her Torah and began reading some more. I'm learning to do just that. Wait on Him. He said pointing to the ceiling. Even though I don't see with my natural eyes what's going on behind the scenes I have assurance that its all being worked out for me. But in His time. So I have to hold on until then. Where did you learn this in Temple? Asked Brad.

No from the woman who wrote the song. Lisa? Said Terry. That's a heck of an insight man. They all nod in agreement. I had prayed that God would bring my girl back home to me, now look. Here she is! It's all by faith, not coincidence, or luck. But by faith. If we learn to trust in Him. He brings rewards that leave us speechless! Like I was when John told me about Lisa. Her father taught us to trust God, no matter what the problem is trust in Him. Hey Word man, said Terry, slapping fives with him. Count me in to man, I need some of that! Said Brad, slapping fives with them both. Brad walks back over to Lisa. Lise, you've done it again girl! Another hit just like all the others you wrote for us. Everyone in Temple loves your music! She stands up smiling. Brad thanks, you don't know what that means to me. I'm so glad that you enjoy what He gives me. Yosef unhooks his bass from the amplifier, and puts it away. He walks back over to Lisa putting his arms around her. Well, we have to get going now. Her Dad is expecting us for counseling. Counseling? What kind of counseling? Said Terry. Premarital Counseling. It's either that, or mess up our lives, by breaking our vows to Him, and to each other. And we're not gonna let anything spoil that man. You mean no, no uh. No Brad no sex until after we're married. Terry shakes his head. How is that possible? I mean in all the time you were together, as well as apart, you never with each other or with anyone else? No I never did, and she never did. Lisa steps away. Honey, I'll be outside when you're ready. Ok, baby. I'll be out in a minute. You guys should've been married a long time ago. Said Brad.

Well maybe we should've , but for every time that we even discussed marriage, something happened. We broke up over that mess with Billy and Helen. Separate colleges. We got back together again, only to break up over some more junk, then her aunt got sick and she had to go be with her. I mean on thing after another kept getting in the way. Then when Lisa sang that song to me for the first time, Then it clicked. It just wasn't time. And now? Said Terry. Now I believe more than anything that it is. And we'll make it this time. And nothing and no one will stop us. It'll happen, just believe my man, believe. Yeah, but how long can you go without you know. Said Terry. Well, I just pray a lot, and take plenty of cold showers. He said laughing. That's got to be tough on you man. Said Brad. It is tough on us both. But we made a promise, and we're not gonna mess that up for anything. Not even sex. If that's all that two people base their relationship on, then they're over before they even get a chance to get started. Lisa walks back into the garage, he takes her by the hand kissing her forehead. Besides when two people really love each other as much as we do. They'll do whatever it takes to make it work. The Scriptures teach that with God all things are possible. He winks at them. Come on baby let's go. Next rehearsal is when Terry? Uh, I don't know. I'll call you, I've got some other possible dates for us coming up soon. I'll get back with you ok?

Solid! He said walking Lisa out to the car. They watched them as they drove off to Lisa's fathers Church.
Brad and Terry still hear Yosef's words ringing in their ears. They savored every word. They never heard him speak like that before. But Yosef himself would soon know the meaning of what he just shared with his friends in a way that would challenge him, and his faith in way that would change him forever. God was getting ready to use him. And Lisa would play a very important part in His plans for him. She would be a part of his Spiritual growth. And even she would have her eyes opened to the deepness of God's plans for their lives, and how it would affect all those around them. Especially Yosef's father.

Lisa was quiet, and solemn, she was thinking of how God worked things out for her to come back to her Beloved. She looked over at him as he drove them to Church. Beloved. Yes baby. Have you made any plans for us tonight? That I have, my girl that I have. He said, kissing her hand. I'm taking you to my favorite restaurant, then after supper. I thought about taking you on a horse and buggy ride. Ohh! She gasped. Then to top the evening off, how about we go over to the beach to watch the Sunset? Oh! Yosef, it sounds wonderful! I can't wait! What time shall I be ready? Well, let's see. We get out of counseling with dad at 6:00. How about I pick you up at 7:00? Sounds like a plan to me. Solid! Lisa? Yes honey.
I have no words to tell you how glad I am that you're back home, and back in my life. I mean , I have no words at all. Beloved? He looks over at her. I Love you. She winks at him. He squirmed in his seat, nearly running the car off the road. Careful honey! She laughed. You ought to be ashamed of yourself doing that to me. They both laughed. They drive on to Church beaming like two fireflies.

Yosef and Lisa finish their counseling session with Rev. Anderson. He happily gives his approval for them to start dating again, as long as they stay committed to their counseling. He was all too willing to give them as much guidance and direction as he felt they needed. Her mother was also in agreement with her husband on the two of them continuing their relationship. Sarah was overjoyed when she heard the news, and blessed the couple. Yosef Puts on his suit coat as he prepares to go pick up Lisa for their first date in over a year. He's dressed causually for the occasion, in a pair of Black slacks, with a matching crew shirt, and matching outer coat. He looked very handsome. But very nervous. Yosef! Get down here boy! It's almost 7:00, what keeps you! I know mom, I'm coming! He hurries down the stairs, meeting her at the bottom of them. Here let me look at you, she said fussing over him. Yosef, where's your tie? No tie mom. Look I have to get going now. If only your father could see you, how handsome you are son. She said wiping the tears from her eyes. Oh, I'm so proud of you and Lisa. So proud son. Mom, now don't start crying. How can I go out tonight if you start crying. He kisses her forehead. He looks up, it was nearing 7:00p.m. Mom? Yes child. Where is dad? I don't know Yosef, he told me that he had another meeting at Temple this afternoon, but I haven't seen him since he left at noon today. Does Rabbi Marcus know about this meeting? I don't know this either. I haven't spoken to him. Your father's not talking to me that much these days. He was all in a huff about Feast coming up this year. Mom, that's not until October, this is only March! His frustration rising. Don't let it bother you son, how will Lisa enjoy you

Tonight if you go to her like this? You're right, you're right. I'm sorry. You ok now eh? Eh. He said looking at her. Her smile cause his anger to leave him But he knew that his mother deserved far better than what his father was giving her. One of his main prayers was that God would work a miracle in his parents marriage. What he doesn't know, is that God heard him. Let's leave it at that for now. You go now, Lisa is waiting for you. But..... No but me son, I'm your mother, you listen to me. She doesn't like to be kept waiting. She said pushing him over to the front door. Go to her and have a blessed time. What about you mom? Deborah is coming over to have prayer with me at 7:30. She's bringing some of the other Prayer Warriors from Church with her. I fix tea and things for them. But I can't if I stand here talking with you all night. Now off with you! Ok mom. He kissed her cheek. Now what was that kiss for there?

You're the greatest mother in the world! Yeah, yeah, you save all your kisses for Lisa . Go on now son.

I'll be fine here. Deborah will be here soon, ok? Ok. He said. He left her with his mind relieved. Having Lisa's family over made him feel much better about leaving for his date. But he was still angry at his father for not being attentive to her. He walks up to the front door and rings the doorbell. Coming! Boomed Rev. Anderson' s voice. Yosef, my dear boy come in, come in. She's nearly ready Her mother and mamie are up with her now. Well don't you look smart tonight in that suit boy. Thank you dad. Very nice. He said. Hey uh, jo,jo. Where did you pick this one up at? At Schmidt's down on 45th and Halstead. I haven't been to Jew Town in a while. Why don't we get down there this Saturday? You think they could make me one like that? Said Rev. Anderson smiling. I don't see why not dad. Good, good. Then we go eh? Eh. He said. Uh, dad. Yes son. Can Lisa come with us? Sure, sure. He said laughing. Here let's go into the den. The girls will be down soon. They walk into the family den. Yosef looks at all the pictures on the wall and on the tables He was mostly in all of them, from the time that he and Lisa were little on up until they both graduated high school. It was like his life with them flashed before his eyes. It was a pleasure remembering all those fun times. He has a history with them, they didn't just see him as a young Jewish boy who was deeply in love with their daughter. But one of them, their family. And he was very proud of that. Even though they differed Culturally, he from a Jewish background, and they Afro-American. They didn't treat one another as Black and Jew. But as family. They've loved each other, laughed, cried, argued, been through hell together. But they still held fast to the bond that cemented them together forever.

Their love for God, and each other. So tell me jo, where are you taking my little girl tonight? He clears his throat. Well, she wants to go to Bernies. Nice place. Interrupted Rev. Anderson.

Then after supper, on a horse and buggy ride. Ohh. Gasped Rev. Anderson. Then I'm taking her over to the beach to watch the Sunset. We should be back home by 11:00. Sounds wonderful son. They sit down to relax. Daddy! Is Yosef here yet? Yes, sweet pea. He's here! He chuckles. Yosef was carrying a small gift box, it was a present that he bought for Lisa. Rev. Anderson noticed that he was a little fidgety. His leg was bouncing up and down. You, uh alright son? Oh sure. He said putting his hand on his leg to stop it's bouncing. Maybe if I sat down I'll feel better. Rev. Anderson turns his head laughing at him. He looks at himself.

Oh, I'm already sitting. Yes, yes you are at that. Chuckling at him. Yosef stood up and began pacing the floor. His nervousness getting the better of him. What is taking her so long? Maybe she doesn't want to go out with me or something. What if she doesn't like the necklace I bought her. What if I say the wrong thing at supper tonight? Rev. Anderson smiled at him. Yosef? Oh, God Lisa! Yosef? He never answered him. I'm alright dad I just need to walk around a little. He then stops in his tracks realizing that he was walking already. Oh dad, what am I gonna do? What's the matter with me? Jo-jo. Take a deep breath, that's right just like I taught you. Son, it's ok to be a little nervous on your first date. Believe me you'll be just fine. You two have known each other all your lives. You should be used to her by now. I know but, why do I do this everytime I see her? If I even think about her, I'm a mess! Don't you know by now

Son? Yosef looks at him curiosity speaking to him. You're in love boy, that's all plain and simple. You're in love. Yosef drops his head. He was in love, very deeply and it felt good to him to love her.

And her love felt good to him. You're right dad, I am in love with her. I've never felt this way about anyone in my life. I can't explain how I feel about her sometimes. I mean. I try to find the words, but I can't. Does that make any sense to you at all? Yes it does jo. When a person is blessed to find the one that they will spend the rest of their lives with. There is a spiritual connecting of the heart that they experience.

I can't explain it myself, but it's more than just a love at first sight. It goes far deeper than that. It's when you look beyond the outer man, and God reveals the true self of that person to you, and you to them. That's when love really begins to flow. That is why people experience what I like to call. Love at true sight.

Yosef walks over and embraces him.   Whoa! That's beautiful dad. Thanks. Anytime son, anytime. He said mussing his hair. Dad......? What, you give me mouth now? I do this to you every since you were a little boy, nothing. Now you talk. And this I need eh? He said parroting Sarah.

You've been hangin around my mother too long. They both bust up laughing. Just then Deborah comes down stairs. Jo-jo, my boy. How are you sweetheart? Kissing him on the cheek. I'm fine mom, just fine.
Hey jo! Said Mamie. Coming in behind Deborah. Oooh Weeee! The man is fine! Lisa, get down here girl and get this boy, before I rob the cradle! Cause this boy's gonna get jacked up!   Not bad, not bad at all. Mamie now you know you need to quit! Said Deborah. All laughing. How you doing handsome? She said kissing him on the cheek. I'm fine mae-mae. How about you? Child I can't wait to get to the Entertainment hall, they're gonna have some new games in soon. Now you know me, I have to be in on the game, know what I'm sayin? She said hitting fives with him. Just then Lisa walked down the stairs, she

She was wearing a soft pink evening dress, it was low cut in the back, with v-neck. Her long dark curls flowed with her every move. Yosef could not take his eyes off her. Whoa! He breathed. His knees wobbled a little, nearly dropping his gift box. My God Lisa, you're beautiful!   His eyes misty.   Isn't he incredible everybody!   To Yosef she looked like an angel descending from Heaven.   They looked deeply into each others eyes.   Rev. Anderson takes his wife and sister by their arms and escorts them into the kitchen. Yosef stared so hard at her, he almost forgot to give her, her present. What's that honey? Huh?
Oh. I have something for you. He gives it to her. I have something for you too Beloved. He looked surprised. She gave him his box as well. They both open their presents. Oh! Beloved! It's beautiful!
It was a gold heart shaped pendant, on the inside was a picture of them. He looks at his gift, it was a gold tie clamp, with a heart in the center. In the center of the heart was a single diamond. Oh baby! This is incredible! Do you like it Beloved? Like it? I love it Lisa, this was so sweet of you. Thanks baby. He kisses her on the cheek. He takes the necklace and puts it on her.   He turns her around. How does it look?

He stares at her again. Hum? The necklace honey, how does it look? He looks down at it. He sees her heart beating. He never answers her. He just deep kisses her. Rev. Anderson still trying to get his wife and sister to leave the den, finally gets them to leave with him. Ok girls that's enough, let's leave them alone now. But Ben I want to see. No dearheart, there's nothing for you to see here. Come on sis, that goes for you too. Your nose is getting too full there. That's right here we go right in here. But my baby.

Whinned Deborah. Honey, the woman is 33 years old now. And uh, I've never seen a baby kiss like that before. Wow! Yosef? Hum? Can we go now? Anything you say ma'mam, anything you say. He takes her by the hand as they leave for the evening. Rabbi Epstien returns home from Temple and from visiting with Rabbi Marcus. He calls to Sarah, he was excited about something. As she enters the room she noticed that he was smiling. Big from ear to ear. The idea that he was smiling period, made her stop and just stare at him. He looked very handsome when he smiled. It reminded her of the way that he used to smile at her when they were young lovers. A warm sensuality rose up from deep within her, awakening her now forgotten senses. She for the moment felt like a young woman of twenty, instead of the aged maiden that she is now. Her heart was beating faster than she could keep up with. It hadn't beat that way in years.

Her body had long forgotten the feel of her husband's touch, his caress, the scent of his body close to hers as they made love. But her memory of these precious moments returned to her flooding her with an overwhelming desire for him. *"Oh Yacov, what you do to me when I look at you!"* she whispered under her breath. Her body not only wanted love, but craved it! But her cravings would go unsatisfied. Her hopes of love with him tonight would all come crashing down on her. He would not tell her that he missed her that day. Or that each second that ticked by without her, was like an infinitum to him. Or that he was even sorry for the cruel way in which he treated her not only that morning, but over the years period. For Sarah would've forgiven him all he had done, just for one night of passion or a moment of

Intimacy. Maybe a gentle kiss, or an I love you Sarah. That would've made her dreams of him sweet that night. But she would once again go to bed the same way that she had gone for years. Heartbroken, abandoned, with only her tears to keep her company. The only voice that she would hear in the silence of the night would be her own wailing for a love that she once knew, that was now gone. There was one question on her mind. Would she ever know that love again? Would she ever experience his masculine body next hers lost in deep intimacy? Would she know again the "Tingle" of love that her son was experiencing with his beloved Lisa? Would she know that love again? Would she? Let's see, shall we?

Sarah! Sarah! Come quick! Come quick here! I have news for you! Sarah was carrying a pair of salt and pepper shakers shaped like two red apples. What is it Yacov? What is this news you have for me? She sounded tired. It's Rabbi Marcus! The news of his medical reports came back today. He does not have the cancer! Isn't that wonderful news Sarah? She was silent for a moment, she now knew what made her husband smile, she was unsure of how to answer him. She was torn between her happiness for Rabbi Marcus. But crushed because that was the only thing that made him smile that night. Her countenance fell like an old condemned building that was demolished by explosives. Yes Yacov, that is good news. How is Connie taking the news, she must be overjoyed to hear this I'm sure. I have not spoken to her. He had not told her at the time that he told me. The Hospital called him at Temple this morning. But I'm sure he's told her by now. He stops and looks around the house. Where is that son of ours. Have you seen him at all today Sarah? She recalls her afternoon with him and Lisa. She smiles a little herself. Yacov! Now I have some good news for you! Well, what is your news for me? Our son did come home today. She squeezes her eyes shut for a moment. Yes, yes, what about that Sarah. He had someone every special with him, someone very dear, and precious to us all. And who might this special someone be? Lisa! Now his countenance fell the same way as hers did earlier. He stops smiling. He walks towards the hall closet to hang up his coat. The weather had cooled off that evening. He turns around to look at her. I suppose our son was thrilled to hear this news eh? Thrilled? He's out with her now Yacov, they have a date tonight.

She walks up to him winking her eye. Why! Sarah! Why does he do this! So many nice Jewish girls, but he picks that one. He said walking over to the big picture window. Sarah walks up behind him. What do you mean by *That one* Yacov? You know what I mean. He said looking around to her. That black girl! Why does he do this thing to us? He has done nothing to us! All he has done was fall in love with a girl who in his mind and heart has every right to be loved as well as he. She told me a long time ago Yacov, that she loves him so much, that she would give her very life for him. I knew then that my son had made a good choice in the woman that he wanted to marry. How could he not love a girl like that? Love should never be denied anyone because of a difference in colour yacov. He loves this girl, I've never seen him this way about anyone before. Their love is strong Yacov, stronger than anything I've ever seen in my life. And not even you with your rantings and ravings can stop it! Not even your hatred can penetrate it! Yacov don't do this to him. He loves Lisa, and she loves him. Rabbi would not hear her reasonings or her pleading for their son. All he heard that night was his own selfishness speaking to him. He walks over to his rocker, still rambling on at Sarah. Trouble, nothing but trouble! Who is trouble to you Yacov? The Black people, they come into our neighborhood, now look. Our son is one of them now. He has left his Heritage behind for that, that girl! He said stuttering. He sits down in his rocker. It was old and creaking like him. We have known that family every since Yosef and Lisa were small children. She comes from a good home. And Yosef from at least half of a good home. He looks at her, he didn't like her remark, but it was the truth. Her parents taught her and Johnathan well, and I have

Done the best that I know how to bring Yosef up the same as Ben and Deborah brought up their children. He jumps up out of his rocker, anger had surfaced in a fury at her. You gave my son to them

Sarah! Yes I did give him to them! I wanted to spare him from the same disease that has blighted and poisoned your soul! That's why I gave him to them. After Michael was killed I feared for my Yosef. I feared so much, that I did the only thing that any mother would've done for her child. I gave him

To the one home that I knew would shelter him from the same demons that torment your tortured life Yacov. I knew that Ben and Deborah would love and take care of him, and instill in his heart and mind the same morals and values that would make him a strong and successful man. Their wisdom and compassion to take a young Jewish boy into their home and lives, and raise him as their own, was what his life needed.

You could never've given to him that love Yacov. You were too busy nursing your hatred, and nurturing your indifference to take the time to love and care for your own children. And me. I could not trust you to teach him what you had not learned yourself. She walks over to the dinning room table. No matter what he became or who he married I knew that I would be proud of him. And I am proud of him Yacov. I'll always be grateful to Ben and Deborah for that, as well as My Lord Yeshua. He brushes her away from him, as he shakes the newspaper open, he was trying to read it hoping that it would make him forget Sarah's words, but they wouldn't let him forget. I don't want to hear talk of this anymore Sarah. No! Yacov! You never do! Because you know I speak the truth! He jumps up out of his rocker causing it to

Sway violently back and forth. Truth! You know nothing of the truth Sarah! For years you hide the truth about yourself from me, then boom! You are not the woman that I fell.... He paused. He couldn't even bring himself to tell her that he had fallen in love with her. She waited anxiously to here those words, but again he would disappoint her. You are not the woman that I thought you were. Why do you blame me Yacov? Why? MY MOTHER WAS RAPED! She screamed, hurt, anger and frustration all surfacing at the same time. You blame me for that Yacov, it's not like she said come and take me you big German Soldier you.! I don't care! He interrupted They are pigs Sarah! Do you hear me pigs! No they are not! They are not pigs, they are people too, just like us. No! No! They are not like us! He said stomping across the floor. They beat my sister, they raped her right before my eyes Sarah, they killed my Mama, and Papa. How can you call them people Sarah! His tears flowing, it was as fresh in his mind as if it had happened that very moment. And what are you Yacov? What? What are you? You hate now just like they did then, you have hated all your life. What are you talking about? I have watched the way you have treated Lisa all her life. Yosef, and I both have watched you hate a child who has never wronged you in any way. Ohhh! He walks away from her. Don't ohhh! Me Yacov. She has always respected you, I have heard her prayers for you many times, she's admired you from afar, because you hated her too much to let get close to you.   And Yosef detests you for it.   Even her parents watched how as their daughter grew.

So did your hatred for her grow as well. When she was a young girl, you hated her for her innocence. Because it was something that she was blessed to enjoy, but you because of the horrible tragedy that was inflicted upon you as a child, was not so blessed to enjoy. And as Lisa grew into a beautiful young woman That our son loves with all his heart, your hatred continued to grow with her. She has never done anything to ever hurt you Yacov, you know this to be true. She sat the shakers down on the table, and started to go upstairs to bed. When she hears a deep groaning sound coming from Rabbi. She turned around to see that her husband had changed! "Do you think that I care how you and Yosef feel about her? Said the deep voice through him. Rabbi's voice had changed, but not only that so did his appearance. He looked as though another being of some sort was looking back through him.   She gasps in horror, His eyes resembled that of a lizard, his face was drawn tight, his hair was sticking out in all directions. Oh my dear Lord Yeshua! She breathed. She backs up the stairs slightly as he crept towards her. He stopped only a few feet away from her. No! No! I don't want to hear that Name Sarah! He turns to walk away from her again. You speak of the Germans like they are angels! But they killed my family! When I look at what you and Yosef have become, I wished they had killed me too! Sarah was horrified, she could find no words to describe what she had felt at his words. They cut to the very core of her heart, which he had broken so many times before. Pigs! They call us pigs! They say. You Sarah speak of them like they have done nothing wrong! You hide the truth about yourself from me. Your father is German Sarah, that makes you like him, like them all. If I am Jew pig them, then you are Nazi pig to me! GET OUT OF MY SIGHT! His words seized her heart like a vice, squeezing out of her all the love that she held inside for him. She grabs her belly shutting her eyes tight. Again she for the moment was unable to speak. She looks at him.   Heh,heh,heh. The demon cackled through him. She walks up to him, an expression of resolve on her face. She speaks to him in Hebrew, she tells him that unless he repents of his actions, that God would surely Judge him for his cruelty. NEVER! Was his answer. Very well Yacov.   She looked up towards Heaven. And begins to pray.   *"Father, God of Abraham,*

Issac, and Jacob. You have heard his words, and seen his offense.
I give him over to You, and for Your Justice to be served upon him.
Do with him whatever You will Father God. He belongs to You
now. In the Name of Yeshua. Amen." Just then there was a loud
rumble of thunder inside the house! The atmosphere had
changed. They both could

Feel it. Sarah turns to go back upstairs, she looked relieved that
Someone Bigger than her had just stepped in to intervene in her
circumstances. Rabbi hears the thunder, it frightened him. He
runs up behind Sarah
Turning her around shaking her slightly. What is it? What is
that Sarah! Don't you know Yacov? Your Judgement. The
thunder stops, Rabbi feels a sense of arrogance come on him. He
smiles laughing out loud. Look at me! I'm still standing Sarah!
Heh, heh,heh! Nothing has happened to me yet! I'm still here!
Your prayers did nothing! No judgement will take me! Heh,
heh,heh! Sarah turns to look at him again. Judgement is never
what we think it should be Yacov, but what He knows it will be,
and always in His time. As I have heard Lisa say so many times.
You just watch, and see what will happen to you. I suppose you
have never heard of the word before. What word? He said his
voice still cocky.

Grace, Yacov, Yes even in His Judgement. He is still Gracious,
and Merciful to us as you will see for yourself. I know nothing of
this grace. He said. Obviously. I'm tired, I need to rest now.
She was tired, but her sleep had abandoned her for the moment.
She goes over to the dinning room table and sits down.
Good night to you Yacov. Rabbi's appearance changed back to
normal. He notices that Sarah puts her head down on the table.
He still could hear her words of God's vindication ringing loud in
his ears. It made him feel uneasy, but yet he still in his hardness
tries to ignore it. He walks away to his study. Sarah is in deep
tears for him. Somehow she knew that God's Judgement would
be severe, yet He would still
Be merciful to him as well. She prays that God will touch his
heart, and release his mind from the demons that have so
tortured him over the years. She weeps painfully for him praying
out of her very soul.
She collapses back onto the table crying herself to sleep.

Oh My Dear Lord Yeshua. Touch his hardened heart.
Help him in whatever way that you can. Help him to
See with Your Eyes. Love with your Love. Make his
Heart like Yours Father.

The Colour Of Love
Anne Hemingway
Chap. 7

Yosef and Lisa finish their dinner, and their buggy ride, after which they drove over to the beach to watch the Sunset over Lake Michigan. They talked about many things, they had a lot of catching up to do. They discussed about the differences in their backgrounds and how they would share, and embrace, and blend their beliefs and Worship God without any fear in Temple as well in Her Father's Pentecostal Church.
Their Love is such a rarity in today's society, which is largely made up of an anything goes belief by some.
Their love is strong and binding, and powerful unlike anything that has ever been seen or heard of. Maybe God through their example can bridge the gap between us all as a Nation, a People. And help us all to realize that true love that comes from the heart, conquers all things. Even Racial, Denominational, and Cultural barriers. It's a lot to over come, even an impossibility to the thinking of some. But The Bible teaches that *"With men this IS impossible. But with God ALL things ARE possible.!"* So you see, it can be done if we through His help will pull together, instead of apart. Let's see what is happening with me and my Beloved shall we?

Yosef arrives home with Lisa, they stare lovingly into each others eyes for a moment. The music playing softly on the radio. It was his favorite. *"If Only You Knew".* Come here. He breathed to her, pulling her close to him. If you only knew how much I Love you Lisa, how long I've waited to hold you in my arms again? He said, kissing her cheek. Honey, I've Loved you the same, and waited for you the same length of time as you have for me. Yeah, you did. Everyday seemed like forever without you! He looks at her. Are you still my girl? Only if you still want me Beloved. He smiled. Oh yes, I want you. More than anything I've ever wanted in all my life! She places her hand on his pinky ring, playing with it slightly. He moves her hand over to his Manhood which had stiffened quickly. Yosef! Shhhh. He kisses her into silence. Their moans escalate as they enjoy a long awaited ecstacy. Lisa stops abruptly. What? He said. Honey

We can't do this. Do what? Look at us, like two puppies in heat or something. He chuckles. Yeah, I guess we did get a little carried away didn't we? Yosef? Hum? As long as we remember what we have up

Ahead of us, and not let anything or anybody get in the way of our getting married. I believe that God will bless our time of Loving that will be beyond words. He does things like that you know. He looks at her

Wonder speaking to him. Unable to grasp the depth of her wisdom. He nods his head in agreement with her. I guess I should take you home now. Yeah, I suppose. She chuckles. They get out of the car. He walks her across the street to her parents house. She puts her arm around him hugging him close to her as they walk. They reach the front yard, standing underneath a flowered tree with pink blossoms. A gentle spring breeze blows on them. I had a wonderful time tonight Yosef. So did I Lisa. She looked up at him his

Handsome face looking like he just stepped out of Heaven Itself. I'll never forget this night as long as I live Beloved. Same here. He said stroking the side of her soft brown face. It's not too late is it? He looks at his watch. It was 12:30 a.m. Look we're both thirty somethings aren't we? Yeah, and I feel that what

We do is no one else's business but ours. I agree Beloved, but we still live with our parents ya know. That's only because they allowed us to until we both get enough money saved to get our own house when we get married. I have enough money saved to take care of both of us. Lisa thought on his words. She remembered how Mamie nearly wiped out all of her savings. Disappointment fills her expression. What's wrong baby? She exhales deeply. I wish that I could say the same thing for myself. Josef smiles a little, but is quickly replaced by a slight frustration at mamie. Your father told me about that. That bothered me at first, but Lisa I have plenty to take care of you. You don't have to work, unless you just want to. But I'll see to it that you never lack anything, you know that don't you? Of course I do Beloved, but I want to help you too, the Bible calls a man's wife his Helpmate. I want to help you in every way that I can. Yosef

Smiles at her, stroking her soft curls. There is no share for you to do Lisa, just love me and be my wife is all I ask. I just want to take care of you and our babies. Babies.... She said in a trance like state. She had

Always wanted children, and Yosef always wanted to be the man to give them to her. Well there will be plenty of time for all that later. She said looking up at the Moon. It's moonlight was shining down on them through the flowered tree they were standing under. It's beautiful isn't it? Not nearly as beautiful as you are Lisa. He pulls her close to him, and kisses her again. He moves her hand down to feel his Manhood again, not only did she feel the stiffness of him, but also that there was a huge wet spot on his slacks. Yosef, you're uh... I know, I know he said softly, still trying to kiss her. Honey.. What happened to you? You happened to me. He said cradling her in his arms. She laughs a little. You're something else

You know that? Look I need to get inside ok? He stops his ravishing of her to look at her. His heart thumping hard inside his chest. Lisa? Yes Beloved. I Love you. She looks deeply into his eyes. I Love you too. She said softly. Does your father know I'm home now? His expression changed. His

Jaw tightened a little. I don't know if he's even home. He wasn't when I left mom. But if he is there, I'm sure she's told him by now. He may not be too happy to hear that I'm back home. She holds her head down sadden about his father's disapproval of her. A single tear makes it's way down her soft cheek.

Yosef looks at her, anger fills him for his father. He pulls her close to him. Shhh... Don't Lisa. Don't cry. And besides that's his problem. Yosef, your father is a man of God. Yeah, right. I know your father is, but I have some serious doubts about mine. Lisa stops crying, to defend Rabbi. Yosef was surprised at her defense of a man who never approved of her in his son's life. She stops a moment. Yosef I believe that he is deep down inside honey. But there has been so much hurt in his life that he has not yet resolved. And that the real Rabbi Epstien is buried deep down underneath all that debris from his past. Somehow, we

have to help him get out from under all that mess and maybe, just maybe he'll be the man, the husband, and father that he's always wanted to be. Through faith in God, and patience. I believe that we can help him achieve that. He's your father Yosef, he needs help, we can't turn our backs on him now. He loves you and your mother, he's old and set in his ways I know. But he really does need our prayers and our support. And I'm willing to give him all that he needs to help him somehow bring some kind of closure to his past.   I will help him, you and Ms. Sarah in anyway that I can. I know his behavior has kept him a bit on the distant side of you and Ms. Sarah. But God has a way to bring him back. Yosef looks at her. His heart filling more and more with love for her. That will take a Miracle Lisa. She smiles at him. Precisely Beloved. He does still work them you know. I really believe that. Seriousness in her expression. I hope you can too. I believe what you believe. He said shaking his head at her. How do you do that?
He said.   Do what honey?   See the good in everyone and everything, no matter how bad a situation maybe, you still somehow see the good side of it? You'll have to teach me that some day. Beloved, we will have the rest of our lives to learn together.   My poor mom Lisa, she goes through so much from him. How in

All of Heaven does she stay with him? Concern for her filling his voice. Yosef, my mother told me that when a woman loves her husband. No matter how much darkness is present in his life, if there is just one spark of light there. She'll do whatever it is in her power to bring that light to the surface. I know, I've seen this happen with my parents. Your mother did this with your father? No, my father did this with her. They both chuckle. No, I'm just teasing you. They did that with each other. See, some men feel this way too. What hurts me for men is that some men sell themselves short in some ways. And what way is that? Well, I believe that men are the most fascinating of God's Creation. He smiles at her. I believe that if they would give themselves a chance. And some of them do. They'll see just how important they are to us. How's that? He said caressing her. Well, I think that they hide too much of themselves from us. That's sometimes understandable, depending on what he's suffered. Just not advisable. What do you mean? You've heard the saying that real men don't cry, that's what sissies do right? Um,hum. Well I

Disagree with that. I think that when a man feels hurt to the point of tears, and shows his wife his true feelings, he's not making himself vulnerable to more hurts. Especially if she's anything of a woman, and loves and cares for him in everyway. But he's making himself available to her to help him resolve what has hurt him so. He's not being weak at all Yosef, but he is really showing her just how strong he is. I don't like that word sissy. Men aren't sissies, just people who need direction, and understanding, just like we do. A man who doesn't view himself this way will tend to cower away, and cover his feelings with anger. He can't trust enough to say. I hurt, but I'm not going to trust you with my hurts so he hides them. But a real man will give expression to those feelings. No matter how much he may fear exposing himself to his wife. He will allow her into his heart trusting that she will mend, and not break his heart. That Yosef takes a tremendous amount of strength. You really believe that? Yes I do honey. Do you really think that being compassionate, and tender, affectionate is limited to old women, and young girls? I think

Not my love. I think that when a man expresses these emotions, these virtues. He's sending a message to
His beloved that says to her. Look, I hurt, but I'm strong enough to go through this as long a I have you by my side to support me. I can face anything, even death itself. As long as I have your faith, your understanding, your love there with me. Beloved, even in her absence, her comfort is there to blanket him in the assurance that all will be just fine. Emotions are not weaknesses to us Yosef, but strengths to us. And we need to have these things expressed to us just as much as you or any man may have a desire to express them to us. And I applaud any man that is brave enough to let them shine, instead of hiding them
Away. What a great injustice we do to one another when we do that. Yosef pauses looking at her blinking
His eyes rapidly. Trust, Faith, Love. They together are the water from which all the other emotions flow.

God did not exclude men when it came to emotions Yosef. I don't believe that for one moment. And any man that will be honest will admit to that too. My God Lisa! Where did you learn that from? From my Father. She said tears forming now. He takes her into his arms and kisses her deeply. Lisa? Yes Beloved. Will you marry me? She nods her head yes. Tears streaming down her soft brown cheeks.

Yes I will Yosef, Yes I will. He smiles big at her, his affection rising more and more for her with each

Moment. I love you. My Beloved. She whispers to him. He smiles more, kissing her tenderly, caressing her close. Yosef? Hum? I have to go now. It's really late. We both have to get up early in the morning for work. I won't sleep tonight Lisa. And I don't have work on my mind at the moment. Honey, please

I have to go now. I know Lisa, but it's so hard to let you go. I've got you back in my life now. I'm never

Letting you outta my sight again. Ever! I need you so much. I have no words to tell you how much

I love you. God! What you do to me Lisa, every time I think about you, I can't explain it. Something happens to me. I want you so bad girl. He hugs her close to him. I Love you the same too Beloved.

Oh God Yosef! They kiss passionately. They stop to rub their noses together. Now Be off with you, before I tear your clothes off and ravish you within an inch of your life. She said to him a cute British

Tone. He chuckles a little. I'll see you tomorrow after work right? Honey, I'm right across the street

From you. You can come to see me everyday ok? Solid! Now I want you to go on home, and kiss

Your mother for me, tell your father I'm praying for him. And I want you to get a good night's sleep.

She looks deeply into his eyes. She felt him for the moment. And he her as well. Tonight, I'll be waiting

For you in your dreams Beloved. Don't keep me waiting. She embraces him. Softly kissing his earlobe.

He sighs out her name. *Oh Lisa.* He watches her go inside, still mesmerized by her kiss. Whoa! He breathed. He leaves to go home. Yosef enters his home only to find his mother sound asleep, her head down on the dining room table. She had been there every since she and Rabbi argued that evening. He

Walks up to her kissing her on the cheek. She stirs a little. "Who is it?" It's just me mom. Yosef?

She awakes, her vision clearing more so she could see him. Yosef, my son! You're home! Yes mom, I'm home now. His voice soft and tender. She stands to hug him hard. It's so good to see you back dear.

She said holding his face in his hands. Yosef could see that she had been crying. Her face stained with tears from this evening's events with his father. How are you dear, are you alright? You look tired to me.

She was fussing over him like a five year old. Mom,mom. I fine, ok? I'm fine. I'm sorry son. Here I am treating you like you were still that thumb sucking little boy who hung on to my dress tail. They both chuckle . So tell me Yosef, how was your date with Lisa? He takes a deep breath. Shaking his head. I don't know where to begin . It's unlike anything I've ever experienced with her. I've never seen her like

This before. What do you mean son? Well, it's like she's matured in a way that I don't understand. The things that she said tonight, it's like wells of wisdom came flowing out of her. About men and their feelings, I mean she really understood how some men think and feel mom. It's like she saw into me, she saw my heart, my soul. She saw me for who I really am. And regardless of that. She still loves me.

After all this time. She still loves me. Sarah smiled as her son continued to share with her his night with

Lisa. We went out for supper, which was nice, then on a horse and buggy ride. She loved that! Then we drove over to Lake shore Dr. to the beach to watch the most beautiful sunset. Then we came back here.

I mean, mom, she's the most amazing girl! That she is Yosef, that she is. But how do you feel about her?

He pauses to think about his mother's question. I don't know how to explain it sometimes. What do you mean child? I felt so different with her tonight than at other times that we've been together. She talked with me about men expressing their feelings, and sharing their hearts with their wives. I mean. I've never been so in love with her than I was tonight. I feel like I tingle all over, she makes me tingle mom,My heart beats fast and out of control. My legs turn to jelly. Then I just get this warm feeling all inside me, and all over me. I'm so comfortable at home with her. She makes me feel like I'm wanted, needed. He paused looking at his mother. She loves me mom, I can feel it. I know it in my heart. She loves me. He said patting his chest. Does that make any sense to you at all? Yes it does child. Why do I go through all that?

It's simple dear. Like I've told you time and time before Yosef. You're in Love child. You're in Love.
And it's a love that you should never take for granted. Lisa is a beautiful girl, a smart girl that one. Yes
She is. And if you treat her right, she'll not only give her life to you, she'll give her life for you. There
Was a pause between them. Did you talk the M word tonight too? She said smiling big at him. He smiles back at her just as big. The M word? He thought a moment. Well yeah, there was some mention of that too. But we're still in counseling with her father once a week until that happens. That's what we promised.
Very good son, very good. She paused looking down at the floor. Mom, what is it? Oh, what can a mother say dear? I'm just so proud of you that's all. So proud. Lisa will make you a fine wife. God's favor is upon you, do not take it for granted. I won't mom, I won't. she kissed him on the cheek. Goodnight son. Good night mom. You have sweet dreams of her tonight eh? Eh. He said to her.
He scales the stairs to his room. Sarah turns off the night light and goes to bed herself. Yosef enters his bedroom taking off his outer coat hanging it up in his closet when he hears his bedroom door opening.

It was his father. So I see you made it home from your date with Lisa. Yosef looks at him, not too pleased to see him at the moment. Yeah, I'm home dad. He takes off his shirt as his father inspects him all over.
I hear you and your mother talk a long time about tonight with, he pauses. Her. Yosef stops and looks at
Him briefly. He was silent, he didn't offer him any information about his evening. What's this talk I hear?
What talk dad? Said Yosef. Going into his bathroom he comes back out wiping his face with a cold towel.
You talk to your mother about this tingle. What is this tingle that you speak about? Yosef's anger surfaces. Something that you wouldn't know about dad. I mean when was the last time that you were
Affectionate with your wife? Huh! When was the last time that you held her in your arms and kissed her
Like there was no tomorrow? Huh! When was the last time that she made you tingle? Rabbi was silent, but his sarcasm decided that it wouldn't be silenced any longer it surfaced in an impish

sort of way. He looked at the front of Yosef's slacks and sees the huge wet spot there. It hadn't dried yet. I see you tingled all over yourself there. Pointing to the front of him. Yosef looks down at himself, he was a little embarrassed. But he smiled anyway. So I did. What of it? This girl did this to you! I tell you she's nothing but trouble. Yosef looks at his father, his temper rising slightly. Dad you've known Lisa and her family every since they moved here from Mississippi, and you treat her like you've never seen her before in

Your life! You seem to forget dad, that I was raised in their home, he pauses. With her. I know what she's like. And I love her. I always have and I always will. Yosef listen to me, I know. They are nothing but trouble! They are nothing but little monkey's in heat! Yosef summoned every ounce of strength at that

Moment to keep from loosing his temper at his father. He had had a wonderful evening with his Beloved Lisa. And he was not about to let his father spoil his mood. Dad I can't speak about every black woman. I can only speak about Lisa. I've never known anyone like her before. She's deeply in Love with God, and her family, she loves me more than I love myself. She's incredibly smart. And, and. He stammers his words. Choking up a little. He looks at his pinky ring. She's beautiful! He whispered. Just like an angel.

She's beautiful dad. And I love her more than my own life. I've never felt this way about anyone, and I know that I never will. Lisa is it for me. And if you can't deal with it, then you might as well spend some time at Temple finding a way to deal with it. Because I will marry her dad. There is nothing that you can ever do to come in between that love. And besides, how can you stand there and lecture me on Black people and their Culture, When the extent of your knowledge about them or any other Culture is about as long as the nose on your face. Rabbi was once again silenced by his son's wisdom. He knew that he spoke the truth. But his heart was still too hardened to accept that truth. Now if you'll excuse me, I'm very tired, and I'm going to bed., My girl is waiting for me in my dreams. And I'm not going to keep her waiting. He walks over to his father, and opens his bedroom door more, he escorts his father outside into the hall. Goodnight dad, God in Heaven help you. He shuts the door. He goes into his bathroom, and changes into his white pj's. He lays across his bed, letting out a gentle sigh. *"I Love you Lisa."* He moans

Before drifting off into a peaceful sleep.

Chap. 8
The Colour Of Love
Anne Hemingway.

Yosef and Lisa spend the weekend together with her parents and
their friends. Her mother told her the good news about her old
boss calling her back to work on Monday. She would then get to
reunite with her good friend Mary Peterson. Yosef awakes early
on Monday morning for work. Always well dressed. Today, he's
dressed in a light beige business suit. He chose not to take an
outer coat with him today, the weather report said that it was to
be 80 degrees that day. He looks out his bedroom window, and
sees Lisa leaving for work herself. She's dressed casual for her
first day back. A dark blue calf length skirt, with matching long
sleeve v-neck under blouse. With suit coat. Which she carried
over her arm.
Whoa! He breathed. She looked beautiful to him. *'I Love you
Lisa".* He whispered smiling at her. He runs downstairs,
grabbing his briefcase, kissing his mother. He takes a roll, and a
few sips of coffee. Yosef! I fix all this breakfast for you and your
father, and you eat that little thing. Sorry mom, I have a very
important business meeting today with Mr. Dennis' client I have
to hurry! What about your lunch dear?

I'm meeting Lisa for lunch today. Bye! He rushes out the front
door. She shakes her head laughing.
Rabbi comes into the kitchen setting his coffee cup on the
kitchen table, he goes over to the counter and stands there
looking at Sarah. She was cleaning off the stove. I see our son is
off on a date with his girl eh?   Don't start this morning Yacov, I
had enough of your doo last night. And no, he is not off to be
with Lisa. He is off to work. He'll be meeting her this afternoon
for lunch. What about it? She said, wiping of the stove. Her hair
was already beginning to droop from the humidity in the air. He
looked at her in disgust, what he saw laboring before him was not
the ravishing beauty that he married over thirty years ago. But

the aged ragged mess that he made out of her. He is Jewish, she is Black! Why can't you see that
Sarah? I do see that Yacov, but when you get to the part where the problem comes in let me know. I'll be in the basement looking for termites or something. They would be better company for me than you at this moment. She throws the dishtowel in the kitchen sink and walks away from him. She goes into the basement, but not to look for termites. But to go to her Prayer Altar and pray. She and Deborah, and Lisa
Made it together a year ago. They would often go down there to have prayer meetings. It was the only time that Sarah found companionship, and closeness. How it would come in handy today. She went down there to pray for her son, and Lisa.

Yosef is seated at his desk when Mr. Dennis calls him into his office. Joseph get in here quick! Mr. Dennis is seated at his computer looking over some graphs. Look at this will ya? He himself is a very distinguished man. Very professional, but also a down to earth kind of guy, that you could tell your deepest secrets to. Which Yosef appreciated. He pulls up the square footage of the land that they were looking into for Mr. Walden for the expansion of his Company. It was located on a beautiful spot of land in southern California. They looked at chart after chart. Graph after graph. They discussed how much money the deal would make for their own company. Now watch this. Said Mr. Dennis. He hits a button on the computer. And an astronomical figure pops up on the screen. Whoa! Gasped Yosef. Whoa is right
My little Jewish friend. He said. That's us? That's us Jo. You do this for me Joseph, do this one thing for me, and we're talking partnership in this Company. Now look at this. He hits another button. This time bringing up another figure. Yosef's salary. This is where you are now. But this is where you'll be after the sale goes through. He right clicks on the mouse. Get outta here! He said his eyes nearly bugging out!
Wow! Said Yosef. Wow! is right! You do this for me, and You'll have your own office right next to mine. Come I'll show you. He takes Yosef through a connecting door. The room was incredible! And very spacious. The furniture was old, but he would have the whole office redecorated for him after the sale. I can't believe it! I can hardly believe it! Said Yosef. Why haven't I ever seen this room before?

I was keeping it a surprise just for you. My top Man in this Company. You've been with me a long time Jo. And you've really worked your butt off for me. I always knew that If I were to put someone here in this office it would be you. He pats him on the shoulder. Yosef was deeply touched by his Boss's faith in him. Thank you sir, I really appreciate that. I really do. I know you do son. Come. They go back into Mr. Dennis' office. He goes over to his desk made out of a beautiful thick Mahogany wood. And opens a small desk drawer. He pulls out a set of keys and puts them into Yosef's hand. What's this? You land this deal for me son, and those are yours. He then nods to the big office he just showed him. Can I pick

My own secretary? Boy, you land this deal for me, and I'll be your secretary! They both laugh out loud.

Yosef hands him back the keys. Mr. Dennis extends his hand to him. Yosef was like the son that he always wanted. He has one daughter, who is married and has two children. He adored her very much, but he couldn't stand her husband. He was an ok guy, he was just a jerk when he drank. But he loved him too. They shake hands, it was strong and binding. You got it sir. He said. Yosef was preparing to leave, when

Mr. Dennis calls him back. Hey uh, Joseph, come back in here a minute will ya? I really need to talk with you about something. It's kinda private. He shuts the office door behind him. Yes sir. Said Yosef, he was concerned a little. Oh, relax son, this isn't about business, well it is but more personal than professional. Yosef was more at ease to hear those words. Mr. Dennis and Yosef share more than just a close professional relationship, they were also great friends. They talked about everything from Religion to

Puppies. But today they would talk about something that they rarely touched on very much. Race, and

Yosef's Intercultural relationship with Lisa. He never spoke about her to him too much. He never even had a picture of her out on his desk. He was concerned about how it would affect the Company. So he chose to remain silent about her. He would talk only briefly about her without revealing her Ethnicity.

Mr. Dennis goes over to sit on his huge desk. Yosef stands waiting to hear what he wanted. I hear you have a girlfriend. Yosef became somewhat defensive. Yes sir I do. A Black girlfriend Yosef? He became even more defensive. Yes sir she's Black. Is there a problem with that Mr. Dennis? No, no. Son take it easy. There is no problem, I mean no harm Jo, believe me. I don't have a problem with that at all. I mean after all this is a new Millenium isn't it not? Yes it is. Said Yosef nodding his head. And aren't all our Racial differences God made are they not? Yes they are, I just wish someone would explain that to my father. Not too approving is he? No he isn't. I don't understand it. He said pacing the floor. Well my mother just adores Lisa. She always have, every since we were kids. She's always loved her. She's crazy about her. Mom has never had a problem at all about Lisa being Black and my being Jewish. But my

Father..... he pauses sitting on a small desk across from Mr. Dennis. He was at a lost for words. He had dreamed of the day that his father would finally accept Lisa. But at this point, it seemed impossible. Give him time Joseph, he'll come around. Yosef smiled to himself. You sound like my girl now. She's more hopeful for him than I am. All I know sir is that I'm so in love with Lisa. I can't live without her. She's everything that I could ever hope for in a woman. In a wife. I've just never been able to see myself with anyone else but her. No matter what colour they are or aren't. Joseph, may I ask you a personal question? Sure but not too personal. I'll be careful. He said holding up his hand. What kind of girl is she? Yosef smiles again. Bigger this time. He walks over to the big picture window over looking the Chicago Skyline
And Lake Michigan. She's warm and sweet. A very caring girl. She has this incredible relationship with God and her family. She's affectionate and very smart. I mean her insight into people and Life period is absolutely amazing! She loves my family, even my father! If you can believe that. Her love for me is unlike anything that I've ever experienced in my life. So pure and deep like her heart. I can't fathom how deep that love goes I've never known anyone like her before. He begins to choke up a little. Mr. Dennis even becomes a little misty eyed himself listening to him share his heart with him about her. It's kinda scary to me to have someone love you like that. I guess we don't see ourselves the way that God allows someone else to see us. I don't follow you Jo. Well I was talking with Lisa's father last week when I

Went to their home to pick her up for our first date. He said something to me that still burns inside my
Mind. What did he say? You've heard of love at first sight right? Sure I have. Well he went deeper than that. He mentioned something called Love at True sight. It's when God reveals the true self of a person's heart to yours. And yours to them. It's when you see all the qualities, all the warmth, the sensitivity, the

Affection, and other things that make them who they are, and you who you are. Then He brings you back to the surface of them to see how He has beautifully packaged them all together just for you. And you just for them. You know I think that we sell ourselves so short when it comes to Love, that we don't take the time to see that Love is more than an emotion, it affects them, but it in itself is not an emotion. It is an action that has a rippling affect on all of our other senses. Touching all the emotions, the compassion, the sensitivities, the warmth. All the things that we have been blessed to experience at that one moment in time. It's then that we realize that we've just fallen in love. That's what I felt when I first saw Lisa. We were too young then to know all that then. But as we grew, they began to show themselves. Not only have I fallen in Love with her Mr. Dennis. I've grown and matured in that love. And so has she. Whoa! Joseph, that is a really deep insight there. I'm impressed, very impressed. I mean every word of it sir. Lisa once told me that love is not an emotion at all. It's an experience, it may touch our emotions without it in itself being one. But an action that is in constant action once it's realized. She has proven this to me time after time after time. He said shaking his head. Getting more choked up with each word about her and their love for each other.
Maybe we feel that this kind of love is just in fairy tales. But I've found out that it's real. We don't see love the way that God does. We sometimes think that He doesn't even exist.
So how could a love like this be real. This is not some fairytale. I mean it's real. I guess maybe we don't see ourselves the way that He allows someone else to see us. And we blind ourselves to the way that He
Wants us to see the other person. I guess fear has a big part to play in all that. Maybe that's why we

66

Can't understand someone loving us this way. I know I never thought I could be loved this way. And what way is that Jo? He said smiling at him. Yosef shakes his head nearly in tears. Unconditionally. Wow! He said to him. Yosef goes back over to the small desk and sits on the corner of it. Pondering to himself what he just said, Mr. Dennis himself feels his own reflective surge surfacing now. Joseph, I remember reading a passage of Scripture in the Bible. I'm sure everyone who has ever looked at a Bible has heard it before. It's John 3:16 *"For God so Loved the World, that He gave His only Begotten Son. That whosoever believed on Him would not perish, but have Everlasting Life."* I thought on that one Scripture, it changed my whole life. In what way sir? Well I thought that if God loved us so much that He would give the only Son that He had just for us, that He through Him would reap a harvest of many sons and daughters that would walk the Earth just as He once did. Then why would he not on this Earth give me

A mate that would love me the same as He Himself? See I was once mad at God when my wife died. I loved her so much I couldn't put words around it. When she died five years ago, I thought, If You are Love. Why would you let someone that I loved so much leave me like that? I didn't understand that He had nothing to do with her death as we have been so religiously brainwashed to believe. Patricia loved God
She was just so sick, that she didn't want to live anymore, she couldn't bear seeing me in agony over her. As well as our daughter Angela. When she died, I closed myself off from God and the world. Understandable, just not advisable. Then what happened to you? Well that brings me to my next point the reason that I wanted to speak with you. Two years later a married couple moved in next to me. Nice people from what I could see. Then all of a sudden trouble in paradise. The husband of this lady began to come home very late at night, then I would hear them going at it about why. Then he stopped coming home all together. I knew then that he was cheating on her. Six months later he divorced her for this other woman, and moved out. That was a year ago. She's been by herself ever since. He paused. She's Black Joseph, about my age give or take a few years. And very pretty. I mean she's beautiful! And I'm very attracted to her. I'm really interested in her, I want to ask her out, but I'm a little nervous that she might say no or

67

something. I don't know how she would feel dating a White man. He said nervously pacing the floor. Yosef smiles big at him. Mr. Dennis, there's only one way to find out. Yeah, and what way is that my young friend? Ask her. He said shrugging his shoulders. He begins to pace more now.

I see her in the neighborhood all the time, She's always polite. She speaks to me all the time. I mean she drives me crazy! I really want to get to know her, tell how interested I am in her. But I just can't seem to get up enough, uh, you know uh. Nerve? Said Yosef. Well let's just say, one part of me gets up, and it ain't nerve. Yosef busted up laughing. What? What's so funny? Mr. Dennis do you like this woman?
Like her? I really like her man! Then go for it man! Yeah, but how? I mean what did you do when you first met Lisa? Yosef quickly flashed in and out of that moment when she lip kissed him for the first time when they were kids. I fainted. He said. Mr. Dennis cocks his head to one side like a puppy does when they hear a funny noise. He looks at him curiosity surfacing. How long have you known Lisa? Yosef smiles. All my life sir. Jo? Sir? Why didn't you ever tell me about her? I was concerned about how
Our relationship would affect the Company, and my employment. That's all. Mr. Dennis walks up to him

Smiling even more at him. His tone serious. Joseph, you really love this girl don't you? Love her? I REALLY LOVE HER! Then son go for it! I'd really like to meet her if that's ok with you and her.
Yosef felt as though a ton of bricks had been lifted from his shoulders. Sure, we're having lunch at Bernies
Today. Great! That sounds great! I'll call my interest, and see if she'll have lunch with me. And I'll send a car to pick them both up ok? Yosef's excitement took an all time high at that moment. Sounds like a plan to me sir. Good, good. I'll see you in about fifteen minutes? Well, I'm expecting a fax from Mr. Walden's Secretary in a few,give me about 45 minutes. Solid. Said Mr. Dennis. I'll see you then. Oh, and uh, Joseph. Thanks. You don't know what this means to me. He said to him. They shake hands.

Mr. Dennis' conversation with Yosef made him feel like he could walk on air. Yosef was more open now in talking about Lisa with him. He had trailblazed a path for him where Interracial relationships were concerned. He felt as though a barrier had been broken down and now he could safely walk through to an uncharted love that he had never known before. Funny how God works that way for us. Mr. Dennis sits at his desk thumbing through his rolodex. He finds Michelle Jennings number. He had gotten it from the phone directory, since it wasn't an unlisted number. He just never had the nerve to call her. But today he had nerves of steel. He dials the number. Hello. The sweet voice said. Hello, uh Michelle? Yes. This is William Dennis, your neighbor. Oh, hello! She sounded excited to hear from him. Hey, uh Ms. Jennings.

I'm having lunch with my Associate and his girlfriend. And I was uh, wondering if you would like to accompany me as my special guest? He said loosening his tie. I would love to Mr. Dennis. You would?

His voice cracking like a pubescent thirteen year old. I mean you would? Sounding more like himself. Yes I would.
Excellent! This is incredible! I'll send a car to pick you and Ms. Anderson up in about half an hour. Is that ok with you? Yes it is. I'll be ready Mr. Dennis. Please, call me Bill. Ok Bill. Bye. He said to her sounding more confident now. He felt as though he could walk on water! He goes out into the outer office Yosef was just getting off the phone with Mr. Walden's Secretary. He had just received the fax he was waiting for. That sounds like a plan. I'll tell Mr. Dennis and thanks for faxing this to us. We'll get right on it. Thanks bye. He hangs up the phone. He notices Mr. Dennis standing there lit up with a florescent glow about him. She accepted. Yosef was looking the forms over. She? She who? Michelle. Who's that? My neighbor, you know the Black woman I was telling you about. Ohhhh. Sighed Yosef. She's agreed to have lunch with me. Solid! Said Yosef handing him the Buy Sell forms that they needed to review before a proposal on the Land in California was made. I'll look at these later. Well son are we ready for operation go get me a woman? Yes sir! Then let's go boy! I'm hungry and horny! Let's go! Yosef and Mr. Dennis pick up Lisa and Michelle for their Lunch date. Everyone hits if off just fine. Michelle was dressed casual in a beautiful light beige dress, with plunging v-neck, and long sleeves. And beige pumps

To match. Her hair was done up in French roll. She looked stunning! Mr. Dennis couldn't take his eyes off her. Yosef, and Lisa chuckled at the couple. After lunch they dropped Lisa back off at work, and Michelle at home. And returned to the Office themselves. Yosef later asked him, what the problem was? She's beautiful and smart. She reminds me of Lisa's mother. Only sassier. They both laugh.

The Colour Of Love
Anne Hemingway.
Chap. 9

Deborah was in the laundry room finishing up the last load of clothes. Her husband was in the living room reading the paper. The back door opens slowly. It was Lisa. She had come home early from work. She was quiet and withdrawn. She was hiding herself. Lisa? What are you doing home so early? Hello, mom. Her tone whispered and trembling. Deborah sensing that something was wrong walks over to her. Baby, what's the matter? Are you alright? Yes, I'm fine mom. She said nodding her head. But she was far from being alright. It was her first day back at work, and what happened there was not what she expected. Her day started out alright in the beginning with her and Mary Peterson, they had missed each other terribly.
They caught up on everything that they had missed out on while Lisa was away. From Church activities, who got married, who got divorced. To who's gonna have a baby, to who's Preaching now. Mary's boss Mr. Webber is a straight forward fellow, who loves his family, and attends Lisa's Church. He's the serious type with a delightful sense of humor. He enjoys his professional relationship with Mary, and Lisa. Even though Lisa is Mr. Wright's Secretary. They all got along great together. There's only one thing. Mr. Webber like Mary has noticed on several occasions Mr. Wright's behavior towards Lisa. All these things

Escaped Lisa's attention, but not Mary's or Mr. Webber. They noticed Mr. Wright a stout sort've fellow about medium height. With slightly graying hair on the sides. He was also balding, causing him to wear a toupee that looked like a pile of wet hay

that somebody just sat on top of his head. You could tell he didn't know how to wear it very well. It would slide off to the side from time to time causing him to go through several hair adjustments to get it back on straight again. His voice was a little on the raspy side. He sounded like he had a terminal case of laryngitis. He looked more like porky pig in a business suit. Wearing a sorry excuse of a toupee. His partial was stained from all the cigars that he smoked throughout the day. Well anyway. They would notice how he would stare at Lisa when she wasn't looking. His oogling eyes that seem to undress her the longer he stared at her. He watched every move her body made When she walked away or towards him. Sometimes he would stand too close to her when he spoke to her, sometimes almost kissing distance. He liked to touch her soft brown skin at times, which caused her to cringe away from him. She never made anything out of it. And just went about her work.
Which she did efficiently and professionally. They decided not to tell Lisa about Mr. Wright's behavior hoping that maybe he would get over his infatuation of her, and remember that he's a married man with
Six children. They also were concerned for Lisa, being such a sensitive girl that it may be too upsetting for her. So they both chose to keep silent for now. Mr. Wright had called for her to come into his office that afternoon after her return from lunch with Yosef and his boss and Michelle. He said that he wanted her to
Review some insurance cases for a few clients, since his associate Melvin Timmons had messed up some of the files. He had very clumsily mixed up all the forms, placing them in folders that belonged to other clients. This guy was the talk of the company. Everyone got a kick out of teasing him. Sweet disposition, he was just clumsy, wearing a huge ball of keys that hung very noisily from his belt. Melvin would sometimes walk into the doors, or not judge his distance right and walk into the wall trying to walk into another room.
Lisa and Mary would bust up laughing at him every time. So would Mr. Webber. I mean a very geeky sort've person. Let's just say if ever there was a dork of the year contest. This guy would win hands down every year! This guy took the cake when it came to dorking. But he totally dorked out that day when he misfiled Mr. Wright's forms for his clients. He called Lisa in there to see if she could straighten out Melvin's mess. That's when all hell broke loose. He had been especially attentive to her that day, since it was her first day back. He couldn't take his eyes off her.

He watched her closely, sometimes he would try to get close enough to her trying to rub his arousal against her soft bottom. When she was in view of him for any length of time, he would often fondle himself a little behind his desk so she would not notice him. Lisa was at a lost for words trying to tell her mother what happened to her that afternoon when Yosef and Mr. Dennis dropped her back at work. Lise, come on honey tell mom what's wrong

Mom, I'll be alright ok? I promise. Why are you hiding from me? What's happened? Mom. Please! Just leave me alone! I'm tired, and I need to be alone. I'm sorry but I don't feel like talking right now! They had never kept secrets from each other before. Deborah was trying hard to understand her daughter's behavior, but understanding was no more talking to her than Lisa was. She makes one last attempt to find out what's troubling her. Honey, please talk to me! She said desperation filling her every word. She had tried to take Lisa by the arm, when she winces in pain. Lisa jerked away abruptly from her. Oh, my God ! Lisa, was there a car accident? No Mom! Please! She cried, running passed her up the backstairs to her room. She closed all the curtains in her room, not allowing the afternoon Sun to shine through them as she usually does. She throws herself across her bed crying uncontrollably. Deborah walks out into the living room fearful for her daughter and the encounter she just had with her. Her mind burning up with thoughts that something absolutely dreadful had happened with Lisa. Ben, Ben? Yes dear. Rev. Anderson was sitting in his easy chair with the morning paper. I want you to go upstairs and talk with Lisa. He looks at her over the top of his wire rimmed glasses. Talk to Lisa? She's here? He looks at his watch. It's 2:30p.m Honey she doesn't get off work until 5:00. I know that, but she came home early today. I tell

You Ben, something's wrong with her. Wrong like what Deborah? Well, she was hiding herself from me.
Hiding? He said startled. Yes, hiding, she wouldn't let me look at her or even touch her. She was quiet and withdrawn! Now get up there and talk to her! I'm really worried about her Ben. She

said looking back at the stairs. She was near tears. Rev. Anderson could see the obvious concern in his wife's expression. He gets up out of his recliner and walks over to her putting his arm around her comforting her.

Deborah, I understand that her behavior is a bit out of her character. But Lisa's a big girl now. And a young woman about to be married soon. Maybe her and Jo-jo had a spat, and she just came home to heal her wounds. I'm telling you she's fine honey, just fine. Ben, they've had words before, and it's never affected her like this. And besides, if they had a fight or something, you and I both know that Yosef would've been here in a matter of seconds to patch things up with her. He would've called her a hundred times by now. Yes this is true too. But he can be a little on the stubborn side sometimes. Ben, please quit trying to make excuses, something happened to her, she was frightened. I know my child. That's not like her at all. A mother knows these things. I can feel her. Honey look, I know the mother's intuition thing, but fathers have insight too. You'll see after a little nap she'll be good as new. He kissed her on the cheek.

His voice reassuring to her. But Deborah was far from being reassured of anything. If I'm wrong, I apologize now. But if I'm right. Well.......? Ok, ok. I'll leave her be for right now. But if she's not down here in an hour, I'm going up there got it? Deal! He said sticking out his large hand. They shake on his offer. Now what I want you to do is go back in there and finish doing whatever it was you were doing. And try not to worry. Ben. How can I not worry about my child? I'm a mother. He smiles winking at her.

She winks back at him. She goes back into the laundry room. He sits back down in his easy chair to finish reading the paper. Ben? He takes a deep breath. Yes Love. I can't reach the whisk broom, will you come and get it down for me? But honey, I just sat down. I'm reading the sports page. Oh, that man! She said in frustration. Just then a large hand reaches over her handing the broom down to her. It was Yosef. Here you go mom. He said smiling. He had gotten off work early himself. He for some strange reason felt that something was not right at all, but he couldn't put his finger on what that was. Deborah noticed that he was

Wearing his Yamika, he had just come from Temple he had, had a time of prayer there. He had finished up early at work so Mr. Dennis let him take the rest of the day off. Jo-jo. What a

73

pleasant surprise to see you! She kissed him on the cheek. I'm so glad you're here. When did I get so blessed to get a greeting like that from you? She was silent for a moment. A single tear made it's way down her soft cheek. Her husband's words about there being a possible argument between him and Lisa surfaced. He could see that

She was deeply troubled about something. Mom? What's wrong? Is everything ok? He said setting his briefcase down on the floor next to the dryer, and his Prayer book on top of it. What's the matter?. He said
A seriousness in his tone. I don't know son. Something happened today that I don't understand, maybe you can help me. I'll try, what is it? She looks over into the living room to see that her husband was still engrossed in his paper reading, glancing up at the television every now and then. She spoke in a soft tone so as not to draw attention to them. She didn't quite know where to start. He could see that she was having trouble speaking, she began to choke up. His fear began to rise. Mom, what's happened? Is Lisa alright?

She looked up at him, it was just the opening she had been looking for. Strange you should mention her Yosef, I was just about to ask you the same thing. Ask me the same thing? What are you talking about?
Did you and Lisa have words today? I mean was there a fight between you two? A fight? About what mom? I don't know son, I'm just trying to make sense out all this that's all. Make sense out of what?
I don't have a clue about what's going on here. Look all I know is that Lisa and my boss, and his new lady friend Michelle all went out for lunch today. We dropped Michelle off at home, and Lisa back at work. I tried to call her later to let her know that I would be over sometime this evening to take her to practice with me. But Mary told me she left early. Did she tell you why? No. She just said that Lisa had to leave that's
All. Had to leave? Said Deborah. Her suspicions had progressed to fear, and fear was speaking at them both loud and clear now. Yosef something happened to her today. Like what? I don't know, she was quite, and withdrawn. Lisa? he said surprised. Yes. Lisa. She was very soft spoken. But she's always been soft spoken. He interrupts her. Yes, I know, but today she was different. She was hiding from me.

What! And what really got my suspicions up. When I tried to touch her arm, she reacted like I had stuck her with a hot poker or something. She cringed at me! She ran upstairs like a scared kitten. I haven't seen her since. That's what's got me so worried about her. Yosef didn't know what to make out of her story the afternoons event's with Lisa. He looked in the living room. Does dad know. Yeah, I tried to tell him, but you know your father dear, he insists that she and you had a little lovers spat, and she'll be fine in a while. Mom, I give you my word, we didn't had a fight this afternoon. I believe you son. May I go and see her? Yes, of course, will you? I'll see what I can find out. Good, the suspense is driving me crazy!

He kisses her on the cheek, and takes the back stairs up to Lisa's bedroom. Deborah looks over at Rev. Anderson again, he was watching the afternoon news now. Hello dear, hi sweetheart. Are you better now? Oh, I'm much better now. She said smiling. Oh, and why is that? Did you find out that I'm right about Lisa? Not really, Yosef is here. He is? I didn't even hear the boy come in. He looks at his watch it was 3:20pm. Yosef didn't get off work until 5:00pm What's the matter with kids these days, doesn't anybody stay at work until quittin time anymore? He's up with Lisa now. See that proves that I was right all along.

He's come to mend their ways. See I told you. Well we'll see dear. Ahhh he grunts at her waving his hand at her. She looks up towards the ceiling, hoping that Yosef could find some answers to Lisa's behavior. He knocks gently on the door. There was no answer. He opens the door and stepped inside. Shutting it behind him. Yosef looked around him, the room was dark. Far from the normal open windows with the Summer Sun streaming through them. He looks over at Lisa, she was lying across the bed crying still. The only light came from a small nite lamp that sat on her night table. It's light was dull and dim. Lisa? He called to her in a soft tone. Yes she whimpered. What's wrong? Your mother told me you came home from work early. Did you get sick or something? No. she whimpered again. Yosef was beginning to get a little frustrated at her, but he retained himself. He came closer to her sitting on the side of her bed.
He touched the small of her back gently. She jerked abruptly. He frowned at her, his supiscions surfacing slowly. You gotta talk to

me honey, your mother is worried sick about you, and so am I. She never answered him back. Would you at lease sit up so I can see you better? She exhales in frustration, and sat up on the bed. The small nite light glimmered off her slightly. We've never had secrets from each other before, let's not start now. He said his anger surfacing at her distant behavior. He scoots a little closer to her, getting a better look at her. He notices that her clothes were ripped and torn, Her blouse was hanging off her shoulder. Her hair was in all directions. She was dirty from a scuffle of some kind. And the slightest noise made her jump like a scared kitten. He looked in horror as his beloved Lisa sat before him looking like someone who had lived in the wilds of the woods for a long period of time. He smelled the fragrance of a man's cologne on her clothes. His breathing became rapid at the moment. My God Lisa! What happened to you? He breathed. I, I. She stuttered trying to find the words to explain, but her mind would give her no help in finding them. She couldn't even look at him. He sat there in front of her looking

Strong and handsome, and she like a small animal that had just crawled out from under a viaduct. His anger got the best of him. He reaches for her startling her. Lisa! He grabs at her arm. She screams. Nooo! God! Noooo! Yosef pleeeease don't hit meee!! Yosef jumps from her bed screaming with her.
He walks away from her bed. He looks back at her, she had buried her face in her hands, cowering up in a little ball. Yosef's heart broke for her. He knew that someone had done something horrible to her, but who, and what? Was the question. He comes back over to her and sits down. Lisa? I'm going to ask you once more, and I want you to tell me the truth. Please Ok? Ok. She said nodding her head at him. When we dropped you off at work, what happened? Well, she sniffs. I went back to my desk, Mary asked me how did lunch go? I told her . At that time Mr. Wright came in and asked me to come to his office, he said that he wanted me to look at some files that Melvin had messed up pretty bad. She goes back to that moment
That afternoon. You might want to grab your note pad, I want you to take some notes for me too. He said
To her. She proceeded to tell him of all that happened. How Mr. Wright got her inside his office, and shut the door locking it. He stood there and stared at her for a few moments. He took his cigar out of his mouth and walks over to his desk, and puts it out in the large glass ashtray next to his desk lamp. He told me

76

that he had admired me for a long time, and that he liked working with me. And he wanted to do things

For me. What things? Said Yosef. I don't know, he started walking towards me. I asked him about the files. He shook his head at me. Later about the files. He pushed the whole pile of them off his desk
Onto the floor. He then asked me to come closer to him.   I backed away, I refused. He said that he had always wanted me from the first time that he laid his eyes on me. Yosef could feel his anger surfacing
In a fury at that moment. And that he, she takes a deep breath, and that he. She whimpered. Yosef looked down at her hands, she was rubbing them together, they were sweaty and shaking. He looks back at her as she struggled to tell him what her boss wanted from her. Yosef he said that he wanted to... she couldn't finish her sentence. Sleep with you? He said finishing it for her. He said through his teeth, he squinted his eyes, his jaw tightens. He clenched his fists. His anger had now showed itself. When I refused him this time, he walked up to me and he, he uh. He, he.. she stuttered. Lisa, did he touch you? Yes. Where? How? What did you he do to you! He said his voice raised. Turn the light on. She said to him. He reaches across her to turn on the large bedside lamp. His horror returns, this time bringing rage with it. Jesus!   He said unbelief overwhelming him. Mr. Wright had assaulted Lisa in a most savage way. Yosef held her face in his hand, turning it from one cheek to the other. She had a large handprint on her cheek where he had slapped her. She opened her blouse, which was hanging from her shoulder, revealing a series of bruises all over her shoulders. She tried to stand up, she fell back on the bed. Yosef extends his hand offering her his assistance. She refuses his gesture. He stands with her to keep her from falling again. She takes her blouse completely off, undoing her bra. She turns around, her back facing him.

Yosef grabs his stomach, nearly vomiting when he sees the large welps on her back. Oh, my God Lisa! She turns around to face him, walking up to him. She was unsteady on her feet.   Come here baby. He calls to her softly. His voice trembling. Tears streaming down his masculine face. She nearly collapses in his arms. They both cry in each others embrace. You see Yosef, I wanted to spare you all this. I never wanted you or my parents to

77

see me this way.   Did you call for help? I tried, but I think Mary
had taken a smoke break outside. Mr. Webber was at a
conference for the rest of the afternoon. I just didn't think to call
the police, I ran out of the back door of his office, jumped in my
car, and came home. Oh Yosef, I didn't even stop for my purse, I
just ran! She said crying heavily in his arms.   Shhh, I'm here
now ok?
I don't know what I did Beloved.   She cried. Lisa you didn't do
anything wrong, it wasn't you alright?
Alright Beloved. Alright. She looks up at him. He tried to kiss
her on her neck, but she abruptly pulls away from him.   What is
it? He walks back up to her. She starts to shake again. She
turns her head to one side pulling her hair back from off her
shoulders. Once again revealing another injury from her boss' s
attack. There on the side of her slender neck were teethmarks.
Jesus Christ! He bit you Lisa! His voice even louder. Her eyes
soft, and tender, full of tears. His heart for a brief second
softened. He takes off his suit coat and puts it around her. He
then picks her up kissing her gently. Lisa curls up in his arms as
he carries her back over to the bed. He carefully lays her down,
staring at her unable to take his eyes off her.
He stokes her hair down, she was quiet, smiling at him slightly.
She was better now. Now that her Beloved was there for her.
Stay here. He said. But Yosef! She said sitting up in bed, fear
returning to her.
Her tears were flowing more. Please don't leave me! He takes
her in his arms, cradling her, rubbing the back of her head. I'll
be back ok? Beloved please! He lays her back down on the bed,
putting his index finger to her lips. Shhh, I'll be back, I promise.
She kisses his finger gently. But, I. She said. Lisa, I promise,
I'll be back alright? He said making her comfortable. Alright
Beloved. Stay here baby. He said softly, winking at her.   I love
you. She mouthed to him. I love you. He said stroking her soft
face, until she slowly closed her eyes. He turned out the large
lamp, leaving her once again in the darkness of her room, with
only the dimness of the small nite light glimmering on her. He
gets up and leaves, he

turns around one last time to look at her before leaving her. He
leaves her door slightly cracked. He stopped out in the hall, his
thoughts filled with her boss's savagely attacking Lisa. His body
begins to swell

as rage had returned to him, his face tightening again. He ran down the stairs. Deborah heard him coming down the stairs into the living room. She jumped up running over to him. Well Yosef , is she alright? No she isn't. Rev. Anderson gets up and walks over to them. What's going on here? His voice now deep filled with concern for his daughter. It was her boss mom. He attacked her this afternoon. He paused, taking a deep breath. He beat her mom, he beat her, then he tried to rape her. The Anderson's gasped as Yosef gave them the same details that Lisa had given him. Oh! My baby! Cried Deborah, I knew it! I knew something was wrong! Oh my God! I Have to get up there to her now! She hurries up the stairs to find that Lisa had curled up in a fetal position on the bed, whimpering like a small lost child. Oh Lisa why did you tell momma honey! Oh Lisa! The cries of both mother and daughter could be heard all the way down stairs by Rev. Anderson and Yosef. Both men now filled with an indescribable anger as they listened to their cries. Who did you say did this to my child Yosef? It was her boss, Mr. Wright down at Webber and Wright Insurance Company. I'm on my way down there to see this jerk Dad he's gonna pay for what

he did to my girl. Wait! Not yet son, I need to think a moment. Well you go ahead and think dad, I've got some business to take care of. No! Yosef! No! Dad you should see her! Go on up there and look at her! He beat my girl. He said whimpering. He bit her, you hear me! That, that scum bit my girl! He said brushing his hair back on his head. Rev. Anderson, walks over to him embracing him, his voice comforting to him. Jo-Jo. Listen to me son, I know how you feel, believe me I do. That's my little girl lying up there wearing an array of injuries caused by this animal. I think that I know why his name stands out to me so. Stay here I have to make a few phone calls down to some friends of mine at the 32nd precinct in town. There was a huge scandal that went down here a year ago, and his name was mentioned in it. Not much, I think. But we should conduct a little investigation of our own shall we? Yes sir said Yosef. He had calmed down for the moment, but his anger had come no where near being calm at all. He watches and listens as Rev. Anderson makes his phone calls. He gives them the name. A file is pulled up on one Wright, Theodore, Allen. Case number 879642. There was a history of criminal sexual assault that went back all the way to the early 80's. Then there was a newspaper article of the local news in their vicinity.

Mr. Wright was part of an attempted rape, and sexual assault against a young woman of her mid 20's a year ago. The charges were dropped because the young woman refused to come forward to identify him as the assailant. He was found innocent of the charge. But there were other cases that were filed against him from years back that he was not found so innocent of. He even spent two years in prison ten years ago
For the same charge in the Wisconsin area. Rev. Anderson after pulling a few strings managed to have the information that he needed faxed to his home. Courtesy of Sgt. Lehman Winston Jr. His father was great friends with Rev. Anderson. They go way back to their war days. I knew there was a reason that he sounded so familiar to me. Here son take this with you, I don't think he'll be a problem to you now. Yosef smiled as he took the nearly twenty page fax with him. Yosef left to pay Mr. Wright a little vengeance call.

He pulls up in front of the huge building. The office is located on the ground floor. Yosef enters the outer lobby leading to Mr. Wrights office. He stands there listening. He hears voices coming from behind his door. Mary Sees him standing there listening. May I help you sir?   He looks at her his tightened features And clenched fists told her why he looked that way. Where is he? He said through his teeth. In there, but he's unavailable. You can't go in there sir.   She said nervousness filling her voice. Watch me! He said walking right passed her. Sir! Sir! Mary really didn't try to stop him. She knew that it was about time that
Mr. Wright got what was long over due him. A good fanny kicking! Yosef walked up to the office door his thoughts filled with this afternoon of Lisa attack. Image after image of her revealing her injuries to him only fueled his anger more. The voices were louder as he got closer and closer to the office door. Suddenly the images of Lisa's welped back, and the bitemark on her neck flashed at the same time.   Yosef, overcome with rage yelled out loudly as he kicked the office door with such force, that it explodes off it's hinges! He attracted the attention of everyone there in the lobby. There were gasps, and expressions of Surprise. He enters the office. The noise had startled the couple. There on the desk was Mr. Wright jumping off his newest victim. A young redhead who Yosef recognized as one of the pros that worked the streets in many of the neighborhoods that he and Johnathan were familiar with. They had seen her on many

Of the corners while they would be on their way to the courts for
a game of one on one.   She even petitioned them once. They
both laughed in her face and kept going. She jumped off the table
and ran
Passed Yosef like a scared rabbit. He watched her leave, shaking
his head in disgust at her. He then turns
To glare at Mr. Wright. You seem quite the ladies man. He said
walking towards him. Mr. Wright becomes indignant at Yosef's
intrusion into his office. He quickly zipped his pants that were
still open for obvious reasons,one of which had just ran out the
door. Who are you? He said. His tone raspy, he fumbled as he
struggled to put his suit coat back on. You know Lisa Anderson
don't you? Lisa? Of course I know her, she's my secretary. What
of it? His raspy voice was beginning to crack like a young
pubescent thirteen year old, as it began to rise at him. Can you
explain to me why my girl came home with bruises, and various
other injuries this afternoon? I want to know how when I saw her
earlier she was fine, not a scratch on her. Now she looks like
she's been in the ring with Mike Tyson. Can you explain that to
me? Yosef's anger rose more and more, as the images of Lisa
kept flashing before him. Your girl! You're her boyfriend? Oh,
I'm much more than that tubby, I'm practically her husband.
Husband? But you're not Black! You're Jewish! That's a good
observation porky, but you still didn't answer me. He said
walking closer and closer to him. Mr. Wright backed further and
further away from him. Mr. Wright's indignation had abandoned
him now, and fear had come in it's place. Yosef walked up to him
standing directly in front of him now. Mr. Wright looked up at
Yosef like he was looking up a tall building or something. He
had stopped there. His anger seething now. I don't know what
happened to her, maybe she was in an accident or something. No
she wasn't in an accident or something. Mr. Wright was trying to
move further back, but

He had no place to go, his desk was right behind him. She said
that you did this to her. Why! Tell me man why! What did she
ever do to you! The man jumped like a frog on a hot plate. Come
on now man, now you know you and me we're the same aren't
we? I, I mean you can't never believe anything that Black people

say. Hey, they all lie! Yosef became so angry at his remark that he jerked him by the collar of his suit

Lifting him off the floor, and just held him there in mid-air, His feet dangling underneath him. He was trying to feel the floor with his feet. Come on man, put me down! Put me down! Yosef threw the man across his desk, his body slamming into the wall. His body hitting it with such force, that it leaves his

Body print there. You, you freaking animal! He said stammering his words. You bit my girl on her neck!

What kind of a sick son of bit.... Yosef catches himself, tears streaming down his tightened face. Look man, I didn't mean to hurt her, I swear, But I couldn't help it! She was driving me crazy! The way that she moved her body when she walked. I just wanted to try her that's all. I always wanted to see what it would be like with a Black woman! I just wanted to have a little fun that's all, just a little fun. You know man fun. He said trying to laugh. His toupee sliding off to the side of his head again, he frantically tried to adjust it back. Yosef walked around the desk where he was, and picked him up again holding him by the collar. I didn't mean it! I swear I didn't mean it! I didn't mean to hurt her! Please believe me! He pleaded with him. Yosef wasn't moved at all by his pleas for mercy. You beat my girl! He said through his teeth. He flashed back again to where Lisa showed him the bitemark on her neck. What kind of an animal are you! Yosef threw the man against the wall again. Harder this time. His body leaving an even deeper groove in it than before. His body thuds hard against the floor. Yosef lost all control of himself, and pounded on the man even more savagely than he beat Lisa. Help! Somebody help me! Please! Help meeeee! He screamed. Mary sat outside at her desk filing her nails smiling as Mr. Wright got his just desserts. She was whistling to herself as she continued on in her nail filing. Yosef's body

Swelled even more as he remembered how Lisa told him how he tore her clothes off her. Yosef finally catches himself, and stopped his beating of Mr. Wright. Slightly winded, he walked back towards the front of his desk. I'm gonna call the police! Fired Mr. Wright. Yosef picks up the phone and throws it at him. Here! Go head and call them, and tell them how you beat my girl, then we can add this to the twenty others that you have already. Mr. Wright looked surprised, His skeletons had come to haunt him and I don't mean the Halloween kind either. How did you know about that! His stiff pile of hair was sliding again. He tries to make another adjustment, it just slid over to the other side. You've really been a busy boy over the years haven't you! All it would take is one phone call, just one. I'm sure your wife and kids would understand right? Mr. Wright's eyes became big as saucer plates. You wouldn't, would you?

Yosef goes back over to him and jerks him off the floor again, dangling him in the air. Listen to me you little hemorrhoid, if you ever touch Lisa again, so help man. He flings him back over the desk again. Yosef walks away from him going back over to what was left of the office door that he kicked off it's hinges. Don't make me come back down here again. He said pointing to him. He leaves the office.

When Mr. Wright saw that Yosef had left the building, his courage returned. Oh yeah, well she's fired! The adhesive that held the toupee in place, lost it's grip on his bald head. And fell off backwards, behind him. His face was swollen, his mouth was bleeding, his lip busted, and both eyes were blackened. He looked like an overweight raccoon with a receding hairline. Oooooh! He sighed before collapsing behind his desk.

Yosef returns to the Anderson's home like he promised Lisa that he would. He goes inside to find Johnathan there alone in the kitchen. He was fixing himself a plate of supper. Jo, come on in man. He sets his plate down on the counter, and goes over to hug him. How they both needed that comfort from each other now. Hey man I uh heard about my baby sister when I got in from work this afternoon. I couldn't believe it jo. I couldn't believe it! He said to him, his pain for his sister surfacing now. Dirty old fart. I can't imagine anyone doing something like this to her man. I mean I know my baby sister, she wouldn't hurt a soul. Not a soul. Then this horny old buzzard jumps her like that! His anger rising now. Yosef was quiet, he listened as johnathan vented his anger. I need to see her John. He turns to go upstairs to her room. Not there! He said. Yosef turns and comes back into the kitchen. Not here? She's not here? No man. After you left, I had come home, Dad told me where you were, and why. He said smiling. Did you take care of business little brother? All the way my bro. All the way. He said, hitting fives with him.

Well when they had told me about Lisa. She was in such a bad way that they had to rush her to the hospital. Yosef thought that his whole world had come crashing in on him. Oh Jesus Lisa! He sighed, tears in his eyes. Which one? Saints Of Mercy. Oh John. He sighed again. Johnathan walks over to console him. Jo, she's a strong girl, you know that. You've known her all your life. She's a trooper, she'll come out of this like a champ. Yosef looked into Johnathan's eyes, seeing Rev. Anderson in them. And hearing him in his voice. Thanks John. I needed to hear that. You bet. Just then they heard the family van pull up outside. They go over to the front picture window in the living room, and saw four people getting out. It was Rev. Anderson, Deborah, Sarah, and Lisa. Lisa was walking better than she was earlier. They open the front door, all coming inside. Johnathan escorts his mother and Sarah inside. Rev. Anderson escorting Lisa. Hello son! Said Sarah hugging Yosef. Here, Johnathan, take this for me will you? Yes ma'mam. He said taking her sweater. He takes his mother's sweater as well hanging them up in the closet for them. Rev. Anderson goes over to shake hands with Yosef, and Johnathan. How is she dad? Asked Johnathan. Fine, fine. Dr. Esman said to keep her off her feet for the next few days, and she should be good as new inside of a week. What's that? Rev. Anderson was holding a small white paper medicine bag. It's a ointment for the welps on her back. Her mother will take care of that for her. Yosef held his head down. He noticed Lisa standing over by the sofa by herself, looking at him. Her eyes full of longing for him. He stared at her the same. Son? Called Sarah to him. He looks down at her. She's alright, sore for a while, but she's alright. He never answered her. He looks back at Lisa. There he goes again staring her face off. They all laugh even Yosef, and Lisa chuckle a little. Everyone leaves the couple alone while

They all go into the kitchen for refreshments. Lisa could no longer stand the anticipation of holding him in her arms again. She runs over to him jumping into his arms. Yosef swinging her around. Oh God Lisa!
I was so worried about you, let me look at you. He put her down looking at her slender form. Come here.
He said softly, kissing her. I'm fine Beloved. A little sore, but I'm fine. That you are baby, that you are.
They walk over to the couch and sit down. What did the Dr. say? Just what Ms. Sarah said. Just take it easy for a few days, and stay away from my boss, and I should be good as new. Yosef laughs a little. That won't be a problem for you will it? No it

84

won't. She looks at him a moment. Yosef? Hum? Are you gonna be alright? I was so scared for you when you left this afternoon. I'm fine now that my girl's home, and doing ok. He kisses her gently on the forehead. He hugs her close to him, pulling her onto his lap. They kiss deeply again. She feels the hardness of his manhood underneath her, Yosef? Stop that. She laughs. I can't help it Lisa, it just happens. I love you so much. I love you too my beloved. She looks down at his hand, he was holding three little booklets. What's that? She said trying to see them. Oh, I stopped at the Jewelers yesterday, and I found these pamphlets. He paused. Would you like to go and look at some engagement rings with me next Friday? Oh Yosef! I would love to. He stares at her again. They started to kiss, but she stops. Let's look at a few in here, maybe we might see something that we both like.

Ok, she said softly, stroking his cheek. They looked the booklets over, and found a design that they both did like. Ohhhh! Gasped Lisa. I really like this. It looks like a starburst of diamonds with a huge one in the center. You like that? Oh Yes I do. Do you like it Beloved? He looked at the design again. Yes, it is beautiful. He said, his heart beating faster with each moment. I want my baby to have only the best that I can give her. Ohh Yosef, That's so sweet of you. Thank you beloved. She whispered, her tone sensual.
Her eyes filled with longing for him again. He looked into her eyes, they revealed to him her heart. *"Make love to me Beloved, make love to me."* It said. He saw what her heart wanted. Oh Lisa!, He moaned, caressing her body closer to him. I love you so much Beloved. She said. Her voice filled with passion. Her moaning was sweet to his ears. He smiles at her tenderly, enjoying her as she enjoyed the throbbing of his manhood underneath her. She squirmed on his lap. Causing ecstacy to surge through him. He felt that tingling sensation flowing all throughout his body. He continues to slow grind her soft bottom, embracing her harder, pushing her deeper into his mouth, as they kissed deeply. Oh Yosef! She winced. What! Oh, you squeezed my arm a little too tight. She showed him the bruised arm that Mr. Wright injured. Oh, baby. I'm sorry, I didn't mean to hurt you. His inflamed passion had cooled now. I got a little carried away. Honey, don't sweat it. I don't break that easy ya know. Here, we'd better get up from here. She said. Yes we better. He said looking at his watch. It was 4:15p Lisa? Yes

85

Beloved. I have to get going now for rehearsal at Terry's at five. I'll try to swing back by here to check in on you before it gets too late. Ok? She looks at him smiling. He steps closer to her. Now what is that smile all about? May I go with you? Lisa, no! He said surprised that she would even ask him such a thing as that. Look, I'd love for you

To, but I want you to stay here, I get worried about you sometimes. Honey, I feel fine, I really do. I just need to get out of this house that's all. Please......? She looked at him, her tender brown eyes melted his heart. She reached up on her tippy toes and kissed gently. He pulled her close to him. Lisa.......? He moaned. He found it nearly impossible to resist her at times. And this was one of them. Alright baby, Go get your sweater. He said softly, smiling at her. I'll be right back! She said. Her excitement was like a small child at a circus. She turns to go upstairs. He looked down at his manhood still slightly swollen. Behave yourself. He laughed, adjusting himself, so he would not be conspicuous to anyone. Just then, his mother and Deborah emerged from the kitchen, they had been discussing the next Intercessory Prayer Warriors meeting.. Yosef, where's Lisa? Sarah asked him. She's upstairs getting a sweater. What would she need a sweater for? It's so humid outside. Well I asked her to get it, she's coming with me to rehearsal. Oh Yosef, do you think that after all she's been through today, that's a good idea? I mean she's still pretty bruised and sore. Said Deborah, her concern surfacing. Sarah looked at her son, standing there strong tall and handsome. She was proud of the man that he had become. She smiled
At him. She also noticed that there was a small wet patch on the front of his slacks. She lowered her head, she was blushing. She remembered the night that he told her about his date with Lisa. She could still hear his voice loud and clear. *"She makes me tingle."* She saw the results of the tingling. She walks over to Deborah and takes her by her hands patting them. It's no use my dear friend. The boy's in Love. But she's not well yet. Said Deborah. Sarah smiles at Yosef. He wondered what made her laugh so. He walks over to her. Mom, are you ok? What's the matter? Yosef, you naughty boy you. Why didn't you tell Lisa no.? I tried to mom, but she begged me. I can't stand to see her beg. She said please, In that little voice of hers. What else?

She, she. He struggled. She kissed me. He said looking up towards the stairs

At that moment, Lisa came back downstairs. She had changed clothes. She was wearing a beautiful floral print sundress, with short sleeves. She had chose her white sweater to carry with her. She let her hair fall to her shoulders. She kept it pulled close to her neck to hide Mr. Wright's bitemark. Lisa, you're not well enough to be outside honey. Don't you want to lie down for a while? Mom, If I lay down any longer, I'm gonna get bed sores. That should make for an interesting honeymoon wouldn't it? Yosef put his hand over his mouth laughing, he and Sarah. Now don't you sass me young lady. I'm still your mother. Lisa walks over to her. Mom, I'm sorry, but I'm fine, I really am. Believe me, I feel a lot better than I look. She kisses her on the cheek. And besides, I'm not three years old anymore. I can take care of myself. Yosef, do something, talk to her will you? She cried to him. He stood there with his arms folded, still smiling at Lisa. Lisa walks up to him. He held her underneath his arm, caressing her gently. Ready now? I'm ready

Beloved. We'll see you in a few hours. He said. Bye Ladies! Said Lisa, as Yosef walked her to the front door. Sarah stop them! Whinned Deborah. Sarah walked over to the big picture window and watches the couple leave. She looks back at Deborah, who was now near tears. She felt about as helpless as a fly in a spider web. Deborah come over here. You see? She watches along with Sarah. While Yosef and Lisa pull off. Sarah, what am I gonna do with that girl? I feel like I've lost her. No, no my child. You've not lost her. She's my little girl Sarah, my little girl. Said Deborah, as her tears begin to flow. Your little girl is

A young woman now. And my little boy, has become a man. Yes? They look at each other. Yes. Deborah nodded. When Lisa kissed Yosef. Telling her no was not what was on his mind at that time. They are in Love Deborah, remember this ok? Let the children enjoy what God has blessed them with.

Let them enjoy their Love. Next to Him, she said pointing to the ceiling. And us. It is all that they have.

Deborah was silent as she thought heavily on Sarah's words, she knew it was the truth. You know what I mean by this eh? Eh. Deborah smiled. Nodding in agreement with her. Come, I go home now. What about coffee Sarah? It's your favorite. Hazelnut Crème. Sarah pauses a moment. It was her favorite, one that she never could resist. I go fix supper for him, then I come back. Ok Deborah? Ok cookie. She laughed. Brad walks into Terry's garage, greeting everyone. Hey what's up! What up man? Said James.

Hey drummer man is back! He said excited along with the rest of the band. Yeah, I'm back! What's up man! He said shaking hands with each other, embracing in brotherly fashion. Drummer man! Said Terry, embracing him like Brad. What's the scoop on the sound equipment in Wisconsin? Said Terry. Cause we could sure use something better than this. I found some stuff up there for us man, that is just too cool for words. But I need the whole band to make a trip up there together to check it out. It's just too much for one person to decide on man. But I did find some great deals up there, I can also pull a few strings with a partner of mine, J.C. He can get us a bit of a discount on the mikes, and amplifiers. I'm talkin top of the line stuff man. James reaches into his pocket and pulls out a few flyers that he brought back from there.

Sound World was the name of the store. He showed them the equipment that he checked out for them. There were no arguments from anyone. Just a lot of oooh's and ahhhh's and gasps and things like that.
The prices were steep, but like he said he could pull some strings and get some super deals on the stuff that they all needed. You get this stuff for us man, and I'll dance at your wedding. Said Terry. They all laughed together. All except Billy. He had come over for a casual visit. He had brought his guitar with him. He wanted to play with them again. But he had been let go from the band when the Incident with Lisa took place two years ago. They never allowed him back in again. He was sitting in the corner strumming his guitar a little. He was quiet, and distant. He seemed to be stewing about something.
But Billy Bravens was always stewing about something. He had a chip on his shoulders the size of the rock of Gibralter. And his head was twice as hard as that big rock. James looked around. Where's my man Jo? Said James. Oh, that's right. You haven't

heard. Lisa's back home now. Billy stops his strumming, sitting up on his stool, batting his eyes like an owl in a hailstorm. His breathing sped up a little.

What! Sweet Lisa's home! Home to stay my man. Said Terry. She is? Said Billy. They all looked over at him. Yeah, she is. Said Terry. I bet the boy flipped when he heard that! Flipped aint the word, drummer man. They boy did handsprings! Said Brad. They've been out every night since she came home. Billy's jealousy began to surface. He hated Yosef being with her. He had wanted her from the time they were kids. But Yosef had won her heart for life. And she's home to stay? Said James. Forever my man! Said Terry slapping fives with him. Billy hid his obvious joy to hear that she was home, by remaining silent, and non-chalant. But in his heart he knew that he was thrilled to hear that she was back. He even thought about how he might try to win her over to him. But there was a problem, a big problem. Yosef. Just then he was shaken out of his fantasy by the tooting of a car horn. It was Yosef and Lisa. They both go inside. What's up people! Said Yosef. The band flocked over to him like bees to a honey blossom.
My man Jo! Bass man himself! Can't nobody play a bass like Jo! What's up bro! Said James to him. Smiling from ear to ear. He embraced him so hard he nearly lifted him off the floor! They shake hands in brotherly fashion. Drummer man! Said Yosef. When did you get back? I got back this morning. It's good to see you man. Said Yosef. It's good to see you too bass man. I want you all to know, this man can make a bass sing like a canary. Don't cha know? That we know. Said Terry. They all stood around greeting one another. They all heard the sweet voice being cleared. It was Lisa. Yosef had left her there in the doorway. They all turned around to look at her. Well, well, well. What do we have here! Lisa, sweet Lisa! Said James. Gimme love, and my squeeze. He said laughing. Hi James. She said. Oh, baby I'm sorry. Forgive me. I didn't mean to forget you back there. No problem, honey. She said laughing.

Yosef goes over to her taking her by the hand. He brings her inside the garage. Hi Lise. Said Billy. They all turn to look at him. He was smiling, his expression was sort of sinister looking. Lisa breathed heavy a little. A slight fear rose up within her. Hello Billy. She said. Her voice a little hesitant. Yosef noticed her reaction. He embraced her close to him, caressing her. He looked at her. Are you gonna be alright? If not you just say the word, and we're outta here. Ok? I'm alright Beloved. He could feel her shaking in his embrace. He glared over in Billy's direction. Billy just glared back at him. The rest of the band members could feel the tension between them rising. Can't you speak man? Said James indignantly.

Pardon my manners. Joseph. He said bowing his head at him. William. Said Yosef. Calling him by his actual name. His mother nicknamed him Billy, because of his father Police Commissioner William Bravens Sr. He spoiled Billy terribly. He was born late in their lives, and was an only child. And he was used to getting his own way. But Yosef drew the line when it came to Lisa. She was his and his alone, and Billy was not going to come in between them. Baby why don't you have a seat right over here ok? He said seating her on a small stool behind him. He felt better with her close to him and the rest of the guys. He trusted them like brothers. He went over to hook his bass into the amplifier. And started tuning up for play. Billy, feeling ignored, allowed his jealousy to get the better of him. His anger surfaced especially when he saw Yosef looking over at Lisa, he bent over to kiss her gently. They mouthed I Love you to each other. Whoooo. Said the rest of the band members. Billy turned his head the other way fuming mad at their display of open affection. He could no longer resist the compulsion to go hemorrhoidal. So he decided to trip out on everybody. His usual impish behavior surfaced in a most cruel way. Hey Joseph, Helen's been asking about you. You know she's still hot for ya man. He said looking at Lisa, hoping to get a jealous reaction from her. But instead all he got from her was her ignoring him. Yosef looked at Lisa. She smiled and winked at him, letting him know, she was not bothered by Billy's instigating.

He winked back at her smiling. He walked over to the other band mates whispering to them. If he starts anything, anything at all. I'm gonna thump him. We got cha back jo. Said James. Whew! It's hot in here! Said Lisa, taking off her sweater. She was a little sensitive to the Sun, so she wore it just to keep from having a reaction from it's exposure. She took it off, revealing all of her injuries of the afternoon's attack. All the band members gasped when they saw her. They could not believe their eyes, when they saw the bruises, and the bitemark. Oh my God ! Said Terry, what happened to her! He told them all of Lisa's attack. Jesus!

Man! I know you took care of business didn't you? Said James. That I did my man, that I did. He said hitting fives with him. Is he still alive? Said Brad, he couldn't take his eyes off of Lisa, it's almost like he was studying her injuries or something. Lisa never heard their conversation, she was sitting there reading a Christian Catalog that Yosef had given her. She was ordering some gifts and books out of it for him. She was filing out the order form as they were tuning their instruments for play. Come on bass man, make her talk for me man. Said James. Yosef began to play a bass run for them. They listened as he played a tune they didn't recognize at first. Then James began to nod his head, he recognized which song it was from. He picked up the beat to the song on his drums. Terry, joined in on Lead guitar, then Brad on the keyboards. They were playing a song that Lisa had written three months ago called. *"I Believe In You."* Yosef had changed the bass run a little. As he stepped over closer to her. She was now

In full view of Billy, he got a bird's eye view of her injuries. His demon began to speak to him. He nodded in agreement. He knew that Helen didn't know that Lisa was back home. And he was going to be the first to tell her. He had always wanted Lisa from the first time that he laid eyes on her. But it was too late. Yosef had already made her his girl. He had tried repeatedly to take her away from him. But all to no avail. Her heart belonged to him, and his to her. Sing a little of that for me Lisa. Said Yosef. Lisa steps up to the Mike, and begins to sing the chorus from the song.

Ever will I stand strong in that day.
Ever will I trust You as I Pray.
Ever will I walk with You by Faith.

I Believe In You....You, You.
Ever in Your Will I Pray to be.
For Your Loving Presence is so
Sweet.
Ever will I linger at Your Feet.

I Believe In You.

The girl be blowin don't she? Said James, smiling at Yosef. That she can, drummer man. Said Yosef. Billy's demon would not be silenced so easily. He spoke to Billy again. It reminded him of how much Helen really wanted Yosef, and how he wanted Lisa the same. Yosef had shunned Helen's every move on him, as did Lisa with Billy.   He saw her injuries, he gasped himself at the sight of them. Just what he needed to fuel his cruelty. So tell me Lisa, let's start over again shall we. I've changed a little since then. Let's start over again. He smiled looking like Dr. Seuss' Grinch. His smile seemed to stretch from ear to ear. James shook his head at him. This boy aint got no luggage, but he be trippin don't he? Said James to Terry. Yosef's gonna give him a one way trip if he don't chill out. How we gonna do something over that never started Billy? And besides, you still talk so much of the same crap, I'm surprised you can stand the smell of your own breath! She said to him, never even looking up at him. Yosef put his hand over his mouth cracking up laughing at him. So did the rest of the band.   Oh, oh. This boy don't want this woman to go home girl on him. Said Terry. I know that's right, the girl's got a temper like a piranha, and teeth just as sharp. Said James. She'll strip him naked. That's real gross Brad. Said terry.   He looked at the injuries again. Hey Joseph, I see you're finally learning how to treat a woman. What's the matter, she wouldn't give you any panty pudding? You knocked her around pretty good boy! Yosef stopped laughing
At him, he nearly dropped his bass, he charged over at him. James, and Terry hold him back. Heh,heh,heh. He laughed in a James dean sort of way. You son of a bit.... James held him tighter. No! Man, he aint worth it. I'll thump you man! You're crazy! I'll thump you Billy! Lisa watched her Beloved

As they held him back from Billy.   Then something inside of her snapped. To her she could feel his anger.
She walked over to them. Yosef? He never heard her. Beloved? She stepped in front of him, palming his face in her soft hand.

92

She spoke softly to him. Let it go baby, let it all go. It's alright, I'm here. Her voice, her eyes seem to mesmerize him. That's right, it's ok. He looked at her somewhat confused as to what was happening to him. His anger totally left him, he was more at ease, like an unknown euphoria had overtaken him.   Better now? Yes. He said to her, his tone softer now.   James and Terry had to sit him down on the small stool that she was sitting on earlier.   She puts her hand on his bass. Why don't you put this away for him will you James? I'll be right back. They all wondered what she meant by that. But she would show them.   ·
She would show them all. Wow! Did you see that! Said Terry. I've never seen anything like that in my life! Said James. Let me take this Jo-jo. He said to him un strapping his bass.

Lisa walked out from among them over towards Billy who was still over in the corner cackling to himself.
She looks at him, this time her anger began to rise. She then turns to look at Yosef who was slowly regaining his composure. She felt a surge of compassion overwhelm her for him. She hurt for him.
She then turns to look at Billy, his words returned to echo in her ears. Her softened features, took on an expression of boldness. You're right James, he isn't worth it. Billy looks over at her. My father told me that Ignorance is an equal opportunity employer, and it'll employ any fool that's stupid enough to work for it. And this boy's working overtime this evening. He stops his laughing and sits up on the stool.   The rest of the band look in amazement at her as she fires at Billy. Ohhh! They all laugh at him.   You know Beloved, some people like for you to feed their stupidity, but Billy will starve to death before I let you feed his. Oooouuuuchh! Said Terry and James together. Ka ching! They said, hitting fist together. James told that boy not to go there. What a Dork! Said Brad.   Yosef and all the members crack up laughing even harder. Billy looks at all of them laughing at him now. He gets up and throws his guitar in the corner, storming passed Lisa. Where ya going Billy boy! She said in southern drawl.   He stops and turns around

Nobody calls me that! I just did, what cha gonna do! He grunts at her, walking rapidly towards her, his fist raised in the air. Yosef gets up his strength fully returned to him now. James , and Terry helping him now.

If he touches her, I'll kill him! He said through his teeth. No, man. Wait, let's see what she's gonna do to him next. This is good I'm enjoying every moment of it. Said Terry. He stops right in front of her, she looks up at his fist. And just what do you think you're gonna do with that! She becomes totally enraged Her eyes seem to glow like red embers in a fireplace. She reaches up and grabs his shoulders, and sinks her knee hard into his groin. He crumples to the floor. Oooohhhh! Yiiiikes! They all said as they wince in pain along with Billy, who actually was in pain. Oh ag-o-ny! Said Brad, as he crosses his legs together. Yosef was shocked as Lisa let Billy have it. She then punches him hard in the face with her fist. Damn!

Said James. Did you see that! Said Terry. I saw that said Yosef. Go Lisa! Cheered Brad. His eyes bugging nearly out of the sockets. Don't you ever raise your hand to me again Billy. My own father doesn't even hit me. What makes you think that you can? You got away with that crap two years ago, but not this time. Just a little retribution on my part don't cha know? He looks up at her, then over at the band

Busting up laughing at him. You're nothing but slime Billy, a worthless waste of human flesh taking up useful space that some decent human being could be using. Oooooh Weeee! Said James. Is she raking him or what? I've never seen her like this before. Said Yosef smiling from ear to ear. Now get out of my sight, and go back to the sewer where you belong. I'm sure there's still a vacancy down there for you somewhere. Go on now slither away, that's a good little slime. Billy glares up at her vengeance in his eyes. Don't you look at me like that Billy, you neither impress or intimidate me with it. I could've made that a lot worse. I won't be responsible for what happens to you the next time, if you ever come near me again. Billy grabs his very sore groin, and tries to stand up. You won't walk away from me if you ever

Try that again. He can't walk now. Said James. Yosef covered his mouth chuckling to himself. The band still laughing at him hard. He makes it to his feet and hobbles out of the garage. She rolled her eyes at him as he leaves. And when you get down there, tell Helen I said hello! She said walking up to the garage door. You Jerk! Yosef and the band busted up laughing again. She looked at them all standing there, they stopped laughing, her expression serious, she was near tears. Yosef 's heart went out to her as did the rest of the band. They hadn't quite seen her like that before. I'm sorry that you gentlemen had to see me like that, I'm not sorry for what I did to Billy, but You saw a side of me that I don't like revealing. But I had no choice, he ticked me off. He insulted my Beloved, and I don't play that! I know that Vengeance belongs only to God, and to Him alone, She hunches her shoulders, but he deserved it. She looked lovingly into Yosef's eyes, he into hers. I will always have your back Beloved. Anyone who hurts you, hurts me, and they will have to answer to me for it. And believe me, I won't be nice about it. You can rehearse now, now that the trash has left. She turns to look outside, The soft spring breeze blowing gently through the

Trees. The Sun shining brightly. I need some fresh air now. She said in a whispered tone. She turns to look at Yosef, who was standing there in a trance like stare at her. She winks at him, mouthing I Love You to him. His knees wobbled a little. James and Terry steady him back on his feet again. She then leaves to go out into the front yard. Wow! Did you see that! Said Terry. Amazement had overtaken them all, but not like it did Yosef. I saw that. Said Yosef. His tone somewhat whispered. You alright man? Asked James. He was still a little unsteady on his feet. Yeah, I got it man. Said Yosef to him. James looked at Brad who was staring at Lisa outside. What's up with you Brad? He said to him. I got a boner. He said in a stupified voice. Shut up man! Said James smacking him playfully on the back of his head. Yosef laughed at them all. Excuse me. He said walking through the midst of them. His eyes never left Lisa for one moment. Come on guys, you heard Lisa, we can rehearse now. Said Terry walking back over to his Keyboards. Who can rehearse now after that man? You got to be kidding me! Said james. Shaking his head. Lisa was standing out in the front yard, she seemed to be lost deep in thought. Yosef approached her slowly. He was filled with a new sense of respect and admiration for her. He quickly flashed to the moment when the touch of her soft hand on his tightened face, filled him with something that

He could not explain. All that he knew was that, he was still feeling the effects of her touch not just on his cheek, but all over his body now. He could still feel the gentle warmth that flowed into him, the gentleness in her eyes that calmed him instantly when he gazed into them. His anger lost it's hold on him the moment he heard the sweetness of her voice. He felt himself falling deeper and deeper in love with her.

God was revealing her heart to him in a deeper way now. He could see things there that he had not seen in her before. And he was falling in love with what he saw. What Rev. Anderson told him about before. Love at true sight. She had stood up to Billy for him, and he wanted to show her his appreciation in more ways than she could ever imagine. Tears form in his eyes, no one had ever done anything like that for him before. But she did, he was filled with so much love for her at that moment that he thought that he would bust! He walks up behind her, stopping a little distance from her. Lisa. He said softly. She turns around. Yosef! She runs up to him jumping into his arms. Oh! My Beloved! He squeezed her into his arms, his eyes closed tightly. Oh! God Lisa! He moaned kissing her all over her face and neck. They stare deeply into each others eyes. He saw everything that God had revealed to him there. He noticed that she had tear traces on her cheeks. She had been crying for him. He caresses her into his arms again. He curls his index finger under her chin lifting her sweet face up to him. I can't believe what you did back there, that was incredible! I've never seen you like that before. He looks up at the deep blue sky, then back at her. She never took her eyes off him. She snuggled close to him, running her hands up and down the hardness of his arms. They felt strong to her. They gave her an assurance, she felt protected by them. An overwhelming surge of Love flowed through her for him. You did that for me? He said to her. Yes, Beloved, I did that for you. I would do anything for you. Anything. She said tears streaming down her face. Her tears made his tears flow even more. He smiled at her words, he felt comforted by them, and assured that she truly

Indeed did love him. Unconditionally. I Love you Lisa. He said to her, his voice trembling. They kiss hard, caressing each other affectionately. They stop kissing to rub their noses together smiling tenderly at one another. Are you going back to rehearse with the boys now? No, I need to get you home. I promised your mother that I would bring you back home after practice. But you didn't have practice yet. She said rubbing his chest. She felt his heart thumping hard against her hand. Yosef takes her hand kissing her palm. He stares at her for a moment. Loosing himself again in the new revelation that God had so graciously given him of her. Their expressions become serious once more, They kiss briefly. Brad saw them kissing. Well guys, looks like rehearsal's over. Let's all go home now. Why? Said Terry. Brad nods in the couple's direction. Oh, yeah. Said Terry. Looks like practice is over. Said James. They were still lost in their intimacy. Well let's call it a day guys. Said James, hitting the cymbal with his hand.

I have to go get my bass ok? Alright honey, I'll be out here. She said. Yosef goes back inside to get his instrument. Looks like rehearsal's over huh? Said Terry. I'm sorry guys, I guess it is. He said unhooking his bass from the amplifier. Don't be sorry Jo, We wouldn't've missed what Lisa did to bad boy Billy for all the world! It was worth it. Said James. He extends his hand out him, they both shake hands. James pats him on the back. She's quite a girl Jo. He said to him. They both look outside at her, she was playing with a butterfly that she had caught. A gentle breeze blew her sundress above her knees, revealing her smooth thighs. Jesus Christ! Jo! How can you stand it! He said to him. Stand what? Said Yosef, putting his guitar in the case. How can you stand being with a girl like that and not, You know, uh, you....
Yosef laughs at him, he knew what he was trying to say. We made a vow J. not to have sex until after we're married. Yeah, but how long is that gonna be? Well when I get the ring, and I ask her officially, we'll have about three months to go. It was April already. What do you mean officially?

The Colour Of Love
Anne Hemingway
Chap 10.

I want to ask her for her hand in Marriage according to our
Jewish Custom. I will have the Ceremony over at my Parents
house. Jo, doesn't that mean that your father will have to
approve of her first? He stops and looks outside at Lisa again.
She flashes a beautiful radiant smile at him.   His heartbeat sped
up a little. Jo? He didn't answer him. Jo! He said shaking him
slightly. Oh, uh. Sorry. What were you saying? Your dad,
Rabbi, won't he have to approve of her first? He takes a deep
breath. Yes, he'll have to. But whether he does or not. I'm still
gonna marry her. He said his tone serious. Will Lisa have a
problem with that?   They both look at her this time. I love you
she mouths to him. What do you think J? He said to him. I
don't think that's gonna be a problem, no problem at all.   Said
Yosef, grabbing Lisa's sweater off the stool.   Yeah, but I'm
concerned about your ole man bro. Why? I'm not.   He won't
approve of her man. Yosef stops and looks at him. Yes he will.
How do you know he will? Because, you know the Scripture.
With God all things are Possible? Yeah, What more proof do you
need? He winks at him leaving to get Lisa.   But Jo! He said
running after him. Where's your faith man! Said Yosef, as he
walks up to Lisa.   He hands her sweater to her. Thank you
Beloved, I forgot all about that.   She kissed him gently on the
lips.   May I take this for you? She trying to take his bass. She
wanted to put in the car for him. But it was too heavy for her.
You're so sweet to me Lisa. I got it baby.   He looks at James.
This is gonna be the longest three months of my life! He said
Putting his bass in the backseat of the car.   Take care man! He
said to James. He watches the couple pull off. James has a
moment to himself. Yosef and Lisa have always been the talk of
the neighborhood every since they were little.   I envy you man. I
hope you're right, I pray that your father will approve of Lisa.
And even more that your faith, and strength will last longer than
his stubbornness. But if for some reason you can't, and you take
her before the time. No one would hold it against you. I know I
wouldn't. God bless you both man. He whispered to himself.

He walks back into the garage with the rest of the band, they had
been standing around talking about what happened. Whew!

What a day it's been. Said Terry. First Lisa's attack, then Billy
nearly gets thumped on by Yosef, only to have his girl tear his
game plan all the way down. Said James, slapping fives with
Terry. Give me some of that! Said Brad laughing. They all five
together. Funniest thing I ever saw in my life! Said Terry. After
the way Lisa downed him, he probably wishes Jo had thumped
him. Said James. Bet. Said Terry hitting fist with James.
Hey uh, Brad. Said James walking over to him in a cloak and
dagger type way. Tell us man, did Lisa give you a boner for real?
Brad hesitates. Yeah, she did. But if any of you ever tell Yosef
about that, I'll deny it until the day I die! If Jo ever found out
about it, dying won't be a problem for you at all boy! Laughed
James. We won't say anything ok? Said Terry.
But If I could, I jump her in a heartbeat man! Said Brad
laughing. Can I get an amen? Amen! Rev! They all said together
laughing. Yosef had heard him earlier, but paid no attention to
him. Brad was not the first or the only man to have his affections
aroused for Lisa. Yosef never felt any jealousy about that at all.

Josef looks over at Lisa smiling at her. You're very quiet over
there. What's the matter? Oh, I was just thinking about all that's
happened today. Trying to make some sense out of it. I'm trying
to figure what it was all about. Which part? He said. All of it
Yosef I don't know why any of it happened. I must admit, I'm a
little confused about it. Do you have any answers? No baby, I
don't, but I'll tell you this. What? You gave Brad a boner! He
said laughing. What! Oh no! My God no! He laughed more at
her embarrassment
He takes her hand kissing it. Yosef please no! Lisa take it easy,
it happens. No, it's not suppose to. She said. Oh brad you
rascal you! She said. Yosef laughed more at her. Lisa, what.
You're a very beautiful girl. What do you expect? I don't know,
but not that? He chuckled again. Look I need to get you home
now ok? Yosef? Yes honey. I don't want to go home now. Your
mother will kill me if I don't get you back! No she won't. Besides,
I'll talk with her ok? Please...... She said taking his index finger
sucking on it gently. Yosef squirmed in his seat. He nearly lost
control of the car. Lisa......? She caresses his hand. May I
Beloved? He looks at her. Again her eyes melting his heart. He
turns the car to the left to go to the Community Park close by
their neighborhood. He looks at his watch. It was 6:00p.m. Just
for a little while ok? Anything you say Beloved. He smiles at
her, they get out of the car, and walk hand in hand to a small

clearing that had a little stream flowing beside it. There was a
huge shade tree with white honeysuckle blossoms flowering on it.
The fragrance fill the air. They liked the nice quiet spot under the
tree, and sat there as it shaded them. They were secluded away
from the crowd of people that were out that evening. The sun still
shining brightly, it's gentle rays streaming through the tree
branches illuminating them. Lisa felt a creative surge coming in
her heart, she began to recite some of her poetry and sonnets,
and odes that she wrote especially for him. She lays his head
gently down in her lap. He rested there as she recited her
writings to him. Oh God Lisa! That's beautiful. You are
beautiful my Beloved. She said softly. Her large breast were
hanging over him, he couldn't take his eyes off them He
squirmed as she leaned over to kiss him passionately hugging
him closer to her.   His face melting inside her soft bosom.
He was able to fight off the urge to caress them in his hands. But
he lost the fight in controlling his arousal. His Manhood pulsated
uncontrollably, he takes Lisa's sweater covering himself. Jesus!
Lisa! Look what you did! She looks at him fighting to hide
himself. I'm sorry Beloved, it just happens. I love you so much.
His words came back through her mouth to him. He smiled at
her, pulling her down to him closer kissing her deeply.   *"Oh
Yosef,* She breathed, her breath coming in short pant's now. *"Oh
Yes My Beloved."* Her arousal was unbearable to her! She thrusts
her tongue deep into his mouth. *"Oh God Lisa!"* He moaned. He
stopped kissing her, stroking her long curls. What are we doing?
He said to her softly.   She smiled at him.   Making love. She said.
He turns his head to one side like a puppy that heard a funny
noise. Yosef, we made a vow not to have sex until after we're
married did we not? Yes we did. But we didn't vow not to make
love did we? I don't follow you. For every time we go for a walk in
the park holding hands, or stare deeply into each others eyes.
We're making love. For each embrace, and every caress, and for
all the times that we said I Love you. We're making Love. When
we sit and just hold each other in our arms, and love on one
another Beloved. We're making Love. As long as we remember
our limitations, and not cross that line until we say I do. I see no
harm in our love making do you? He sat up

Thinking on her words, they were beginning to arouse him more
than her breast were earlier. I never thought of it like that. That's

beautiful! Do you remember our first date, after I came back home?
How can I ever forget that night Lisa? Well there you go, we made love all that evening. Starting with dinner by candlelight. The carriage ride, watching the Sunset on the beach. You were making love to me the whole evening long. I mean each event after the other was an event of nothing but pure love making. That's incredible Lisa!   I never looked at it like that before, but from now on I will. They stand up together. He kisses her. Thank you. He said to her. Thank you for what Beloved? Thank you for being my girl Lisa. For always being there for me. For being so understanding about my father. Loving me and my mother. She really does love you, you know. I know Beloved. And I love her too, and Rabbi. He looked surprised to hear her say that. And It is I who thank you for giving me the privalige of being your girl, for sharing your beautiful Culture with me, and receiving mine as your own too. For loving my family. Thank you Beloved. To me it is an honor to be your girl. Which I will be always. I Love you.
His eyes fill with tears. I Love you so much Lisa, I would die without you. They kiss briefly. I'd better get you home now ok? Alright Beloved. They walk back to his car arm in arm.   Her love made him feel as
Thought he could walk on water. They reach her home. They go inside. Everyone there had just finished up with supper. Hey Jo-jo. They all greeted him. Hi angel. Hi Daddy. Lisa! Lisa! Brace yourself girl here comes your mother. Oh Lisa! Let me look at you. Hi mom. Are you alright? Yes mom, I'm fine.

Lisa looks at Yosef. She does this all the time when she hasn't seen me for a while. Yosef and Rev. Anderson laugh. Where's Johnathan? Oh He's in there in the kitchen having a slice of 7-up pound cake that Lisa made yesterday. Just then Johnathan comes out of the kitchen with crumbs around his mouth.
So I see you found the cake. Said Rev. Anderson. What cake? He mumbled his cheeks full. He looked like an overgrown hampster. Lisa shakes her head laughing at him. He managed to swallow it all down.
So tell me man, how was rehearsal? Interesting. He said to him. Lisa lets out a gentle yawn, sleep was coming on her. I think you need to get up to bed now young lady. Yes ma'mam. Good night daddy.

She kisses him on the cheek. Good night angel. Night john-john.
She said to johnathan. Goodnight, and quit calling me that. She
laughs as she walks up stairs.   Goodnight Beloved. He looks up
at her going up the stairs she looked just like an angel ascending
back into Heaven.   Her mother follows her up to her room. I'll
be right back boys. Said Deborah. Yosef, make yourself at home
dear. They all sit down and discuss this afternoons events.
Deborah returns down the stairs five minutes later. Jo-jo. Lisa is
asking for you. It's not too late, he said looking at his watch, it
was only 7:30p.m. Just for a few mom, then dad wants me to
whip him at chess again. Whip me! Oh,oh. I feel a challenge
here. Said Johnathan. I'll be right back dad. He said taking off
to Lisa's room. He enters in. and sees her standing in the middle
of her room wearing a beautiful v-necked night gown with
matching blue robe. Whoa! He breathed. He shut the door
leaving it slightly cracked. Mom said that you wanted me. Oh
yes, I want you Beloved. They walked up to each other. He pulls
her to him by her slender waist. Kissing her forehead. What is it
baby? I can't sleep. You can't sleep? No. I can't, and my head
hurts. It does? Yes. So does mine he said. You too Yosef? She
said rubbing his temples. Not that one Lisa. She smiled. Oh, no
not again. He picks her up taking her over to her rocking chair.
He sits down with her in his lap rocking her back and forth.
Relax ok? Ok Beloved. He cradled her in his arms humming a
tune that he had in his heart for her. He had the music but no
words. They hummed it together.   You like that Lisa? There was
no answer. Lisa? She had fallen asleep.   He got up taking her
back over to her bed, laying her down gently. He covered her with
a light blanket, kissing her forehead once more. He turns out her
lamp, leaving only the small nite lite on.
I love you baby. He said stroking her hair. He leaves to go back
down stairs.   How is she jo-jo? Said Deborah. She just had a
little headache that's all. But she's fine now.   You sure? I'm
sure, she's sleeping like a baby.   That's nice son. She said. She
went into the kitchen to bring out some refreshments for them.
Rev. Anderson had talked him into to staying for a few games of
chess. Deborah returns with the refreshment tray. And Yosef's
Siddur, he had left it there that afternoon.   They all sit down
together for cake, and chess. Enjoying the rest of the evening.

Where is that boy of ours Sarah? Sounded Rabbi. He was very
irritated at Yosef. He thought that he had missed him at Temple
that day. Which he did. But not because Yosef had failed to
show. But because Yosef got there before him. And had prayer
with Rabbi Marcus, and discussed their plans for the up coming
Feast of Tabernacles in the fall. He told him that he would not be
available for the concert that he wanted his band Daystar to play
for. Because it fell on the same Saturday as Pastors Day
International Conference. Rabbi Marcus had forgotten about
that, he attended the Conference every year himself.
And they quickly scheduled another Saturday that they were free.
Yosef gave him a rough draft of the program that he did on his
home computer. Both were excited about the Conference. Rabbi
arrived two hours later after Yosef had left to go over to Lisa's
parents home.   What's the matter now Yacov? What has the boy
done now? He was to meet me at Temple today, I waited for him
to come, and he never showed up there. It's that girl that has
him all twisted I tell you! I will never know what he sees in that
girl! Obviously everything that you don't Yacov.   And if anybody
here is twisted, it's you! She sounded tired, she was not up to
his words tonight. All she wanted was to take a hot bath and go
to bed. She was fed up with her husband's constant complaining,
his faultfinding with Lisa. His non-acceptance of Yosef
relationship with her. His bickering about his past issues, and life
period! I tell you Sarah I've had it up to here with them! He said
waving his hand over the top of his head.   He continued on in
his tantrum.

Sarah puts her hands over her ears as she walks slowly towards
the stairs. She stops, and turns around.
Why did you marry me? He stops his rambling on looking
startled. What? You heard me. Why did you marry me Yacov?
She said her eyes filling with their usual tears around this time
every evening.   What are you saying Sarah? He said stepping a
little closer to her. ANSWER ME! I WANT TO KNOW, WHY DID
YOU MARRY ME!!! Rabbi Epstien was stunned to hear these
words. For the first time in a long evening of arguments, he was

at a lost for words. I, I. He stuttered. He couldn't even say it. He couldn't even say that he loved her. His bitterness refused to let him utter such words to her.

Or to their son. He just stood there wordless. God made even a dumb ass to speak Yacov, I'm sure you can speak without His help. She knew what it was that he could not say. She just smiled a little, and began to walk towards the stairs again. She wiped her eyes with the corner of her apron as she walked away. She stopped again at the foot of them, to explain why he missed Yosef at Temple today. Yosef had called her to tell her that he had already met with Rabbi Marcus, and that planning for Feast was well under way.

He waited for his father, but when he didn't show up like he said, he left word with Rabbi Marcus to tell him that he was there, but he had to leave. Rabbi Marcus left the message on Rabbi Epstien's desk. He never saw it, because he never went to his office there. You missed him not because of Lisa, but because of another one of your meetings that no one seems to know about but you. She never even told him about Lisa's assault that day, she kept it to herself. Somehow, she felt he wouldn't care one way or the other. Yosef did attend his rehearsal, and yes he did take Lisa with him. Our son is more of a man than you'll ever be Yacov. I have watched him grow over the years, grow from a shy timid little boy. To the fine, strong handsome man that he is now. And I have watched his growth Spiritually as well. He is well versed in the Torah, more than you could ever know Yacov, and Lisa has taught him well in the Holy Scriptures as did her father. He looks away from her in disgust when she mentioned her name. Why do you hate her so much Yacov! What has she done! Again he was silenced, he had no reason to hate Lisa at all. He had known her and her family every since she was a little girl. What happened to you to trigger such hatred to wards your best friend's child? His voice would not let him speak that to her. You spoke of Yosef leaving his Culture for Black Culture. Well I disagree with you! I say that he has enhanced his Culture more by embracing Lisa's. So instead of complaining about him. You should be proud of him, as I am proud.

Rabbi stands there listening to her. She know she was right, but his indifference would not let him receive her words. He didn't know what to say or do, he looks away from her at first, then back at her again. You know I look at him sometimes and I find it hard to believe that he is the son of your loins I find no resemblance of you in him at all. And you know what? I thank Yeshua for that everyday. Good to you Yacov. Rabbi felt sorrow pierce his heart like a double edged sword. His wife's word's cut to the very core of his heart. He felt the pain of them, because he knew that she was right. There was no resemblance of Yosef in him at all. He didn't act like him in any way of his character. He remembered how she gave him over to Rev. Anderson, and Deborah the night that they buried their oldest son Michael. He saw her seated in Michael's room rocking in his rocking chair, the same one that she used to rock him and Yosef to sleep in. Sorrow and grief both attacking her at the same time, in the worst way. She had lost a son to death. But she had lost him long before death came. She had lost him to the same demons that had taken her husband away from her too. The demons of hatred, and prejudiced. They had been his companions long before he knew she even existed. He also welcomed a few others as well. Indifference, and intolorance, unforgiveness, also took up residence in his soul. Their contagion of racial bigotry had spread through him and Michael like a cancer, eating any and all compassion in their hearts. If there was one shred of humanity left in them. It too lost it's battle to the racial monstrosity that had invaded their hearts and minds. Any hopes of them having the slightest bit of compassion or humanity left for their fellow man

Was practically nil. He remembered how Sarah watched it consume him and Michael to the point of no return. He saw in his mind how Michael left the house in a fit of rage over Racial issues that had people glued to their sets on the evening news. It was during the Bombing at the Ebenezear Baptist Church where the four young black girls were killed. The Riots that broke out in Watts, the Black Panther protests, these were events that covered nearly every channel on television. Oh! How he hated whites, Germans, and Blacks! His hatred ran the entire colour spectrum of man. He walked into an all Black neighborhood at night looking for trouble. But instead trouble found him. Coming around the corner was a White gang with an even bigger chip on their shoulders than he. They surrounded Michael, picking, and mocking him.
They were ready to assault him, when coming up the street, there were two young Black men about the same age as the gang

members. Early to mid twenties. Michael was in his late teens early twenties himself. They came to his rescue, they pleaded with the gang not to harm the young Jewish man.

But Michael refused their help. He was also confused as to why two Black men would want to help him anyway. What dealings did Jews and Blacks have with each other anyway? He didn't understand why the Black men didn't take off and run away from the White men, since White people at that time hated Blacks As much as Germans hated Jews. Why would they want to help him he wondered? He hated Black people, thanks to his father. Back off nigger! This aint your fight! There were six of them, one of Michael, and two of the Black men. There doesn't have to be any fight man. Said one of the Black men. I told you once, I aint telling you again Boy! Back off! Said the White member again. You know, there're plenty
Trees to hang you from out here! The other Black man's expression changed, his fury rose, and they saw it! Sir, this aint Mississippi, and it aint the 1800's either! He fired back at him. Look all we want you to do is back off the young man, leave him be. Go away little boy, I don't need your help. I can take care of myself! Sounded Michael. The young White men continued to taunt, and poke at Michael, when one of the gang members pulled out a switch blade. I'm gonna cut me a slice of kike! As he raised his knifed hand in the air, one of the Black men quickly grabbed his wrist swinging him around like a rag doll, breaking his wrist. At that moment, all hell broke loose in a fury of racial slurs, and violence. Michael
Stepped back and watched as the young men took a beating that was meant for him. Sirens and flashing red and blue lights speeding from around the corner as four police cars closed in on them all. Freeze Nigger! Yelled one of the Officers. Two of the members managed to hide away from view of the police.

Michael himself managed the same thing, but remained where he could see them. He watched to see what would happen next. The young Black men froze in place with their hands raised high in the air. He listened as one of the younger White members told that it was the Black boys who tried to beat up the young Jewish boy. Michael cracked a sinister smile as the boy told lie after lie on the boys. Just then with his back turned, not knowing that

106

two of the White members had snuck up behind him. One of the members pulled out a small pistol, aiming it right at the back of Michael's head. As the boy cocked the pistol, it's clicking sound was heard by one of the Black men. He raised his head up to see the boy about ready to shoot Michael. "Look out!" He yelled. Shots rang out from three of the Officers, killing both of the Black boys instantly. Michael was shot in the crossfire, as was the member that tried to shoot him. All four of the men were pronounced dead at the scene. An Officer walked over to see the gruesome sight.

Blood was everywhere, eyes staring blankly into the night. As Michael, and three others lie dead on the cold black cement ground. He saw that it was one of the White gang members with pistol still clutched in his dead fingers that tried to shoot Michael. He knew then that the White boy had been lying to them all along. He called for two other Officers to come over. They huddled briefly. Then one of the Officers walked back over to the scene. He looked from right to left to see if there were any witnesses to what he was about to do. He bent down and took the gun from the boy's hand and placed it inside of one of the Black boy's hand. He then went back over to the boy who had been lying to them. He was used as their witness of the incident as he took his report. But what they didn't know was that there had been another spectator. She saw the whole thing from across the street from her bedroom window. She was on the Mother's Board at their Church. She was horrified at what she had seen. She didn't have her glasses on, and things were a little blurred, but she saw well enough to indentify the true murderers. She decided that she would go out to see for herself. She felt a fear that she had never known before rise up in the pit of her belly. She approached the scene slowly, looking at all who were looking at her. Their expressions said something to her. There were head shakes, and looks of sorrow for her as she looked at all who were looking at her. For the mayhem attracted many from around the neighborhood. As she moved in closer to the scene, she looked at the bodies of the young Black boys stretched out on the ground. As she approached further in she began to recognize the bodies, they were covered in blood, their eyes blankly staring into the night sky. They were twin brothers, and they were both her grandsons! Lord God Almighty! Nooooo! Nooooooooo! Not my babieeeeesssss! She wailed. One of her White neighbors caught her as she collapses to the ground in a heap. She looked at the

Officers Why! Whhhhyyyyy! I saw you kill my babies! I saw you!
Everyone then looked at the Officers. Rage on their faces. Her
grandsons had just come from Church, when they stopped to be
Samaritan to another human being whom they saw was being
victimized because of a racial difference. And they as well as
Michael ended up being casualties of that same injustice and
race hatred. When the case went to trial, it was her testimony,
not the young White gang member's testimony that was used to
bring justice, where there was once injustice.
But even then there was still injustice as prejudice had it's day in
the same court. Still there was no fairness shown for her
grandsons.

Even though she was an eye witness as well as the other officers,
and the White gang member. The officers were only suspended
until further notice. As a result of that Verdict. Many race riots
broke out all over the city. Yes, he remembered it all. How he felt
when the news came to he and Sarah, He felt that at that
moment, his rage would not be quieted until he served his
vengeance on all Blacks for his son's death.
To him, if the boys had minded their own business, Michael
would still be alive. He hated Germans for the cruel murder of
his family. Now he hated Black people for what he called the
"unfair killing" of his son.
And he would not rest until his rage found another victim. And it
did. Lisa. He hated her with the same passion that his son loved
her. He was jealous of their love. How could he allow himself to
feel, and experience love again. Never again! He thought. What
he love and held dear to his heart was brutally taken from him.
And there was nothing he could do about it. His memories of his
past that he kept buried in his heart poisoned the life out of him.
The constant reoccurring images of Michael in his casket, the
faces of his mother and father and sister in the Chamber as their
bodies were gassed, haunted him every single day of his life. He
felt there was no way to escape this hell that he had made for
himself. He thought back to the night that Josef came home
from his date with Lisa. And seeing the wet spot on his son's
slacks. How it filled him with such a longing desire to feel that
same kind of love again for Sarah.

But he held fast to his memories. He had showed them more affection than he did his own wife. They had become his mistress. Sarah watched him as he silently courted them with the same ferverant passion that she longed for. Yes, he courted them by day, and slept with them at night. When he would go into his study, Sarah could hear his song of sorrows, as his mournful dirges made their way to her ears. He wrote about his memories in his journal. His writings reflected not his love, but his hatred. He had built a home in his bitterness where he and they could be alone. He totally alienated Sarah and Yosef from his love, but not from his cruelty. He lowered his head as his wife had once again gone to bed in her misery, with only her tears to keep her company. I'm so sorry that you do not understand my pain Sarah. Just then the door opens. It was Yosef. He was beaming like a firefly. He walks into the front room where his father was still standing at the foot of the stairs. He sat his bass on the floor. So I see you made it home in one piece.
Said Rabbi, his sarcasm surfacing. Where's mom? He made a head gesture telling him that she had gone upstairs to bed. Were you waiting up for me? You're usually in bed by this time. He said looking at his watch. It was 11:30 p.m. His father looked away from him. Yosef took a deep breath, he somehow knew that his father had abused his mother again. His anger rose in him. Don't tell me dad. You had another round with mom, and she went to bed in tears as usual. Right? Rabbi never answered him, he knew that Yosef was telling the truth, that's exactly what had happened. Yosef walked in the living room a little further standing face to face with him. Rabbi walked down into the living room aside from Yosef. I suppose you waited up so you could inspect me for any noticeable signs of romantic involvement?

He said taking his jacket throwing it back across his shoulder, picking up his bass. He walked towards the stairs. Well as you can see dad, I'm all dry tonight. He said looking down at his groin. His father looked embarrassed. But he had stayed up to see if there was anything visable on his clothes. I'm going to bed now, that is if I've passed inspection. Rabbi felt his demon speaking to him at that moment. It surfaced in a very vulgar way. You were gone a long time tonight Yosef. He said in a deep legato tone. Yosef turned around to see the very same creature that his mother had seen a few weeks ago. His features had changed.

109

Yosef could not believe his eyes at what he saw! Heh,heh,heh. The demon laughed. No, uh what you say. No hanky-panky? He said sarcastically. Yosef's anger rose at that moment. He spoke back to the spirit that was speaking through his father. Oh, she was very affectionate tonight dad. So affectionate, I could hardly control myself. But you are dry tonight, why is that? Did her hand get tired? He said in a teasing type of tone, moving closer to Yosef. Yosef glared at his father for that remark, he now felt his own sarcasam surfacing. He felt one good turn deserves another. He took a deep breath, speaking softy back to the spirit. No, dad. Her hand didn't get tired. She just swallowed this time. He said smiling, winking at him. He turned and went upstairs. The demon's voice wailed through Rabbi Epstien, as he ran into his Study slamming the door behind him. Yosef ran upstairs, and stood outside his bedroom in the hall, unsure as to what had just happened. He began to feel horrible for making such a vulgar remark about Lisa

And he detested his father even more for the innuendo that he made about her as well. He goes into his bedroom and sets his bass on the floor. He hears a gentle sigh coming from his mother's bedroom. He goes into her. He watches her toss and turn on her pillow trying to find a dry spot. It was it's usual wetness. Oh, mom. I'd give anything to see you happy again. Anything at all. He bends down next to her, kissing her on her cheek. He tastes her tears. He closes his eyes tight nearly breaking into to tears himself for her. She stirs a little Yosef? She opens her eyes focusing them on him. Oh Yosef! My son! You're home! Seeing him at that moment made her forget the misery that she had encountered earlier.

I didn't hear you come in dear. I'm so glad you're here son. Me too mom. Me too. His voice trembling.

His expression told her that something was troubling him. What's the matter son? Are you alright? Uh, yeah, I'm fine. I just didn't mean to wake you that's all. He said playing in her hair. Oh, that's alright child, you've been doing that to me every since you were a little baby. Yes? He chuckles a little.

I guess so. Where's your father? His expression changed to one of frustration. He was fine until she mentioned him. He's in his study feeling a little sick that's all. She becomes concerned for him. Sick?

Why is he sick Yosef? Is it something that he ate that disagree with him? She was trying to get up, but he wouldn't let her. You could say that. He just had a little too much humble pie mom, that's all. Humble pie? What is this pie Yosef? She rolled over

110

again changing her position, still trying to find a dry spot on her pillow. Mom, stay here, I'll be right back. Where you go Yosef? She said. Stay here. He goes out to the hall closet, he pulls out a fresh pillow case. He goes back inside the bedroom. Here, let's change this ok? Ok son. She said. She sat up in bed while he changed her pillow case. He lays her gently back down. There better now? He said tucking her in underneath the light coverings on the bed. It was still for some reason unseasonably warm out that night. A very humid 70 degrees. I can sleep better now that you're here Yosef. How was your date with Lisa tonight? Awesome as usual. And that's all I have to say about that. Why? She said. He usually tells her most of the details of his dates with her. Because, If I start talking about her, I'll never get to sleep tonight. Ok? Ok son, I understand. She's a beautiful girl. That she is mom, that she is. I love you. I love you too son. Goodnight dear. Night. He said

Walking out into the hall. His father had just come upstairs. They traded looks, their minds flowing at the same time to their vulgar moment downstairs. They went into their bedrooms. He felt sorry for his father
But felt that there was nothing that he could do. He went into his bedroom and shut the door. Standing up against it, he ponders in his mind what all had happened that day. From Lisa's assault, to the garage incident where Lisa stood up to Billy for him. And now this. What did this all mean? He sighs for his father. Dad I'm sorry for what I said to you tonight. It was disrespectful to you and to my girl. I pray that God will forgive me for what I said about her to you. For give me! He whispered walking over to his window looking up at the Moon. It was full and bright that night. His thoughts of his first date
With Lisa returned to him. He remembered what she said about that one spark of light. He felt that maybe it was there, but he just didn't see it yet. Oh Lisa I hope you were right baby. I hope you were right. He changes for bed. Little did he know, that he was about to have an encounter of the Divine Kind. He gets into bed and drifts quickly off into a deep sleep. After he had been sleeping about a while, he hears his name being called softly. *"Yosef, Yosef."* Ummm. What is it? He said sleepily. He tosses and turns more, as the voice called to him again. *"Yosef, Yosef."* Suddenly, his eyes began to open slowly. As he awakens to the

111

voice, his eyes opened to see a light shining in his room. He sits up in bed, his voice had left him briefly. His eyes batted rapidly, his breathing was as rapid as his batting eyes. He could not believe his eyes as he gazed at the figure shining like the brightest star. Standing over in the corner of his bedroom was a huge Angel! He was at least 8 feet in height! With a white robe trimmed in gold. There was a huge gleaming sword hanging down from his side. He was wearing golden sandals. He was awesome looking! He smiled at him. Yosef was startled as the Angel spoke to him again. *"You are Daniel Joseph Epstein."Yosef."* Yosef stuttered trying to find words to speak, but his fear wouldn't let him. Finally,

After much struggling, his voice returned to him. Jesus! He said. *"No, I'm not my Master, but I am His servant. Here what it is I have to say to you son. For I have been sent to you from The Most High. For there is a time approaching when you will know the true Essence of His Power in your life. For He has chosen you to work His Will."* What am I supposed to do for God, why would He choose me? I'm just a
Real Estate Executive with a band. That's all. *"Yes, but you are much more than that to Him Yosef. There will come a time when a great sacrifice will be made on your behalf. But fear not, for the enemy has lost, and all will be done for His Glory. Remember son. ALL THINGS ARE POSSIBLE TO HIM WHO BELIEVES." All things, all things......"* The angel begins to vanish. Wait! Said Yosef. He returns to him. What is it that He wants me to do? The angel was standing there smiling even more at him. His robes flowing softly almost like in slow motion of some kind. *"In His time, so stay faithful, prayerful. Seek Him Yosef. His favor is upon you. In time all will be revealed For it is such a time as this that she was given back to you."* Who was given back to me? *"LISA....." In time, in time, in time......."* The angel's voice echoed into silence as he vanished out of sight. But his words lingered in Yosef's heart and his mind.
What did he mean about Lisa? What did she have to do with all this? Whoa! He breathed. He didn't know quite what to make out of the angel's visitation. He never had anything like this happen to him before. He slowly laid back down, trying to sleep. But sleep for the moment had abandoned him. His emotions were mixed. A little excitement, some confusion as to why God

112

would choose him, how did Lisa fit into this thing? Then there
was the fear of not knowing what he was to do. What if I fail him?

He thought. I was never taught anything like this in Temple! He
turned over and finally drifted back into a deep restful sleep. He
woke up early that Saturday morning, his thoughts still on last
nights Angelic encounter. Yosef wakes up abruptly breathing
rapidly. Lisa! He shouted. He brushes his hair back, he had
dreamt the whole thing he thought. Yet he could still see the
Angel, and hear his voice as clear as he heard him last night.
He could still feel his presence as his radiance filled his room.
He goes over to the window, the Sun was shining brightly that
morning. He looks at his watch. 9:45a.m.   Jesus! I have to get
ready! It was the day that He and Lisa were going to Shineway
Jewelers to look at engagement rings.   He was to take her the
next Friday, but he talked her into going today.   It was a
gorgeous day! And very warm. Unseasonably warm , the forecast
said 80 degrees for April. He took a quick shower, and went
downstairs into the kitchen to find his father sitting at the table
drinking a cup of coffee. Good morning Yosef. He said in that all
too familiar legato tone. Yes, his demons were up with him, and
ready to lash out at him more. Yosef goes over to the refrigerator
to get the juice pitcher. He takes a small juice glass out of the
cupboard, and pours himself a cup of juice.   Is your mother up
yet? No, uh she's still sleeping. She's been tired lately. He said
drinking his juice. She's usually up and has breakfast ready and
on the table for me. Heh,heh. Yosef glared at him, walking back
to the fridge to put the juice pitcher back inside.

He takes another sip of coffee. No matter, I guess she's entitled to
one day of laziness. Yosef nearly breaks the juice glass he was
holding. He takes the last sip, setting it down on the table. I'm
outta here!
What did you say son? I'm not your son! He said threw his teeth.
What is it with you dad. I mean every night, every freaking night
mom goes to bed in tears because of you! Rabbi never
acknowledged his son's anger, as a matter of fact, he was rather
enjoying himself. And to think that I came down here to apologize
to you for the way that I spoke to you last night. His father's
cruelty surfaced in a most vulgar way that morning. Apologize

eh? For what Yosef. He said smiling. Yosef looked away from him. He remembered the remark that he made about Lisa, and the sexual innuendo that he made about her. It hurt him deeply. He was silent as his father became even more cruel to him. You said something about Lisa swallowing something Yosef? He looked away from him again. His father then looked down at Yosef's groin laughing. How could she swallow anything from you? You don't have enough there to get passed her teeth! Yosef was stunned beyond words! You sick bastard! He fumed at his father. He picked up the juice glass and threw it into the kitchen sink shattering it into pieces. He then grabbed his jacket and stormed out of the kitchen slamming the backdoor behind him. Rabbi sat there at the table cackling to himself at Yosef's anger. He gloated as he sipped away on his coffee. Yosef walked into the garage, and got into his car. He started beating the steering wheel with his fist. He then laid his head down and began to

Cry. Sarah came downstairs, she had heard their raised voices. What has happened? Where is my son? Her voice filled with anger. She knew that he had done something to upset Yosef. She saw the shattered juice glass in the sink. Where is he Yacov? He looked at her, his contorted features were worse this morning, his eyebrows met in the center of his forehead. The voice deep and demonic spoke to her
Mercilessly. *"In hell where he and that whore of his belongs, maybe you should join them there too!"*
He spits a yellowish looking substance at her, it splatters on the night clothes that she was still wearing.
He then lets out a deep gutteral laughter at her. Sarah looks at him, her expression not one of fear, but of faith. She spoke out of her heart to the spirit. In the Name of Yeshua Get out of my sight! At that moment, the demon wailed through Rabbi's voice, he jumped up out of the chair with such force that it knocked the chair over. He ran into his study slamming the door behind him whimpering to himself. Sarah sets the chair back up at the table sitting down in it. Oh my Dear God, in Heaven. What has happened to my husband? Where is he Father? Please do whatever it is that You have to, to help him. Help him to rid himself of this hell once and for all. I can't take anymore of this. I'm tired and old. Either help him Lord, or take me out of this world. I refused to live like this any longer. Watch over my child and his girl. In the Name of Yeshua my Messiah. Amen. She

cups her face in her hands and sobs painfully for her husband.
But even more for her son. She went upstairs and showered and
changed her clothes. She took the night
Gown and robe that Yosef and Lisa had given her for Christmas
two years ago, and threw it into the garbage. The stench from the
yellow substance that Rabbi spewed on her was horrible. She
went downstairs into the basement for a time on Intercessory
Prayer. Lisa came out onto the front porch, she could see that
Yosef was already in his car, she thought that maybe he was
waiting for her. She smiles.

She went over to the garage. As she approached inside the
garage, she noticed that His head was down on the steering
wheel. He was crying. She walked up to the driver side of the
car. Yosef? He never looked up at her. Go away Lisa. Honey
what's wrong? He sits up getting out of the car, slamming the
door.
Beloved, what's the matter? She tried to touch him. He jerks
away from her. Get away from me Lisa!
His anger surfacing in a fury. He walks away from her pacing
back and forth. How does she put up with him! Lisa tried again
to console him, but he kept refusing, pulling away from her. No!
No! I said leave me alone! He glares at her. His face tightened,
that man is hopeless! You hear me hopeless! Who? What are
you talking about Yosef? The angrier he got the faster he paced.
On, and on. Lisa gave up trying to keep up with him. She hoped
that he would tire himself out and sit down in the car. But he
never did. Can I do anything to help? She asked quietly. I don't
want your help! You wouldn't understand anyway ok?
Oh, now don't even go there with that mess! She said. Her anger
surfacing now. I'm not in the mood for this at all Lisa. Honey
please talk to me. She said trying to hold his arm. He thought
on what his father said about his groin, then laughed at him for
it. His anger surfaced savagely, and lashed out at Lisa. No!
I told you once already, I don't want your help. It doesn't concern
you ok! Just stay out of it! You hcar me! Now leave me alone!
Oh Yosef! She breathed, grabbing her stomach.

She had never seen him like this before, he never in his life spoke
to her like that. She knew something, or someone upset him
terribly. With tears in her eyes, she turns and runs out of the
garage. Lisa wait! Lisa! Jesus! What's the matter with me! He

said brushing his hair back. Baby I didn't mean it! Lisa! She never came back, she ran out of his sight. He gets into his car, and drives out to look for her. He had forgotten all about the angel visitation last night, and their date to go look at engagement rings that day.

His mind in a turmoil, he gets into his car to go look for her. She had gone back home to get her work keys

She had already received the news that she had been terminated from her job. Hurt and confused, she walked back to her former job to clear not only from there, but to cleanse her mind and her heart as well.

She prayed for Yosef and their relationship as she walked. Yosef returned back home still not seeing Lisa anywhere in sight. He notices coming down the street Rev. Anderson out for a stroll. He slows his car down, blowing the car horn at him. He pulls the car over parking it along side of him. Rev. Anderson raises his hand waving at him. Rev. Anderson gets inside the car. He looks at Yosef, and he could tell right away that something was deeply troubling him. He could see the dried tear traces on his face, his

Breathing was rapid, his hands shaky. Yosef? His voice deep and comforting. Yes. What's the matter son? I don't understand any of this. Any of this at all. His voice trembling. I don't understand me or my father. Why does he treat my mother so, so. He broke down in tears. He hates me and my girl. I can't understand why dad. You'v e been more like a father to me than he could ever be. As far as I'm concerned you are my father. Rev. Anderson smiled at those words. Is he on to you again? Asked Rev. Anderson. Well it's like he's changed in a way that I find hard to explain. What do you mean? Well his voice, it didn't sound like him at all, and his face. It's as though someone else was looking back through his eyes at me. It's like he's not my father anymore. I don't really know who or what he is now. You know what I mean? Yes, I believe I do. But what's important is what are you gonna do? What can I do? I've never seen anything like this before. Jesus Christ! He said, breaking again. Now, there, there son. I'm here for you, you know that right Jo-Jo? Yes sir. I know that. Rev. Anderson puts his hand on his shoulder consoling him. Yosef, I've known you and your family every since you were a young lad. I have loved you just like you were my own son. As far as my wife and I are concerned. You are our son. This time Yosef smiled at those words. To know that someone did love him, made all the times that his father denied him of that love vanish from his mind and his heart. I have never known a time that you and I could not sit down and talk things out. Now, from the beginning tell me what brought all this burah on? Yosef takes a

Deep breath. Better now. Yes. He said nodding his head. Rev. Anderson listened attentively as Yosef told him everything.
From the vulgar remarks they made to each other. To his father's abuse towards his mother. The jealousy that he felt towards him and Lisa. By the time that he finished explaining everything to him. Rev. Anderson was quite annoyed with Rabbi. I will deal with your father myself.
This is something that I need to discuss with him in private. I know that he's been through quite a lot, but his behavior is inexcusable to me. I should've spoken to him a long time ago. But God always provides an opportunity to make things right does He not son? Yes, yes He does. I understand now. He had calmed down more now. Rev. Anderson looks around him enjoying the sunshine, it was warm again that day. It's such a beautiful day out this morning. Why don't you go and get Lisa and have a good time today, and forget all about this morning ok? Ok dad, and thanks. He looks at his pinky ring. It was a beautiful gold
Ring with their initials Y & L. in the center instead of an amperstand, there was a small diamond in the center. He then remembers his date with Lisa.

Jesus! Lisa! What's the matter? Said Rev. Anderson. I was supposed to take Lisa to the jewelers today to look at engagement rings. But I got so mad at my father that I took my anger out on her. She'll never go with me now. She's probably not too happy with me I'm afraid. He said lowering his head shaking it in disappointment at himself. Rev. Anderson closes his eyes, his words disturbed him deeply. Yosef. Sir.
So strange. What? Does the fruit fall far from the tree son? I don't know what you mean dad. Well your father takes his issues out on you, your mother, and the world. And this morning you

did the same thing to Lisa. I ask you again, does the fruit fall far from the tree? Yosef stopped a moment thinking on his words. They found a place in his heart, as well as his mind. You're right, I became just like him for a moment didn't I? The question is son, how long will that moment last? Yosef paused again. I have to find Lisa, and make things right with her dad. That you do son, that you do. Now get going boy! Get going! Yosef smiles. As Rev. Anderson leaves. Dad! Yes Jo. Thanks. Rev. Anderson smiles at him. Anytime son, anytime. Go find her ok? I will Yosef pulls off not knowing where Lisa might be. She had a way of disappearing without a trace when she was troubled about something. His fear was that she wouldn't forgive him and agree to marry him. But he knew her better than that. At least he hoped he did. He asked around for her, no leads at all. He was really beginning to worry about her now. He came back to her parents house to see if she had come back home. She wasn't there, but she told her mother where she would be. Deborah told Yosef her whereabouts. He then sped off to her former workplace after her.

Lisa had arrived at her   former place of employment, to her surprise Mary, Mr. Webber's Secretary was there waiting for her. She knew about Mr. Wright firing her. Mary was a bit of a straight laced girl. A little on the plain side, but very nice. She and Lisa were good friends, they got along well together, personally as well as professionally.   She was deeply hurt about Lisa's termination.   Lisa walks inside to see Mary sitting at her desk playing with a picture of them from an outing that Lisa had invited her to at her parents house two summers ago. Lisa could tell that Mary had been crying for her. Mary, what are you doing here? She said walking slowly inside. I thought that you might be back here after your things. I couldn't just let you leave me without saying goodbye. She gets up bringing the picture with her. You gave this to me, remember? Lisa takes the picture smiling. Yeah, I remember Mary, we had such a good time that day didn't we? Mary nods her head, sniffling a little. Lisa hands the picture back to her.   You're so sweet to me Mary, I will always be grateful for what you taught me here. I wouldn't've made it without you. Really? Said Mary. Yeah, really.   Things just aren't going to be the same without you here to brighten up the place. Oh Mary! She said hugging her. How sweet of you to say that. Thanks, I need a friend about now.   Mary could also tell that Lisa had been crying, but she didn't know about what.

There was a pause between them. Uh, it's sure gonna be lonely around here. I miss you already Lisa.

I always feel so good when you're here. You make me laugh so hard my face hurts. And the way you do that cute little munchkin voice just bust's me. Lisa laughs and cries at the same time. Mary will you stop it. This is hard enough for me as it is. I'm sorry, but I can't help it! You're my only good and true friend in the whole world Lisa, I'm never gonna find another friend like you. And I love you too Mary, and it is I who thank you for being my true friend. I don't have many of those. But I have you. My buddy. Mary breaks down in front of her. Mary please stop this honey ok? She said going over to her taking a tissue out of her purse. She takes it and wipes Mary's tears for her. She looks at Lisa. Yosef is so blessed to have you. I hope he appreciates what God has given him in you. Lisa flashes back to where Yosef blew up at her. She begins to cry. Did I say something wrong Lisa? If I did, I'm sorry. No dearest, you didn't say anything wrong. Lisa couldn't tell her about her and Yosef having words between them. But Mary now knew why Lisa had been crying. So do I, so do I. Now you stop all this ok. I'm never far away from you. And You can come and see me anytime alright? Really? Yeah, really. We'll keep in touch, I promise. Now I better get in there and get started. Ok? There was another pause between them. Lisa? Mary walks

Over to her embracing her. I'm really gonna miss you! I miss you already sweetie. Now quit making me cry ok? I'll try. Said Mary. Lisa goes inside her office and shuts the door, she turns around to find that Mr. Wright was in there waiting for her. She felt a nauseating fear well up inside of her. It nearly paralyzed her. Ms. Anderson, will you uh, come in? He was still pretty bruised as well as embarrassed. I was coming to clear out my desk. Sure, sure. Go ahead. He said stepping out of her way. I just wanted you to know that I apologize for crazy way that I behaved the other day. I was way out of line, and I'm sorry about it all. He held out his hand to her. She jerked away from him. He looked at his hand pulling it away

From her. Of course, how foolish of me. Just then Yosef pulled up in front of the building. He goes inside. He sees Mary sitting at her desk still holding the picture of her and Lisa. She was still crying.

He goes up to her. Mary? She looks up at him. She's in there. Thank you. He said to her. He turns to walk away. Mr. Epstien? Yes. She gets up walking up to him. That girl loves you, I've seen it. I've never seen a woman love a man like this before. She truly loves you. You'll never find another like her in the world. She is like a rare jewel. And precious to God. I hope she is to you too. She is Ms. Peterson.

She is. He smiles slightly, not knowing what to make out of her words. But he appreciated them. Thanks.

If you have trouble finding another job, I'll give you a good reference ok? Lisa never answered him, she had found a small box in the supply closet, she had already started to fill it with her personals. She looked up at him. Thank you Mr. Wright. He paused a little. Or you can consider coming back here. I mean if you want to. I don't think that she wants to. The voice said from behind him. It was Yosef. Mr. Wright stumbled backwards nearly falling down. Ok, ok. Just letting her know that the door is open, and no hard feelings that's all. Yosef just glared at him. His expression telling him to get lost, he wanted to be alone with Lisa. Well uh, I'll just be going. Leave you two alone. He walks out shutting the new door behind him, since Yosef destroyed the other one.   What do you want? She said. In an indignant tone. Lisa, you have every reason to be mad at me. I was wrong for the way I treated you this morning. He tries to walk over to her, she walks away from him. She went over to the front window to get more of her personals, throwing them and everything she got her hands on into the small box. She was still very hurt. Seems like everyone takes their frustrations out on me. I feel like that blockheaded boy that everyone picks on. Yosef saw her irritation,her pain. He felt guilt sitting on his shoulder speaking bitter nothings to him. She understood that there was a fight between him and his father, but there was no reason for him to take it out on her. But that is where we all live isn't it? What did I do to you? What did I do? She wept. His heart broke for her. His mind quickly flashed to the other day when she told him about her attack, his father's cruelty to her, and how she stood up to Billy for him. How those memories felt like they weighed a ton, crashing in on him at the same time, making his guilt even more heavy to bear. His eyes filled with tears

As he watched her break down in front of him. Lisa please don't cry, you're breaking my heart. She looked up at him. I'm sorry that your heart is broken Yosef, but you broke mine first. He walks over to her no! Yosef no! he backs away from her. Lisa please! I have no excuse for my behavior today. All I know is that I've been worried out of my mind without you. I'm really sorry. Why did I ever start seeing you again? She said to him. What! He gasped. Those words hurt him deeply. You don't really mean that do you Lisa? She looks down at the floor dropping her box. I'm tired of being hurt because of someone else's problems! You hear me! I'm tired of, of... she cries into her cupped hands. Yosef walks up closer to her snatching her into his arms kissing her deeply. She struggles, but not to hard. No, Yosef! No! Oh yes! She moans. She began to suck gently on his earlobe. Oh God Lisa! He breathed his eyes rolled upward. He pulls her closer to him He slides his tongue deeper into her mouth, and hers into his. I'm so sorry baby. Please forgive me! She looks up at him. Her expression telling him all was forgiven. There's nothing to forgive Beloved. She kisses him again. *Lisa.* He moans out her name softly. She stroked his earlobe with her soft tongue, it felt warm and good to him. His eyes close tighter as she messages his body next to hers.

"Oh Lisa, yes! God Yes!" He moans louder. Mary had been listening at the door when Mr. Wright walks up behind her. What's going on in there! He said. His voice loud and raspy. Don't ever do that! She said.

He startled her making her jump like a scared cat. Shhh! I don't hear anything. She said. She listens again. Nothing. She quietly opens the door just a crack. What's happening in there? He said. Mary sees the couple lost in their deep moment of intimacy. Kissing and caressing passionately. She smiles to herself. Her face a beet red colour. She shuts the door the way she opened it, sighing out loud. Well, are they busy or what? He said. Oh yeah, their busy alright. She said walking away in a dream state. What's the matter with you? Are you nuts or something? She never answered him. He looks at the door then back at her. She had sat down at her desk swinging herself around fussing in her hair. He opens the door slowly. And sees the same thing that she saw. Yosef and Lisa still lost in their passion, his hands running up and down her soft buttom, their moans like soft music fill the air. He closes the door abruptly, and straightens his tie, and his sorry pile of hair. And walks away from the door. Oh God I Love you Lisa!

He breathed, and I love you too my Beloved. Come on, let's go now ok? I still have to get you to the Jewelers. Really? You're still gonna take me? Of course, that is if you'll still marry me? Yes, Yosef, Yes. Well, then let's go. Oh, what about my things? We'll come back for them later ok? Ok. He takes her by the hand. They emerge from the office smiling at each other. Bye Lisa! Lisa looks over at Mary who was in tears again, but for a different reason this time, she was happy for the couple. Mr. Epstien, remember what I told you? He nodded, he did remember. I will, and thanks once again for the advice. Bye, bye dear. Said Lisa winking at her. Ms. Anderson. Said Mr. Wright walking up to her, with his arms outstretched, he wanted a hug from her. But Yosef stood in front of her folding his arms, glaring at him. He backs off. Sorry, uh, take care kids. He laughs, all pretended of course. Yosef takes Lisa by the hand and walks out. Mr. Wright watches the couple as they get into his car, and drove off. Lisa has left the building! Said Mary. He looks back at her smirking. Lisa has left the building. He said parroting her. Why are all the good ones taken? Darn it all! He goes back into his office shutting the door behind him. Mary busted up laughing.

The Colour Of Love
Anne Hemingway
Chap 12.

Rabbi Epstien prepares to go to Temple today. His demons had freed him for the moment but he was still full of himself as he is most of the time. He goes out into the hall closet to get a light spring coat to take with him when he feels a slight discomfort in his chest. He shakes it off. Just gas I think. It hits him a gain a little stronger this time. He rubs the middle of his chest trying to soothe it away. It leaves him. He clears his throat. There, that's much better. Just gas that's all. He grabs his Siddur and leaves for Temple.
Yosef and Lisa arrive at Shineway Jewelers. They walk inside. Lisa gasped as she looked at all the beautiful gems of all shapes sizes and colours. Mr. Epstien, good morning! Said Madeline. Her tone was
Somewhat flirtatious. Yosef and Lisa both knew that she along with Helen and a few others had been trying to get after him for a

long time. But he never paid her or Helen or anyone else any attention at all.

Lisa. She said to her in a snappy tone. Hello Madeline. She said in a soft tone, her demeanor friendly as she always is. You look very pretty in that dress Madeline. It was a yellow long sleeve dress with floral prints on it. Madeline was wearing her white smock unbuttoned in front. Thank you. She said still snapping at her. Yosef looked at her, he didn't like her tone of voice. But he remained quiet about it. I have the designs that you had drawn up Yosef. You tell me which ones that you like, and We'll have it done in about three to four weeks. Well let's get her measured up first shall we? Oh yes of course, how silly of me. She reaches underneath the counter and pulls out what looked like a huge key ring, with several others linked together all of different sizes. Left hand third finger Lisa. She puts her hand on the counter. Madeline saw that Yosef was thumbing through one of the brochures. Madeline snatched Lisa's hand hard across the counter. There was a loud cracking sound. Ow! Be careful! Cried Lisa. You did that on purpose you little cow! Lisa yelled at her, her anger surfacing at her. Yosef saw out of the corner of his eye what she had done to her. He looked up at her dropping the little booklet to the floor. His expression spoke to her, his anger had rose in a fury. He looked at Lisa wincing in pain. She had just cracked Lisa's wrist out of place. He looked back at her. I would never in my life hit a woman. I wasn't raised that way. But so help me, if you ever touch her again. Not only will I break all my Traditions, but I'll break every

Bone in your body! You hear me! He yelled at her, his face clenched tight. Madeline swallowed hard. I'm sorry, I guess I was a little too rough with her. I didn't mean to hurt her. The hell you didn't, you nearly broke her wrist! He yelled louder. What goes on out here! We heard the Scchreeem! Said the voice in a thick Yiddish accent. It was Mr. And Mrs. Wawsczyk. The owners of Shineway Jewelers. They were a

Beautiful couple. Both short in stature. He a few inches taller than she. Her hair nearly white, his nearly bald. They by far are the nicest people on the block down the Jew Town stretch. They've known Yosef's and Lisa's family for years. Rev. Anderson asked him once when he had come to purchase a new bridal set to celebrate his twentieth wedding anniversary. Why did you give your store another name other than your own? He said to him. Well I remember when we got the first shipment of gems in. me and my wife laid them all out on the counter. They sparkled and twinkled like the stars. My Jenna said to me. Ed, look at them, look at the way they shine! It's like Heaven has come down to us in many colours. That's when I came up with the name Shineway. And besides, it's easier to pronounce than Wawsczyk. Yosef had flashed quickly in and out to that moment, he remember when Rev. Anderson had told it to him when he was younger.

They both had come over to Lisa, she was still in a lot of pain. Tears streaming down her face. Yosef was frantic trying to calm her down. Jenna takes Lisa's hand into hers gently. There, there dear. It will be alright. Yes? Yes ma'mam. She said nodding her head. She almost fainted from the pain. Madeline, you Do this to her? Why! Jenna looked at Lisa's wrist it was a little out of place. Ed come quick look see here. She showed them her wrist still somewhat disjointed. He looked at Madeline in disgust. I should fire you for this! You injure our customers like this! If you didn't have a brood of kids at home that needed to be fed, I would kick you out now! He yelled shaking his fist at her. His accent was so thick, that spit flew With each word that he spoke. Come Yosef, I show you a trick that I learned from my father. Jenna, you stand behind her eh? Eh. She said nodding her head, as she stood behind Lisa. He took Lisa's hand into his. Look at me Lisa, he said pointing to his eyes. She looks at Yosef first. It's ok baby, I'm right here ok? She nods at him. She looks back at Mr. Wawsczyk. He gently starts to massage her wrist back and forth. Close your eyes child. She does. Tell me what you see there? Lisa begins to smile, so did Yosef.

He knew she was thinking of him, of them both. I see me and my Beloved sitting near a beautiful waterfall Having a picnic. And we...her next word was interrupted by a cracking sound again. She jumped a little. So did Yosef. He still continued to massage her wrist. Lisa? Yes. Open your eyes now dear. She opens her eye slowly. How does it feel now? She looked at her wrist. It was good as new! It was back in place How did you do that! Said Yosef taking her hand into his rubbing it gently. I never felt a thing, I just heard this cracking noise. I learned this from my father. Yosef, you learn from me too eh? Eh he said nodding, smiling at Lisa. Mr. Wawsczyk turns to look at Madeline, who was still standing behind the counter looking at all that had taken place.   He looks at her in disgust. You go home now, I finish up here today. But what about her measurements? She will have no fingers left for him to put the ring on if I let you touch her again. I do this for her, you heard my husband, now you go on home maddie. Said Ms. Jenna, calling her by her nickname. I finish up here today. Please go now. She said. Lisa, come up here to me child, let's see what you take ok? Ok Ms Jenna. Lisa gets her finger measured. Ahh. A 6 you take

Eh? Eh. She said smiling.   Ms. Jenna records the measurements down on the order form, Then all of a sudden Lisa begins to cry under her breath. She didn't want Yosef to hear her. What is the matter child? What makes you cry like this? I'm sorry Ms. Jenna. I guess I don't understand why certain things happen to certain people. What do you mean dear?   Lisa turned around Yosef and Mr. Wawsczyk were looking

At some of the pictures of his family from the old Country, they never heard the ladies talking. She looks back at Ms. Jenna. Well, it's like now. Why did Madeline hurt me? I never did anything nor would I ever do anything to hurt her or anyone. Now there, there child. Don't trouble yourself about someone elses problems. She said trying to comfort her. It's not just her, it's been this way most of my life.   Things happen to me, and I don't understand the why of any of it. Well Child, I don't understand many of these things myself. But I do know this about you Lisa. And I've known you every since you were a small child.

You have a call on your life, by God Himself. I look at you, and I see that He's preparing you for something. But you must be patient, and allow Him to take you through whatever it is that He's leading you into. But why me Ms. Jenna, why me? I've not been too happy with these things. But yet through it all I can't hate, I mean I simply can't hate anyone. No matter what they've done to me. I can't hold a grudge, or retaliate against them. I really in my heart feel the need to pray for them. Is that stupid of me?

Ms. Jenna laughs at her, taking both of her hands into hers. No, my dear child, no. Lisa your heart is like pure gold to Him, and precious in His sight. She said to her, pointing to the ceiling. Whatever you do, don't ever let anyone tell you, that you are foolish for the way that you are. What is foolish to men, is wisdom to God. Stay that way, Yosef needs that from you. He's been through a lot himself. Without His faith in God, and you, as well as the prayers of his dear mother. He would not have made it this far in his life. He needs you Lisa. And I need him too Ms Jenna. But I feel like even he doesn't love me sometimes.

Ahh! She said waving her hand at her. You are all he talks about. I've had to glue my ears back on many times because he talked them off me talking about you! She said laughing out loud. Lisa laughed with her.
There, that's the smile that won his heart eh? Eh, she said. Now you remember what I said to you ok? Ok Ms. Jenna, and thanks. She kisses her on the cheek. Yosef, these rings will not pay for themselves! You come now! She called to him. Yes ma'mam! He said. He takes out his check book and writes out a check for the deposit on the rings. They had already picked out the design that they both liked. It was cluster wrap that resembled a starburst of diamonds. With the huge three karat diamond ring in the center. It was absolutely breathtaking! Here is your receipt son. It should be in, in about three to four weeks, I'll call you at home. Do you have my work number? No I don't think so. Yosef took a scrap piece of paper and wrote it down for her. Call me there if you can't get me at home. Ok son. Excited Lisa? Said Ms. Jenna. Very. Said Lisa. She bent down to look in the window where there were all sorts of necklaces, and lockets and pendants. Yosef looks down at her admiring the other jewelery. Lisa? She seemed mesmerized by them.

Lisa? Yes. Let's go baby. She takes his hand. As they begin to walk away. Mr. Wawsczyk calls to him. Yosef? Yo. He turns around taking Lisa up to him. Pay it no matter what people say about you and Lisa.
I know that people talk about these things, and many don't approve. But to me. If God approves, then what they think matters very little in His sight. Yes, I know. I've seen the stares, and heard some of the talk that goes on around here. But I say phooey on them all. This is a new Millenium now. And it is time for the wall that separates us to come down. Right Lisa? Amen Mr. Wawsczyk. Son, you just take care of her, and she'll take care of you, she is good for you, and you for her. It matters not

about her colour or yours. Just love each other eh? Eh. They both said together. His expression was tender, and sincere. Yosef felt his words ooze all over him like a warm salve. They brought comfort and encouragement to both he and Lisa. That had at first been a concern of them both. But they were quickly learning that when one is truly in Love, colour, culture, is not a factor. For it is a matter of the heart. They learned that true love really doesn't see any colour. Any colour at all. I will sir, I will. They shake hands. She's good for you! He said. That she is sir. That she is. Bye Ms. Jenna! They said to her. God bless you children! She said. Yosef and Lisa left the jewelers feeling assured in their hearts that God had truly blessed them in their relationship. But all was not over yet. For there was still more opposition, persecution that awaited them. Would their Love stand strong in the heat of it all? Well let's see. Yosef dropped Lisa off at her parents house, she had to help her mother with more planning for Pastors Day International coming up in June. He would be back to pick her up later. He had asked her out on another date. Mom! Mom!

I'm home! She yelled. I'm in the kitchen! Deborah yelled back. Her mother came out into the dinning room drying her hands on her apron. She had just finished up the dishes from that morning. Well, how did everything go with the rings? Oh mom! It's going to be beautiful! You should see it, I've never laid my eyes on anything so beautiful in my life! Well, I have. She paused. My Beloved. Deborah takes her into her arms hugging her tightly. I'm so happy for you dear. There's only one problem though. Oh, what's that? Madeline tried to break my wrist measuring me that's all. What! She gasped. Yes. She did. She cracked my wrist out of place. Oh my goodness Lisa. She said taking her hands into hers looking them over. Which one is it honey? This one. She said holding up her left hand. Deborah looks at her wrist, it was still slightly

swollen, not too much. Careful mom, it still hurts a little. I wanted to thump her one for that. She did it on purpose you know. I understand how you feel Lisa, but you know what the Scriptures say about turning the other cheek. Oh, I would've turned the other cheek alright. I just would've made sure it was hers that's all. There's a saying that I just heard that goes. If you don't touch my cheeks, I won't touch yours. Deborah laughs. Who said that? I did, just now. They both laugh together. Mr. Wawsczyk was so sweet to me and Yosef, He massaged my wrist back into place, just like magic he did. Deborah was silent for a few moments. Mom? What's the matter. She looks at Lisa, stroking her long curls. Her eyes filled with many things for her daughter. Excitement, joy, fear, and confusion. They all spoke to her at the same time. Mom, what is it? Oh Lisa, I don't know what to feel for you sometimes

It seems like every since you've been back home, all sorts of misfortune has made it's way to you. Billy, your boss, now this. She said rubbing her hands. I'm scared for you dear that's all. I feel like something really drastic might happen to you. And if it does, I don't know what I'll do. Lisa looked in her mother's eyes, and saw all the same things that she was feeling for her. She saw her emotions, Now they were trying to speak to her too. But she selected only the ones that she would listen to. Mom? Her voice it's usual sweetness. I've learned so much from you and daddy over the years. But do you know the one thing that I appreciate the most? No angel, what is it? You taught me that in hard times, no matter how mild or severe. You taught me to pray. Deborah smiled at those words. She and Rev. Anderson had taught her to pray for others. She was a true Intercessory Prayer Warrior, just like her mother. I remember when you invited me to my first intercessors prayer meeting, Lisa how could you remember that? You were only
A baby? Mom, I was five years old. And I do remember, well anyway. I watched as you and Ms. Sarah,
Ms. Carolyn, and Ms. Jenna were all in prayer. You were interceding for this Community. I was trying to pray along with you all. You were so cute Lisa, with your little hands folded together.   Your little eyes closed so tight, I didn't think you'd be able to see when you opened them. They laugh together. As I remembered mom, you were praying for togetherness in our neighborhood. Being that it's about 70% Jewish, about 15% White, and what other percentage left over after that is mostly all Black. We were all

Pretty leary of one another back then. But now look at us all. We're more than just a Community, a neighbohood. We're more like family. We've entered a New Millenium mom, and I believe that it
Brings with it a glorious fulfillment of your prayers that night. I've never forgotten that, never. With
God all things are possible. Amen. Sweetheart. Said Deborah. I see that racisim is loosing it's hold

On many Cultures, and Churches now. And instead of shunning
one another, we're beginning to open up
To learn more from each other. Embracing instead of rejecting.
It's happening all over the world mom.
I believe that God has been longsuffering with mankind long
enough. And this racial, and Denominational
Apartied has to stop. Or His Judgement will fall. If you can pray
for something as seemingly impossible as Intercultural
togetherness. I'm sure that God can and will help you direct your
prayers where your family is concerned don't you? Deborah was
stunned at her daughter's wisdom, as well as proud. Lisa's words
effected her in ways that she never imagined, tears began to flow
from both their eyes. There was a special bond between them,
they often prayed together, studied together. Their love was a
intimate love, that only a mother and daughter shared. It was
special to them both. Thank you Lisa. She said sniffing still.
Thank you for what mom? Thank you for being my daughter, I
love you so much dear. She said, her tears flowing more now. I
love you too mom. And it's I who thank you for being there when
I needed someone. I would not be the woman that I am now if it
were not for you. For that, I'll be forever grateful to you and my
father. She pauses. By the way where is daddy? Oh, uh he's at
the Church. He and Johnathan left a while ago. They should be
back shortly. Which reminds me. I have to get dressed. Get
dressed? For what? Your father's taking me out to dinner
tonight. Go head mom. Where
You two going? To Chae's. Wow! I've always wanted to go there.
But it's so expensive. Yes, it is, and I'm worth every penny of it.
She said snapping her finger in the air. Well, alright then lady.
Said Lisa, snapping her finger in the air. Would you like to see
the dress I'm wearing tonight? I would. Then let's go my
daughter. Let's go! They both go upstairs arm in arm to her
mother's bedroom. Rev. Anderson drops Johnathan off at his
girlfriend's house, after they had finished looking in on the pipes
down in the basement. They had been leaking for sometime now,
and were going to need some fixing. They also had to meet with
two of the Elders there. Elder Watkins, and Elder Jones. More
Planning for the upcoming Pastors Day. They asked Johnathan if
he would resume his position as Head Deacon. He was unsure as
he had been out of Church for about four years now. He was still
undecided but would let them know before the Conference. The
position was still open to him if he still wanted it. Rev. Anderson
went on to Temple

To speak with Rabbi about his behavior that morning. As well as to his entire family. And especially to stop his tormenting Yosef and Lisa. But even more his wife, Sarah. He pulls into the Temple parking lot.

It was vacant, all except Rabbi Epstien's Van. He goes inside. It was cold, dark, and very uninviting. Rev. Anderson looks down the hall to the left of him, and he notices a glimmer of light coming from the a small room. He walks toward it, there was laughter coming from the inside. He recognizes one of the voices. Oh no. He breathed. The door was slightly ajar. He stepped up to the cracked door to peek inside. She was a young woman about 25-30ish with firey red hair. It was the same woman that Mr. Wright was having an affair with when Yosef caught him in the act not too long ago. He peeked in further, holding her by the waist was Rabbi Epstien! Jesus! He whispered, his eyes filled with tears. He thought of Sarah, what this would do to her if she knew. Yosef more than likely would never have anything to do with him ever again. He just stood there watching them. His anger rising, not at the girl. But at him. A Rabbi, a Servant of God committing adultery! Rabbi was just about to kiss the woman when he heard a deep grunting sound. He looked up right into Rev. Anderson's eyes. He could tell Rev. Anderson was deeply hurt, and furious at him! The girl never heard him, she continued on in her whinning, and trying to undo his slacks, and kissing at him. Rabbi was speechless, stunned scared. You name it, he felt it at that moment. Rev. Anderson didn't want to bust them in the act. So he thought that he would just let Rabbi see him standing there. He knew then that Rabbi would come to him to talk later. Rev. Anderson thought about all that Yosef had told him that morning, they came back to remind him that it was for his daughter
And soon to be son-in-law, and their right to marry that he was fighting in their behalf on. Rabbi saw the
Disappointment in his expression, he saw Rev. Anderson's hurt for Sarah and Yosef. It cut him deeply. He looked down at the girl, then back at his friend. Rev. Anderson never said one word, he just turned and quietly walked away. Rabbi for the first time in his life came face to face with the sprit of fear. It gripped him like a vice. He was paralyzed by it. Myriads of thoughts ran across his mind like a scroll marquee, flashing images of his life in happier times with Sarah and their sons. As well as the Andersons. They were all just like family. He saw it all flash

before him in a matter of seconds. He began to sweat profusely, his laughter stopped abruptly. I'm very sorry my dear, but I can't now. I have to go. But Jacob, you promised. She whinned. No! I can't! Now go, please get out of here! She snatches up her purse and leaves his office slamming the door behind her. The girl left him alone with all his feelings, all of his fears, all of his sorrows. Things that she knew nothing of. For all she knew, he was just another john paying her

For a favor. He sits down at his desk, burying his head in his hands, and sobbed. My dear God in Heaven. What have I done! He wept as he had lived. Bitterly.

The Colour Of Love
Anne Hemingway

Chap. 13

Rev. Anderson returned home, his thoughts all on what had happened that day. He now found it difficult to enjoy the rest of the day as he had told Yosef to do earlier. His best friend committing adultery, his best friend, a bigot towards his daughter, his best friend emotionally abusive towards his wife and only son.
Why! Jacob? Why? He sobbed in his car for his friend, whom he loved dearly. He finally gathered himself together, and went into the house. Deborah was not there, she was across the street at Sarah's. Good. He thought to himself. He didn't want her to see him in his present state. He didn't want to have to tell her what he had witnessed that morning. He looked at his watch. It was 12:45p.m. He knew that Rabbi would either call him or stop by. He just patiently waited for whichever came first. He was hurt for him, as well as angry at him. His jaws tight, as he paced the living room floor. The phone rings out loud.

Anderson Residence. His deep baritone voice answered. There was no answer. But he knew who it was.
Hello Jacob. His tone even deeper now than it had ever been. I need to talk with you Ben. He sounded desperate. I'll meet you

downtown at Grant Park. Said Rev. Anderson. Thank you Ben, thank you. I don't think you know what this means to me. Thank you my friend. Rev. Anderson paused a little. Hum He called me friend. I haven't heard that in a while. He thought. He smiled a little before answering him.

Of course Jacob, see you there. They hang up. One half hour later, they meet at the park. Nearly arriving there at the same time. One pulling in right behind the other. They walk together looking for a park bench that was somewhere private. It was hot and sunny out that afternoon. The park was full of families, and bikers, and lovers picnicking together, joggers etc. They find a park bench and sit down next to each other.

Rabbi takes a deep breath. Where shall we begin Jacob? Rabbi knew that from the sound of his voice that he was not in the mood for any attitude from him at all. I don't where to begin, there's just so much. Why

Don't you start with this morning. He said fanning himself with the morning newspaper. This morning?

Yes, why you made such an ass out of yourself this morning, upsetting Yosef so much that he took it out on Lisa. He was in tears, she was in tears. It was not a good scene between them. His anger was slowly surfacing. I don't know Ben. I can't explain my actions lately. I feel like someone completely different. I didn't mean to upset my son. I can't explain a lot of anything anymore. I don't know if that makes any sense to you, but it does to me. I would like to talk out these things, but I don't know how. Ben saw his friend's obvious frustration, his anguish, his misery. He had never been able to live a normal life since the deaths of his family. And he had not been the same towards Sarah since she told him the news about her

Parents either. Rev. Anderson paused. Jacob, the young girl. Yes that. Rabbi interrupted. Do you know who she is? I just know her by the name Lorraine. Do you know what she is? Just some silly red head girl I met at in the store one night. Jacob, she's a prostitute. Rabbi lowered his head. I'm not surprised. Oh, and why is that? I kinda felt that she might be this type of woman, when I began to experience a sickness sometime ago. I went to the clinic, they said that I had an infection and I would have to take a medicine to clear it up. And? The medicine cleared up the infection. What did you have? Asked Rev. Anderson. Gonorrhea. Said Rabbi. Rev. Anderson was now even more disgusted with him than before. Jacob? Yes.

132

How do you feel about Sarah? Rabbi chuckles a little. He shakes his head. You might not believe what I'm about to say. But I, I. He struggled to say the word even in the presence of Rev. Anderson. I love my wife. They both look at each other. I do Ben, I do. I love her. He hadn't said those words in such a long time, they felt like a bucket of fresh water was just poured all over him. It felt good to him. Rev. Anderson notices his reaction to saying them. He knew then that he was telling the truth. Then why Jacob? Why adultery? The words hit him like a bolt of lighting. I don't know! I don't know! Do you

Love this Lorraine? Jesus no Ben! I do not! She was someone who was just there when I needed a place to unload my frustrations. That's not all you unloaded. Said Rev. Anderson. Rabbi was quieted by those words. Yes, I know this. There was a pause between them. What are you going to do about cookie? I mean Sarah? Ben I told you, I love my wife! I love Sarah! I have no intentions of leaving her!
Then why did you do this to her? Do you know what it would do to her if she knew about this? And I don't want to even think about Yosef.. Rabbi was silent. I never got over what she told me about her parents. She is half of a people that I love, and half of a people that I hate! He shouted. That was not her fault Jacob! Her mother was raped! That is no excuse for adultery man! Shouted Rev. Anderson even louder, beating his fist in his hand. His voice boomed throughout the park attracting attention to them. He settles down some, lowering his voice a little. Look Jacob. I've known you and your family for a long time, every since we moved up here from the South. You were the first people that we met. We've been through a lot together. We've even raised our children together man. Rabbi nods his head in remembrance of those times. You mean you and Deborah raised Yosef. Rev. Anderson knew what he was talking about. He remembered that night too. The night that Sarah brought him over to their house in desperation. A last attempt to save her only son. He remembers hearing the doorbell ringing frantically.
Ok, ok. I'm coming! He opens the door. It was Sarah and Yosef. She was carrying a suitcase filled with all his belongings. Benjamin, may I come in please! Yes of course cookie. She pushes Yosef gently inside
Closing the door behind them. She set his suitcase down on the floor, and goes over to the large picture window and looks out.

133

She was trembling all over with fear. Cookie what is it dear? Deborah had come from in the laundry room to see what was going on. Sarah? She said in a soft tone. Come here my dear. Sarah goes over to her. Deborah embraces her. What is all this? Why are you and Yosef out on a night like this? It was raining hard out that night. She was still dressed in her mourning clothes. Today I buried my firstborn son. Michael. They had heard about Michael's death, and was deeply grieved for her and Rabbi. The Anderson's were quiet as Sarah explained her actions to them. Yacov has left us. I don't know if he will ever come back. He was devastated over Michael's death. She takes a deep breath. He blames me for this. The Anderson's look at each other. Disgust filled their expressions. Now my only

Child has no father to look after him, and no older brother for him to look up to. But you have an older son. Johnathan will be good for my Yosef. The are the best of friends already. You take my child, you take my son. Take him and raise him well in your home. I trust no one else to do this for me. I cannot stand around and hope for Yacov to return to me, while he goes without a father. I've already lost one son. I will not loose another! Her tears streaming down her soft cheeks. Rev. Anderson and Deborah felt their own tears flowing as well. She bends down to Yosef. Go, go to Rev. Anderson, and Deborah. He is your father now. And she is your second mother. Oh Sarah! Cried Deborah. No! No! I've made my decision! Please take him! And love him! I know in here, that you will raise him like he was your very own. She said pointing to her chest. I'll come to see you everyday mom! He cried to her. I know you will child, I know you will. Yosef looks at his mother, she looked as though all life had been drained from her. He runs over to her, throwing his arms around her neck hugging her hard. Tears streaming down his face. I love you mom! I love you my son! They each cried. She gathered him into her arms embracing him hard.

She was somewhat torn in her feelings for both her sons. Having to decide which hurt worse. Burying Michael, or parting with her only living son. She felt they each hurt the worse in their own way. It was the hardest thing that she had ever done in her life. To part with the only person left in her life that ever really loved her. Please understand Yosef, I do this not for me, but for you eh? Eh, he said crying hard for her. Always know, that no matter what happens, My love is always with you. And my love is always with you too mom. I know my dearest. She takes him by the hand, walking him over to Rev. Anderson, and Deborah. He looks at them, looking down at him. All their expression speaking to one another. Here, take my son, he's yours now. Give him what Yacov denied him, teach him what Yacov never learned himself.

Raise him, and love him the way that he deserves. This home is full of love, and I know he will be happy here. May God in all His Glory bless you both richly for this. Give me your hands. They both stretch out their hands. She puts Yosef's hand in theirs praying for his new family.

"Father, God of Abraham, Issac, and Jacob.
I ask that you bless this home, bless this family
I ask that Your Will be done, as I give my only
Child to Rev. Anderson and Deborah. Oh Father
Crown their heads with Your Wisdom, and Your
Understanding, as they raise Yosef in the fear and
Reverance of the Lord. And may he find peace, love
And joy in his new surroundings. We love
You, and honor You. And Father I ask you to
Watch over my child, that he will be obedient
And give them the respect that they deserve.
Make him the man that You want him to be.
This I ask in the Name of our DearLord and
Savior. Yeshua. Amen."

Amen. They all said after her. Johnathan! Rev. Anderson calls. Sir! Come down here son! Coming! Johnathan runs down the stairs Yeah dad. Take Jo-Jo upstairs to your room. He's going to be living here with us for a while. Son, go get your things. Yes sir. He said. Wow! My own little brother! This is going to be neat! Come on squirt! He said playfully to him. Yosef goes to get his suitcase. He looks back at his mother, who was still in tears, but for a different reason this time. She felt as though a hundred ton burden had been lifted off her shoulders, as well as her heart. Johnathan takes Yosef upstairs. Rev. Anderson and Deborah step closer to Sarah, embracing her warmly. There was a loud boom of thunder outside. Sarah, your husband is gone now, but he'll be back. I'm sure of it. He just needs time to heal

That's all. You should not be alone tonight. I want you to stay here with us tonight ok?   He said to her.

Now don't say no to me cookie. She looks at Deborah, nodding in agreement with her husband. You can sleep in the guess room next to Lisa's room ok? Said Deborah. Ok. She said. She sounded tired, Michael's funeral, Rabbi's ranting and raving about his death. Had taken an awful toll on her. She looked aged, and worn down. The only thing that made her smile, was giving Yosef over to the Andersons. How that made her heart glad to know that Yosef would be taken care of, and surrounded by a loving caring family, that accepted him. His being Jewish, and they being African-American was never a problem to them. They loved each other deeply. Now you come with me dear, I'll get you some dry clothes to put on. Then we'll go into the kitchen for some macadamian, chocolate chip cookies. Sarah's expression changed. Her weakness was cookies. She never could refuse them! And Deborah made the best in the neighborhood. How can I refuse when you offer me my favorite things Deborah. They all laugh together.

Rev. Anderson hears the laughter echoing in his ears. Yosef has always been a good child Ben. Said Rabbi

His voice snapping him from his memories back into the now. He was never any trouble to me or his mother. You and Deborah did well with him. Please believe me when I say this. I'll always be grateful for what you both did for my son. Very grateful. He has grown up to act just like his father. He looks over at Rev. Anderson smiling. They both smile. Thank you Jacob. I appreciate that. My wife will too. Rev. Anderson held off telling him about Yosef and Lisa's pending engagement for the moment. Jacob, I'll help you in any way that I can. But you must tell cookie about your, uh. Indescretion. Yes, I know. But you must let me choose the time and place for this telling eh? Eh. Said Rev. Anderson. They both get up off the bench to leave. And about our son. That little remark you made about his, uh. Manhood. Yes, that. Said Rabbi. I was wrong to say that about him. I'm sorry Ben. Truly I'm sorry. You can tell him yourself when the time comes. Yes, when the time comes. Said Rabbi. He was somewhat remorseful for his treatment of him that

morning. I just want you to know, that I've seen him the buff. And he's not, uh.
Lacking at all if you know what I mean.   Said Rev. Anderson, winking at him. Yes my friend, I know what you mean. Said Rabbi winking back at him. My poor daughter! He said as they each leave to go home.

The Colour Of Love
Anne Hemingway

Chap 14.

Yosef had called Lisa to tell her that he'll be a little late picking her up for their date that night. Terry called him asking him to come over for a quick rehearsal. And that he would be by later. Pastors Day International was a very important Conference. It was more than a festivity. It was a time for Pastors from all over the World to come together for a time of sharing what God was doing in their Churches, regardless of the Denomination. It was a powerful time of everyone opening up their hearts and embracing each other in the Spirit of Love and Unity. Which was this years theme. *"Unity Through Love."* All the visiting Pastors were praying for a Spirit of Revival to sweep this years Conference. And that God would move in their midst. Little did they know that God heard that prayer, and would answer them in a way that all would never forget.

Jo, has Rabbi ever been to Pastors Day? Asked Terry. He didn't answer. His mind was thinking on his girl, his mother, and his father. He knew that his father would have to except Lisa in order for him to marry her. But that wasn't a worry to him. He would make her his wife regardless. And Rabbi knew it.
The other band mates noticed his strange mood. He seemed distant for some reason. James walked up to him. Tapping him on the shoulder. Yosef was putting his bass away. You ok man? His voice snapping him out of his mood. I'm sorry, what were you saying? You ok? he asked again. Yeah, I'm fine, just thinking that's all. The rest of the band knew who he was thinking about more than anybody. Lisa. James looked around for her. They didn't even notice that she wasn't with him like she

normally is. Jo? James calls out to him. What. Where's Lisa? She's at home. I dropped her off, we have a date tonight. But Terry called me for a quick rehearsal. So here I am. And Lisa didn't mind that even though you're taking her out tonight? Why should she mind bro? She is about the most understanding woman I've ever seen in my life. She amazes me man. You broke your date with that angel to come over here to rehearse with us? Said Brad. I didn't break our date, I just told her what happened that's all. And what did she say? Said James. Yosef picks up his bass and prepares to leave. She said ok. I'll see you later. That's it? Just like that? Said Terry. That's it. I bet you five dollars she'll be mad when you get over there to pick her up.

No she won't J. Look, I know my baby. She's not like that. She loves you guys you know that. She understands believe me. Yeah we do know that. But there's just something about standing up a sister
Jo, no matter how understanding she is. They don't like it! James said. I'm not standing her up J. What is it with you guys tonight? Can we just see for ourselves? Said Brad. What! Would you like to make a small wager, sister will have a serious tude when you get over there man. Said James. Yosef nods his head laughing a little. Sure why not, I don't mind making a little extra money. Just more for me to take her out with tonight. I want in. Said Terry. Oh I gotta have some. Said James. I want a taste too. Said Brad. They all place there bet. Now let's go gentlemen shall we? Said Yosef. Lead the way bass man. Said James. They follow Yosef over to Lisa's parents house in Terry's car. They reach Lisa's home. Yosef and the rest of the band get out of their cars Like I said, and I reinterate. Sister's gonna have a tude man. Said James. I know Black women. You gonna get jacked up! They all break up laughing. Yosef laughs with them. You don't know my girl James. And thanks for the extra cash, I'm sure she'll appreciate it. He walks to the front porch. Stay here. He said to them. Hope you make it out in one piece boy! Said James.

The door wasn't locked, so he just let himself in. The fragrance of fried chicken, and buttermilk biscuits filled the air. Lisa's father had come home to get her mother, they had a few errands to run before their date tonight. But Lisa had forgotten about that. So she prepared dinner for them as a surprise. She was in the

kitchen finishing up the last of the dishes. She liked to clean as she cooked. She never heard Yosef come in.
Yosef's stomach begins to rumble at the dinner that she had prepared. Her back was to him, as he walked
Silently up behind her. He slides his hands around her slender waist, kissing her on her cheek. Hello baby. He said softly in her ear. Ohhh. She moaned sweetly. Beloved. She breathed, turning around to kiss him. Now how did you know it was me? He said smiling at her. I recognize your touch, and besides.
No one can make my heart beat like that but you. She kisses him again. Whoa! He said shaking his head.
You ought to be ashamed of yourself kissing me like that girl. He picks her up kissing her again. Yosef put me down, I have to finish getting dinner fixed before my parents get home. I'm surprising them. Just then, the front door opens, it was her parents. Rev. Anderson takes a deep breath inhaling the aroma of the dinner that Lisa had fixed for them. I can tell by the smell, that someone forgot that we were going out tonight. Said Deborah. Do we have to go out now? Said Rev. Anderson, looking at Deborah. He inhaled deeply at the dinner that Lisa had made. He smiled as he savored every whiff of garlic roasted potatoes, Mushroom onion gravy buttermilk biscuits, and deep fried chicken. Fresh garden salad. And Sun tea.
With honey and lemon. Yes we do, I know it smells good, but you promised me. I know love, but she made homemade biscuits, and gravy and taters. He said whinning. Never mind that big boy, you come on with me. She said taking him by the hand into the kitchen. They go inside, Yosef and Lisa were still kissing. Her parents laugh a little. Rev. Anderson clears his throat loud. Lisa jumps in Yosef's embrace.
They both turn around seeing her parents there smiling at them. Hello kids. Said Rev. Anderson. Mom! Dad! They all greet one another. Yosef shaking hands with Rev. Anderson. Kissing Deborah on the cheek. Hi angel. Said Rev. Anderson. Kissing her cheek. Hello sweetie. Said her mother kissing her the same. What's all this? Said Rev. Anderson, looking around at all the food that she had prepared for them.

I thought that I would surprise you and make dinner. Surprise! She said. Laughing. Yosef laughs at her.
Honey, here tell me how they came out. She said handing him a hot biscuit dripping with melted honey butter. He takes a bite.

Ohhhh! Oh, baby this is Heaven! Rev. Anderson drools at the biscuit. Yosef offers him a bite. Deborah tries to stop him, grabbing him by the arm. Benjamin. She said to him. Now, now if my angel wants us to sample her biscuits, what kind of a father would I be to her if I said no? He takes a bite off Yosef's biscuit, Yosef ate the last bite himself. His reaction was the same as Yosef's. They both stood there moaning to themselves, honey butter dripping from the corner of their mouths. Deborah turns to look Lisa. Lisa look what you did. I'll never get to Chae's now! Mom. Chill, chill. Yes you will. Honey looks like you forgot all about your father's and my dinner date for tonight. Lisa smacks her forehead. Oh, that's right! I did forget. She looks at the dinner table. What am I gonna do with all this food now. Yosef was still standing there licking his fingers, and wiping his mouth with a paper towel.Have you had supper tonight yet son? Asked Rev. Anderson. No, I haven't been home yet. Looks like you and the band have just been invited over for supper. I mean you wouldn't want to disappoint Lisa after all the trouble she went through to make this fantastic meal now would you? Yosef looks over at her. No sir, I wouldn't want to do that. Go call them in. We have to get ready and going. But I just want one more taste. Oh no you don't Benjamin. Deborah interrupted him. Yosef go get the boys honey. And as for you biscuit lips you come on with me. Said Deborah pulling him by the arm. Rev. Anderson laughs out loud.

Will do said Yosef, laughing at them. Well, what do you think? Should we go in there and rescue the poor guy? Said terry. Just then the front door opens. You guys hungry? Said Yosef. He waves his hand for them to come inside. They all stand around looking at one another. What did she do to you man? Said James. Yosef stood there chuckling at them. She kissed me, then she gave me a biscuit. Now she wants you all to stay for supper. Let's go! You know how she doesn't like to be kept waiting. He said punching James playfully in the shoulder. They all go inside. Lisa had set a beautiful dinner table. From the centerpiece down to the silverware. Everything was ready for them to enjoy. Whoa! Said Brad. Look at this! Lisa you did this all by yourself? All by myself Brad. Here sit down. She said sweetly offering him a chair to seat himself. Gentlemen , please. Be seated, I have to go get the tea. This is incredible! I haven't seen a table like this since last thanksgiving. Said Terry. Yosef smiles at them all. Lisa returns to them carrying a huge pitcher of tea, filled with lemon slices. It's fragrance was heavenly.

Baby would you say Grace for us please. My pleasure said Yosef. Our Dear Heavenly Father, We thank You for this food that we're about to receive. We ask that You bless that hands that prepared it, and to Lisa's parents for their hospitality offered to us tonight. Watch over them and us Now . We ask in the Name of Yeshua our Lord. Amen. Amen. Said the rest. Everyone seated themselves. Yosef seated Lisa.
Then they began their dinner. Everyone filled their plates with everything. Lisa took only small portions of some things. Is that all you're having Lisa? Asked Brad. I have to be careful. I have to watch my figure. She said. Oh, I forgot the salt and pepper. I'll be right back. She got up from the table. Yosef's eyes followed her into the kitchen. He squirmed in his chair a little. He noticed that he wasn't the only one watching her figure. He smiled to himself. She returns to the dinner room. Everyone was watching her as she approached the table. Here you go guys, sorry about that. she sat back down next to Yosef. Her soft breast bouncing up and down with each movement. Yosef squirmed more this time. Her presence made it difficult for him to enjoy his supper. It was hard for him to take his eyes off her long enough to even eat anything. Lisa was taking a sip of water when her father calls to her. Lisa! We're leaving now! She gets up again from the table, walking into the living room. All eyes were on her again. Especially Yosef's Whoa! He breathed. Whoa, is right. Said James. Shaking his head at him.   How much longer will it be before you guys are uh, official bro? Asked James. Yosef still in a trance. Too long! He said. But I'm cool, I can do this. He said snapping back into the now. Taking a sip of water.
Dad you look wonderful! Thanks baby. He was dressed in the suit that he and Yosef had made for him from Schmidt's the same suit that Yosef wore on the night of their first date. They both look up Deborah was coming down the stairs. She looked like she just stepped out of a fashion magazine. Wow! Mon, you look incredible! I do? She said playfully. This old thing? Yeah, right. That old thing cost my credit card $500.00 dollars. But I'm worth it, she said. That you are my dear. But to me. You are priceless. Come here woman! He kisses her. Honey, Lisa. She said nodding over at her. Lisa was blushing. To see her parents kiss like young lovers, did something to her. She at that moment

was filled with an overwhelming desire for her Beloved. We have to go now. Ok mom. Be good angel. I will daddy. He kisses her on the cheek. If you see Johnathan tonight, tell him I need him to help me down at the Church tomorrow. Some leaks that need fixing in the basement. Ok daddy. Have a good time you two. By Mom. Bye sweetie.

I love you both. Her father turns to wink at her as she shuts the door behind them. She smiles to herself, she felt like she could walk on air. She walked back into the dinning room, her face flushed from the
Arousal that she felt for Yosef. He and the band had nearly finished their dinner, they were just sitting around talking about writing some new material for the Conference. Lisa seated herself next to Yosef, she didn't feel like eating now. Her mind was on her parents. They both looked like prom night to her.
Both of them dressed in black. He in his new tailor made suit. And she in a black scooped necked sequined dress, with long sleeves, and a split that went all the way up to her knees. She looked gorgeous!

The band stared at her for a moment, she looked different to them. She had that "In Love" expression on her face. She sighed softly. Seeing her parents tonight, made her realize how deeply in love with Yosef she is. She starts to play with the food on her plate. Yosef was talking with Terry about the new songs that he and Lisa, had written together, and he wanted to introduce them to the band. James was watching her.
Yosef was so deep into his conversation, he never noticed her at that moment. Jo? He never answered James. He was still talking with Terry and didn't hear him. Yosef! What is it man? Look. Said James nodding in Lisa's direction. She was still playing with her supper. She was thinking of her and Yosef. She was wondering if they would be that much in love when they reached her parents age. Or even more so.

Yosef didn' t know what to say, he too just looked at her. Lisa? She never answered him. Baby, what's wrong? He put his hand on hers. The feel of his hand sent a surge of passion through her body. She moaned sensually. Still no answer. All of a sudden, she looks at him, a radiant love in her eyes for him.

142

She moves in closer to him.   Oh,oh. Said Yosef. Oh,oh is right said James leaning over to Terry.

Lisa, no! said Yosef. Too late! She deep kisses him right in front of everyone! Her soft tongue sliding down this throat. Gasps came from all over the dinner table.   She stops kissing him, and looks deeply into his eyes. His breathing was heavy, he dropped his water glass to the floor.   I love you, Beloved. She whispered. Yosef was more shocked than any of them, she never kissed him like that in front of anyone before.   He was speechless. She gets up from the table, her soft tender breast gently stroked the side of his cheek. Brad quickly grabs his water glass, gulping the water down fast. Terry and James sat there with their eyes wide and staring, and their mouths opened just as wide.   They looked at each other in silence.   Did you see that! Terry whispered to James. I saw that he said.   They looked on to see what she would do to him next. I think I'll go get dessert. She said in a breathy tone, walking away. She stops and turns back to look at Yosef, who never took his eyes off her. He was still in shock over that display of unihibited affection from her. She winks at him sensually,   As she walks into the kitchen. Her every move seem to be in slow motion.   Her soft round bottom bounced with every move. "Oh God Lisa!" Sighed Yosef. He ached terribly in that all too familiar way for her again. Brad reaches over to get the water pitcher. But Yosef beat him to it. So Brad reached his water glass to him expecting him to fill it. But instead, Yosef pours the whole thing into his lap! Ahhhhhh! He sighed loudly. Brad was still holding his water glass out. Hey man! He shouted to Yosef. Leave me alone man, I'm in pain here! Said Yosef. He lowers his head down on the table beating it up and down gently.   He ain't gonna make it. He aint gonna make it at all. Said James. He and Terry shaking their heads at him.   Brad sat back down, setting his glass back on the table. Did you ever see anything like that in your life? He said, still not knowing what to make out of what he just saw. Yosef lifts his head. I'm not gonna make it! I'm not gonna make it! Please! Please! Pray for me! He said. The water only gave him just enough relief, so that he could get up from the table without embarrassment. But of course all the guys knew what happened with him when Lisa deep kissed him. It's ok man, it's ok Jo! Said James trying to console him. Tell that to him! He said pointing to his manhood. You're on your own there bro. Said James laughing a little at him. It'll be alright Man. Said Terry. Yosef lowers his head back down on the table again. Oh God help me! He sighed. Just then Lisa emerges from the kitchen carrying a medium sized serving dish. She sat it down on the table.

Lemon pound cake anyone? She said in a sensuous tone. They never looked at the cake, all eyes were on her. Especially Yosef's His breathing still rapid. He squirmed a little again.   She went about them all clearing the table of the supper dishes.   I have to go do the dishes now. Enjoy your dessert gentlemen.
Her voice the same sensuous tone.   She looked at Yosef, I Love you. She mouthed to him, flashing a beautiful smile at him.   She disappears inside the kitchen. Everyone was silent, no one knew what to say.
Cake anyone? Said Brad.   His voice trembling. No one answered him. No one even had their minds on cake at that moment.
Especially Yosef.   I'd like some cake. He said. Still no answer.
He clears his throat, pulling his shirt from around his neck. Is it hot in here or what? He said.   Oh look. She even cut it for us guys. Total silence from them all.   Brad looked at everyone at the table. Terry and James still in a trance. Yosef, had that same "In Love" expression on his face that Lisa had earlier. Terry looked at him.
Yosef had propped his chin upon his hand. Still staring blankly into nothing.   The guy's so gooey, you could slurp him through a straw. Said Terry. Bet man. Said James hitting fists with him.
James shakes his head
A little. Come on man! Come on! Let's enjoy this! She went through all the trouble to make this for us.
He said a little frustrated. He as well as all the rest expected a nice quiet fellowship supper. They had never figured on getting a birds eye view of a young woman making love to her beloved right before their eyes.   She can't do this to me and get away with it! Said Yosef. He gets up from the table to go into the kitchen after her. Noooo! No man! Don't go in there! She's not safe to be around Jo! Said James.

She's still hot Jo! Said Terry. She'll burn him alive. Said Brad shaking his head.   He never answered them. He walks into the kitchen. They hear Lisa scream. Run for your lives! Shouted Brad. Let's get outta here! Said Terry. They all scatter out of the house, leaving the front door open. All of a sudden there was the

144

sound of soft moans, then gentle laughter filtering out of the kitchen. Yosef and Lisa came out together holding hands to let them know all was well. But all they found was an empty dining room., they had left, not one of them touched any cake. Where'd they go? She said looking around. I guess they couldn't stand the heat. He said laughing. Going over to shut the front door. But they didn't have any cake. She said shaking her head laughing some. Look, I have to be going myself. My mom is probably worried about me. No she isn't. now how do you know that? Because I called her when you went out to get the guys. That's why not. He takes her by her slender waist, smiling at her. I love you Lisa. I love you so much, I can hardly stand to look at you sometimes. He said stroking her long curls. You just read my heart Yosef. I did? Yes you did. She said getting closer to his lips. I love you the same. They kiss
Gently. I have to finish the dishes now. Ok. He said softly. He found it even more difficult to leave her there alone. Come on, I'll walk you to the door. She said taking him by the hand. Will I see you tomorrow Beloved? You know you will Lisa. He said. Night. Goodnight baby. He said to her. She goes back to finish her dishes.

The Colour Of Love
Anne Hemingway
Chap. 15

Josef returns home to find his father at the dinning room table. He seemed quiet tonight. Yosef. He called to him. He never answered, he just stopped to look at him. Your mother told me you were at Lisa's parent's house for supper. That's right dad, I was. What about it? Is there a problem? No, no. I was just wondering. Wondering what? Jewish food not good enough for you any more that you go over there to eat their weird fixings. What! Since when is eating fried chicken weird dad? And besides, you've eaten there yourself, many times. I don't recall you complaining about that! No matter! You should still have dinner here with your own family! What family! The only family I have besides my mother. Is Lisa and her family. Rabbi was stunned to hear that. It kinda hurt almost like an electric current. But instead of letting Yosef know that he had gotten to him. He allowed his demon to surface again in that all too familiar way again. He noticed that the front of Yosef slacks were drenched. He didn't know that it was just water this time. I see that you and Lisa have been at it again. His tone sarcastic as usual. What did she do to you this time? Yosef just walked away from him. He never answered him. I'm tired, and I'm going to bed. After I check in on mom. Yosef walks passed him to go upstairs. Rabbi follows him. That is quite a spill there, what are you trying to do to the poor girl? Drown her? Heh, heh,heh! Yosef turns to look at him. Rabbi's face was again that contorted creature, that he was a few days ago. I didn't know you were so full boy! Be careful, or you'll blow her head off! Yosef was about to fire at his father again, when he heard this voice come from inside his spirit. *"If you'll say My Name, It will leave him."* "Heh, heh, heh." The demon laughed through him. "In the Name of Yeshua, get out of my sight!" "Nooooooo!" cried the spirit through Rabbi. He then took off running down the hall into his study slamming the door behind him.

Yosef stood there tying to make sense out of what had just happened. But it was only the beginning of a series of tests that God would allow in his life, to prove him, so He could use him. Not only him, but Lisa would play a very important part in Yosef's growth, as well and he the same with her. God was about to use them both. He would use them to bridge the gap between the diversitiy of Cultures in their neighborhood, as well as their Churches. Yosef already saw this with his boss, and his new girlfriend.
He wanted the wall of Racial predjudice torn down, and He would use them to do it. This should be interesting. Yosef went upstairs to check in on his mother like he said. She was sleeping soundly. She looked peaceful, more peaceful that he had seen her sleep in a long time. I love you mom. And I'll always take care of you. You and Lisa. He kisses her forehead gently. Then goes to his room to bed.

Three weeks later on a sweltering Wednesday morning. Yosef goes off to work. He has on his dark blue business suit, and his Yamika. He would go to work a little late this morning, because Mr. Wawsczyk had
Called him last night to inform him that Lisa's rings had come in. And he could pick them up at anytime.

Yosef couldn't wait for anytime, as far as he was concerned, the time was now. He called Mr. Dennis
To let him know he would be late, that he had to stop at the Jewelers. His boss was happy to oblige him. After all every since their lunch date, Mr. Dennis was getting quite close to his new found love. Yes, he had fallen very deeply in love with Michelle. And she with him. It had become very serious between them. Yosef and Lisa had inspired something in them both. He saw from their example that love at true sight really does exists. He saw beyond Michelle's colour, and saw her heart, and she saw his. Their love, like Yosef, and Lisa's didn't know any colour. Just love. Pure, true and real. Sarah was in the kitchen putting the last of the breakfast dishes in the sink, she would wash them later. Rabbi was in his study
Preparing to go to Temple that afternoon for Seder. He is seated at his desk, when he feels a slight discomfort in his chest again, just like the one that he felt a few weeks ago. He rubs it just like he did before. It leaves him for the moment. He clears his throat standing up to gather his things to take to Temple with him. A slight dizziness comes on him. He shakes his head, it clears. He takes his brief case and prepares to leave. When out of the darkness of his soul, his tormentors surface again. Bringing with them all the hellish memories of his past. It's as though Satan himself had summoned every demon in hell to this Earth to torture him. Image after image flashed before him. Lashing his mind with horror after horror. He jumps up out of his chair, grabbing his Siddur. He fumbles it back onto the desk. He picks

It back up again, then puts on his round wire rimmed glasses, and heads out for Temple. Sarah is in the kitchen wiping off the stove,and the cabinets. While listening to a Messianic Praise tape that Lisa had made for her. It was some of the same songs that she wrote for Yosef's band. She hears the front door slam
She stops her cleaning abruptly. Yacov? She calls out. There was no answer. She walks out into the living room. Yacov? She calls again. He had left without even saying goodbye. She goes over to the picture window, and sees the car pull off in a hurry. She drops her head, and goes back into the kitchen.
The telephone rings snapping her out of her tears. She wipes her eyes, as she answers. It was Deborah.
She lets out a sigh of relief as she sits down on the little chair by the phone to chat a little with her best

Friend. Rabbi pulls into the parking lot. There were many cars there today, among them was Rabbi Marcus. He would be glad to see him there. Since he received the good news that he was in good health.

All throughout his mind he is plagued with his holocaust memories, they show him no mercy. Just as he had been merciless to his family, they now repay him for his cruelty. They once again flash the image of his sister and his mother being tortured by the Squad. Another demon flashes the image of his father being shot in the forehead, he sees himself standing there feeling his father's loosing it's grip on his. He sees his mother lying dead in a pool of blood. Laura's brutal rape and murder. Laura Nooooo! He screams, and flinches at the same time with his mind child. He then watches in renewed horror as his family is taken one
By one to the gas chamber to be gassed along with the others. He can still see the Squad members flinching at the stench of death as it's foulness overwhelms them. He can still himself smell the odor of rotted and burning human flesh and hair, as the huge cloud billowed out from the chamber, causing him and the Squad members themselves to nearly loose the contents of their stomachs. He can still see Laura's eyes staring at him, as her body is thrown onto the body of her mother. His memories were like swords, like cold blades of steel that sliced into his mind, his emotions, cutting every nerve that he had.

He felt powerless against them. Each memory flashed was like a sharp dagger that had been thrust into his heart. Reopening wounds that he would never allow time or anyone, not even God Himself to heal. Now they were about to kill him! He gets out of his car and enters the Temple through a narrow hall which leads into the Sanctuary. He hangs up his outer coat in the foyer. And walks down the long hall. It seems like it went on for infinitum before he finally reaches the Altar. He loosens his collar some so he could breathe clearly. Just then another flash hits him like a lightening bolt. He remembers his son Michael lying
Dead in the walnut casket, his wife taking Yosef over to the Anderson's . Yosef kissing Lisa out on her front porch. It's as though his entire life was passing before him. Usually people see their life flash right before death. But he was still alive. How could this be? He wondered, am I dying? He wondered to

148

himself. Tears were beginning to well up in his eyes. Beads of sweat formed on his brow. The same demons that used him to torture his family, were now torturing him in a most savage and deathly way.

But isn't that how the enemy works? To seduce one into evil, then he turns on that one to torture them even worse than the people they have been the most cruel. Then he mocks their pain, the highlight of his treachery.

Rabbi? The meek voice called. He drops his Siddur to the floor. It was Rabbi Marcus calling him. It's time to start now. Rabbi stood there, his voice had left him again, just like it did when he was ten years old. He tried to find words to say to him. But they had abandoned him once more. He was just as alone now as he was then. Would you like to start, or shall I? Rabbi Marcus asked him. He bends down to pick up his Prayer book, and stands up again. I, I. He stutters. Yacov, are you alright? Finally his voice returned to him, his words jumped out of his mouth forcefully. I can't talk to you right now, not feeling to well I'm afraid. You,you cover for me will you Marcus? Yes, yes I will Yacov. You go home now alright? Yes, yes. I go now. He said nearly out of breath. He takes out a white hankerchief to wipe his brow. All of a sudden he feels a cough coming on. He puts the cloth up to his mouth coughing hard into it. As he pulls it away, he notices that he had coughed blood and phlem into it. Rabbi Marcus was still standing there watching him unsure as to what to make out of his friend's condition. Rabbi puts his hankerchief back into his vestment pocket. He feels his hand loosing it's grip on his Siddur, it drops to the floor. He reaches down to pick it up. Rabbi Marcus is horrified at what he sees next. As Rabbi stood back up, His face had changed again. There were darkened circles underneath his eyes, his face was a pale ashened colour, his hair a salt and pepper colour had turned snow white! His lips were drawn and chapped.
His eyebrows met in the center of his forehead. Merciful God in Heaven! Yacov! What's happened to you! Rabbi never answers him, he pushes his way pass him and runs out of the Sanctuary down the long hall that leads back out in the parking lot. He reaches into his pocket for his car keys, he fumbles them in his hands. Just then a sharp pain shoots through his chest, just like the one that he felt that morning. But only this one was stronger than the first. He grips his keys in his hand tightly, like the pain

gripped his heart. He places the other hand over his heart clutching his chest tight. His voice left him again, he was unable to utter any sound at all. His breathing was labored and coming in short gasps. The pain then decides to be merciful for all of a few seconds allowing him time to get into his vehicle. He opens the door throwing all his belongings inside. He fumbles again trying to stick the key into the ignition. He finally starts the car, and pulls out to go home. Rabbi Epstien, driven by desperation, drives his car the same way.

Desperately trying to get home. As he comes to a stop sign, he breathes a sigh of relief as the pain leaves him alone for a while. But that while was very short lived. But as his pain leaves him, his memories return to him in a fury! He sees the day when Rev. Anderson caught him with the redheaded prostitue Lorraine. His arguments with his wife driving her into tears nearly every evening. His hatred for Lisa, when he saw Yosef kiss her on the front porch again. No! No! Please leave me alone! Please! He is snapped back into the now by the honking of a car that had pulled up behind him. He drives off again in desperation, to him home seemed like it was on the other side of the world. A repeat of his sister in the chamber with his parents flash across the screen of his mind. It repeats the scene where he was watching the Star of David necklace that the Leader member threw at him. He was watching it as though he was mesmerized by it. He reaches the driveway of his home, pulling the car in violently. He turns off the ignition, his head falling upon the steering wheel. He takes out his hankerchief to wipe his brow again. His breathing slowly calming down. But his memory flash has not released him from it's torture yet. It again repeats the scene where he is watching the Star of David necklace, a brisk wind blew causing the Star to turn to face him; When he looks at it this time it reveals Laura's blood on the other side of it. He looks over at her face down in the mud. Her eyes fixed in place. She is dead. Laurieeeeee!!!! He screams with his mind child. Now his pain had decided that it has missed him long enough, and returns to him in a fury!

It shows him no mercy, it begins to radiate down his arm. He grabs it with his other hand. Oh My Lord Yeshua! What is it! What's happening to me! He fumbles the latch on the door trying to let himself out

Of the car. He reaches over grabbing his Siddur. His head feels like someone drove an icepick through it. His heart pounding like a jackhammer. He finally unlocks the door, and emerges from the car. Everything around him swimming out of control, saliva drizzles down from the corner of his mouth. Tears streaming down his ashened face. He staggers dizzily into the front yard when another pain squeezes his heart again.

His brow becomes fevered, sweating profusely. The pain becomes even more excruciating as it seizes his heart. He drops his prayer book in the grass. He tries to bend down to pick it up, but lunges forth into the lawn. He grips his chest in agony rolling over and over in the grass. It's moisture providing his feverish agony with only a temporary relief. His demons now return to him all at the same time in one final fury of hell, as they unleash one torture after another. Before his eyes close, he sees in his mind the night that he and Sarah argued about Yosef and Lisa's date. He hears Sarah's words echoing in his mind over and over.

"Unless you repent of your ways, and forgive Yacov. God will judge you for your cruelty." Oh, my God! Don't let me die! He prayed. Please don't let me die! Fear had come on him now. And he wanted mercy.
In one last act of desperation, he screams out his wife's name. The same wife that he had been unfaithful , and cruel to for so many years of their marriage. Now he calls upon her for help.

Sarahhhhhh! He screams! There was no answer, he didn't see her come to the window to see that he was lying out there dying. She was in the kitchen finishing up the last of the breakfast dishes. She is humming to the CD that Lisa had recorded for her. It was a Messianic tune that Lisa had wrote for their Passover last year before she went away. It was one of Sarah's favorite songs. *"How sweet is Your Word unto me, sweeter than honey to my mouth.. My heart delights in the Word on Life. How sweet is Your Word unto me."* Such a sweet voice she has, that little one. She chuckles to herself, as she shuts off the faucet. Clanging the last of the dishes in the dish holder to drain. Steam rising off them and her hands from the hot water. She walks over to turn the sound down on the stereo, when she hears a voice calling to her. Sarahhhhh! What! She said, turning around. She walks into the living room still wiping her hands on the dish towel. She goes over to the big picture window, and in her horror she sees her husband lying out on the front lawn rolling over and over in the grass. She drops the drying towel to the floor. Yacov! She runs to the front door, and down the porch steps nearly falling down them all. She falls over to Rabbi, picking his head up into her hands laying him down in her lap. Yacov! What has happened to you! He struggles to speak to her, but his voice it's usual abandonment, has left him again. Oh my Dear Lord Yeshua! She cries, her tears dropping down into his face. His expression filled with agony and fear.

He looks up at her, and for the first time in a span of years, he feels the need for his wife. He reaches up to her trying to rub her cheek. Just then his voice interrupts him. He..help meeee! He stutters. He then slips into unconsciousness. Dear Lord! Yacov! She gently lays his head back down in the grass, and runs frantically into the house to dial 911. She struggles desperately to push the buttons, her heart racing as fast in her chest as her tears were falling from her eyes. Her hands trembled and fumbled over the buttons. She finally makes the call. "911" the voice spoke. Hello! Hello! This is Mrs. Yacov Epstein. My husband is having a heart attack! Please come quickly! What's the address? Sarah broke down in tears. Ma'mam, your address please. I live at 6254 N. Grove Dr. My husband is out on the front lawn, she cries and whimpers again. Hello! Sarah cries louder. I'm right here ma'mam. Please hurry! I have to pull you up in the computer, the dispatcher said. HE'S NOT BREATHING!! She screamed. As fear overwhelmed her. Ma'mam Please! Try to stay calm. I know you're scared. But I promise you, I won't leave you until the Ambulance arrives ok? Sarah calms down a little. Ok dear. I'm sorry, I did not meant to shout at you.

Not a problem at all. I have you up on screen now. Your number Mrs. Epstien. Sarah breaks down in tears again. Stay with me honey ok? I need your phone number. Sarah gives it to her. Thank you. She said to her. I'll have an Ambulance to you in about five minutes ok? Ok dear, You still with me? Asked the dispatcher. Yes, I am here. Said Sarah, as she regained her composure. While she was still giving her some additional information, they both hear the sirens wailing down the street. I must go now to be with my husband. Said Sarah. I can hear the Ambulance, go ahead ma'mam. Thank you so much miss. Not a

problem. You take care now. Bye dear. Sarah hangs up the
phone, she goes to the hall closet to get a light sweater. She digs
into her purse for her house, and car keys. She runs out of the
house locking the door behind her. Back down the steps onto the
lawn, where the Ambulance pulls onto the grass very near to
where Rabbi was lying. The EMT's emerge from the Ambulance
carrying their bags of equipment. Sarah fills them in on what has
happened, they approach him. His face had taken on a grayish
colour, his eyes were half closed. He still breathing, but just
barely. One of the tech's listened for a heart beat, Mr. Epstien.
He is a Rabbi sir. Said Sarah. Excuse me ma'mam. Rabbi, can
you hear me sir! He said loudly. There was no response. They
checked for a pulse, there wasn't one. "I'm not getting a pulse
here." Said one of the Tech's. They tear at his vestments to get
him prepared for defibrillation. Once they get the probes into
place, the other Tech turns a small knob on the Defibrillator.
Clear! He shouts. A slight blip
Appears on the screen. Then flat line again. "Ok, once more."
Said the Tech, as he turns up the knob a little. Ok, Clear! He
shouts again. Another blip appears on the screen. Come on
Yacov, your heart is too stubborn to quit now. Said Sarah under
her breath. The blip turns into a steady beat. "We got a rhythm!"
said the Technician. They work to get the stat IV's into place, and
phones ahead to the hospital. Sarah

Buries her head in her hands crying uncontrollably, her heart full
of relief for the moment. He was still alive! She watches the
EMT's strap her husband onto the gurney, the tech comes over
to her. 'Let's get him to the hospital now ma'mam." He said
softly. She nods her head in agreement, while he helps her into
the Ambulance. The sirens wail again as they rush Rabbi Epstien
to Saints of Mercy Hospital.

The Colour Of Love
Anne Hemingway
Chap. 16.

Rev. Anderson is seated at his desk in his study, and is unaware
of what has just taken place across the street.   He, like Sarah
was listening to his daughter's CD.   He takes his earphones off.
Only to hear Deborah vacuuming the floor across the hall in the
family room. She too unaware of Rabbi's dilemma.
He was preparing for Bible study tonight, he had to bring the
message. It was to prepare them for the up coming Pastor's Day
Conference. He glances over at a photo taken of him and Lisa
when she was little
At the South Haven lighthouse, in the beautiful city of South
Haven, Michigan. They have a lovely summer cottage there,
where they always went when they needed a place to relax, and
unwind. Or to just get away for a weekend. The picture made
him smile big. He was proud of his daughter. How she had
grown over the years. A tear made it's way down his masculine
cheek. He sniffles a bit as he has a reflective moment about
Lisa's childhood. He chuckles as he sets the picture back down
on his desk. He begins working on his Sermon notes. Unity.
Would be the subject for tonight. Yosef and Lisa attended an
earlier Bible study which was taught by Associate Pastor
Raymond Jeffries.   All of a sudden, he hears footsteps coming
down the hall. "Knock, knock." Said Deborah. She was carrying
a small serving tray

With two medium sized coffee mugs filled with Cappuccino. Rev.
Anderson looks around to see his wife
Standing in the doorway holding the tray. He takes off his
glasses, smiling bigger now than he did before.
"hello Love." He said, his deep baritone voice sounding a bit on
the sensual side. Hello sweetheart. She said. She too sounding
sensual. It was their display of affection towards each other that
they instilled in Yosef and Lisa. "Never be afraid to show your
woman how much you love her. Because if you don't love her.
Someone else will." He said to both Yosef, and Johnathan. Yosef
learned very quickly, and took his advice to heart. Johnathan
was still coming along. Just not there yet. Deborah walks inside
setting the tray down on his desk.   What have we here? He said
looking up at her. The sun shining on her face. She looked like

a golden angel. She seemed to glow all over. I thought that you might what to have a drink with me. A drink? Yes my Beloved. A drink, it's your favorite. It's English Toffee. She hands him a cup, she taking the other. He inhales it's fragrance deeply. The aroma of the beverage fills him with thoughts of where he just came from a moment ago. The sweet memories of walks with Deborah, and the children on the beach. Drinking English Toffee Cappuccino, and watching the spectacular Sunsets on the beach. Walking out on the pier to the Lighthouse. All came back to fill him with a joy that he had almost forgotten. They both take a sip together, just like they did when they would sit on the beach in South Haven. Ahhh. That's the best yet. He said setting his cup back down on the desk next to his Bible. He then reaches up and takes Deborah's cup setting next to his. And you're right Love, I did need this. He said, pulling her down onto his lap. Woman I love you so much Do you know that? Yes, dearest, I know that. And I love you the same. I've never been so blessed in all my life as I am now. I was just sitting here

thinking about us over the years. All we've been through, yet we still managed to keep our marriage in tact. Our Ministry prospered, and to top it all off. God blessed us with two beautiful children. Our son, a fine young man. I'm very proud of Johnathan. He worries me though. Oh, and why is that? Said Deborah. The man is fourty two years old, and he has no wife. Now when I was his age, I had a wife and children. He should've made me a grandfather long ago, now his baby sister is about to beat him to it. Deborah laughed out loud, rubbing his head. Well don't give up on him yet dear, he'll find the right girl, or she'll find him. Like Yosef and Lisa found each other. She said. He detected a slight melancholia in her tone. She too was thinking about Lisa and Yosef, and that he would soon ask her daughter to marry him. The thought of it made her smile big. Now what is that smile for? His voice rising in a falsetto tone. Oh just a mother and her thoughts that's all. My baby has now grown from that precious little angel, and blossomed into a beautiful young woman. She said, her eyes fill up with tears. Rev. Anderson curls his index finger up under her chin lifting her face to him. He wipes away her tears. There, there now. What's all the tears for? He said. His voice still in it's falsetto tone. I'm so proud of her, but I feel like I'm loosing her Ben. Ahh. He said waving his hand at her. You're not loosing her, you're, I mean we're gaining a son.

And what a son he is child! She said to him laughing. Oooooh! That boy knows he loves him some Lisa don't he? She said laughing harder. Honey, what you talkin about! They stop laughing for a moment, and stare lovingly into each other's eyes. Talking about Yosef and Lisa's love. Reminded them of how deeply they loved each other. They kiss tenderly. Oh Ben! I love you so much dearest. I love you too my Love.

They kiss passionately. Deborah stops abruptly. What's the matter dear? He asked her. But Ben, what about your Sermon notes? He smiled at her again. That's for tonight, I'm seizing this moment now! He said kissing her passionately again. Lisa is upstairs getting ready for Bible study, their's was earlier than the study that her father taught. Their's started at 5:30pm. And Rev. Anderson for the Seniors at 7:00pm.

It was now 5:10. She know that Yosef would be by any minute to pick her up. He had planned to take her out to Chae's. It will be there that he will propose to her. It would be the surprise of her life! She hears giggling coming from downstairs, It was her parents. She didn't know that they had just had a time of loving. She just shrugged it off, and kept on getting ready. She was just straightening out her dress when she hears their giggling again. What in the World is that? She said. Her parents emerge from her father's study, and go into the family room smiling at each other, still laughing, holding hands, and caressing. They sit down on the love seat, Lisa comes downstairs. She hears their giggling again. She follows their laughter into the family room where she finds her parents seated close together on the love seat. They seemed to sparkle all over, there was an inner glow that emanated from them. Whoa! She breathed. They looked beautiful! Just then there was a knock at the door. Lisa could not take her eyes off her parents. It's opened! She said, still not able to take her eyes off them for fear she may miss something.

She had never seen them like this before. It was Yosef that had come for her. He walked up behind her putting his hands around her waist. You ready baby? Shhh. She said. Look at them! She whispered.

Her tone one of unbelief. Yosef steps up beside her, holding her hand. What's the matter? He asked her.

She points to them. Look! Yosef looks at her parents, and his reaction is the same as hers. He sees the soft glow emanating from them. Whoa! He breathed. That's what I said too. Said Lisa. What's the matter with them? She asked him. I don't know Lisa, I've never seen anything like this before. This is about the most awesome thing I've ever seen in my life! What is that! He said. Do your parents look like that? She asked him. Yeah, right. He said, not even one spark or a flicker between them. He said. Lisa chuckles. You big silly. It's old age I think. She said. No, it's not old age. Being old don't make you smile or glow like that. There's only one thing that I can think of that will make people shine that way. And what way is that Yosef? She asked him. He turns her to him, his expression serious, as his voice. They both gazed into each other's eyes. Love. He said softly. Love. She echoed in a trance like tone. She reaches up to him, he picks her up by her slender waist. They kiss briefly. So it's not an old thing Beloved? No baby, it's not an old thing. He looks back over at her parents. It's a love thing. He kissed her again gently on the lips. They look at her parents again. Mom, Dad. We're getting ready to go now. They stop their gazing for the moment. Hello baby girl. Said Deborah. Hi angel. Said her father. Jo-Jo, my son. Said Rev. Anderson. Hi jo-jo. Said Deborah. She was still chuckling a little, they were still glowing. They then return to their gazing. Well guys, we'll see you later after Bible study ok? She said. They never answered

Her. They didn't even look at her. They couldn't take their eyes off each other. Aren't you two even listening to me? She asked them, her voice raised a little. Hummmm? Did she say something dear? Said Deborah. Who? Said her father. Lisa gasped. Yosef busted up laughing at her. Yosef gabbed Lisa by her arm, pulling her away. Baby, come on. I think they want to be alone. I think they've been alone too much already. She said. Yosef began to feel the same thing for Lisa at that moment that her parents felt for each other. He looks at them, then back at Lisa. Will they be alright? She said concerned for them. He looks at them one last time. I wouldn't worry about them, they'll, be just fine. But we have to go now ok? Lisa turns to look at Yosef. He felt love's overwhelming power for her come on himat that moment. They pause, they now gaze into each other's eyes. Their minds flowing ahead in time together. Their thoughts were the same. Will we be that much in love when we're their age Beloved? She asked him. Even more so Lisa, even more. He said softly to her. He felt that he would do anything for her. Your eyes are telling me something Yosef. They're telling you how much I Love you Lisa. He pulls her closer to him, kissing her tenderly. Her parents look over in their direction, smiling and shaking their heads at them. I think that we're rubbing off on them. Said Deborah. We'd better go. Said Rev. Anderson. They quietly get up and leave the couple in their intimacy. Yosef and Lisa never even noticed that they had left to give them their privacy, and to have a little more of their own. What's that! Said Lisa pulling away from him slightly.

She felt something in his suit coat pocket. Nothing, nothing. He said. He puts his hand in there to move the ring box over.   Let me see, she said like a young child at Christmastime.   She was trying to reach inside his pocket. He takes her hand kissing it, smiling at her. I think we'd better go now. We don't want to be late. He looks at his watch, it was 5:25pm. You know how Ray gets when people come into Church late. Alright, let's go. She said.   They leave, taking her car to Church. Since his was vandalized a couple of nights ago. He had a feeling who the vandals might be. But he kept it quiet so as not to upset Lisa.

But is was Billy and a few of his gang boys. They punctured his tires, and put sugar in his gas tank. They did many other things to his Cherokee, that would've cost him a piece of change to fix. But he chose to say and do nothing yet. Lisa gladly gave him her car to use, since she was no longer employed now. But Yosef knew that Billy was after him to get his revenge on him and Lisa. Little did Billy know, was that God was watching him, and in his time. His Judgement call would come to pay him a visit, just like it did Yosef's father. Even more. God would use the next series of events that would change the lives of everyone in their Community. It would be etched on the hearts and on the pages of their minds forever.

The Ambulance arrives at Saint's Of Mercy Hospital. Rabbi
Epstien is rushed inside. All the formalities are taken care of as
they rush him to the Emergency Room, and started on I.V. drips
of saline. The E.R staff work feverishly to stablize him. He is
then hooked to the monitors and watched by the E.R. nurses.
Dr. Kaplan arrives. He is shocked to see that the heart attack
victim that he was phoned about was his own Temple companion,
and friend for over twenty years. Rabbi Yacov Epstien! Dr.
Kaplan himself, a devout Jew, he was more modern than Rabbi
who leaned more towards the Traditional aspects of his faith.
Steeped in religious Customs, and Traditions. He didn't adhere to
them like he should've himself. Yet he could talk them very well.
Dr. Kaplan never argued with him about them, he just listened to
him, knowing that he would live his faith his way, while leaving
Rabbi to live his faith his way. He quickly grabs Rabbi's chart
and begins to read carefully. He then orders the staff what to do,
then monitors him closely to look for signs of any change in his
condition. His beeper sounds off, he has another emergency call
on floor five.

He answers the call, a head injury from a car accident has just
arrived. He leaves for the emergency. No visitors! He shouts. I'll
be back shortly. But Dr. His wife is here. He stops a moment.
Sarah? Mrs. Epstien is waiting down the hall. Tell her to wait for
me, I'll be back as soon as I can. The Nurse nods her head.
Sarah is pacing the floor in the waiting area, nervousness taking
it's toll on her. In her pacing, she remembers the happier times
between her and her husband, and the children. He was good to
them, and loved them deeply. How she missed those times. They
brought a slight smile to her sweet face. Oh Yacov!
Please not now. You can't die now. I know there's still love there
for me and Yosef. I feel it there. She was about to break down,
when she heard foot steps coming down the hall. It was an
orderly. He was at least six feet in height, his hair dark, and
curly, with olive toned complexion. Oh son? Yes ma'mam. He
said in the Italian accent. Do you have a Chapel here? Yes we do
ma'mam. If you'll follow the yellow line down this hall, and turn
right. It's the third room on the right. Thank you dear. You're
welcome ma'mam. Have a nice day. He said. His politeness was
pleasant to her. She went down the hall to the Chapel, and walks

inside, gasping at the surroundings. It was as though she stepped back into time, almost like the Biblical days. It was dimly lit, and warm. She looked at the ornate decorations, the stained glassed windows. It smelled of some kind of potpurri that had a pleasant fragrance of apples and cinnamon. But there was one thing that caught her attention more than all the other intricate decorations. There in the center of the Sanctuary hung a huge Cross with Jesus hanging from it. His thorned crown buried deep in side His brow, blood streaming down His face. On His side was the open would where His tormentors pierced Him. The Nails in His hands and feet. It's as though she could at that moment, hear the Choir of Heaven singing softly in the background. She was overcome with an overwhelming sense of Reverence for Him. She remembered what God told Moses as he stood upon the Mountain where he saw the burning bush. *"Take off thy shoes from off thy feet. For the ground on which thou standest, is Holy Ground."* She took off her shoes that very instant. Clasping her hands together, she got down on her knees. She looks back up at the Cross shaking her head. My Lord Yeshua, I am here. She whispered.

Her face stained with tears. She gazed at His wounds again, feeling like she was one of the women at His Crucifixion. One of the ones who wept for Him. *"Weep not for Me, but rejoice For it was this that I was sent. If you can only believe, you will see the Glory of God!" For I AM He, Who was dead, but now I AM alive forevermore! Can you believe this?"* She heard the voice say from within her.

She gasped, thinking that the voice came from the Cross. Her face fresh with new tears now. Yes! Yes! My dear Lord Yeshua! I believe! I believe! She weeps. Just then a radiant glow shone all around her bathing her in it. There over in the corner to the right of the Cross stood the same Warrior Angel that had appeared to Yosef back in march. It was mid May already. He looked at Sarah, he felt for her. His expression tender, and understanding. *"Sarah"* He called to her. She opened her eyes, and nearly fainted at what she sees. She was speechless almost like Yosef when he saw him. *"Daughter weep not, and do not fear. For the Lord your God has seen your tears, As He has said in His Word."* The angel then quotes Psalm 56:8-9 to her. *"You number my wanderings, put my tears into Your bottle, are they not all in Your Book? When I cry out to You, Then my enemies will turn back."* He then took out a medium sized crystal jar. It's beauty was indescribable! Sarah gasped at the object. It had a golden glow about it. It had something that seemed to be moving around inside of it. They sparkled like small stars, so many of them that they could not be numbered by any man. What is that you are holding Angel? She asked, her voice trembling. *"These are your tears Sarah. All the tears that you've shed over the years. They are so Precious to the Master, that he sent me to collect them for Him. He collects the tears of all His children. Not one of His Saint's tears fall to the ground. Not their tears, or their prayers. He has heard your prayers. For He has seen your tears, and He has felt your pain. He truly has seen your sufferings, and knows your sorrows. Know this daughter, that his suffering is not unto death, but that the Glory of God be revealed in him. For all shall be done in His time. So be encouraged, and strengthened. For I have appeared to your son at the request of your prayers, and I was sent to watch over him. For he will be used in the Great Work that God*

Has for him. For your prayers, as well as the prayers of Lisa have touched the very Heart of God Himself! Not one of your prayers will go unanswered. Only remember this, do not tell him that I appeared to you, for I will come again three times more to visit him, to show him what he must do before his time comes. If he will only believe, all things are possible to him who believes, who believes, who believes......." Sarah listened intently as the being shared what God had told him to share with her. What time? She asked, unsure of what he meant. *"In time daughter, in time, in time....."* said the Angel as his voice echoed away with him, but his words lingered with her mind as well as her heart. Darkness quickly overtook the Chapel again, except for the dim light. But Sarah was still bathed in the warm glow from the Angel's radiance. She looked a little younger now, and stronger in her spirit. His words returned to her rememberence *"His suffering is not unto death, but that the Glory of God be revealed."* She knew that he was speaking of her husband. She didn't quite understand what all this meant, or why an angel would even appear to her. But she feeling the same as Yosef when he appeared to him in March. Said the same thing. " I was never taught anything like this in Temple!" She left the Chapel with a renewed sense of faith that was soaring about now. She felt strengthened, and ready for anything. The presence of a heavenly euphoria was upon her. She went back to the waiting area to await the news on Rabbi's condition.

Yosef, would you start us off in prayer? Asked Rev. Jeffries. Yes. He said. He was looking tenderly at Lisa, she was watching him the same. Yosef stood to his feet, they all take hands, every head bowed, and every eye closed as they say. Yosef prayed a brief prayer. Our Dear Heavenly Father, we are gathered here together in this place to give thanks and praise around Your Holy Word. Father You said, that where two or three are gathered in Your Name, that You are there in the midst of us. Holy Spirit, we welcome You,come into this study tonight and have Your way in this service. Reveal Your Holy Presence to us, that we may receive all Truth from You tonight. In the Name of our Lord and Savior. Yeshua. Amen.   Amen said all those present. Yosef then sits back down next to Lisa. He grabs his Bible, the one that Lisa gave him for Christmas three years ago. It was kinda mark up like hers. He learned to study the Bible just like she did. He puts it on his lap, and pulls Lisa closer to him caressing her. She looks at him smiling. I love you. He mouthed to her. She mouthed the same back to him. He kisses her on her forehead. He had never felt affection for her before like he did at this moment. Honey, let's listen now ok? Said Lisa. Ok. He said. He found it difficult to listen to Pastor Jeffries, and his thoughts about her at the same time. So his thoughts of her won out over Pastor Jeffries. Who started out that night's Sermon with Psalms 133:1   *"Behold how good it is and how pleasant it is for brethren to dwell together in UNITY!"* That's what my father is preaching on at Pastors Day. Said Lisa. She was all excited about the Conference, Yosef was as well, he had written some new songs and couldn't wait to minister them.   Lisa felt Yosef's eyes all over her, she looks over at him. He was staring at her again. He couldn't take his eyes off her. His expression told her many things. How deeply in love with her he is, how much he wanted to make her his wife, and how he

Would do anything for her. He wondered if she felt the same way about him? He felt down in his suit coat pocket and felt the ring box there. He smiled at her a little. Yosef, what's the matter? Nothing baby, I'm alright. You're sure? Yes. He nodded, he was near tears, his love for her was overwhelming him. He began to stroke her hair. He never thought that he could feel so much love for anyone. It was like he was being filled with surge after surge of love and affection for her. Rev. Jeffries voice echoed away as his memories came for a brief visit. He remembered as his mind flowed back in time to the first time that he met her. It was Easter Sunday, and her and her family had just come back from Church. She was wearing a pastel pink dress with white lace, and a satin sash that tied in the back. Her hair hung down her back in soft curls. She was beautiful! Whoa! He breathed. He clenched his chest trying to soothe this heart's thumping. Lisa spotted him out on the front lawn, and decided to come over to say hello. They had only been living in the neighborhood a little while, and she wanted to be friends. She looked like an angel coming over to him. His eyes never left her at all. He had seen many Jewish , as well as Black girls in the

Neighborhood, but none of them affected him the way she did that day. It's like the Song Of Solomon.
8:6 *"Set me as a seal upon your heart, as a seal upon your arm. For Love is as strong as death."* It was at that moment that God had branded her not only upon his heart, but in his heart forever. There was just something about her that left an unforgettable impression upon him. She looked over at him, and flashed a most radiant smile. It was that smile that captivated his heart to this very day. As she walked over to introduce herself to him, he became nervous. She 's coming over here. He said to himself. He froze like a tall statue. He himself was tall, and very handsome! He was dressed in blue jeans, and a white sweat shirt. She walked up close to him. She herself was just as spellbound by him as he was by her.

Hi. She breathed. My name is Lisa. It's Elizabeth, but my nickname is Lisa. She held out her hand to him. He was so mesmerized by her, he just stood there unable to speak. Are you alright? She said to him. His voice had left him for the moment. But it returns one syllable at a time. Seemed like. Huh? He said.

163

My name's Lisa. Oh, uh hi. He said taking her hand in his. He sighed out a little. The touch of her soft hand in his. Made his heart thump faster. He stuttered a little answering her. Mmm,my name is Yosef.

It's really Daniel Joseph. My Hebrew name is Yosef. I like that. She said to him. You do? He said, his voice was hi pitched and cracking. I mean you do. Lisa chuckled a little. Yes, I do. It's really neat. They both stared into each other's eyes. It was as if they each knew they would be together always. Lisa! Lisa! The voice called. It was her mother. Mrs. Deborah Anderson. That's my mom Mrs. Anderson. She walked out onto the front yard. She was tall her hair done up in a flip hairstyle, pretty stylish in the 60's.

Yosef looked at her then back at Lisa. He could see where she got her looks from. She was graceful and very beautiful. Lisa! Come in the house to change your clothes! Tell your friend you can come back out after you put your play clothes on. I have to go now, but my mom says I can come back to play with you after I change my clothes ok? You're leaving ? He said somewhat frantic. Lisa puts her hand on top of his.

I'll be back, I promise. I won't leave you for long. Then she said something to him that made his mouth hang open.

I like you. She said. His eyes now wide and staring at her more. He had hoped to hear that. He clenches his chest again, his heart pounding more and more. Are you sure you can come back? He said. Worried that she won't. She steps up to him, and what she did this time, was etched in his mind and his heart even to this day. She steps up to him, and gently kisses him on the lips. The soft moistness of them sent a surge of passion throughout his ten year old body. I never break a kiss. She walks away to go home.

Yosef's eyes roll upward in his head, he then falls dizzily to the ground in an ecstatic faint. "Now is the time for all this racisim in the Church to stop people! Fired Rev. Jeffries. His voice snapping Yosef back into the now. Black brothers and sister not being able to Worship in White Churches, and vice-versa. Pentacostals not able to fellowship with Baptist's. And etc. Look around you here! There are many of us that differ from one another as far as Culture is concerned. By the time that Yosef had regained himself. He had missed Rev. Jeffries entire Sermon.

Lisa was standing to her feet as well as the rest of the study group.

Rev. Jeffries had preached everyone happy! Even himself! There were applauses, and shouts and praises going up in agreement with his message. Yosef stood to his feet clapping his hands along with the rest of the Congregation. We the Church will have to answer to God for this! Racisim does not belong in the Church! Oh, I feel the Holy Spirit wanting to move in our midst today. He said. His voice trembling.
Oh, Heavenly Father, please forgive us, we've been so wrong, so many times that You've wanted to move in the Denominations of Man to reveal Your Will to all Your people. But we shut You out, not allowing those that You've sent to us to teach us, and to train us how to dwell with each other in unity. How to walk in the Love of Your Holy Spirit. Father God, help us to grow together, and not apart. Show us how to open up to the Holy Spirit. He is here with us in the earth today. He will come and Fill us when we yield to Him. Show us how to break down the wall of racial indifference and intolorance of those of different Cultures. Let Your Love blanket the Churches, Baptize us in Your Holiness Father. Forgive us, forgive us! He prayed ferverantly, weeping before them all. Yosef looks at Lisa, tears streaming down her soft brown face. His heart wells up with love for her again. His eyes just rested on her for the moment. He knew that he would ask her to marry him today after Church. But just as he was about to tell her that he loved her. His memories of the past paid him a visit. This one not about his meeting her for the first time. Or even his more recent encounters with her. This one God sent to him. He could see a clear picture of people from all walks of life coming together to listen to Dr. Martin Luther King Jr. give his famous I have a Dream Speech. He could see people worshipping God together in one accord, loving one another, regardless of Ethinic background, or Colour of skin. He heard the part where Dr. King spoke of his children not being judged by the colour of their skin, but by the content of their character. Dr. King's words echoed away with Free at Last, free at last! Thank God Almighty. We're free at last! The crowd
Thundering with praise for him, and his powerful words of Unity and Togetherness for all mankind.

His mind then flows back in time to April 4, 1968 when Dr. King was assassinated. He sees scores of people filing by to see Dr.

King at his funeral. He remembers Rev. Anderson and his family and how it affected them, as well as the whole world when he was taken from us. He remembers Lisa crying uncontrollably, she refused to eat for three days. He remembered the togetherness that they all shared that day, and how Rev. Anderson declared that he would do whatever it was in the power that God gave him to treat all mankind as fairly as God Himself would treat them. No one would ever be turned away because of skin colour or a Denominational difference. He would embrace all Cultures of people, from all walks of life. His own voice snaps him back into the now, as he breaks down in front of the people. Forgive us Lord! He shouts. Lisa looks over at him gasping at what she sees. Yosef began to glow all over, she had never seen him do that before. Tears were now streaming down his masculine face. An intense expression of worship took him over, his heart was now tender, and just right for God to speak to him directly. Which He did! With his eyes closed, he hears these words in his spirit. *"Son, tell my people that it shall come to pass in this time, that you will see many of my people come together in complete unity. For I have desired to see this for many years, but because you let Denominational and Cultural differences get in the way of true love and fellowship. They would not allow others to come and Worship Me. For did I the God of all Creation, Create man in My own Image, and My Own Likeness? Did I not Create the Jewish man, the Black man, the White man, The Native American man? I Created all of Mankind for My Glory, not his. And the eyes of man will see My Will done in the Earth as never before. My Spirit has been grieved because of prejudice, and He could not move in their midst. But I AM is saying to the Churches today. If you'll cleanse yourselves from the filth of prejudice, and indifference,then I will tear down this wall, and utterly destroy it once and for all!*

Then I can move freely in your midst, and MY Glory, not the glory of man, but the Glory of God will be manifest for all to see. Tell my people son, tell them. For I desire ferverantly to bless the Nations, and the Churches. Tear down the wall of Racial, Cutural, Denominational, indifference. Let love replace all hatred and strife among yourselves. Remember,

166

man made Denominations. But I made man. Says Yeshua"
Yosef heard the words in his heart. And thundered out the
Prophecy
All remained silent as he spoke. Many wept with him and Lisa.
Rev. Jeffries trembled in the Pulpit. It's as though the whole
Congregation was hushed as the Word came forth. When he
finished speaking, there was a thunderous applause from the
people. Lisa wept into her hands. Yosef opened his eyes, not
sure what had just happened to him. He never did anything like
this in Temple! As he opened his eyes, standing to the far left in
the corner was the Huge Warrior Angel that had appeared to him
back in March.
He nodded at him smiling big. *"Well done."* The being spoke. He
waved his large hand, and six people fell to the floor! Bam! Bam!
Bam! One right after the other! Rev. Jeffries, his wife Mary.
Rita Jenkins, a friend of Lisa's, and two other people in the back,
and then Lisa! All fell under the power of the Holy Spirit. A
beautiful wave of Glory had swept across the Church, taking six
people with it! Yosef caught Lisa in his arms. Lisa! He
screamed. He looked up the Angel still standing there smiling at
him. *"Fear not son, for this is a move of God's Spirit, He is
speaking to them, but especially to her. Fear not son. For I will
return to you two times more."* In time, in time......." His voice
echoed away with him again. But Yosef could not ignore that
something was definitely different about him. He sat Lisa down
on the pew
She sighed a little then she began to come around. So did many
of the others that had fallen down. Baby,

Can you hear me? He asked her, tears steaming down his face.
Beloved? I'm right here baby, I'm right here! He said. He had
never seen this in his life. In all my years of being a Jew, have I
ever seen anything like this before. What happened to you? I'll
have to explain it to you later honey. She said, her voice sounded
weak. She looked over at him. He looked handsome to her. Her
heart racing, her breathing rapid. Lisa are you alright? He asked
her. Oh, yeah, my Beloved. Oh yeah. I love you Yosef. More
than I do my own life I love you. He looked at her surprised, he
smiled gathering her up in his arms. He embraced her hard. I
love you too baby. I love you too! He was near tears himself.
Look, I have to talk to you, it's important ok? We have to go now.
Everyone else that had fallen had totally regained themselves,

they were standing around talking about what had just happened. Yosef stood her to her feet, as she looked at him, she could see that light was shining all around him. She knew what that was. Her father shone like that many times when God's Power would come on him strong. So did her mother when she was in deep intercession in prayer. What Lisa didn't know was that the same light also shone from her as well when she laid hands on people for healing. Come on Lise, We have to go now. There was an urgency to his voice. Ok honey, just let me get my Bible. Just then Jamal, and his wife Rita came up to them. He was a big man with a big singing voice. But a loving and gentle heart. As was his wife Rita.

He pats Yosef on the back. Man if that wasn't a word for the Church today, I don't know what was. He stops and looks at Yosef a moment. Not bad for a Jew, not bad at all. You keep hanging around us man, you're gonna become a Pentecostal Jew. Lisa laughs out loud. I can deal with that. Said Yosef. They slap fives. Rita then staggers up to them. She was still feeling the effects of God's move upon her. Jamal catches her in his arms. Oops there girl. He said. She's still a little hung over I think. He said. I guess said Yosef. I'm ready said Lisa. As she and Yosef were about to leave, she calls out to her. Hey Lisa!

Yes Rita. Said Lisa turning back around. I'm sorry that I wasn't at Choir practice for the past few weeks, I haven't been feeling well lately. We don't know what's the matter with my baby man. I'm really worried about her. Said Jamal. Yosef then looks at Rita and smiles. *"She's seven weeks pregnant. A boy!"* The voice spoke from within him. I guess it's one of them women things right Jo? And a man thing too Jamal. What you talkin' about man? She's seven weeks pregnant. They all gasped at him. What! Said Jamal. Come on baby I need to talk to you now. He said taking Lisa by the arm. Jamal was about to ask him what sex the baby was, before he could say anything. Yosef turns around pointing his finger at them.
It's a boy! He said smiling, taking Lisa out to the car. Honey, what is it Lisa? I sense so strongly in my heart that you're being prepared for something. I'm not sure what, but it's something big. Lisa I don't know much about what just happened back there, but I'm about to tell you what I'm being prepared for. It's big too! He said smiling. But he was very serious. Yosef don't joke this is serious. She said.

He stops and looks at her opening the car door, she gets inside, then he lets himself in on the other side.

Now what is it that can't wait until after our date tonight? She said. He almost didn't quite know how to begin. His heartbeat sped up a little. He strokes her soft cheek, his love welling up inside him again for her. Lisa, we've known each other all our lives. She nods. Yes, yes we have. I've never loved anyone like this before, I've never been loved like this before by anyone. Neither have I Yosef. I want us to spend the rest of our lives together. He said reaching into his suit coat pocket. He pulled out the ring box

Opening it. The huge three carat diamond sparkled like he reached up into the Heavens, and picked the largest one there. Ohhhh! Gasped Lisa. I want us to spend the rest of our lives together as Husband and Wife.

He said tears streaming down his face. As he placed the large diamond on her finger. Lisa could not control her tears. Oh, my God! Yosef! Do you like it? She looks up at him. Next to you Beloved, I've never seen anything so beautiful in all my life. I love it. But not as much as I love you! She threw her arms around his neck kissing him deeply. Will you marry me Lisa? Her emotions had taken her voice from her. She couldn't speak, so she nodded yes, crying into his arms. Well is that a yes, or what? He said smiling at her. Her emotions finally released her to speak again. Yes! Yes! They cry into each others arms. I love you Beloved. I love you too baby. They kiss passionately. He takes her hand and kisses the diamond on her finger. She looks lovingly into his eyes stroking his cheek. God! You're beautiful Lisa!

So are you beloved, so are you. He kisses her again. He moans out softly. I'd better get you home, other wise we'll be marching to the tune of rock-a-bye baby, instead of here comes the Bride. They both laugh together.

The Colour Of Love
Anne Hemingway

Chap 18.
A man about 5 foot 11 inches in height, wearing light blue hospital scrubs. Emerges from MICU. Mrs. Epstien, your husband will recover from his episode. He has suffered a mild heart attack. He said a thick Yiddish accent. Dr. Kaplan, may I see him now? Sarah, he's had quite an ordeal there. He needs his rest.
No excitement now eh? I just want to see him, I won't disturb him. I just want to look at his face. I know Sarah, But I'm afraid that I cannot. Please Alton, please! Just for five minutes is all that I ask! Please! She cries into her hands. He exhales in frustration. But he gives into her. Most Dr's would not allow this,
But he's been a family friend for years. He simply couldn't stand to see her cry like this. Wives, wives!
Why do you do this thing to us huh? You don't get your way, you cry like the babies do! I have wife too Sarah, she does the same thing to get her way. I'm Sorry Dr. He's my husband. She pause looking up at him. I love him. She whispers softly. He smiles a little at her. Yes, I know this to be true of you. He looks at her giving her a thumbs up, then an open hand meaning that he will only allow her five minutes.
I have to call our son first. He doesn't know about this. Yosef? He said. How is the dear boy now? I haven't seen him since he was knee high to a pup. He's grown now, a fine young man. He has the most beautiful girlfriend. Her name is Lisa. They are thinking about getting married. She said smiling at him. Well if Yacov ever wants to see his son get married, he should get rid of whatever it is that's killing him,

Or you'll bury him before Yosef walks his new bride down the aisle. The only thing that saved his life today, is that he is still in good shape that one. But something has a hold of him squeezing the life out of him. He better take my advice and take it easy. This I give free. Go now Sarah call your son. He turns to walk away, he turns around to look at her. Remember. He holds up his hand reminding her of her time of five minutes. She smiles nodding at him, she then leaves to find the pay phone.

Come on Lisa, I'll walk you to the front door. They get out of the car, he puts his arm around her hugging her close to him as they walk across the street to her parents home. I'll see you in a few hours ok? I have to go meet the guys, they'll flip when I tell them. Then, I'll be back here for you alright? Alright Beloved. They stared at each other briefly. They couldn't bear to let each other go for even a moment. Their love was just that strong, and it was getting stronger, and stronger. Their love could even be felt by others that were around them. Even when they would walk down the street in their neighborhood, all in the Community would wave smiling at them. What a lovely couple they are. Some would say. Their love generated a sort've "Feel good" kind of feeling all throughout the neighborhood. Yosef looked at his watch, it was nearing 6:15pm. I should get going now baby ok? He said to her. I'll be ready when you get back. She said. She couldn't take her eyes off him, nor he her. He was silent for a few. I Love you Lisa.
He said, his voice trembling again. He pulled her close to him embracing her hard. I Love you too Yosef.

I'll be right back. Ok. She goes inside. He turns to go home to tell his mother the good news. Rev. Anderson comes out of the kitchen carrying his Bible, Deborah right behind him drinking a cup of cappuccino. Lisa comes through the door. She looked as though she could walk on water! Her expression was serene, her face a flushed, and reddened in colour. Oh,oh said Rev. Anderson. Oh, oh is right said Deborah. Lisa seemed to be floating on cloud nine, she glowed all over. What's the matter with her? He said in his falsetto tone. I don't know, but I have a hunch what would make her look like that. Just then, they heard shouts coming from outside. Whoooo! I'm in Love! Yessss! It was Yosef, he was rejoicing over his engagement to Lisa. They all go over to the window to look at him out in the street. Lisa! I Love you! She places on hand over her heart, while blowing him a kiss with the other. She was near tears again.

Go on boy! Laughs Rev. Anderson. I wonder what got into him? I wonder what could make him so happy? At that time, Deborah notices Lisa's hand, she picks it up gasping at the huge diamond engagement ring adorning her daughter's finger. She smiles at Lisa. You can stop your wondering Ben. Huh? He said. Look.

She puts Lisa's hand in his. He looks at the diamond smiling big at her. So my baby's getting married. He said his voice deep, and tender. Deborah sets her cup down on the small table next to the large picture window. Come here sweetie. Said her mother. They embrace tenderly. Are you happy dear? I have no words mom, no words at all. He's a good man angel. I tried to teach him the same things that I taught Johnathan. By the way where is that boy? He said to her. I don't know, never mind him, he'll be in sometime. I just can't get over my baby here. About to become the most precious treasure on the face of this Earth. A Man's Wife. She kissed Lisa on the cheek, tears streaming down all their faces now. Congratulations dear. Thanks mom, Daddy. She said throwing her arms around his neck. He laughs out loud. Daddy, Mom. Do we have your blessing? He looks at her, his moment returns when reflected on her earlier. He embraces her tenderly. Baby girl, you have more than our blessing. We have a little something that we've been saving for you and Yosef every since you both were teenagers. We saw this coming for years. And we knew that there was no talking the two of you out of marriage. So we prepared

For this time. We want to give it to you together. Ok? Lisa was shocked to hear her parents words. She didn't know what to make out of them. We have something here that we want you and him to have with our blessing. But I need to speak with him alone first ok? Then we'll speak to you both eh? Eh. Said Lisa. They all laugh. I can't wait to tell aunt mamie. Is she in her room? What's tonight Wednesday? Asked Rev. Anderson. Yeah. Said Lisa. Not there! They both said together. Well, where is she? At the Entertainment hall. Tonight is Powerball Bingo. Said Deborah. Powerball Bingo? What is that? Said Lisa. Oh, child something about how the balls fall or something, I don't know. Said Deborah. Lisa smiles a little looking at her father. I aint even going there so don't look at me. He said holding up his hand. He goes back over to the small table to get Deborah's coffee cup. They all bust up laughing. Deborah, are you ready we have to get going now. Yes, I'm ready honey. I just want to speak with Lisa before we go.

Well Hurry up now, I don't want to miss opening prayer. Deacon Wilson's gonna open up for us. I love to hear that man pray! He takes another sip of Deborah's cappuccino, it was still very warm. Ummmm. Good stuff. He said, walking back into the kitchen.

172

Deborah takes Lisa by the hand walking her back over to the picture window. Oh, I can't get over it! Let me look at you! Said Deborah. How do you feel dear?

She asked Lisa. Tingly sensation all over me mom, I can't explain any further, I can't find the words. I've never felt like this before. It's all new to me. You're about to be married. She said. Her excitement returning to her. Yes we are mom. But I'm a little scared of something though. What's that baby?

If I can be a good wife and mother. I've never been neither before. Don't worry angel, you'll be the best wife that he's had in his life. And the only wife that he's ever had in his life. She said in a home girl tone.

Lisa laughs. Oh, mom. I pray that God will do just that. Make me the wife, that my husband's life needs. And that He'll make Yosef the Husband that my life needs as well. He already has dear. He already has.

Said Deborah. A tone of assurance in her voice. Yosef wants to ask you and daddy for my hand according to their Jewish Custom mom. He's taught me about their Traditions, Oh, mom. They have the most beautiful Customs. As well as we do. He'll be over tonight after we get back from our date. Where's he taking you? I don't know, he wouldn't tell me. He said it's a surprise. So is it ok? Said Lisa. Is what ok dear? Said Deborah, she was thinking a little herself about Lisa when she was a little girl. For Yosef to ask for my hand tonight? She smiles at her. I'm sure it is honey. She pauses looking at the floor. Mom, what is it? Oh nothing. She said. Well, I was looking at you, you remind me of myself when I was your age. And your father asked me for my hand. I was glowing just like you, and he was jumping around like a flea on a hot plate like Yosef was earlier. I mean that boy was happy! I love him so much mom. She said tears flowing a little. I know you do dear, it shows. And he loves you more than anything Lisa. Cherish that love, never take it for granted. I won't mom. I won't. She pauses. It's like a dream come true for me. I've waited all my life for him. Yes, you have angel. And he the same for you too. It's wonderful what God will do when we just trust Him isn't it? That's all He's ever asked of any of us. Just Trust Me. I can move on your faith if you'll just trust Me. With God all things are possible! They both quote the Scripture together. Deborah's face began to glow slightly with the glow of faith. They both look towards the kitchen, how do you think dad feels really about Yosef and I getting married mom. Please, it's important to the both of us. Oh, Lisa. Don't you know by now? Lisa looks at her, curiosity surfacing. Your father loves Yosef just like he was his own child. And You know how Jo-Jo feels about your father. Lisa lets out a sigh still not convinced. What's the matter dear? Well, it's dad. He looked happy for us, but I

Could still detect a little disappointment there. Deborah smiles at her. Honey, he's a father, you're his little girl, his angel. He doesn't want to give you up, but he knows the time is drawing near for him to let you go now. But I can tell, he's so very proud of you and Yosef. Really? Yes, angel. Really. She kisses her mother. If you only knew what this means to me and I'm sure Yosef would appreciate it too. Thank you mom. She whispers to her. I love you so much, you and daddy. And Johnathan. And we love you too baby girl. Oh, oh. Said Deborah. What mom? Call of nature again. That darn water pill. Woman are you ready to go? Said Rev. Anderson, walking back into the living room. You're gonna make me late. Tell it to my bladder Ben. She said walking into the downstairs bathroom. Lisa chuckles at them. They're so cute. She said under her breath. She begins to admire her ring again. Her father looks at her smiling, tell your mother I'll be out in the car. She never answered him. She never even looked at him. Lise, I'll be...
He waved his hand at her. Never mind, must be a woman thing again. He smiles walking out to the car, to wait for Deborah. Leaving Lisa lost in her moment, he knew all her thoughts were on her Beloved.

Yosef returns home, he calls out to her. Mom! Mom! His excitement was building so, he thought that he would burst! He couldn't wait to tell her the news. Mom! The telephone rings, he runs over to answer it.
Hello. Yosef! She said. Mom! He answered. Where are you? I've just got back from Bible study with Lisa. Mom, are you ready for this! I've got the most incredible news for you! Yosef! Listen to me please! She interrupts him. It's important that you hear me son please! Yosef was quiet for the moment, he could hear the urgency in her voice. Mom, what is it? This afternoon your father had a heart attack. He's in intensive care. Wha, what! He stammers. He was filled with pleasure earlier about his

engagement. But now that pleasure was abruptly snatched away from him. His heart felt as though someone drove an icepick through it. No! Mom, No! Yosef, please. The Dr. said that it was a mild one, but severe enough for him to be put in MICU. He will recover, but he's in intensive care for now, they have to watch him close to see how he does. Yosef's mind flows back in time to where his father caught him and Lisa kissing behind the house. They were in their mid teens. She was fifteen, he was seventeen. What is this? Said Rabbi. You kiss her Yosef? A Black girl. The two of them look at him. Rabbi You've known me and my family for a long time. Is that all you see is Black? Said Lisa. Yosef moves her behind him, as his father walks up on them. He moves Yosef out of the way leaving Lisa unguarded. I talk to you for the last time girl. Go be with your own kind, I'm sure there are lots of nice black boys for you lay with! He said, in his legato tone. Lisa gasped at his remark. Yosef steps back up to him taking Lisa by the hand. Let's get outta here Lisa. No! He said breaking them apart. He pushes Yosef down with such force that his kippot fell off his head. You can't have my Yosef! Never! Rabbi, she said in a soft tone. We love each other, and

You'll never keep me from him. What do you know about love? You both are too young to talk of such things! What do you know about love little girl! He fires at her. Enough to respect him and his faith, without letting our differences divide us, But even deeper still, enough to where I don't let him being a Jew be the only thing that I see every time that I look at him. Whoa! Breathed Yosef. Does that answer your question sir? Yosef steps between them his gaze transfixed on Lisa. He turns to look at his father. I love you dad, and I have nothing against our people, and our Customs. But you can't stop me from Loving Lisa, I'll love her until the day that I die! Then I should kill you now and be done with you! Yosef and Lisa gasp at his remark. Why do you do this thing Yosef? Why can't you find a nice Jewish girl?

Like I said, I don't have anything against our people, but I didn't fall in love with a Jewish girl. Or any other girl. I fell in Love with Lisa. He turns back to look at her again. I'm gonna marry her. He said tenderly. Marry her! No! Fumed Rabbi. He pushes Yosef out of the way again. There will never be any marriage between my son and a Black girl NEVER!!!!! Said his father in an outrage. I told you before Yosef this is our way, and you cannot break our Traditions. This is not our way dad! He fires back at him. It's your way! He turns back to look at Lisa, she could see the rage in his eyes. Go home! He is twisted because of you! Go home Lisa! And never talk of marriage to my Yosef again. We can never be family.

That's not what you told my father Rabbi! You can never make me stop loving him! You hear me never!
I'll give my life before I stop loving him! She shouts at him. No! He shouts back at her, slapping her to the ground. Yosef couldn't believe his eyes. LISA!!!!! He screamed. He ran up to his father spinning him around, hitting him hard in his face with his fist. Rabbi stumbles to the ground blood oozing out of the corner of his mouth. He raised his hand to hit him again, when Lisa takes his hand into hers. Beloved, he's wrong, but he is still your father. Don't do this. Rabbi gets up off the ground. Smirking at them. Yosef was out of breath. If you ever touch her again I'll kill you! He looks at Lisa' s face, she was bleeding slightly from where Rabbi back slapped her. Yosef became enraged again. He turns to look at him. I hate you! I hate you! You hear me! I hate you! He screamed at his father, crying into Lisa's arms. Rabbi walks back towards the house, he stops to turn to look at them. I'll never agree to any marriage between you, ever! He walks inside slamming the door behind him. Yosef looks up at him as he walks inside. Yes you will. He said softly. Yes you will.....
His voice echoed away, as his mother's voice snapped him back into the now. Yosef, are you there son! Yes, mom. I'm here. I have no way to get home, the ambulance brought me. Mom, I'll be right there ok? I just have to call Lisa to tell her and her parents. We'll be right down to pick you up alright? Ok son. He hangs up the phone. His mind swirling out of control. He regains himself, and leaves to go get Lisa, and tell her and her parents the news.
He pulls Lisa's car into the driveway. He never noticed Rev. Anderson out in his car, he walked right by him into the house. He gets inside to find Lisa and her mother discussing wedding plans, since they only had nearly two months to go. Lisa, mom, I have some news for you. He said his voice sounded distant.

They both turned around to look at him. He was in a daze somewhat. Jo-Jo. What's the matter son? Said Deborah. Lisa looked at him, she too sensing something wrong. Honey, what's the matter? He looked at them again. I just got off the phone with my mother. This afternoon, my father had a heart attack

Both women Gasped. Oh, Rabbi! Sighed Lisa, Sarah! Said Deborah. They both embraced him. My mom is down at the Hospital with him now. Oh son, I'm so sorry to hear this. He couldn't say anything, he just nods his head. Where's my dad? He's out in the car waiting for me, he has to speak tonight. Look you and Lisa wait for me, I want to ride down to the hospital with you. I just want to go and tell my husband before we leave alright? Ok. He said. Lisa, lock the door for me will you baby? Ok mom.

Lisa looks up at Yosef, he looked as though he would break at any moment. It'll, be ok for him beloved.

Believe me. He'll pull through. He smiled at her. You'll have to teach me how you do that someday Lisa.

My pleasure Beloved. He pulls her close to him. I'm so glad you're a part of my life Lisa. I don't know what I would do without you. Let's go she said taking his hand. They leave together. They get outside. They go down by her car. Lisa looks at him, her expression seem to speak to him. She wanted to tell him something. What? He said to her. She shakes her head. I know that you and he haven't been on good terms in a long while, but he's still your father. How did you know that? He said to her. I could hear your

Heart Yosef. And I can see it in your face. You love him, very much you love him. He's not allowed you to get close enough so that he could see that love. But it's there. And you know what? What? He loves you too! She said smiling. In spite of his behavior, he really loves you Beloved. Yosef cried into her arms again. Oh, God! Lisa! I love you so much! He looks at her. What is it? She said. What you just said.

What did I just say? That I love him. Yes, you do. She said. I never gave loving my father much thought until now. He's been a hard cold, and bitter old man to live with all these years. It's just like living with a stranger. But now that you mentioned it. I really do love him Lisa. I love my father. He smiles at her, tears

in his eyes. They embrace tenderly. Rev. Anderson was sitting
out in his car listening to a new CD recording that Lisa had just
cut. The song filled him with an overwhelming faith. Just then
his wife hits the car door startling him. He jumps hitting his
head on the car ceiling. I'm sorry honey, I didn't mean to frighten
you, but we have an emergency! He turns the CD player off.
What is it love? He said, seriousness in his tone. Ben, this
afternoon, Rabbi had a heart attack, Yosef just got off the phone
with his mother. He's at Saint's of Mercy Hospital. Sarah's still
out there. He gets out of the car. Oh, no my Lord no. He said
sorrow overwhelming him for Rabbi. He embraces Deborah. He
looks at her. He's my good friend Deborah. My good friend. I
know sweetheart. He needs our prayers, we must cover him. She
said.

Yosef and Lisa stood gazing at each other for a moment. They
knew each other's thoughts. They were both torn between sheer
happiness over their engagement. But yet at the same time,
deeply hurt for Rabbi, as well as For Sarah We'd better go now.
My mom is waiting for us. Said Lisa. He takes her by the hand
They walk back over to Rev. Anderson's car. Ben stared off into
the darkness of the night, his thoughts on Rabbi. Ben? Are you
alright? Hum? Oh, uh yes. Of course. Where's my son?
Deborah looks around Yosef and Lisa were walking back towards
them. Here they come now. Yosef! She calls to him. Yes
ma'mam. Come here son. Said Rev. Anderson. Don't you worry
now ok? Try to be strong for your mother. She really needs your
strength. She really needs us all. But especially you. He said to
him. Yosef embraces him hard, tears in his eyes. Lisa goes over
to her mother, she was crying for Rabbi.

I love him dad. I really do I love my father. Lisa pointed that out
to me tonight. She made me realize just how much I really love
him. I've always known that son. Believe me, I have. We'll all
pray for Jacob tonight at Church before we do anything else, we'll
pray for him first. Thanks dad. I appreciate this more than you
know. But something I don't understand. What is that son?
How could you still love him after the way that he's treated Lisa
all these years? You said it yourself son. Love. We all love Rabbi,
your father has survived an ordeal that many of us would have
lost the battle with a long time ago. But he hung in there. He
tried the best that he could. And we understood. I'm not making

excuses for him. But his past has played a very big part in what has led him up to this. Now let's see what Miracles God can work through this to get his out of it ok son? Yosef thought hard on his adopted father's words. They touched him deeply. I'm so glad to become a member of this family. He said. Choking up a little. Become? Said Rev. Anderson.

Jo, you've always been a member of this family, and you always will be. How can I ever thank you and mom and Johnathan for all that you've done for me? Rev. Anderson looks back at Lisa, her mother holding her in her arms. He reaches out his hand to her. Deborah brings Lisa over to her father. He takes her by the hand giving her to him. He embraces Lisa close to him. You just take care of my little girl for me and her mother ok son? He winks at him. Not a problem at all dad. He winks back at him. Rev. Anderson gets in his car, Yosef lets Lisa and her mother, then himself in her car, and leaves for the Hospital. Rev. Anderson drives off to Bible study. Rev. Anderson's mind is filled with memories of how he came to meet Rabbi Epstien. It was during the late Sixties, when their children were still very young still single digit age. As the children grew, he remembered what Rabbi Epstien told him after their first meeting, he could still hear his words echoing in his mind. "Your family is my family now, and my family is your family." A single tear makes it's way down his masculine cheek. You honery old coot, you can't die now. Our kids are about to be married. Come on my friend, hang in there. Help is on the way. Rev. Anderson remininces about the time that he saved Rabbi from four hoodlums that tried to hold him up one night.

Rev. Anderson was trained in combat martial arts when he was in the Service. And he was able to ward off the boys with no problem at all. "Come now my friend, let's get you home." He said , his deep baritonc voice was soothing and friendly. He held his hand out to Rabbi to help him off the ground. Rabbi extends his hand out to take Rev. Anderson's. He pulls him up and help dust himself off. Rabbi was a little unsteady, one of the thugs managed to cuff him a good one underneath his right eye. His cheek was a little bruised, and bleeding some. Whoa there! Said Rev. Anderson as he catches Rabbi, he stumbled into his arms. He had had a little dizzy spell. He looked at him. There was

blood coming down from his forehead, he had been hurt pretty bad. Rabbi was somewhat hesitant at first, but he sensed that this man meant him no harm, and went with him. Rev. Anderson puts him into his car first, and takes him home with him, instead of taking him to his home. He needed looking after first, and he would take him home later. Upon reaching there, Mrs. Anderson hears the doorbell ringing frantically. Ok! I'm coming ! I'm coming! She said wiping her hands on her apron. She opens the door. Why are you ringing the doorbell like that Ben?
She said, then she notices Rabbi Epstien in her husband's arms. Oh my God! What has happened? She takes her husband's briefcase, and Bible and sets them on the baby grand piano. They bring Rabbi inside, he was still a little wobbly. Deborah, help me with his coat will you dear? Yes, of course I will. She said.

They walk him over to the couch, and set him down,making him comfortable. There my friend just relax, and make yourself at home, you are among friends here. He said making him feel more like a King instead of a neighbor. Deborah returns with a medium sized first aid kit. She had used it many times to bandage up her husband and their children. Even Yosef, which he didn't even know about yet. But Yosef and Lisa had already met, as well as his wife Sarah and Deborah. He himself never really felt the need to get too close to the new family who by this time had been there for nearly three months. He would see them from time to time, but never initiated an aquaintance with them. Deborah prepares all the bottles and other contents of her kit on the cocktail table. She was a Registered Nurse at Saints of Mercy Hospital. And was very well respected by some, while shunned by others. A Black Nurse during that time wasn't too well accepted by Whites in the Medical Profession. But nonetheless, that's how it was back then. "Here we go now" She said as she prepares a cotton ball with some sterile water. She daps a little on the areas where he was injured. then she takes out a small bottle of antiseptic from the case. She daps a little of it onto the cotton ball. Now this might sting a little bit Rabbi. He smiles at her a little, unsure what to make of her kindness to him. He was a Jew, and they were Black. Is there supposed to be a connection here? He thought to himself. "I'm a big boy ma'mam. He said chuckling. He sticks out his cheek to her, she gently applies the cotton ball to his face. He winces slightly. He looks up at Rev. Anderson who was watching them smiling.

Deborah specialized in bandaging up injured folks. She worked in the Emergency room at the Hospital, and this was a piece of cake to her. She enjoyed her work and put her heart and soul into everything that she did. She even received an award for Excellence in Nursing care, And was given a bonus in her salary! Talk about coming a long way! She's right, it does sting a little. He said smiling. He was beginning to open up more to them. She cleanses him dapping on this and that. She then secures a small bandage underneath his eye, and on his forehead where he took the blow from the boys. There just keep those on, and you'll be good as new in a few days ok? Yes ma'mam. He said. Well I hate to get bandaged up and run, but I must get home now. Leaving so soon Rabbi? Said Deborah, as she cleaned up the mess she made cleaning up their new house guest. Rabbi would you please stay for dinner? I made chicken and dumplings, cornbread, and a fresh garden salad. And for dessert, I made homemade apple pie, and butter pecan ice cream. Rev. Anderson pats his tummy. I can hardly wait for that! He said. Rabbi my wife makes the best chicken and dumplings this side of Heaven! Oh go on you. She said. How was your day dear? She asked him. Just fine love. He kissed her cheek, as he hung his coat in the hall closet. Rabbi? She called to him again. Would you please stay with us for supper? We'd love to have you as our special guest. Well I was just uh. She struggled to find the words to answer her but there were none. He looked all around him. His head swimming out of control a bit. But now he was beginning to settle down. Rev. Anderson walks up to his wife putting his arm around her waist. They traded looks at each other. As far as

They knew, they hadn't been rude to him in any way. He was still looking around him. He looked as though he was trying to figure out something. He was just attacked by four Black hoodlums that tried to rob him. They assaulted him in doing so. Then he was rescued by a Black man, and brought to his home and treated like something that he never thought anyone would ever treat him as. A human being! Now he is seated in the home of a beautiful upper middle class suburban Black family. He a Reverend, and his wife a Registered Nurse. He watched the love shared between the Reverend and his wife. It touched him a

little. He then spoke. Yes. He said. Yes? They both said to him.
Yes, I accept your offer, that is, it if I'm still invited. Deborah help
me with him. Smiled Rev. Anderson. They both go over to help
him off the large sofa. I don't know how to repay you for your
kindness to me. Being so hospitable to a middle aged man like
myself. Oh stop that Rabbi! Said Deborah. They stand him to
his feet. He wobbled a little.

Steady there. Said Rev. Anderson. Rabbi accidently touched his
sore eye. Oooouch! He said . Both Rev. And Deborah winced in
pain with him. Careful, they both said together, They each take
one of his arms and escort him into the dinning room.   While
eating, both men trade Ministry stories, Rabbi shares of his
experiences in one of the Synagogue's while he lived briefly in
New York. There was some personal trouble with one of the
Rabbi's that he knew about. And he had to make a decision
about the wrong that he saw, or resign from his position there.
He chose to resign his position, and relocate to Chicago.

His resume was immediately accepted and he was listed as one of
the most highly respected Rabbi's there at his Temple where he
and his family currently attend faithfully.   Rabbi spoke much
about the Torah, and their Temple observances, and customs.
Rev. Anderson shared much about the Bible, and some of his
stories in the Military, before he became an Ordained Minister.
Johnathan listens as the two men talk amongst them. Deborah
prepares to clear the table getting ready for dessert. Lisa! Come
and help me.
Lisa? Rabbi asked. I'm coming momma! She shouts back. She
runs into the dinning room smiling big at Rabbi, she saw Yosef in
his expression. He smiles slightly at her. Lisa, go and get all the
silverware from the table and put it in the kitchen sink for
momma honey. Ok. She said excited. Sooooo, this is the lovely
young lady who has my son's heart thumping a mile a minute!
He chuckles out loud. Excuse me Rabbi I have to take your
silverware in the kitchen for my mom. You're going to have
dessert with us! She said smiling even bigger at him. Oh she is a
dear girl, and very beautiful, just like Yosef said. Lisa takes off
into the kitchen after her mother carrying a handful of silverware.
I have to help my mother now Rabbi.
Yes child of course. He said. They both smile at her. Yosef used
to be a quiet child, then boom! Now my wife and I can't get him
to shut up! He talks of her all the time. And the same here with

her. She's more gabby now than I've ever seen her. Lisa's got a boyfriend. Oh, stop it Johnathan. At least I got a friend, boy! She said. Come here squirt! He said chasing her into the family room. Lisa screams running from him. Both laughing. You have a beautiful home, and family Rev. Anderson. Oh, stop the formalities. He stands up extending his large hand to him, and introduces himself to him properly. Reverend Benjamin

Anderson. Deborah comes back into the dinning room with pie plates, and fresh silverware preparing to serve them dessert. This is my first lady, my wife. And to me the most beautiful woman in the world.
Deborah Anderson. We Pastor Faith Pentecostal Center down on Halsted ave. Deborah sets all the dishes
And silverware down on the table. She extends her hand to shake his. Rabbi, I'm so delighted to meet you.
You are welcome here anytime. Rabbi extends his hand to Rev. Anderson. I'm Rabbi Jacob Epstien, my wife Sarah and I are members of Bethel Temple Hebrew Church on Washington Blvd. Down by that chicken place. Uh, what's the name of that place again?.... Henry's? said Rev. Anderson. That's the one I know where it is, I pass there all the time on my way to Rexall drug store. We have two sons. Our oldest Michael is 20, and our youngest Daniel Joseph is 10. Just then Deborah looks around for Lisa. Where is that little girl of mine, she was suppose to come and help me. A roar of laughter sounds out from the family room, as Johnathan and Lisa played hide and seek. Thank you Rabbi, uh, that uncouth racket you hear coming from the family room are our two children. Johnathan and Lisa. Cut it out back there! He said to them. Then another roar of laughter sounds out from the family room. Rev. Anderson and Deborah look at each other. Them your children. They said together, pointing at each other. They all laugh together. Rabbi, you take your seat there, and I'll cut you a slice of apple pie. Said Deborah. He

Looks at all the neatly arranged dessert on the table. And takes a deep breath. Well I would love to stay for this delicious dessert, but I can't eat another bite I'm afraid. He said patting his very full tummy.

Not a problem Rabbi, just stay right here. I'll be right back. Said Deborah. She takes all the dessert dishes and silverware back into the kitchen. She later returns with two large plastic containers. One filled with large slices of apple pie the other filled to the top with butter pecan ice cream. She hands them both over to him. Here you are Rabbi, I hope that you and Sarah and the children will enjoy this. She said smiling big at him. I'm sure that they will. Now once again, I really must be going now, and thank you for inviting me to your home, and meeting your dear,dear family. I have enjoyed myself immensely. And I'm sure my family will enjoy this. He said smiling holding up the containers. Rev. Anderson goes to the hall closet to get his coat. He and Deborah help him with it. Now Rabbi don't forget. Just keep those bandages on, you'll be fine in a day or two. He bows his head to her. As you say ma'mam. At that time, Lisa comes running out from the family room, Johnathan still chasing her. Rabbi! Rabbi! She shouts at him. Deborah stops her. Lisa, no running in the house. Johnathan will you stop chasing her! She said swatting at him. He laughs and runs back into the family room. Sorry mama, she walks up to Rabbi Epstien. He was tall and handsome, a very dignified man. Yosef looked like him sort've. He looked down at her. What is it my child? He said smiling at her. Could you tell Yosef to come out to play by our favorite spot? Kick ball tomorrow. Yes I will dear. The tender look of innocence in her expression, touched his heart deeply. Her smile captivated his heart, as well as it already had his son. Come now sweetheart, Rabbi has to go home now. It's time for your bath. Ok mama. Good night Rabbi. Goodnight child. He said to her smiling. Goodnight daddy. Goodnight angel she reaches up to him. He picks her up. Give daddy sugar. She kisses him on the cheek. That's my girl. Go with your mother now. Goodnight Rabbi. Said Deborah.

Goodnight Deborah. They watch Deborah and Lisa leave, then walks Rabbi out onto the porch which was decked with an assortment of hanging flower baskets, and a porch swing. It has been an absolute pleasure

Ben. I hope to see you soon. Same here Jacob. Can I give you a lift home? He said offering to drive him to wherever home might be. He smiled at him. He knew where he lived, he was teasing him a little. Uh, no unless you wish to drive me way over there across the street. Said Rabbi chuckling himself. They both look at each other, and bust up laughing. He pointed to a beautiful home right across the street from them.

It was a big white two story home, trimmed in yellow. It had a screened in porch, with a various assortment of porch pots scattered in different places. They both laugh again. As Rev. Anderson turns to walk back inside the house, Rabbi calls to him. Ben? Yes. Rabbi extends his hand to him. They shake hands. I've never been treated this way before. I don't quite know how to feel about now. He said.

All that I know is that it feels good, I'm confused as to how good feels I've not felt it in so long, I've forgotten how to feel good, I'm not sure if I even deserve to feel this way or not. Rev. Anderson himself
Felt sorry for him at that moment. Now no talk like that Jacob. Of course you deserve the right to feel good. We all do. I believe that I know what you are talking about. I'm glad somebody does. You and your family have treated me very kind. My people are not usually treated so well, or accepted by some people. But you accepted me, and treated me as if I have known you for many years. And this is only our first formal meeting. Rev. Anderson nodded his head in agreement with him. He knew all too well himself about the stinging irritation of discrimination. I know what you are feeling Jacob. Believe me I do. When I was a young man, I use to travel with my parents when they had just started out in their Ministry. We were called to Minister in small towns. Back then we had to enter In through the back door of the Church.

Jacob listened to Rev. Anderson tell him of his experiences as a young aspiring Minister, following in his Father's footsteps. He told him of how even back though his father was a man of God. He was still Black, and the White people there did not take too kindly to a Black man speaking to them about anything. There were stares of disapproval of a Black man preaching to a group of White people. I remember one night when my father was preaching to a very harden group of white folks. They were spouting their anger at him. My mother, who was a strong Intercessory Prayer warrior, covered my father in her prayers as they shouted something like "Get out of the Pulpit Nigger!" more than Amen Preacher! Rabbi shakes his head when he heard that. It seem to hit him right in his heart. They didn't want to hear his message. But he preached on through them anyway.

Just then as he fired away at them preaching to them about the Power of God through Love. One old timer walked up to the altar. Tears flowing from his eyes. Pappa's message touched his heart. The man said nothing, he just looked at my father. Dad, then looked up towards Heaven and closed his eyes. And Lifted his hands, and I tell you Jacob, that man prayed a prayer that I'll never forget as long as I live. He prayed that God would move in such a way so as to soften the hearts of this hardened people. He prayed. "Father God, Melt them!" I never heard of such a thing as melting human beings before. But now I know what he meant by that prayer. He asked for God to melt

Away all the indifference, all the prejudice, and the hatred from their hearts. And fill them with Himself, with His Love, and His Kindness. He took his text from the 133 Psalms. "Behold how good and how pleasant it is for brethren to dwell together in Unity." And when he said. "Father let Your Glory come down!" Something that I've never seen before in my life happened. I saw coming from the back of the Church. What looked like a huge cloud! Ahh! Jacob, it was beautiful! It was luminous, and the radiance was nearly blinding! It made it's way to where the people were ranting and raving against my father. When he saw it coming, he told me and my mother to stand back and watch God move in this place!
And He did! People started falling all over the place like dominoes. It's what the Bible calls the Shekinah
Glory of God Himself! His Presence had entered the Church, and the people began to fall and weep before Him. Women began to wail out of their spirits. The old timer that I was telling you about lifted his eyes towards my father. And asked him to forgive him! "I'm so sorry" he cried. Just then, the man fell to his knees, then bam! He was out like a light! This man was "slain" to the floor. He was completely overcome with the Spirit of God. He laid there for about fifteen minutes. I noticed that there was a rattling in his chest. Before he went under. When he got up off the floor, even though he was a man of about fifty years old then. He looked ten years younger! He was dying of TB, what they called Consumption back then. When God touched him, he was completely well. The rattling stopped. 'Son receive God's Blessings on your life!" My father said to him. He barely touched him with the tip of his finger, and he was out again.
Where he stayed for the rest of the Service. I want you to know Jacob when that Service was over, those people had a very

different opinion about my father. Where there were first stares of hatred, and disapproval, there were now looks of total amazement and acceptance.   And get this, they never made us come through the back door again! When people heard that Minister Hezekiah Anderson was coming to town. People came in droves to see him! He was a man that truly understood the Love of God. And he shared that love with people everywhere he went. He vowed to God that he would never treat anyone unfairly because of a difference in skin colour, or that they come from a certain Denomination or Church.

To him all peoples belong to God, Denominations were man's idea. But the Race of Man was the heart and desire of God Himself. He knew that God would hold him accountable for all those that He entrusted to his

Ministerial care. And he loved all who came to him. He never turned anyone away. He was a bold man, a man truly blessed of God. Before he died, he asked me to bring my daughter to him that he wanted to see her one last time. I didn't understand what he meant by that. But me and Deborah obliged him. He wanted to Christen Lisa for us. She was only a little over a month old at the time. She was a beautiful baby. "Just like an angel" He said. Well anyway, he took her into his arms, and began to pray over her like I've never seen him pray before. He laid his hands upon her little head, she was sound asleep at the time. He prophesied to us that God would use her mightily for Him. He spoke something to her in a language that my wife and I didn't understand. Then he prayed this over her "A Double Portion of Thy Spirit Father!"

It was then that he passed his Mantle on to her. You see, God used him greatly in the Healing Ministry.

I mean healing flowed from him when the Spirit cam e upon him. Jacob, there was never a time that I watched him lay hands on someone that God didn't heal them either instantly or over a period of time, and believe me that time was not very long. Now I'm beginning to see that same ability in Lisa. She's too young to know about all this now, but when she comes of age, He'll begin to show these things to her.

But then he said something else to me that bothers me to this very day. And what was that Ben? He said that Lisa would have to make a sacrifice a choice of some sort.   And that from her choice, her sacrifice, the lives of many would come to know Him.

They would be changed, saved. Every time that I look at her, I can't but feel concern for her. My wife and I are very guarded over her. Especially her mother. But I guess we'll see when the time comes. I still don't to this day know what he meant by that, but it's going to be interesting to find out. Were you treated differently in the Military ? Asked Rabbi. Yes I was, I was treated with the same prejudice in the Service as I was in the Ministry. I along with many other black men were treated with the same disgust and indifference. It matter not that I was there for the same purpose as

Were. To serve my Country. To them, I was just a nigger in a uniform. But I remember something that happened that changed all that too. What happened my friend? Well I was belaboring my plight about being in this outfit with a bunch of white boys who meant to do me and some fellow comrades some serious harm one day. When out of no where, there was a middle aged Chaplain who walked up to me. He
Heard me complaining about this unfair business of which I could do nothing about. We were about to go up for another flight the next day. See I was a pilot in the Air Force. And I was worried about not coming back. The Chaplain said to me something very strange. He said. *"Remember the Lamb, and death will Passover you!"* Rabbi nods his head. I didn't understand at the moment yet, but then when I couldn't sleep that night. I got up and went to my Bible. I read in the Book of Exodus about the Children of Israel
Covering their doorposts with Lambs Blood, so when the death angel came that night. All the first born of Egypt died, but he passed over all the Israelites who were covered in the Blood. I went to the supply shed and got some red paint, and blessed it. I then marked my plane and the others with it. A few of the white boys saw what I was doing, and began to mock me. They told me that I would not be back the next day.
I told them that it would help us, and that God would protect us. They laughed even harder at me. And rather insisted that I don't touch their planes with my "Blood." I mean they meant business. I finished my business with my fellow comrades planes, I then said a prayer, and blessed all of our planes, Even the white boys who didn't want me near them. But I blessed, and prayed for them anyway. When the time came, it was combat as usual. But do you know, all of us whose planes were covered in the Blood were never harmed! We were shot at, but we were able to do

some fancy manuvering to dodge the fire that was coming at us. I believe we had a lot of His help up there. Two of the other men were shot down. But all of us who were covered, all survived without harm to us or our planes. But instead we took out more enemy fighters than anyone in our Company. The white boys called us the fighting Lambs after that. They too had a different opinion about me and my fellow pilots. After all, those boys were gonna sabotage our planes the night before to make certain that we never came back. If anything they were so stunned at what happened up there that day, that they began following our example. They even let me pray for them. I never had anymore trouble after that. I guess not Ben, that is quite a story. Yes it is, but every word is true.

Every word. He said. Well Jacob, it's been my pleasure. He said to him shaking his hand once more. And mine too. Said Rabbi. I should go now. I think my ice cream is melting. They both laugh. They part their ways, but their friendship had only just begun. That brief moment in time seemed like hours to Rev. Anderson. But it only lasted a few minutes. He drove on to Church, where he made known to all about Rabbi's illness. And they should immediately cover him in their prayers. They all gathered around the Altar in a circle, and began intense united Intercessory prayer for Rabbi. There were tears streaming down the faces of everyone there. Especially Rev. Anderson. He broke for him. His Deacon's gather around to lift him up in support of his love for his friend.

Yosef and Lisa, and Deborah reach the hospital, they see Sarah down the hall in the waiting area. Mom!
Mom! Shouts Yosef. Here! Yosef, I'm here! She shouts back. She was glad to see him, all of them. Especially him. They all embrace her. They walk down the corridor leading back to the waiting area, Sarah had run up to meet them. As they reached there, they all sat down and Sarah began to tell them about Rabbi. How is he? Yosef asked. She looked tired to him, but yet he could see a difference in her appearance. But he said nothing to her about it. He felt that his mother could use a good long rest, he kept that to himself as well. He held himself together long enough to hear the report that Dr. Kaplan had given her.

He's still in intensive care son, But Dr, Kaplan says that he'll recover. Can we see him? No, they won't allow any visitors right now. I just barely got in there to see him myself. But Alton was kind to me, and let me see your father for only five minutes. But you can see him through the window. Come and see Yosef, Lisa, Deborah come. At that moment a Nurse came over to Rabbi's room. She stopped them for the moment, and went inside to close the curtain a little more. She stepped back outside to speak with them briefly. She informed them that she had her orders from Dr. Kaplan that Rabbi's condition had improved in such a way that he gave them permission to move him in about an hour to the recovery room. He didn't quite know himself how he was able to pull through such a crisis as his, but he didn't question it any further, and gave the staff the go head to move him. But he needed to check him one last time to make sure

That there were no changes first. She assured them that if they would wait until she finished getting him ready they could see him briefly before the orderly's took him to his room. They all agreed to wait. She went inside to get Rabbi ready, as she shut the door. The breeze from it caused the curtain to fly up off the window. They Went over closer, and caught a glimpse of him lying there with tubes, and monitors everywhere. The sight of him caused fear to grip Yosef like a vice. It spoke to him that his father would die, and it's all his fault, and Lisa's. "You broke your father's heart by getting with that black girl, now he's gonna pay for it with his life because of you!" He's gonna die, and it's all her fault, and yours. He tried to tell you, but you wouldn't listen to him You never should've started seeing her again! Break it off! And he'll live! Yosef shook his head at first. He remembered when Lisa said those exact same words to him only a few weeks ago. "Why did I ever start seeing you again." He remembered. He's your father look out for him! The demon spoke to him. His anger began to rise at Lisa for his father's illness. His mind had tricked him into believing an obvious lie. The same lie that his father believed for so many years.

Now he was about to do the same thing to Lisa. His mind was in a daze, as was his heart. His deep love for Lisa, and his love restored for his father. His thoughts spoke lie after lie to him. Confusion had began to speak to him, and it was beginning to take it's toll on him. He looked back up at the more aged nurse as she prepared to remove most of the tubing's, and the oxygen from Rabbi. When she saw them all staring in at him. She

190

mouthed. "I'm sorry." To them, then closed the curtain. Nearly ten minutes passed by when the door opens. The nurse and two other orderly's emerged from the MICU room with Rabbi. He was still sleeping, he never knew they were there. They followed after her. She took him to recovery room 7. Just

Then Deborah senses the urge in her spirit to go pray. I have to find a Chapel. She said. I know where it is. Said Sarah. Follow the yellow line down to the right. It's the third room on the right. Thanks dear. Said Deborah. I'll be back soon. She said. Yosef felt a host of feelings overwhelm him all at the same time. Anger, hurt confusion, fear of loosing him, when they never even had a chance to mend their ways.

All speaking to him at the same time. He could no longer contain himself, he broke at that moment! Nooooo! He shouted. He starteled Lisa and Sarah. Mom! It's my fault! It's my fault! His outburst attracted the attention of a few others in the lobby area. Yosef, what is the matter with you! Shouted Sarah. He fell up against the wall beating it with his fist. He was crying painfully for his father. Lisa stood there in confusion as she watched him, not knowing what to make out of his behavior. She calmly walks over to him. Usually her presence calmed him, but he would not be so easily consoled by her this time. Yosef. She calls out softly to him. Putting her hand on his arm. No! don't touch me! Get away from me Lisa! This is your fault! What! She said. My fault! If I had done like he wanted in the first place this wouldn've never happened to him! Do you understand that! No, I don't. What are you talking about? She said, tears in her eyes. He walks over to his mother, who was just as confused as Lisa, but her anger was beginning to rise at Yosef for his behavior. Mom, I'm sorry that I wasn't here for him when he needed me. He tried to tell me not to do this, but I wouldn't listen. Yosef, you aren't making any sense to me at all, tried to tell you not to do what? Sarah asked him. Me and Lisa. What about you and Lisa? Yosef couldn't speak, his words had left him for the moment. Yosef, please, tell me what did I do wrong.

Pleaded Lisa. She again tries to console him, he snatched away from her His thoughts spoke further to him. His moment returns again in a fury bringing with it rage this time. And he unleashes them all on Lisa. Who had gone over to Sarah to speak to her about the engagement. Lisa felt that with all that had happened, the news would cheer up Sarah. Yosef, was quiet at the time as she spoke to his mother. Ms. Sarah, I don't know what all this is about, but we have some news for you, and Rabbi. I mean when he's well and out of here. Yosef then walks over to her and snatches her away from his mother. Are you crazy! You can't tell them about the engagement now! Jesus, Lisa! He's been through enough because of us, didn't you see him! If you thought he was messed up before, this will kill him! Yosef please listen to me.

She pleaded with him again. No Lisa! I'm through listening to you! My father is in there dying, and all you can think about is making wedding plans! How selfish can you be? He said through his teeth to her.

Lisa and Sarah gasped at him. He pauses looking at the floor. He looks at her. Maybe you were right.

We never should've started seeing each other again. He takes a deep breath. The engagement is off.

What! Lisa breathed. Yosef you can't mean that, you can't mean that! She said tears streaming down her face. He backs away from her. No! Yosef, tell me what I did wrong! He grabs her hard by her arm shaking her. Yosef you're hurting me! Would you just leave me alone! Huh! Just get outta here and leave me alone! I don't want to see you anymore! Sarah stood there shaking her head. Yosef! Where are your senses boy! Lisa grabs her stomach, she felt nausea rising up in her. She looks back at him one last time.

She tore her dress from the shoulder, and turns to walk away. She stops to look at him again, he turns away from her, I love you. She mouthed to him, and runs out of the hospital. Lisa! Shouted Sarah. Yosef walks back over to one of the lobby chairs to sit down. He buries his head in his hands and breaks down in tears. He was unable to grasp what he had just done. He for the moment had become just like his father..

Sarah comes over to Yosef, calling to him. Stand up son. She said, her voice more authoritative now. He stands up to face her. I can't believe what you just did. Neither can I mom, neither canI. You behaved to Lisa, just like your father has been to me. How could you do this thing to Lisa? To Lisa? What about me huh? What about my father? I have to look out for him! He said raising his voice to her. Shhh! Yosef, don't you raise your voice to me child. I'm still your mother. He calms down a little. I think we need to talk now. She said softly. I can't now mom, please not now. He walked back over to the chair and sits back down. Sarah sat down beside him. Compassion speaking to her. Yosef look at me son. She smiles at him a little, clearing her throat. Did I hear you say something about engagement? He smiled a little himself, before his tears came surging forth. Oh God! Mom! What have I done! He buries his face in his hands weeping bitterly for Lisa. There, there now dear, it's alright. She said patting his back. No it isn't, she left me! No she didn't leave you, you threw the poor girl out of here like an old shoe or something.

Yosef, this isn't like you. He remembered at the moment insulting Lisa again. The demon that had tricked him returns to mock him now. He can hear his own words, and how they seized Lisa mercilessly. She clenched her heart as her Beloved's words savagely beat upon her. He saw the look on her face as he called off their engagement, a day they both had been waiting their whole life for. She looked as though all life had been drained from her in a matter of seconds. He watched his girl walk down the long corridor, disappearing through the lobby doors. It all came flooding back to him. He then could hear Rev. Anderson's words asking him. *"How long will that moment last?"* Oh Jesus! I've lost her mom! I've lost Lisa forever. No you haven't child, I know Lisa as well as you. She'll be back. Sarah saw what Lisa did when Yosef turned away from her. She said. "I Love you." To him. She smiled at that little gesture.

Yosef gets up from the chair pacing back and forth, every now and then looking at the lobby doors to see if Lisa would walk back through them. I broke our engagement off, a day that I've been waiting my whole life for, as well as her. Then when it finally comes. He brushes his hair back. He pauses. She'll never forgive me, I know it. Never. He said shaking his head. Sarah smiles at him. How blind can you be Yosef? What? How blind am I? I don't know what you mean mom. I hear you call her selfish, no son.

Lisa's not selfish,and you'll come to know what this means very soon. But I want you to know this. I'm very disappointed in you for the way that you handled things with Lisa. It's no different than the way your father has treated me all these years. Yosef held his head down, remorse speaking to him now. Sarah saw his obvious pain. She was surprised that Yosef could be so protective over his father, in that he was so abusive to him over the years. For that she was proud of him. He thought on her words for a moment.

I didn't meant to hurt her mom, You know I love Lisa more than I do my own life. I'd never ever hurt her mom! He said his voice rising slightly. I didn't intend for any of this to happen between us. Yosef, it's not a matter of intent, but a matter of fact son. You may not have intended to hurt Lisa, but the fact is, you did. Now you must fix what you have done. Deborah had just walked back from the Chapel, she had been in Intercessory prayer for Rabbi, she missed the whole incident. How mom? I don't know son. I don't know.

Fix what? Said Deborah. They both turn around to look at her, they had forgotten that she was in the Chapel. She could tell from their expressions that something had happened. I was praying for Rabbi, what's happened? She looks around. Where's Lisa? Answer her son. Said Sarah. He takes a deep breath She's gone mom. What! She gasped. Gone? Gone where Yosef, why would she leave like this? He looks at her. Because of me. You? Her frustration begins to rise. Yosef tell me what happened here. Her tone a bit more demanding. Yosef's frustration rises even more, but at himself. I broke our engagement off mom alright! I broke it off! His voice loud, and trembling with fear. But I don't understand why you would do this? Why! I mean you were the happiest I've ever seen you in your life, now this. You haven't been engaged a good hour, and now it's over just like that? She said snapping her finger. My God Yosef, Lisa must be devastated! She said near tears, Sarah comes over to comfort her. Yosef holds his head down as the two woman embrace each other. Oh Sarah! She cried. Deborah wiping her eyes, calming her down.

Come here Yosef. He walks over to her. You know I've loved you like my own son. I raised you in the same house with my children. He nods his head. I don't know how to feel over what you just did to her and yourself. Look at you now. Guilt had sat upon his shoulder now, mocking him. His sorrow was inexpressible, he was quiet as Deborah spoke to him further. She could tell that he was deeply disturbed about Lisa. I may not know how to say what's on my mind because I'm confused, I can't make sense out of this at all. But I do know how to say what's in my heart. And that's this. She walks up to him closer.

I know with all that's in me that you love Lisa more than anything. And she loves you the same. He began to cry in her presence. I don't know what brought all this on in you, but I do know this, you are nothing like your father. Why son? Why did you do this? Especially on a day like today. A day of all days. Your engagement day. What did she do? That was so horrible that you would call the whole thing off in a matter of minutes? Yosef began to stutter, his words left him again. He tried to get the words to answer her, but he was loosing the battle in finding them. While my son is trying to find his tongue Deborah, I'll tell why. Said Sarah. He thought that Lisa was too soon in telling us about the engagement, which she had not planned to do with Yacov until he was well and out of the hospital. But He misunderstood, and something took over him just like his father. He yelled and screamed at her, they had words between them, Then he broke the engagement off, she was stunned beyond words. He then told her he didn't want to see her again, then he made her leave. I never seen a child so hurt in all my life, and I've never seen my son like this as well. I must say this, I somehow don't believe that he meant what happened, but still, it has happened. Lisa left the hospital in tears, almost like she had just experienced death. We haven't seen her since. Oh Yosef! Is this true son? Deborah sighed. Yosef looked up at her, tears streaming down his

Face. Yes ma'mam, it's true. I guess I overreacted. You guess? Said Deborah. I thought that I was doing the right thing by my father. His voice was beginning to rise. I'm sorry, but I was wrong! Ok! I was wrong! He walks away from them leaning his face up against the wall. "Oh God! Lisa, I'm sorry! I'm sorry! He cried out loud. He wept painfully for her. Both women stood there watching him, compassion filled them both for him. She's out there mom, he said looking at Sarah. I blamed her for something that wasn't her fault. How could I've been so stupid! He said. Sarah then walks up to him. Isn't that what your father has done to me for years Yosef? What do you mean? He's been through a lot in his life mom.

Yes he has, but that's not Lisa's fault or yours or mine. All that he's been through is his own fault!

Mom, his family was murdered in front of him! Said Yosef, his anger rising. I know that! She fired back at him. I don't blame him for what happened to them or him. It's what he's done to us all as a result of that Yosef. He's carried their deaths with him all his life. He's refused to live because they died, he never Forgave himself for surviving what they did not. And since then, he would not allow himself to forgive.

He never learned how to care, or, or. She stuttered. Or to Love son, to love. She cried. Deborah cried under her breath. She saw Sarah's pain many a night when she would go over to have prayer meeting with her down in their basement. Yosef turned to look at his mother, he felt his mother's hurt at that moment. But he loved you didn't he? Did he? She said. Yosef looks at her confused as to what she meant by that.

Sit down son, I need to tell you something about me. They all sit down together, with him in the middle of them. Yes, it's true at one time your father did love me. At Least I believed he did until I told him about my Real Parents. Your Real Parents? He echoed. Yes. I still don't understand mom. I never told you about your real grandfather Yosef. You were just too young to understand such things, and I wanted to spare you all the same hatred that your father has carried inside him all this time. I wanted to protect you from that. I was too late in helping your brother Michael, but I vowed to Yeshua that I would not let Yacov take you from me the way he took Michael. What happened? He takes a deep breath. Yosef my

Father, my real father was not Jewish. He was German. What? He breathed. Yes, it's true. He looks over at Deborah, she nods her head in agreement with Sarah. It's true son. He was a German Squad member. My mother was raped by one of them. She never said which one of them it was, I guess it didn't matter. She was raped while her husband was forced to watch. There was nothing he could do. Yosef held his head down unable to grasp the reality that as he sat listening to his mother's, he was face with the fact that he too was part German, as well as Jewish. So was Michael. He looked back at her. Is there more? Yes son there's more. He nodded his head. Go on with the story. They came to their hut one night where there were many families of Jews together. My mother and her husband were the only family each other had. Anyway, one of the Officers came to her while she was sleeping in her husband's arms. He hit her and woke her up. He was standing over their bed speaking to them in his language. They didn't understand what he wanted. He then told one of the other officers to come over to them. He did. They talked amongst themselves. When they were through talking. The member who woke my mother, motioned for her to get out of bed. She refused. He slapped her, then snatched her away from her husband, and threw her to the floor. He then snatched her up, then her husband. He was silent, as he watched. He was cold, starved, and scared to death. He thought that they were about to be killed. But they forced them out of the hut into the cold of the night. They were taken to the back of the hut and held at gunpoint. The officer who woke my mother began to tear at her clothes. Her husband stood there shivering from the cold night air, he wanted them to just kill them and get it over with. But that was not what they wanted from them. There were two

Members that held him at gunpoint, and made him watch everything that they did to my mother. Right before his eyes, the member raped, beat and then spat on her. When they were through, they took her to
Another hut that night. She didn't say what for, they just did. They were separated for a little while. Then later that week, they were told that they were being moved to another camp fifteen miles away. For some reason they rejoined my mother's husband to her before they were to leave. The next day, they were awakened early that morning, and lined up. Then they were marched for miles down the dusty roads, they didn't even know if they would survive the journey there. She was weak from

hunger, tired, and in terrible pain from her rape and beating only the day before. She never wanted death so bad in her life, as did her husband. Anyway, while they marched on, they were taken to a clearing in the woods, where there was a huge pit dug in the ground. The men were forced to dig these pits. They knew what they were for. It was then that they knew that they were not being taken to another camp. But they had been marched to an open grave where they were to be executed and buried. Jesus! Mom! Said Yosef. Well all of a sudden a whistle blew from somewhere close by, where we all could hear it. It distracted the Soldiers. Then the ones that could, began to scatter all over the woods. Some of them got away, some were not so fortunate. They were shot and killed, they were drugged back to the pit and thrown in. They ran, and ran, they did not know where they were going, they didn't even care. She said her emotions rising with her voice. They just

Wanted freedom, and their lives. Finally my mother and her husband came upon a small cottage on a large farm. They went up to the house to beg the people living there to let them stay until the Germans left the area. The older polish couple agreed to let them stay. It was not the first time that Jews were hidden from the Soldiers. They had done it before. So they hid them there until the search was over. Later on my mother became sick, they didn't know what was wrong. When the lady looked closely at my mother a few weeks later, she found out that she was with child. She told her husband. He looked at her with disgust.
He knew that he was not the father. He felt an extreme hatred towards her. He could not see himself raising a child that was fathered by a man that he hated. He told my mother that he had to find a place for them to live for when she has the baby. He left. He never returned for her. Yosef held his head down.

The couple let my mother stay there until she was well and strong. Later on my mother met this young handsome Jewish man that also lived in a small house in back of the couple's farm. He saw my mother, and fell in love with her. The couple told him of what happened to her. He didn't even care. He loved her and wanted to take care of her. He asked my mother to marry him. He didn't even care that I was fathered
By a German soldier. To him I was his child. When my mother fully recovered, her caretakers gave him permission to marry her.

After they were married. I was born six months later. He raised me with all the loved and nurturing that Benjamin and Deborah gave you. He loved me as if I were the child of his loins, even though he knew Jewish as well as German blood flowed through my veins. He loved me and Ben and Deborah loved you the same. That my dear child is true love. Yosef shakes his head at his mother's story. Whoa! He breathed. Does dad know? Yes he does dear, he knows. That has been the reason for so many of our problems. She pauses. He blames me for what happened to my mother, just as he blames Lisa

For what happened to Michael.   That was not your fault mom! Sarah looks at him. He then realizes what he did to Lisa was just as unfair as what his father did to his mother. Nor was it Lisa's fault about your father. Grief weighed heavily on his heart now. All his thoughts on Lisa. He turns to look at Deborah.
You're like a second mother to me. And I love you both just about the same. What I did to Lisa was wrong, I know that. And I'll do whatever it takes to make this right with her. I'm sorry mom, please believe me, I'm sorry. In hurting her I hurt you. He stands up, they stand up with him. They both embrace him. I know son, I know. Just then the door to Rabbi's room opened, it was the Nurse. They had finished with Him, and they were now ready for them to come in. They began to walk inside his room. Yosef stops and looks at the lobby doors, his mind on Lisa totally. He closed his eyes tight. His heart felt like it would stop any moment now. He was deeply, and doubly heart broken now. For his father who nearly died, and for the only woman he has ever loved who looked as though she just did. A single tear makes it's way down his cheek. Oh Lisa! I'm so sorry. Please forgive me. His heart falling deep within him. His mother heard him. Yosef? She called to him. Don't make the same mistake with her as your father did with me.
He never forgave me for being what I am. Part German, part Jew. He is torn between his love for me as one, but his hatred for me as the other. After you see him, go to her son, go quickly! She said. I will mom. I will. He escorts them inside. He took one last look at the lobby doors, before going in himself. He's still weak ok. Dr. will only allow ten minutes no further ok? Said the nurse, then she leaves them. I understand. Said Sarah, shutting the door after the nurse. They walk over to Rabbi, he was still sleeping. He looked a little better than he did at first, his colour was returning to him.   Oh, Yacov! Sighed Sarah as she breaks

down in tears. Yosef embracing her close, comforting her. He reached out his hand behind him

Deborah walks up to him taking his hand into hers. He pulls her to him and Sarah embracing her to them. They all look at him. Yosef's tears began to flow more and more, as he looked at his father lying before him helpless. Suddenly something strange began to happen. He started to stir a little. He blinked his eyes, then opened them slowly. Sarah? He whispered. She hurries over to him sitting on the bedside.

Yacov! Sarah! His voice a little stronger now. He looks up and sees Yosef and Deborah. An expression

Of surprise on their faces. He holds his hand up to his wife. Sarah takes his hand into hers. He looks back at Yosef, and an even stranger thing happens. Tears began to well up in his eyes! Yosef! He whimpers.

My son! They all looked at each other stunned at what they just heard. Come here to me please. Yosef goes over to him, and sits down on the other side of the bed. Rabbi reaches his hand up to him. Yosef extends his hand to his father. He wanted him to shake hands with him. So he did! It was the most meaningful thing between them in years. Yosef wiped his eyes, he could not believe what he was seeing.

His father showing something that he hasn't be able to show in years. Affection! Hh,how are you son? He stammers a little. Yosef tried to answer him, but his memories of his break up with Lisa would not let him.

It took his words away from him. He flashes back to that moment, the way he yelled at her, he could still hear his own voice and the savage way that his words assaulted her. He sees himself snatching away from her as she tried to console him. The look of devastation in her expression when he broke off the engagement, telling her he never wanted to see her again. The way she looked when she left the hospital, she looked as though death had come to drain her very life from her. He felt a slight nausea rise up in the pit of his belly. He rubs his stomach getting off the bed. He couldn't take his mind off her. He closes his eyes tightly. Yosef? Calls to him. What's the matter son? He never answered him. Sarah, what is wrong with him? Now don't you worry yourself over him Yacov. He's a big boy now. He can take care of himself. Yosef turns around, his memories leave him for the moment, as they leave, his voice returns to him. I'm ok dad. Just something I ate that's all. Rabbi listened to him, but he knew that it was not something that he ate. But that something was eating him. And It was Lisa. Rabbi tried to raise up in

Bed a little, but Sarah wouldn't let him. He seemed to be looking for someone. He looked all around the room. He then noticed that Lisa was not with them. Yacov lie still now. I want to ask him something. Where is she? Where is who? Answered Yosef. His father stammered again. Li,Lisa. He breathed.
His mention of her name hit him hard, his memories came flooding back in on him again. She's not here dad. But didn't she come with you? No one answered him. Sarah and Deborah looked at each other. Yosef couldn't take it any more, his thought savagely assaulted him, the way his words did her earlier.
He grabs his stomach and runs into the bathroom, slamming the door behind him. He turned on the cold water splashing it onto his face. Nausea had returned to him again, but quickly left him after he splashed himself with the cold water. Sarah knocked on the door. Yosef are you going to be alright son? Yes, mom. I'm ok now. He comes back out into the room. Yosef, is Lisa home? Rabbi asked him. He tried to answer him once more, but again his grief had taken his words away from him. I, I. He stammered. I can't talk now dad. I can't talk now. He said, His tears returning again. I'm sorry, but I can't. Mom. He kisses his mother on her cheek, I have to go now. He takes Deborah by the arm, and pulls her away from them. I have to go now. I've gotta find her. Sarah heard him, and nods her head, as does Deborah. He steps back up to his father's bed. I'll be back to see you tomorrow dad. He leaves his room. He reaches into his pocket pulling out Lisa's car keys. He hadn't even realized that he chased her off with no way to get home. He had her car! Jesus! He said out loud. What have I done? He again realizes that his mother
And Deborah need a way back home as well. He goes back into his father's room, he calls to Deborah.

She goes out to him. Yosef what is it? He gives Lisa's car keys to her. I'm sorry mom. I forgot to give them to her. You'll have to drive yourself and my mother back home. But what about you dear, how will you get home? I don't know, but I have to try to find her ok? Be careful baby. I will, you drive safe. Tell my mother and my dad that I love them both. And I love you too mom. We love you too. She said nodding her head. He runs out of the hospital. He had no clue as to where Lisa was. He walked to all the places that he thought that she might be. No leads at all. He looked at his watch. It was 7:30pm. He looked all around him, not a trace of her insight. Fear rose up in him, speaking to him. She'll never marry you now! You might as well find you somebody else. She'll never come back to you! The same spirit that lied, and tricked him into chasing Lisa away, was now speaking the same lies to him again. But this time he wouldn't listen. He shook it off, as he looked all around him. Oh baby, where are you?

The Colour Of Love
Anne Hemingway
Chap 20.

God help me find her please! Yosef began to walk, he didn't know where he was going, he had lost all sense of time, and what was around him. He just walked hoping that he might run into her on the street.
But just as God would have it. *And He did.* A blessing from above comes to him. Yosef hears a car horn blowing at him. It was Johnathan! He pulls the car over to him, getting out. Yosef hits the car with his hand. He was glad to see him. Johnathan goes over to him, they embrace. Man, am I glad to see you big bro! Said Yosef. I'm glad to see you too little brother.
Johnathan looks around. Yosef it may be none of my business, but what the hell are you doing out here, and where's my little sister? Yosef didn't know that Lisa had taken a taxi home, and informed her father and johnathan of the day's events.
Johnathan felt that it would be best if Yosef told him himself about what had happened. And he did. Come on little bro. Lets get you home ok? Get in. He opens the car door for Yosef, getting him inside. Whew! He said shaking his head. I can't believe this man! What were you thinking? Yosef let his head fall back onto the headrest rubbing his face. I wasn't thinking at all John. What the hell am I going to do? She'll never forgive me, she'll never marry me now! Oh, you think! Said Johnathan. I don't

blame you for being ticked off at me man, But I'm truly sorry, I'd give anything to change this. But I can't. he let's his head fall back again.

That's for sure. Said Johnathan, but I'm not the one you have to convince man, It's my Dad. Yosef had forgotten all about Rev. Anderson. Jesus Christ! He said. They looked at each other. I'm dead, you're dead man. They both said together. Johnathan takes a deep breath. Look all's not lost. I'm sure she's around here somewhere. He said trying to be hopeful for him. Where is somewhere John? Well I don't know, Jo, she came back to you before, I know my baby sister man. She'll come back to you again.   But you don't know what I said to her. Said Yosef, grief returning to him again. That's what you think. Said Johnathan under his breath. What! Said Yosef. Nothing, nothing. Yosef looked at him as though he knew he was keeping something from him. Do you know where Lisa is John? He paused. If you know please tell me where she is man! Please tell me! Johnathan was silent for the moment. I wish I knew man, I wish I knew.   Yosef fell back on the headrest again. Nearly in tears. Jo? What is it man? For what it's worth, I know that Lisa loves you, she does man. Trust me on this one. I know she loves you, she'd do anything for you. Yosef's heart felt a little at ease for the moment. He even smiled at Johnathan's words. He looks over at him. How do you know that john? He asked, his tone soft and saddened. Because she told me.

Told you? Yes she did. Did you speak to her? Did she tell you where she was going? I need to know man
Please John tell me! Yosef was getting frantic, his anxiety over her was getting the best of him. Yosef! Stop trippin man! Johnathan yelled back at him. He relaxed a little. I'm sorry. I just want her back with me that's all, I need her. I can't breathe without her man. She's everything that I could ever hope for, Lisa is it for me don't you understand that John? I mean she's the total package. I won't rest ever until she's back in my life again. I don't care what I have to do. He said. Wow! Man. You really do love her don't you? Yosef pauses, looking over at Johnathan. More than I do my own life! Johnathan rubs his shoulders comforting him. He felt a deep sorrow well up in his heart for his adopted brother. We're here.

Come. My Father is waiting. Yosef was somewhat hesitant about seeing Rev. Anderson, But he knew that it was inevitable And they would have to talk some time. Yosef gets out of the car. He looks back in the window at Johnathan. Aren't you coming in too? No little bro. I've been given search detail. He said laughing. What's that? Said Yosef. Operation go find your girl. Yosef smiles at him. They shake hands.

God bless you man. Said Yosef. Go on Jo, it'll be fine ok. You know dad. Lisa is his heart. But I'm his main man. If anybody can find Lisa, I can. Now get in there. Find her for me John, please find her for me.

I love you man. Ditto little bro. Yosef hits the car as Johnathan pulls off. But the thing is, not even Johnathan knew where Lisa was. And he would come up just as empty handed as Yosef did. But it was more than Yosef's hands that were empty, his heart was even more so. As Yosef approached the porch, he sees Lisa's car pull up in the driveway. Deborah, and Sarah had returned. Yosef! Sarah yells to him. Mom! He hugs her hard. Have you heard anything yet? No ma'mam he said. Grief filled his voice.

Don't loose heart child, she'll come back to you Yosef. This I know. She's a smart girl, just a little hurt, she's healing that's all. And when she is better she will come back home. I promise you this. She winks at him. He smiles winking back at her. Just then, Deborah comes up on the porch. You ok son? Asked Deborah. No, mom. I'm not ok. You heard anything yet? He asked her. No baby not yet. I feel like you, but in the worse way. Yosef looks at her. How could that be possible? How could you feel worse than me? She looks at him she smiles a little. Because, I'm her Mother son. Her Mother. She said. A single tear makes it's way down her cheek. Come on cookie, she said to Sarah. Don't stand out here too long ok Jo-Jo? Ok mom. She kissed him on the cheek. She stops after she let Sarah in the house, and speaks with him. We do love you Yosef, you and your family. More than you could ever know. As far as we're concerned. You are our family. Please Jo-Jo, if you can, find my baby girl. Please. Find her. Yosef stands there his heart breaking more and more for Lisa. I will mom, I promise I will. Thank you. She then walks into the house. Yosef stands there on the porch, looking up at the night sky. The door opens, it was Deborah. Here. she holds her hand out to him. I didn't need to use this. She said handing him back his cell phone. Just in case something happened, or if Lisa called him on it. He takes it and puts it in his suit coat pocket. Thanks mom. She steps back inside. He looks up at the sky again. All his thoughts on her.

It was a warm and comfortable night. Oh! How he would've given anything to be out with his beloved Lisa on the night of their engagement. Oh! God! Help me! Help me find her Father. I'm so sorry that I misunderstood her tonight. I didn't mean to hurt my girl, so help me I didn't. I need her Father, and she needs me. I'll do anything, anything at all to get her back, Please Yeshua, let Lisa know how much I love her, I've done wrong in Your sight, and her family. If You'll help me find her, I'll serve You more with all my heart. With all my life Father. She didn't deserve what I did to her tonight. Please let her know wherever she is how much I need her. I'll do whatever it takes to make this right with her, and her family . Just bring her back to me Father, help me find my girl. Amen. Tears were streaming down his face. Rev. Anderson was standing at the door listening to his prayer. It touched him deeply, he smiled, nodding his head in approval at his adopted son's prayer. But he felt that Yosef also needed to be taught a lesson for his behavior. And he would be just the man to teach him such a lesson. See Rev. Anderson confronting Yosef about his behavior towards Lisa would be easy for him. But the real test is not in how well he would stand toe to toe with Rev. Anderson. Self confrontation is never easy for anyone. It is never a pretty sight for one to behold of one's self. All the imperfections, and character flaws, shortcomings. Things that we would never speak to anyone about ourselves. In the privacy of our lives when no one else is watching. How do we live really? In that time of privacy,do we let that be a defining moment of our character? Or does it define us as a character. If we were to behave in public the way we do in secret. Most of us would be friendless. It is here where God will sit as the Refiner in not only Yosef's life, but Lisa's as well. He would teach her through her pain that running away is never really an answer to a problem. She seems to do every time there is one. What about assertiveness, standing up for your integrity, and believing in oneself, that no matter what difficulties she or anyone faces, there is more than enough faith in God, and in His Promises to see you through whatever the circumstances maybe. She and Yosef would learn a great lesson in their separation. For him. He would learn the value of self control, and gentleness, and she would learn of the firmness of faith, and how to stand strong in the face of difficulty. No matter how the winds of adversity blow she'll stand undaunted by it. It is these forces of God's attributes that are resident in the heart of every believer, that will cause them to soar above all the circumstances of life, and become

More than conquerors, instead of a "Victim" of circumstance. It is here that Rev. Anderson will see for himself just how much Yosef truly loves his daughter. He will make Yosef stand face to face with himself. Let's see whatelse happens. Rev. Anderson smiles more. He clears his throat, and jerks the front door open. Yosef turns around. Come in here! he said to him. Yosef swallow hard as he walked inside.Deborah had gone into the kitchen to fix refreshments for them He could tell by the tone of his voice and the look in his eyes. That Rev. Anderson was very angry with him. I don't know what it is with you kids these days! He said slamming the newspaper down on the coffee table causing the all the what-nots to shake. What's the matter with you kids huh? Yosef holds up his finger to answer him. Shut up! He sounded not letting him answer. He was pacing back and forth. Can you tell my how two people who have loved each other as deeply and as long as you two have? Go through all that you have gone through, finally get engaged and go through all this "Whooo, whooo." I'm in love! I'm engaged! Yessssss!
She loves me! He loves me! Whooo! Whooo! Stuff. He said jumping up and down like an overweight fairy. Deborah comes in just in time to see her husband's evening aerobics show as in live that is. She was carrying a refreshment tray. She stops in the middle of the living room watching her husband carry on. Skipping around the room. Her head follows him up and down as he jumped all over the place. She looks over at Yosef, who put his hand over his mouth to keep from busting up laughing at him, he could hardly keep a straight face. She looks at Yosef, her expression asking him what's the matter with her husband. He shrugs his shoulders. He didn't quite know himself. She makes an attempt to come further in and set the tray down on the table, but he jumps in front of her. She steps back a little. She attempts to set it down again, this time she makes it as he prances off in a different direction. She looks at Yosef who was nearly

Ready to bust at any moment, she walks over giving him a cup of tea. She then sits down on the arm of the easy chair next to him. They watch together as Rev. Anderson continues on his moment. Whoooo! I'm getting married! I'm in love! I'm engaged! I'm about to pass out! He said as he stopped skipping around.

He sat down in his recliner out of breath clutching his chest. His heart pounding from his prancing episode.

He looks over to find that his wife, and Yosef were laughing at him. Boy! Did he look goofy! She whispered to him. He nods his head. It was the most he laughed since Lisa left. Hey! Snapped Rev. Anderson. They both stopped laughing abruptly looking at him. He was still out of breath, About my little girl! Deborah pats Yosef on the shoulder. Honey have some tea, before it gets cold, it'll make you feel better. Yosef inhales the aroma as he takes a sip. It was still hot. It was Lisa's favorite. Chamomile. Oh! Lisa he sighed as he set the cup back down on the table. He clears his throat. Yeah, dad. I'm here to find Lisa. He could see the hurt in Rev. Anderson's expression returning. There was just something about the bond between a Father and his daughter. A special bond like no other. And when she feels pain, her father too feels the magnitude of her pain a hundred fold, in ways that simply cannot be explained. I want to know what you intend to do about my daughter? Why you ask her to marry you, then in one hour you break the whole thing off! His voice boomed throughout the whole house. Deborah was in the kitchen praying for Yosef, she could feel his fear. The fear that he had lost Lisa forever, and that maybe Rev. Anderson would never agree to him marrying her at all now. He gets up pacing the floor again. Yosef holds up his finger to answer him. That's enough! He interrupted him again. Kids! Well just don't sit there boy answer me! I'm trying dad. I thought that she might be here,that's why I came over so I could talk to her. Well she's not! He shouted at him. I can see that! But I have to find her dad! I'm going crazy without her! He gets up and walks over to the big picture window. He turns around to face him. Don't you think that I feel terrible about what I did? It's been on my mind all day since it happened. I'll never forget the

Look on her face as long as I live. Never. His pain for her returns to him, as well as his tears. Rev. Anderson calms down now. He walks up to him. I know how you treated her at the hospital this afternoon.

Yes sir. He said crying. Jo-Jo, this isn't like you at all son. What happened? Yosef shakes his head. I don't know dad. I don't know. Remember what I told you about that moment? Seems like it's returned.

What moment? Remember our talk a month ago, when I talked with you about your father? Yosef thought on his words, flashing quickly to that time when he lashed out at Lisa because of his father. Then it all came back to him, he lowered his head crying harder this time. Yes, you do remember don't you? Yosef nods his head. Do you have any idea what you've done to her, and to this family? No dad. All I know

Is that my girl is out there somewhere, and I'm not with her. And the thought of what I did to her makes me sick! His anger returns again. At himself that is. He knew that what happened at the hospital was nothing to break their engagement over.

Yosef, what I want you to do is to go home and have a nice long think about what you've done to yourself and Lisa. Go home! I can't go home now dad I can't! Go on now Yosef. What about my mom? she's staying here with us tonight, My wife put her to bed a long time ago, she's had quite an ordeal herself today. I didn't want her by herself tonight. No need for you to worry, we'll take good care of cookie ok? Off with you now. Dad Please don't make me go home

What am I going to do? I don't know son, you have to sort this thing out for yourself. What about Lisa? She's a big girl now, she can take care of herself. I thought that I could trust you to do that Jo.

Those words hurt him deeply. Go on now. Yosef leaves the very home that he was raised most of his life in. He never felt so empty as he did at that moment. He goes home like Rev. Anderson said. He goes into his bedroom and falls backward onto his bed. All his thoughts flood in on him all at once. His engagement to Lisa, his breaking it off, the look of total devastation in her expression. His tears flood from his eyes like his memories flood his mind. Oh! Lisa! He could feel her hurt, he could see her in his spirit. But where was she? At the same time. Lisa could still hear her Beloved's words as they seize her heart, the anger in his eyes at her. Him snatching away from her. All came flooding in on her as they were him at that same moment. Oh! Yosef! Why! Why! She weeps painfully for him. Unable to sleep, Yosef gets up from his bed, and leaves the house. His heart breaking for her with every second that ticked by. His every thought on her. Her absence overwhelms him. Oh! Lisa! I'm so sorry. He never went back home, he just walked the streets for the rest of the night.

The Colour Of Love
Anne Hemingway
Chap 21.

Thursday morning comes in a little cooler this time only 85 degrees today. Rabbi Epstien, here's your breakfast. Said the homely nurse that came in to do her 9:00am bed check, and to give him his morning medication. She sets the tray down in front of him. She adjusts his pillow making him comfortable. She removes the lid from the plate, he frowns at what he sees. A bowl of oatmeal, coffee, and toast with no butter, and small glass of orange juice. Where are the eggs and the ham, and potatoes? My wife cooks like that for me all the time. Well I'm not your wife sir, and besides, it's your Doctor's orders not mine. So be nice! She said in a husky voice. She was a stocky pudgy sort of woman, with bushy brown hair, and a cratered face. She was also a heavy smoker,and smelled of tobacco. She wore dentures that looked like they were about to fall out of her mouth every time she talked. But she was a nice old girl that knew her stuff. Rabbi looks at his watch, it was nearly 9:30am. He never touched his breakfast, he just stared out of the window, a myriad of thoughts flash across his mind. His thoughts take him back further than just yesterday. But to when his family were killed, then Michael, he thought on how all these tradgeties left him feeling, and what was it that he could do about them. He still didn't have an answer yet, but he was certain that there was one out there for him. There was a knock at the door, snapping him out of his moment with himself back into the now. It was Dr. Kaplan. He comes in to see him. Good morning! Yacov! He was glad to see his patient doing so well after the severity of his condition. He was sure that Rabbi would not survive. But somehow, he did. Good morning Alton. He said. He grabs his chart to review his prognosis. I don't understand this at all. Yacov. And what is it that you do not understand this

Morning? How you could recover like this?   I mean, I've seen heart attack cases all of my of my Medical Career, but never have I ever seen one like this! He was amazed at the speed of his recovery. Well what is the matter my friend? Laughs Rabbi. I look at your EKG, and your Echocardiogram. Normal, all normal. There was no tissue damage at all, the muscles were weakened a little but with a low-fat diet and strict bed rest, and NO stress! That should all repair itself in no time. Rabbi nods his head in agreement with Dr. Kaplan. Here, let's listen to you. He walks over to his bedside, putting his chart down at the foot of the bed. He takes his stethescope, and listens through his hospital gown. He nods his head. Sounds good eh?

Said Rabbi. Inhale. He takes a deep breath. Exhale. He breathes out. I can't understand this. He said. Putting his instrument back around his neck. He takes his wrist and takes his pulse. A steady 74. Incredible! He breathes. He takes his chart and records his vitals down inside, and hangs it back at the foot of the bed. I would have to say that somebody up there likes you, if you keep healing like this, you'll be out of here in no time at all Rabbi. But there is something about your healing this way that puzzles me.

And what is this puzzling Alton?   You are here, in recovery, what are you doing here Yacov? I don't know what you mean. I mean this, the heart attack you suffered, you should still be in ICU, but you are here! why is that Yacov? Rabbi thought on his words himself, Why was he there in recovery? I don't know Alton, maybe you can tell me this eh? No eh my friend. This one is out of my league. I would have to say this though, You were spared for a reason, and don't ask me what that is cause I do not know this.

But I will say this to you. Take it easy, I tell your wife this first, now I tell you. Bury the past or your past will bury you. His voice seemed to echo in his ears. He turns to leave. Rabbi thought on his words, he knew himself that it was his lingering in his past that was the cause of all of his problems in his life. Privately with his wife, with his son. And with Lisa. He wasn't like this with everybody. Just with his wife because she is closest to him, and with Lisa, because she is closest to Yosef. He knew that it had been the very wedge that had driven his family away from him. And that things had to change if he were to ever get them back again. But he somehow was still hanging on to that

210

one little shred of bitterness. He clung to it for dear life. He felt that it was all that he had left from his past. He felt that by holding on to his bitterness, it was his way of preserving his love for them. How wrong he was! Sarah would be on her way up to see him that morning, and he knew that she would want to talk to him. She held off telling him about Yosef and Lisa for the moment. She wanted Yosef to tell him anyway. He reaches over to grab his Siddur and begins his morning prayer.

What started out as being a cool 85 degrees became a sweltering 95! The weatherman lied to us! Yosef went to work that morning, still unable to get Lisa off his mind. He thought about her all night. He was quiet and withdrawn, unshaven, he hadn't even been home to change clothes. He just went in the way he was. He was seated ad his desk with his head down. Mr. Dennis comes into his office to speak with him on the status of the land deal. Everything was looking good so far. He and Yosef had been working their bottoms off to make sure everything that Mr. Walden wanted was in order. He comes in and finds him sleeping at his desk. He couldn't believe his eyes. This was not the Yosef he knew. Always clean shaven, and very well dressed. Today he still had on yesterday's suit. His hair had begun to grow longer, he hadn't shaved since yesterday. He looked like he had been pulled through a knothole backwards. Yosef? He whispered. No answer. Yosef! He called louder this time. Shaking his shoulder. Yes sir! He jumped in his seat. He wipes his face, brushing his hair back on his head. My God in Heaven man! What happened to you? You look like you've been up since the butt crack of dawn! You look like, like hell! Yosef lets his head fall back down onto his desk. Yosef begins to sniffle a little, he had hoped this had been a bad dream, and when he woke up everything would be just fine. But this is reality, everything was not fine., and it wasn't a bad dream. Mr. Dennis pulls up a chair and sits next to him. He could tell that something awful was wrong with him. What's the matter Yosef, this isn't like you? My life is hell Mr. Dennis, hell!

What are you talking about? He was a little frustrated, mainly because he was worried about him. Well for starters. I got engaged to Lisa yesterday. Engaged! Why that's wonderful boy!

211

Then I broke it off in lest than an hour. Oh that sucks! He said.
Then he caught himself. What! Broke it off! Are you nuts! What
the hell did you do that for! Yosef looks at him. Sliding his index
finger across his forehead. Can you say DORK! DUFUS! IDIOT!
Want me to go on? Stop! Mr. Dennis interrupts him. I don't
understand. Yosef takes a deep breath. Yesterday, while me and
Lisa were getting engaged. My father had a heart
Attack. Oh, Yosef. I'm so sorry son. I'm so sorry. Yosef shakes
his head. Lisa and I and both our moms
Went out to see him. Lisa was so excited about our engagement,
that she wanted to tell my mother the news. I guess I
overreacted. I yelled at her, and blamed her for his illness, I said
some other stupid things to her. I don't remember what. Yosef,
wait a minute. I can't see you doing anything like that.
Especially to an angel like Lisa. I don't know what happened to
me. First I was enjoying the happiest day of my entire life, the
next thing I know I felt as though all of my life had been snatched
away from me. I will never forget the look on her face when I
asked her to marry me. As well as how my heart felt when she
said yes. Well have you talked to her at all? Yosef gets up and
walks over to the window staring up at the sky. It was a beautiful
deep blue with puffy white cumulus clouds. No, I chased her out
of the hospital, and I haven't seen her since. She was so hurt,
I've never seen her like that before She was, so, so. He breaks
down beating his fist against the window. Mr. Dennis goes over
to console him. Yosef listen to me. He said turning him around
to face him. I know you well enough to know that what you did
was the result of over work here at the office. I've watched you
every since we started this venture with Mr. Walden. Who by the
way is very, very impressed with your work. He can't wait to meet
you. He said that himself.

Yosef smiles a little. And pressures at home with your parents,
that can be very trying especially when you're trying to have a life
all your own. Then last but not least. Wanting to marry the most
precious girl in the world. He looks at Mr. Dennis. Yeah, she is
precious to me. Sir. I can hardly put words around how I feel
about her. I know son, I know. They paused. Look, I called Mr.
Walden last night, we spoke by teleconference call about the
deal. He's more interested than ever now. He really wants us to
do this for him. He informed me that he's gonna be away for a
few days, he'll call me when he gets back to New York. Why don't
you take today, and tomorrow off, and let me take care of things

212

here. I need to check into some things for him anyway. Go and get your head back on straight, get your life in order, and most importantly. Go find Lisa. She needs you about now. She'll never marry me Mr. Dennis. I don't believe that Jo. But what I said to her. There's nothing you can do about that now. But somehow I get the feeling that she's a lot more forgiving than you give her credit for. I'm so disgusted with myself. I can see that.

Jo, Yosef looks at him. Are you sorry? I mean really sorry? More sorry than I've ever been in my whole life. He said threw his teeth sir. How well do you know Lisa? Like the back of my hand sir . He said holding his hand up in front of him. And her of you? More than I know myself. What more do you need?

Go find her son. If that girl's all that you said that she is, then she'll forgive you of this just like she's forgiven you of everything else. Here. He hands him his suit coat. Go and find her now ok? Yosef smiles at him. Ok.

The Colour Of Love
Anne Hemingway
Chap 22.

All the spring days seem to come in hotter, and more miserable. And this Friday is no exception to the rule. Lisa is seated at the concession stand table watching families, lovers, and all sorts of people down on the beach having fun. Laughing, swimming, playing volleyball. And just waiting to watch the sunset. Her mind burning up with thoughts of Wednesday's events. She looked tired, she didn't sleep well last night, she was weak, some as well. She hadn't eaten since the break up. Her thoughts would only give her a little rest before they would return to her to torture her again. Would she ever see her Beloved again? He said he never wanted to see me again. But that can't be true. I know with all that's in me he Loves me. She reasoned within herself. She looks down at her now empty ring finger She left her ring in her room before she left to come to South Haven, Michigan. A single tear falling from her eye splashing on the finger where the beautiful ring had once adorned it. It sat there for a moment, the Sun shining off of it. It sparkled like a huge liquid diamond itself. Then it spilled over off her finger onto the concrete floor beneath her. Oh Yosef! How could you! She wept uncontrollably, one convulsion after another followed. She looked over to the beautiful cottage that her parents owned. Where she had stayed since she left Chicago. She looked back down at the little pierhead lighthouse, the spectators watching the sailboats and the Yachts that went sailing by. She listened to their oooohs, and ahhhhs as they sailed beautiful Lake Michigan. She looked at her empty ring finger once more, before another wave of tears flood her again. Oh! Yosef how could you! With her vision blurred of tears, she wipes her face dry, as she leaves the

Beach. She wanted to be alone away from the crowd. It was now high season there in South Haven, and tourist from all over the Country had flocked to the tiny resort city for the Summer Festivities. As she walks to the porch, she goes back inside the house, shutting the door gently behind her. She inhales deeply, the aroma reminds her of when she and her family come there every year to vacation in the Summer when she was little. She walks down the hall into her bedroom. Everything still in the same place where she left it. Her toys, and her dollhouse, her dishes of when she would have tea parties and invite her parents. She invited Johnathan once but he brought one of his tanks with him to the party and ran over one of her dolls with it. She never invited him again. The memory of that moment make her chuckle slightly. She goes over to her bed, bouncing up and down on it. She looks over at a picture of Yosef and the whole family at his Bar Mitzvah. He looked handsome to her. She had always dreamt that they would come there to consummate their marriage. An eruption of tears burst forth, heavier this time. She falls over onto her side on the bed, and painfully cries herself to sleep.

Yosef returns to Rev. Anderson's home to find him with Deborah and Sarah. They were preparing to leave for the hospital to see Rabbi. He had been home to shower and shave, and change his clothes, his hair was still long he never thought to cut it yet, so he left it. Yosef, you home from work already? Asked Sarah. No mom, Mr. Dennis gave me the rest of the week off. She came over to hug him. I've missed you so much son. He hugs his mother tightly. She felt good to him. Her embrace brought

214

much comfort to him about now. He needed that from her. I've missed you too mom. How are you feeling? I'm fine dear, Benjamin and Deborah take good care of me here. You want something to eat son? She asked him. Uh, no, I'm not hungry, I just thought that I would stop by to see if you heard anything from Lisa. They all looked at each other. I'm sorry son, not one word from her. Said Rev. Anderson. Jesus! Where is she? He said brushing his hair back. His fear returning. Yosef, calm down, take a deep breath. Breathe. I DON'T WANT TO TAKE A DEEP BREATH! I DON'T WANT TO BREATHE. I WANT LISA! CAN'T YOU SEE WHAT THIS IS DOING TO ME!! He shouted back at Rev. Anderson. They all were silent. As he broke down in front of them. They hurt for him deeply, Sarah, covered her mouth, weeping under her breath for him, as was Deborah. His misery was unbearable. Rev. Anderson, could see that, but
He still needed a little more time to be convinced that Yosef truly loved Lisa. Yosef, would you like to come up to the hospital with us to see your father? His mother asked softly. I'll, I'll. He stammered. I'll stop by to see him later ok mom? But I have to try to find her. I don't care what I have to do, I have to find her. If you hear anything from her, anything at all you call me. You have my cell number, please call me alright? Alright son, we will. I promise. Said Rev. Anderson. His tone reassuring to him. He felt Yosef's pain. He smiled knowing that what he looked for in him brought him the satisfaction that he needed. And that was knowing that his future son-in-law, was worthy of his daughters hand in marriage.

They watch him leave. Rev. Anderson smiled to himself. He knew when a man was truly in love. And Yosef was one of them. How much longer are you going to do this to him Ben? Deborah's voice snapping him out of his moment. I know love Ben, and I know my son. Said Sarah. We both do as well as you too. He's suffered enough. Rev. Anderson was silent. Ben this is killing him! Said Deborah. Yes, I know. He said. Ben, said Deborah softly. He loves her, and what about what this is doing to her. You will tell him won't you? She said poking him in the side. I think that tonight should do it. He said smiling at them both. Then you will tell him when he comes back eh? They both said. He exhales deeply, smiling at them.
Eh. He said. Good! Now lets go my husband is waiting for us. They all leave for the hospital.

Yosef goes to Temple for prayer. He puts on his prayer shawl, and kneels down in front of the altar.

Oh, God in Heaven, God of Abraham, Issac, and Jacob.
Father I ask you to forgive me for the unfair way that I
Treated my girl. I was wrong for what I did to her. And If
You'll just give me one more chance with her, I promise not
To do this to her again. I've learned my lesson, teach me how
To be more considerate of her, and to cherish every moment
That I spend with her, and never take her for granted ever again.
I just want to love her and make her my wife, that's all Father.
In the Name of my Lord and Savior, Yeshua, Ha mashiach.

Amen.

Just then his cell phone rings. He jumps up off the floor. Yo! Hey Jo, it's Terry. Oh, Terry it just you.
He said in a disappointed tone. Well, I'm glad to hear from you too man. I'm sorry Terry, I didn't mean that the way it sounded. I have to keep my line open. What's up man? What do you mean keep your line open, is something wrong Jo? Yosef takes a deep breath. Lisa and I broke up Wednesday. What! Are you serious man? Serious as an execution bro. That's serious alright. I can't explain all the details now, but I can't find her anywhere man. It's driving me crazy! Have you or any of the guys seen her at all? No, we haven't but if we hear anything, we'll call you ok? Thanks man. Oh, what was it that you wanted ? nothing really just wondering if you were coming to rehearsal today. But, you have other business to take care of now. You keep us informed Jo, and well pray for you and Lisa. I'll tell the guys ok? Bless you man, I really appreciate this. Just then he hears static in his phone. I have to go now ok? What! I can't hear you! You're breaking up Jo! Bye Terry! They shout at one another. He hangs up. He looked at the window in his phone. "Low Battery." He forgot to recharge it last night. He didn't want to leave and go home, he needed to still try to find her, his beloved. He goes back to Lisa's car, her parents let him keep it until she comes back home. He went place after place looking for her. Not a trace of her in sight. His heart falls deep within him again. Oh, baby

where are you? He finally goes up to the hospital like he told his mother. He looked at his watch. It was now late evening around 5:45pm. He goes to the reception area to check in. I'm here to see Rabbi Jacob Epstien. Right down this center hall second room on the left. He's still in recovery room 7. Thank you miss. Yosef inhales a little, he's unsure what kind of meeting this will be with his father. He opens the door walking inside. Rabbi turns to look at him. Yosef! Hello son. Dad. He said walking further in the room. He was sitting up in bed, he looked better, still a little weakened, but he was doing well. His voice was not it's usual sarcastic tone, he was truly glad to see him.

Yosef nods his head at him, he pulled up a small chair, and sits down. You missed your mother, and Benjamin, and Deborah, they left here about twenty minutes ago. Yeah? Said Yosef.   His depression had returned to him. There was a pause between them. Yosef? He called to him. He looks up at him. May I speak with you? He nods yes to him.   What about? Things, I need to talk with you about things. He was trying to smile at Yosef, but Yosef's expression wouldn't let him. He somehow felt his son's hurt. He

Couldn't himself explain what he was feeling. What things dad? He takes a deep breath. Things about me, you and your mother, and....and.... There was a slight pause. Lisa. Yosef looked up at him when he mentioned her name. Has she been here? Tell me dad has Lisa been here today? No, no son. She hasn't I've not seen her. Is there something wrong? Yosef gets up out of the chair, and walks over to the window, looking out. He didn't know how to answer him. He had never been concerned about her at all. But now all of a sudden, he was taking an interest in her. Yosef, I know that I have been rather difficult and hard on you, and your mother. I wouldn't blame you if you never spoke to me again. But I feel something inside of me that is not easy for me to explain. I know that you are a man now, and you really don't have to listen

To me if you don't want to. What I'm trying to say is that. I want to help you in anyway that I can. Yosef turned around, he was shocked at what he just heard. You want me to talk to you about a personal problem in my life? He said shaking his head at him. Well, I don't know if I can do that or not dad. I mean you're right. You haven't been exactly father of the year lately. But I'll tell you what you have been. How about

Abusive! To me, and to my mother! Cold, hard, unfair. Oh and then there's this one. Racist! That one word hit him deep in his heart. It hurt almost as bad as the pain from the heart attack. Do I need to go on dad? Huh? Do I! I can understand that loosing your family left you deeply scarred, that would happen to anyone who came through what you did. But my God dad, there comes a time in a person's life when we have to go on with life, even when those closest to us die. Life for us shouldn't stop for us because it ends for someone else. I know that's not easy for you or for anyone dad. But it's possible. We simply have to make a choice. Rabbi nods his head in agreement with him. Sometimes Yosef, that choice is not an easy one to make. His tears returning to him. I never said that it was easy. Just that it's possible. Look at what you've cheated me and mom out of because you stopped living. You closed yourself off from us entirely, you wouldn't even give us a chance to love you, and you stopped loving us. I never stopped loving you and your mother Yosef! Then what do you call it then! Huh! What do you call it. How long has it been since you've been with mom? And you know what I mean. He said threw his teeth. Don't you?

Rabbi held his head down. He did know what Yosef meant. He hadn't slept with his wife in five years.
Do you know what that did to her? The only thing that she slept with in all that time was her own tears.
That you caused her dad! And what about me! Huh! Didn't you ever stop to think how I felt knowing what you did to her day after every freaking day, night after night. How could you do that to her? He said shaking his head again. Rabbi thought on Yosef's every word. He knew that he was right about it all, and there was nothing he could do except listen to him. You know something dad. I take my hat off to my mother. The reason why I say that is because. Most women Jew or non-Jew would have left you a long time ago. But my mother, she stayed with you, and you know why she did. He looked at Yosef, he still couldn't say the word just yet. Because she loved you so much. Mom loves you dad. I've never seen a woman so in love with her husband. Especially with the way that you've treated her over the years. Well I do know of another woman who loves like that. He begins to choke up a little as his thoughts of her flood his mind again. Rabbi holds his head up looking at him. He looked as though he

had lost best friend. He didn't know why, but he felt compelled to ask him about her. Where is she? He asked him. Yosef looked at him. Where is who? Rabbi hesitated. Lisa, where is Lisa Yosef? You're asking me where my girl is? I want to talk about her. Yosef looked even more stunned than before. He laughs a little. Alright then, let's talk about her. What is it that you want to uh, talk about? I know how close you are to each other. I thought that she would've come with you to see me. She has always shown a like for me, that I've never shown for her. No dad that's where you're wrong. Lisa doesn't just like you. She loves you. You hear me! She loves you! Rabbi was the stunned one now. He never thought about Lisa loving him, after the way he treated her all her life. Yeah, surprised to hear that? A girl that has never done you any wrong, who has respected you, and our people, our teachings, and our ways. She knows the Torah backwards and forwards. And she knows our Customs, speaks our language better than you! You have done nothing but make racial remarks about her and her whole Culture of people. Of which you know

Nothing about. Black people have been more embracing of our people than we could ever be of them! And not just us dad. Black people have this beauty about them that I've come to learn and respect. They can fit in with any culture, it doesn't matter who they are. They can embrace another Culture of people, without ever loosing integrity in their own. They are a proud people dad, and I'm so glad that they have taken me in as one of theirs, while at the same time. Teaching me how to love my own people as well.
They give so much of themselves to others, without ever taking away from the ones that they give themselves to. I've never seen anything like that in my life! And I honor, and respect them for that.
And for what they've done not only for me personally. But for what they've done to help shape this Nation.
And you know what dad, they as well as our people and many other Cultures of people are still being unfairly treated. No not like it was in your time, no one is gassing Jews any more, or lynching Blacks.

But there are many other subtle ways that people give voice to their racisim without ever saying one word.

Just chew on that for a while dad. I would say it bears a lot of thinking with all of us. And if we'll all be honest with one another. We'll see it in not only others, but ourselves. Rabbi once again was silenced by his son's words, he again knew that every word he spoke was the truth. I understand son, I understand.

Oh, do you? You don't understand anything about me or her at all! You think that you know me so well, do you know what I've been going through for the past three days? Not only that, but most of my life with you as a father! No, you don't understand anything about me at all. Since you think you know so much about me I ask you again? What do you think that it did to me, the first time that I wanted to bring Lisa over to have family supper with us? Do you remember what you did that night? You made me bring her around the back of our house. Like you were ashamed of us or something. Then you wouldn't even let me bring her inside. I've detested you for that every since. You've never made her feel welcome in our home, or your life. Her father has been your friend every since they moved up here. And don't you think that it's escaped their attention of how you've treated Lisa over the years. And to you her only crime was the colour of her skin. As though she had a choice in the matter. Or we had a choice being born Jewish.

The Colour Of Love
Anne Hemingway
Chap. 23.

There was a pause between them. I want you to know one thing dad, I love Lisa. So help me God I do. And no matter whether you accept her or not. I'm going to find her. And when I do. I'll apologize for the stupid way that I treated her, I'm not going to make the same mistake with her that you made with mom. Then, I'm going to ask her marry me again. And there's nothing you or anyone can do to stop me. He was preparing to leave, when his father calls to him. Yosef! He stops at the door. He turns around. Come, please sit here. He offers him a place on the bed beside him. You are right about me, and my ways. The way that I've been to you and your mother. And to Lisa. Said

Yosef. Yes, yes to Lisa. He said nodding his head. I have no explanation for my behavior Yosef. I've been selfish, hard hearted. A stubborn old fool I've been. I wish I had been killed with my family, then I would've spared you and your mother all this trouble I've caused you both. So much pain Yosef I've caused you and Sarah. He looks up at Yosef.
I'm so sorry son. Please forgive me, if you can. I know I can't erase what I've done. But maybe I can start
Over if you and my wife will still have me. Yosef was stunned at what he just heard. His father admitting that he was wrong, and asking forgiveness as well. You asked me earlier where Lisa was. Yes, I did. Why didn't she come with you? I know how close she is to you. Well that's the thing dad, we haven't been close in three days. Is there a reason for this? Yes, and that reason is you. Yosef got up off the bed, and walked back over to the window. Night was approaching the city now. The Sun beginning to set. The colours were brilliant and bold in the sky. He becomes a little misty eyed as he thinks of her at that moment. He remembered how the two of them would go to the beach to watch the sunset. This one reminded him of her. Yosef. His father called softly. Yeah dad. Where is she? He turned around to look at him. Gone dad, she's gone. He was choking up again. Why is that? Why would she leave? Because I

Chased her away alright! You hear me! I chased her away because of you! His anger had returned in a fury. Yosef, please come and sit here. Please. Yosef calms down a little. He walks back over to the bed sitting down beside his father. I don't understand what I had to do with you chasing her away, but I will listen if you tell me. Yosef looked at him. Ok. I'll tell you what happened. Wednesday while you were going through your ordeal, I asked Lisa to marry me. She accepted, I've never been so happy in all my
Life when I heard her say yes. I took her home so we both could get ready for our date that night. I went home. When I got there the phone was ringing off the hook. It was mom. She was calling to tell me about you. When she did, I didn't know how to feel for you. I told Lisa and her parents, we all we shocked, and scared for you dad. I started not to come see you at all, but Lisa talked me into it. And for the first time in many years, I began to realize something. He paused, looking up at his father. I realized that I love you.

Rabbi's expression changed to one of surprise to hear his son tell him that he loved him. I really love you dad. And I have Lisa to thank for that. She made me see just how much I really care for you. I've always loved you dad. When we were allowed to see you. I broke, I'd never seen you like that before. I hurt for you. I would've given anything at that moment to gather you up in my arms and let you know that you're gonna make it,everything's gonna be alright. Rabbi listened to Yosef tears streaming down his face. His heart breaking for him. Well Lisa was so excited about the engagement, that she wanted to tell mom. I felt that with all that had happened that it was too soon, and not the right time or place for that. But she just wanted to cheer mom up that's all. She thought that it would make her feel better. I don't know what happened to me. I lost my temper with her, and called the engagement off. I told her that she was selfish, and something else stupid to her. I don't even remember what all else I said. But then I chased her away

And told her I didn't want to see her again. I can't believe I said that to her. Never want to see her again?
I'll never forget the look on her face as long as I live. She looked as though she just died. She tore her dress, then she left. She stopped to turn to look at me I guess for one last time, but I turned away from her.
I didn't want to see her. Mom said that she said something to me before she left, I don't know what. I saw her lips moving, but I didn't hear anything. All I know is that I haven't been the same without her. I feel myself dying a very slow and painful death. I've never felt anything like this in my life dad. I need her back , I'm going crazy without her. If I don't find her soon.. Rabbi listened to his son's story. I can't believe that I blamed her for your being here. I blamed her just like you've been blaming mom all her life
About being half Jew, and half German. He looked up at Yosef. Your mother should not have told you that Yosef. But I understand why she did. Now you see dad? Do you see why she's not here with me?
She's out there somewhere, and I don't know where somewhere is. But I've gotta find her, and find her now. Yosef walks back over to the window again. Night had nearly overtaken the city now. The colours in the sky were even more beautiful than they were before. Why can't we all be like that? He said. Like what

son? He steps aside so his father could see out the window. Like that! He said pointing to the sunset. It was breathtaking! See how all the colours blend together? No clashing at all. They just blend. They all differ, yet they still blend beautifully in the sky together. If Nature can do this why can't we? Why do we as humans put up barriers? What are we trying to prove by building walls that separate, instead of building bridges that bring together? We seem to have this Superior-inferior attitude about ourselves, that blinds us to the truth about each other. Anyone not like us is inferior to us, or vice versa. We so cheat ourselves out so much when we stop at the surface of a person, instead of looking a little deeper into the heart of that person. The surface can only tell you so much dad, and even that in itself can be deceptive. But the heart can tell you much more, it can reveal everything that the surface may hide. What will it take dad? Huh? What will it take? I believe that God is giving all Mankind a wake up call to realize something about ourselves. If He Himself doesn't have a problem with Intercultural, Interracial harmony. Then should we?

He made us in His Image, and in His Likeness, and if we claim half as much as we do to "Love" our fellowman, our fellow brothers and sisters in Christ. Then why do we have all this Separation in the Churches? Why do we make distinctions of those who differ from us Racially, and Culturally? Why do

We have all this hatred, and indifference between the Denominations. We can't fellowship together because Blacks worship with Blacks, and Whites with Whites. Catholics with their people, and Baptists with their people! Who do we all think we are to do this to one another! What right do we have to say, you stay with your kind, and we'll stay with ours? Where is the Agape, the God kind of Love that the Bible speaks about dad? How many Churches will be brave enough to be honest and say there isn't any!

But we don't know what to do about it. Well, they had better do something about it, because I believe that this is the one place that God will severely deal with and Judge people is in the Churches. And He will start with it's Leaders, all the way down to it's pew warmers. You would at least think that prejudice would not be allowed in Church. But not only is it allowed, it's even practiced by some! Lisa told me of a

Place where she was thinking of just going to it's Temple, just to learn. To see what would happen. She walked up to the Temple steps, and the greeter told her. I'm sorry but we're not having Service today! And very quickly slammed the door in her face! Dad, it was a Jewish Temple, It was Saturday, our Sabbath, Lisa had already seen many people filing in before she got there. So she knew the woman was lying. But what she meant was that. Our Services are not open to Black people. She said that the woman looked like she was scared to death that a Black woman had shown up on their Temple steps. What the

Heck did she think? That Lisa was going to come in there, and make all them Pentecostals or something? All Lisa wanted was to come and listen and learn from them. And she was denied that opportunity all because of the colour of her skin. How will we answer to Him for the inhumane and cruel way that we've treated each other and those that differ from us? Why are we so afraid of each other? Now I ask you the same question dad. Why are you so indifferent towards Lisa? What has she ever done to you to make you feel this way about her? Rabbi could not answer him. He just held his head down. He didn't quite know himself. But he knew that Yosef was right about him. That it was long since past the time for all the race of man to wake up and put an end to racial prejudice, and intolorance, and indifference. And practice true love, and brotherly fellowship. And practice embracing instead of alienation. We've come so far dad, but we still have a long way to go. He then walked back over to the window to look out. Night had completely taken over the city now. Yosef? Rabbi called softly. Yeah dad. I think that you should find this girl and marry her. Yosef turned around, and looked at him. What? He said in a breathy tone. I think that you should find Lisa and marry her. That is what I said. He was smiling a little. Yosef walks over to him, his expression was a cross between surprise, and unbelief. Don't tease me dad, I'm sick enough over loosing her already as It is. Don't make matters worse ok? I'm not teasing you son. His tone more serious now.

I mean this from my heart. I know how much you have loved Lisa all this time. I was just hard and jealous of you both Because this is how I wanted to love my Sarah. I never let myself get over her news about her parents, or my own misfortune with my family. I never let myself feel love for my own wife the way you do for your girl. I was selfish and stubborn, and I'm sorry Yosef. I'm

224

so sorry. Yosef stood there speechless as his father poured out
his heart to him. Then Rabbi said something to him that stunned
him even more beyond words. Yosef. Yes. I want to love again.
Yosef came over to him and sat down beside him on the bed.
What did you say? I want to love again, I want to love the way
you and Lisa love. I've always wanted to love my Sarah this way.
Please son, let me love you and my wife again. All I ask for is
One more chance before I leave this earth. Let me love, just let
me love Yeshua! He cried into his hands.
Yosef could not hold back his tears. I tried to love you both, but I
don't know how. I just don't know how son. He cried painfully.
Yosef saw his father's heart breaking, as his went out to him.
Yosef, listen to me.
Find her son, and marry her, don't make the mistake with her
that I made with your mother. Are you serious? He breathed.
Yes! I'm serious. Serious, how you say as a heart attack! They
both laugh together. That's serious dad. You mean you accept
me marrying a Black woman? Rabbi shakes his head. I accept
you marrying who you fell in love with. He pauses. If you want to
marry Lisa, then I accept her in your life, as well as into our
family! You were right son, you were right. It's not the colour of
her skin, but a matter of her heart that is important. There was
silence between them. I don't know what to say dad.
Say yes son, say yes! He said excitement surfacing now. Do you
love her Yosef? His tone more serious now. More than my own
life. More than my own life. He paused some. But what about
our Customs and our Traditions dad? What about them? I know
that I and your mother raised you to respect our ways and things
Yosef, and I will forever be grateful to Ben and Deborah for the
way that they too taught you to stay established in our teachings.
But Yosef, Many a home have been broken when it comes to
Traditions

And Customs. Don't let it break yours before you and Lisa even
have a chance to build it yet. And I'm not saying that they don't
have their place in our lives. But when it comes to love son, true
love. Even these things themselves must not come between the
love that God has placed in the heart of any man and his woman.
Yosef paused, this time it was he that was silenced by his father's
wisdom. He looks up at Yosef. Go find her, and marry her and
give me and your mother lots of grandchildren! Yosef smiles
taking him in his arms, they embrace warmly. Dad, you don't

know what this means to me. I still don't know what to say. Tears streaming down his face. Say nothing son, I'm a little surprised myself. But I mean this from my heart. You and Lisa have my blessing! Thank you dad, thank you so much! Yosef gets up to leave. Yosef! He called to him. Yeah dad. May I come to the wedding? He comes back to sit down again. He grabs his father in his arms hugging him hard. Dad! I love you son! I've always loved you! I'm so sorry that I hurt you and Lisa. And my Sarah. Can you ever forgive such a stupid fool!

There's nothing to forgive dad. Nothing at all. Thank you son. Thank you. And as for the wedding. Lisa and I wouldn't have it any other way. I would be honored if you would come dad. Rabbi nods his head yes. Now look, that ugly nurse will be back to kick you out of here. You should leave now and spare yourself that trauma. They both laugh. I'll be out of here by next week sometime. Good just in time for Pastors Day at Lisa's Church. You mean you want me to come there? It wouldn't be the same without you dad. Will you come? Yes, I will how you say with the bells on! He said laughing. Alright! Said Yosef jumping off the bed. He turns back to look at his father. Dad. Yes son. You mentioned earlier that you wished that you had been killed with your family. Well for what it's worth. I'm glad that you weren't Rabbi's expression changed, he looked surprised. I can't think of a better person through whose seed that I Came. And I'm very proud of that dad. Thank you for my Existence, and my Heritage. He winks at him.

Rabbi nods his head winking back at him. Rabbi at that moment was filled with a new respect for his son, an overwhelming sense of love and pride for him. His baby that he used to call, his treasure from heaven.
Standing before him, just like Sarah told him many times before. A fine strong young man. Just as Yosef opens the door, the nurse busted the door all the way open, nearly knocking Yosef off balance. "Excuse me." She said, as she clumsily entered the room. Rabbi turns his head in disgust at the sight of her. Yosef puts his hand across his mouth trying to stifle his laughter. He shuts the door behind him. Yessss! Yessss! I'm in love! He screamed as he jumped up and down like a child who just found a lost toy or something. There were two night clerks sitting at the front desk. They watched Yosef walk by, when another

moment hits him. He jumped up in the air, his tall slender body stretching up as he hits the sign
With his hand that was hanging down from the ceiling. I love you Lisa! He yelled. They looked at each other. "Issues." They both said, as he walked out the building.

The Colour Of Love
Anne Hemingway
Chap. 24.

.   *(1)*

Yosef left the hospital feeling like he could walk on water! Things had come together for him and his Father. It seemed like to him that all that took place over the years between them never even existed. Both men had just had a tremendous load lifted off their shoulders.   Rabbi watched his son leave floating on cloud nine. As he was left there alone with the nurse from hell, that made him sicker than his heart attack.
Even though Yosef was about as happy as a bird in a cement pond, he still didn't have a clue as to where Lisa was. His happiness was beginning to dwindle as reality spoke to him about her. He returns to her parents home. He goes inside. Hello, anyone here! We're in the kitchen! Said Deborah. She walks up to him, and kisses him on the cheek. Hi sweetie. She said glad to see him. Hi mom. He looked around. What's the matter dear? Is my mother here? No, honey, she went home today. She wanted some time to be alone. But she'll be back tomorrow. He nods his head. Is dad here? No he and Johnathan went down to the Church to fix those leaky pipes in the basement. And to answer your next question coming up, no, we haven't heard anything from Lisa at all. Yosef felt all his joy drain from him at that moment. Nothing mom? No, baby. Nothing at all. And it's driving me up a wall, this is totally not like her at all. How are you holding up honey? I know this must be very hard for you. He pulls up a chair and sits down at the kitchen table. He sighs in exasperation. You just don't know mom how hard it's been for me, I mean it's like she's dropped off the face of the earth. Honey if it's any consolation to you at all. You're not alone in

This ok? Lisa will either come back on her own. Or somehow, or another. God will provide a way for you to find her. But please

227

son. Don't give up on her. He looks up at her. Her words did comfort him. He smiled. Never! I'll never give up on my girl mom. That's my boy. She said kissing him on the cheek again. Deborah, where's my marker case? Said Mamie shouting from the back room, she was looking for her things to take to bingo tonight. Mamie, you're going to bingo this late at night? Mamie walks into the kitchen. Hello handsome. She said kissing him on the forehead. Hey, mae,mae. Come on now Deborah, help me find it, I have to get going. Sal, and Jimmie Lee will be here in a minute to pick me up, and I can't find my marker case anywhere. Mamie for the last time, I haven't seen that thing honey. Well I know it didn't just suddenly grow feet and walk on outta here. She said in a sassy tone. Yosef laughed a little. Where did you see it last girl? I don't know, I've looked for it everywhere. Do you have your keys? Yeah, I have those right here. She said reaching into her purse. She then stops and looks at Yosef and Deborah a funny expression on her face. She felt a small velvety object in there. It was her marker case, she had forgot that was where she put it. She pulls it out. Oh child, I'm dangerous tonight aint I? Deborah looks at her. Now don't you look at me like that Debbie, don't say nothing to me. I didn't say a word woman. You better get going, or you'll miss the way the balls fall. Just then they hear a car horn tooting out front. I'm going, I'm going. She said grabbing her sweater off the back of the kitchen chair. She

Walks out of the kitchen. See y'all later. Alright sis. Yosef looks at Deborah. It's power ball bingo.
Power ball bingo? Yeah, yeah child. The way the balls fall? He said smiling. Now don't you even look like you want me to explain that so just shut up and leave me alone. He laughs out loud. It's the most he's laughed in three days. Deborah went to the stove to pour herself another cup of coffee. You hungry son? Uh, no mom, I'm not. I just want to find Lisa that's all. Yosef, she'll be back, I know it like I've never known anything else in my entire life. He looks at her. How do you know that for sure? Deborah thought back to the moment where Sarah told her what Lisa had done before she left the hospital. Honey, didn't you see what Lisa did before she left? I don't know, I know she tore her dress she was so mad at me. Not that part you big silly. He smiled at those words. Lisa would call him that at times. She said she loves you. She loves me? Yeah, she said nodding her

head. She loves you, and she really does Jo-Jo. He gets up out of his chair walking over to the window, looking out into the blackness of the night. Then why won't she come back! This is killing me! I can't stand this much longer! I'm about to loose my mind!

Where is she mom! Where is she! He shouted crying into her arms. Deborah's heart broke for him. Yosef. She said softly. Yeah. Look at me. He looks at her. Do you think this is easy for her? She's just as miserable without you as you are without her. How do you know that? I birthed her son. I know my child, I can somehow feel her hurt she's very heartbroken. She probably thinks you don't love her anymore. Jesus mom, How could she think something like that? Didn't you tell her you didn't want to see her anymore? His mind flashed back to that very moment when he told her that. Oh, God mom! What have I done? He breathed. Yosef, it's not easy for me either not knowing where my child is. All I know is that God is with her, and He'll bring my baby back home to me, and to you safe and sound. You'll see. Everything will be alright Yosef. Trust me. But even more son, trust Him. She said pointing up at the ceiling. Ok? Now please if you can sweetheart, try to be patient, she will be home again. I promise she will. Ok. He said nodding his head. Coffee? No, thanks I need to check on my mother, I haven't seen her in a while. She's probably worried about me. No she isn't Yosef looked at her. I called her when you came over, she knows you're here. He smiles at her. You and Lisa, and my mother are three of the most amazing women I've ever seen in my life. And I love all three of you. And we love you too son. She embraces him. Go check in on Sarah for me. You're welcome to come back here if you want to, you have your key
Just let yourself in. Thanks, but I need to stay with her for tonight. Alright son. I'll tell Ben and Johnathan
That you came by. Ok. He said, kissing her cheek. He then leaves to go home. He enters his home, it was dark inside. No sign of life anywhere, it was totally unlike where he just came from. A home that is full of life, and warmth, and love. He felt as though he just stepped inside of a mausoleum. He shivered even on a Summer night as he felt the coldness the deadness of a home that was void of love, life and warmth. He

Felt sadness come on him. How he wished his home was more like Lisa's. he went upstairs, his mother's bedroom door is cracked open. He stepped inside, she was sleeping soundly. He kissed her gently on her temple. I love you mom, I love you so much. But I have to find Lisa. He whispered to her. She never stirred. Watch over her Father, and help me find my girl please Yeshua. He prayed, as he left shutting the door behind him.

Yosef left not knowing where to look this time for Lisa. He had already turned the whole city inside out looking for her. Where are you Lisa? He whispered. Yosef came over to the neighborhood where Billy and Helen lived. She wouldn't be over here, But I'm desperate. He thought to himself. To his surprise he sees Billy and Helen out for a late night stroll. He pulls the car over locking it then getting out. Well, well. If it isn't Mr. Goody two shoes himself. Helen stares at Yosef. Her face lighting up like a firecracker. Hi Yosef. She said. Hello Helen. And uh. What brings you to this neck of the woods? Asked Billy. He was leary about telling them that he was looking for Lisa. I'm uh. He was struggling hard to answer him
Oh, Joseph, what's this I hear about you and Lisa breaking up or something? Is that true? He said mocking him. Helen smiled a very sinister smile, just the break that she was waiting for. She thought that he was there to see her! NOT!! She still wanted him, even though her and Billy had been dating for years. But that's all it was. Dating. It was deeper than that with Yosef and Lisa, they have a relationship, a history with each other. And both Billy and Helen knew the history of their relationship. They truly love each other. Billy felt the same way for Lisa. He still had a terrible crush on her, which he never got over. And he was still determined to take her away from Yosef. NOT!! Again. I'm looking for Lisa. Have either of you seen her? Why would she be all the way over here? Said Billy his tone mocking him. Yosef glares at him. Don't toy with me man, not tonight . I'm not in the mood. Have you seen my girl? His body swelling with rage at him. Helen was staring at Yosef, she puts her hand on her chest to soothe her heart's pounding. No, no, I uh haven't seen her. But if I did, I wouldn't tell you. He said cackling out loud.

Helen looked over at Billy. I would. She said. Yosef looks at her. Thanks Helen, I appreciate that. Yosef was about to leave when she called to him. Yosef! Yes. If things don't work out with you and Lisa. Whoa there! He said backing up from her. Don't even go there lady, I told you once before, and I'll tell you again forever. I'm not, nor will I ever be interested in a relationship with you. No offense. But my heart has always belonged to Lisa, and it always will. She felt her heart sink deep within her. As reality spoke to her again I Told you. NOT!! Billy looked at her. His anger seething at her. He grabs her by the arm snatching her away. We have to go now! He said as they walked away from him. Yosef turned to leave, when Billy stops and follows in behind him. Hey Yosef! He stops and turns around to look at him. You look a little down. He steps away from Billy, and starts to leave again. What's the matter? Did the little woman break your poor little ole heart? He said. In an Elmer Fudd tone. Heh,Heh, heh. He laughed. Billy's mocking reminded him of how his father used to tease and taunt him. Hey don't sweat it Joseph.

So what if you lost one little blackberry, Just go over on the South side of town down on Ashland Dr. And just pick yourself another. Heh, heh, heh! He laughed out loud. Yosef lost control of himself. He grabs Billy by the throat with one hand, and punched him hard in the face with the other. Billy crumples to the ground in a heap. Helen screams. No! No! Yosef! He didn't mean it! Billy gets up off the ground as Yosef was walking away. He jumps on his back and sucker punches him in his side. Yosef falls to the ground in pain. Billy then kicks him the stomach. Yosef falls over on his back gasping for breath. Helen tries to pull him off Yosef, but he pushes her away. I knew you were a nothing but a little Jew wimp! No

Billy! Stop! Get away from me! He shouts at her. I'm gonna enjoy this. Come on Jew boy! Come on! I've always wanted to take you Joseph! Yosef stands to his feet, he had regained himself. He looks at him. Come and get some Billy. Just as Billy was about to charge at him. They hear the sound of Police sirens blaring down the street. Yosef was still a little weak, and in pain. His face was bleeding where he scraped it on the sidewalk. The car pulls over to them. The officer gets out, and walks up to them. Ok people what's going on here? He said. He was a tall Black man about six feet four, two hundred plus pounds. He took out his note pad. Billy walks up to him. This jerk tried to kill me! I want him arrested!

He scribbled down Billy's accusation as he walked over to Yosef. Who didn't care about anything at that moment except finding Lisa. He asked him for his side of the story, Yosef didn't even try to defend himself. He just stood there shaking his head. He was still a little out of breath. The officer noticed the

Injury on his face. That's a bad abrasion there. You sure you don't want to go to the hospital to have that looked at? He said nothing to him, he just shook his head again. Don't you have anything to say sir?

Yosef looked at him, tears in his eyes. No sir, I just want to go home, all I want is to just find my girl and go home. Well, I'm sorry about you and your girlfriend sir, but I'm afraid I'll have to take you all down to the police station for questioning. And a report will have to be filed. Yosef nodded his head. I understand sir. I want to press charges for assault and battery! Fired Billy. You just wait until my father hears about this! The officer goes over to Billy. And just who is your father sir? Police Commissioner Bravens. He said in a cocky tone. The officer's expression changed. He knew Billy's father. He pulled him and Helen aside and talked briefly with them. Yosef watched them slowly walk away as the officer came back over to him. Come with me sir. Come with you? Come with you for what? You're under arrest for assault and battery. Billy stood there with Helen laughing. Helen felt sorry for Yosef. But she was silent about her feelings. They watched the officer cuff Yosef and place him in the back of the squad car. She dropped her head, as guilt came on her. She knew it was not his fault, but that Billy had instigated the whole thing. Her silence was what caused him to go to jail. I'm so sorry Yosef, I'm so sorry. She whispered. But not silent enough. Billy heard her. What! You're sorry! For who! That Jew wimp!

He grabs her tightly. Billy you're hurting me! Shut up! Don't ever do that again Helen, you hear me! He shouted shaking her violently! Yes, Billy, Yes! I'm sorry, I'm sorry ok? He releases her. I didn't mean it.

She said. He takes her in his arms and kisses her. He takes her by the hand. Come on lets get outta here, I need a drink. They leave together.

Rev. Anderson and Johnathan return home, his wife greeting them at the door. They were exausted from the days events of pipe fixing in the Church basement. Hello dear. He said to her kissing her cheek. Hi sweetheart. Give me that John. She said, reaching for his coveralls. She takes them into her arms. How did things go at Church? Did you get the pipes fixed? She said taking more dirty clothing from them.

As fixed as we're gonna get them. Said Rev. Anderson. I don't believe we'll drown down there. They all laugh. I just hope we don't have to start holding Service on an Ark or something. They laugh again. Any coffee honey? I could sure use some about now. I'll put some on fresh. She said taking the clothes into the laundry room. I'll start these while you boys wash up ok? Ok baby. He said to her. Mom, Yes John.

Do we have anymore leftovers? Yes, I'll be right out. Come on son , lets get cleaned up. Right behind you dad. They followed Deborah into the kitchen, each taking turns washing their hands and faces with

The paper towels. They sit down at the table and talk a little about Pastors Day coming up in a few weeks

It was already late May, they still had just a little time left for some last minute planning. Deborah comes back into the kitchen. She goes over to the refridgerator, and prepares a late night dinner for them. Here are some left over ribs and potato salad. Boy that sounds good. Said Johnathan. She warmed up all the leftovers in the microwave for them. As they all sat and ate dinner, she told them that Yosef had stopped by, and that he went to look in on Sarah. Just then the phone rings. No, dad I'll get it. It's probably Deniece calling for me. At this hour boy? His father said. It's nearly midnight. Hey, call of nature dad Don't cha know! He said smiling. His parents laugh, as he runs to get the phone. What are we gonna do with that boy? He said. I don't know honey, that's your child. She said getting up from the table. What

Do you mean? He said in his falsetto tone again. He walks up behind her grabbing her by the waist. I have to was the dishes now. She said smiling. I'll wash you. He said playfully. Oh will you now?

They kiss tenderly. Ok, ok. I'll be right down. Take it easy man. I'll be right there little bro. What?

No dad isn't gonna kill you Jo. Just be cool, I'm on my way ok? Ok. Bye. He hangs up the phone and goes back into the kitchen, his parents still kissing. He blushes a little, clearing his throat. They look at him smiling. Mom, dad. I have to go now. Call of nature with Deniece? No, I have to go into town to bail Jo out of jail. JAIL! His parents said together. What happened? Said Deborah. I don't know, he said that he'll explain when I come down and get him. Rev. Anderson sticks both his hands in his pants pocket in frustration. Kids! He fumed. Deborah looks at him, her frustration rising at him now. Johnathan would you leave me and your father alone for a few ok honey? Ok mom. He looks at his father.

Oooh, you gonna get it...... He teased his father. Get outta here boy! She said laughing. He leaves going into the living room. What's the matter love? He said. Ben, now you know good and well this isn't like Yosef. The boy's never been arrested in his life. He's always been a good child. You know that. We

Raised him right here in this house with our own children. Now all of a sudden this? And you know what brought all this on. I don't know what you're talking about. He said in a childish tone walking away from her. Oh yes you do Benjamin Anderson. The boy is sick over Lisa. He misses her, can't you see that! He loves her, and she loves him. I can see it whenever he is with her. I can feel his love for her, and hers for him. I've never seen love like theirs before. It's the most purest, beautiful, and strongest thing that I've ever seen in my life! You know this to be true. You feel it just like me. She pauses. You know where Lisa is and you won't tell him. My God Ben. I'm her mother, and you won't even tell me! Do you know what this has done to me? To Yosef? You promised me and Sarah that you would tell him tonight. If you had only told him in the beginning, this whole thing would never have happened. She begins to cry. His heart breaks for her. He nods his head in agreement with her, walking over to embrace her in his arms. I'm

Sorry dear, I'm so sorry. You're right, you're right. I was so crazy over him hurting my angel, that I just lost it for a moment. But I felt that he had to be taught a lesson. Look, You know I love Yosef, just as much as I love Johnathan. Sometimes a little more than John. And you know I would never do anything to

Hurt Jo-jo. But I had to be sure that he was worth all the love, time and effort that Lisa was putting into him. I had to see for myself just how much he really loves her. I would never hurt him love you know that.

But that's just the thing, you did hurt him, by not telling him where Lisa is. And what about all the time and effort that he's put into her? I mean, how many young men do you know that would've waited for a girl as long as he's waited for Lisa? Doesn't that mean anything to you? Yosef could've had any girl he wanted. But something happened to him when he saw our Lisa. His heart hasn't been the same since.

And she loves him the same. Doesn't that count for something? He pauses thinking on her words. He looks at her. You asked me how many young men would've waited for a girl like he's waited for Lisa?

Yes. She said. I know of only one. Yeah, who? Me. Deborah looks at him. He reminded me of myself when you and I broke up that one and only time. I thought that I would die! It was the closest to death that I had ever been. And I never want to go through that hell again. I never want to feel like that again Deborah.

Then you understand what he's feeling now, what he's going through don't you? Yes, I know, I understand. Don't you think you've punished him enough? If this doesn't prove that to you that he really loves this girl, I don't know what will. Don't hurt him any more Ben, He's like our own child. Yes, he is. He said. Give him a chance. He needs her, and she needs him. She pauses. They need each other.

He pulls her close to him. I'm sorry dear. I'll tell him tonight, just like I promised. Oh God thank you!

Cause I can't stand to see him like this. I have a confession to make love. Yes, what is it? He was getting to me too. I couldn't stand to see him like that any more either. He really does love her doesn't he? Yes, yes he does Ben. I'll tell him ok? Good, now go and get him, so he can go and get Lisa. Alright love. He kisses her on the cheek. Johnathan! Come in here son. He walks back into the kitchen. Yeah, dad. Lets

Go and get your little brother before something else happens. Lets go pops! They leave together.

They get into to town and bail Yosef out of jail. Thank you for getting me outta this place. What happened man? Said Johnathan. How did you get yourself arrested? He asked. They

leave in Johnathan's car. To go home. Well I had stopped over in Billy's neighborhood, I knew that it was a long shot, but I was desperate man. I saw Billy and Helen out for a walk together. I asked if they had seen her. They had heard about the break up. Billy and I had words, then. Rev. Anderson could see that it was getting difficult for him to go on. He stops him. That's not what's important son, the main thing is you're outta there, and safe with your family now. Those words brought comfort and belonging to Yosef, he appreciated them. I'm sorry dad, I didn't mean to be such a bother to you and mom, and to you too big bro.
This is not your fault son, I have something to tell you. Oh, oh. I forgot! Forgot what? Said Rev. Anderson. I forgot Lisa's car. I left it over in Billy's neighborhood. We have to go over and get it dad, there's no telling what he'll do to it. Johnathan drives them over to get Lisa's car. It was still parked where he left it, it was still locked, and in tact. He gets out and goes over to the car. Johnathan follows him. Why don't you follow us back home man. Said Johnathan. No, I don't feel like going home right now john. I can't. going there only reminds me of Lisa. If I go there, I'll, I'll. He stammered, breaking a little. Johnathan felt sorry for him. Yosef puts his head down on the top of the car crying hard. I think that I know what you need about now. Yosef lifts his head looking at him. Yeah, and what's that my man? A

Little pick me up. Yosef shakes his head laughing. Look, stay right here. I'll be right back. Yosef unlocks the car and gets inside. Hey dad. Me and Jo have to make a stop first before we come home ok?
We shouldn't be long. Rev, Anderson looks at his watch. It was 12:30a.m. Rev. Anderson gets out of the car. He looks at Johnathan. They felt a bond at that moment that they hadn't felt in a long while. He takes him in his arms embracing him. What's that for dad? Oh, just to say I love you son. And I'm so darn proud of you. He kisses him on his bald head. Thanks dad. I love you too man. He said patting him playfully on his shoulder. We'll be home soon. Ok son, but no foolishness ok? Ok. He said. You take care of one another, be careful. We will dad. Tell mom not to worry. Get outta here boy! He said laughing at him. Johnathan goes back to the car, Yosef had already started it and was waiting for him.

He gets inside. Now my little brother. I want to take you to this little spot I know. A place where I go to unwind when I have some things that need sorting out. Where is this place? Just follow my finger. He said, they both laugh. They pull up to a small hole in the wall kind of place. A cross between a café and
A night club. It was dark and quiet. It was called the Night Owl. It opened only dusk, and stayed opened until daybreak. I've never seen this place before. Yosef said looking around. There were all sorts of people there that frequented the little club. Especially forbidden lovers. It was a hot spot for this kinda thing. Yosef and Johnathan go inside. They find that it was even darken in there, than outside. The lights were dim, the music was playing softly in the background. It was a real laid back atmosphere. Towards the back is were the smokers lounged and played their games, slow dancing and whatever else they do back there. They find a small booth over in a corner just before the entrance into the back lounge. They sit down a their table. A very tall and handsome young man approaches their booth. He was around six feet three, lean, muscular, with curly black hair. Between 25-30ish. He was their waiter for the morning. His voice was deep, and sexy. The kind of voice that would melt the heart of any woman. As well as his light brown hazel eyes. What can I do for you gentlemen this morning? He said. His voice attracted some of the women there. One woman sighed out loud when she heard him. It was almost as if you could see her poor little heart pounding in an uncontrollable frenzy. Yosef and Johnathan laugh a little. I'll have your best house champagne please my man. Said Johnathan. Very good sir. He said. Champange! What for?

Said Yosef. To celebrate your official membership into our family little bro. We love you boy! Don't you know that by now? Said Johnathan smiling at him. But I'm not married yet John. So. But you will be soon. He said smiling at him still. Yosef smiles a little himself. I hope so man, I really hope so. Yosef stares off blankly for a moment his thoughts all on Lisa. What was she doing about now? What was happening to her? Johnathan noticed his moment. Where are you man? He asked him. Yosef looked over at him. What? Yosef answered. What's up with you? You look down. You know what's up with me John. I'd give anything to change what I did. His mind flowing back in time to his break up with Lisa at

237

The hospital. Johnathan could see his depression returning to him even more now. I have no words to describe what I'm feeling at this moment man. I can't stand it, everytime I think about what I did to her.
I feel sick all over. Johnathan looks at him nodding his head. It's called the Blues man. That's when the

Heart of a man experiences true brokenness over his one and only true love. A love that he never forgets, it's like his whole being has just been pulled out of him when she's gone. Yosef looks at him. That's what I feel like John, like all of my insides have just been pulled out of me. I feel so empty man. I can't sleep, I can't think. Well, she's all I think about when I do. It's like I'll die if I don't get her back man. I just hope she takes me back John. He holds his head down, his eyes misty . he resembled his mother a little, in her agony over her husband. I remember the last time that I cried over her John, it's as clear as a bell in my mind. We had broken up over some junk about her and Billy. Me and Helen. It was the night that he attacked her. Come on man, don't go there again. Said Johnathan. We're already there bro. I'll never forget that as long as I live. Yosef reminds John of that night that he and Lisa broke up over a misunderstanding. He accused her of sleeping with Billy, because Billy had spread a nasty rumour bragging that he had slept with her. Yosef wouldn't listen to Lisa's side of the story, he left her in a rage

In his haste, he happened upon Helen, who was as heart broken over Billy as he was over Lisa. So to spite Lisa and Billy they went out together. This is what Helen had been waiting for most of her life. She always had a crush on Yosef. Just as Billy had on Lisa. He took her to his and Lisa's favorite restaurant Bernie's. But the whole time they were there. He thought of nothing and no one but Lisa. He remembered he and Helen sitting at the table, her thoughts on ravishing him, his mind on Lisa. Come on Jo, forget about her. She was never any good for you anyway. And besides, it never would've worked. A Jewish man, and a black woman? People did talk about you two you know. What did you have in common with her any way? He never answered her. Once we've been together, you'll forget all about little ole jemimah. Yosef glared at her for that remark. She

reaches over to try to squeeze his thigh. He pushes her hand away. No, Helen. I can't do this, I just can't do this! But come on Jo, please. I'm hot for you, I always have been.
I want you! He looks at her. Well, I don't want you. Look Helen, no offense, I'm sure you're a nice person in your own way. But I'm in love with someone else. I 'm in love with Lisa, I always have been

And I always will be. Don't you understand? I could never love you, I will never love you! She felt her heart sink deep within her, she knew it was the truth. She stands up from the table. How could you love somebody like that! She slept with Billy! She fired at him. She attracted the attention of some of the people there. No she didn't! she tried to tell me, but I didn't listen to her. It was all a lie to break us up
And you know it! He turns to leave. No! Please don't go Yosef, I'm sorry for what I said about Lisa! I take it back! I take it all back! She said grabbing his arm. Don't touch me! He said snatching away from her. He beckons for the waiter to come, he gives him a twenty. Keep the change. Thank you Mr. Epstien. I hope to see you and Lisa back soon sir. Yosef smiles at him. Thanks Maurice, thanks man. He puts a ten dollar bill on the table for Helen to take a taxi home. Jo please! She reaches for him again, stumbling over the chair. She had been drinking and smoking heavily. I'll get you for this! You both will pay for this Yosef! You hear me!! She screamed. Everyone in the restaurant was looking at her shaking their heads.
Yosef returns home early from his date from hell with Helen. He gets out of the car, he looks over at Lisa's parents house. The lights were off. He wondered what Lisa was doing about now. He starts to wonder about her date with Billy. What he didn't know, is that she was just as unhappy with Billy as he was with Helen. He starts to walk over but turns to go home. Just then he hears a scream coming from the Anderson's backyard. It was Lisa's voice. Lisa.....? He whispered He runs back there to find that Billy was viciously attacking her. Come on Lisa you want it, You've always wanted it. Now I'm gonna take you! You'll never want that Jew boy again after you've had a taste of me. I'd rather kiss a snaggle toothed jack-ass Billy. He glared at her snatching her up off the ground. Yosef heard what she said to him, he smiled big at her. He tried to kiss her. No! Billy! No! she struggles to get away from him. He had been drinking just as much as Helen. Yosef thought for a moment to where Helen tried

to kiss him at the restaurant, the thought of her kissing him, made him just as nauseated, just as Billy made Lisa. I'm sure you would. Come here! He snatches her close to him trying to kiss her. Stop! Please Billy Stop! He slaps her to the ground again. Ahhhh! She screams. Louder this time. A light comes on upstairs, it was

Her parents bedroom light. Deborah jumps up out of bed, and runs over to the bedroom window. To her horror, she sees Billy assaulting Lisa. Oh, dear Lord! Ben! Ben! Get up quick! Hurry! It's Lisa, Billy's beating her! What! Oh my God! Said Rev. Anderson. He fumbles in the dim light of his wife's night Lamp from her bedside table to find the switch on his own bedside lamp. He turns it on. He can barely see, his eyes still not focused from his sleep yet. He fumbles over his eye glasses finding them. He puts them on getting out of bed. He grabs his robe, and puts on his slippers. They both run down the stairs to the kitchen. Somebody help me please! Billy tears and rips her black blouse off of her shoulders. He slaps her again, throwing her to the ground laughing sadistically at her. Heh,heh,heh. Lisa then notices Yosef standing over in the darkness looking at them. Yosef help me pleeeeaasssseeee! She cries. Help me! Beloved! Help me! At her cries, Yosef's body then begin to swell with rage, his eyes tight. His fists clenched. He started walking slowly towards them. Billy never heard him. Your Jew boy aint here brown sugah. He's with that little cow Helen. So what if she takes him from you, Chicago's a big place. There's plenty of fish in the sea right? Heh,heh,heh. Yosef, help! Her cries for his help sparked something in him for her. All he could think about was getting to her, and killing Billy. Shut up! He said slapping her again

Harder this time. Knocking her unconscious. He undoes his belt and zipper. I'm gonna enjoy this. He said. Just then a large hand reaches out of the darkness and spins him around abruptly. It was Yosef. A look of savage anger in his eyes. Rev. Anderson had taught Yosef and Johnathan some of his combat martial arts when he was in the Service. It paid off. Yosef punches Billy hard in the face knocking him to the ground. Billy jumps up and charges after him like a wild bull. I'm gonna kick

240

me some Jew butt. He said spitting out the blood where his mouth was bleeding. As he charged at him, Yosef stood in a defensive
Martial arts stance and beckoned for him to come on. Billy screamed out loud charging at him. Yosef then executes a beautiful roundhouse kick, three of them in a row. Knocking Billy to the ground again. Billy crumpled in a heap to the ground. He looked dazed, he tried to get up, but couldn't manage it. At that time Rev. Anderson and Deborah had already come outside, they saw the whole thing. Deborah had picked up Lisa's head placing her in her lap fussing over her. Rev. Anderson watching over them both.

Yosef walked over to Billy looking at him in disgust. If you ever touch her, if you so much as even look at her again Billy. I'll Kill you! You hear me! I'll kill you man! He shouted at him. Yosef was so angered at Billy his whole body vibrated with rage. Billy fell back to the grass unconscious this time. Yosef walks away from him and over to where Deborah and Rev. Anderson was. Deborah was still crying over Lisa.

Oh God Lisa! He mother cried. Rev. Anderson walks up to him. Shaking his hand. That was quite a display there son. Well done. Well done. He was proud of him. Thank you dad. I was just.... No need to explain son. I know what you were doing. He interrupted him. They walk over to Lisa and Deborah. She was still crying over her. Oh Ben, I can't get her to wake up! I think she's dead. She's not breathing!
She's not dead mom. Said Yosef softly, his long hair flowing gently in the night air. She looks up at him. How do you know that? Look at her! How do you know she's not dead? He looks at Lisa his tightened features had begun to soften now, as his beloved Lisa lay helpless in her mother's arms. How do you know she's not dead Yosef? She asked him again. Because I'm still alive. He said softly smiling a little. May I? He asked Rev. Anderson. He bent down and gently took Lisa's limp body from her mother's arms into his. Deborah runs ahead of them to get the backdoor for them. They all go inside the house as Yosef carries Lisa upstairs to her bedroom. He gently lays her on her bed. He kisses her on her forehead. She was bruised a little from Billy's assault. His heart broke for her. He begins to cry painfully for her. Oh, Lisa! How could I go out with that girl when I have you? He cried. I'm so sorry. Her mother returns to her

room with her first aid kit to clean and dress her wounds. Jo-Jo, let me get in here baby ok? I have to tend to her. He brushes his long hair back stepping away. Ok mom. May I stay here with her? Please dad, this is all my fault to begin with. If it wasn't for me, this never would've happened to her. I never should've left her dad. Please! Please let me stay! He looks at Deborah busy fussing over Lisa. Ok son. But no uh.... Of course not! Said Yosef. I just want to be near her that's all. I'll sit right here. I promise.

He goes over by the window and gets Lisa's white rocking chair and pulls it up next to her bedside. When Deborah had finished, Rev. Anderson took her outside the room. He's gonna sit with her for a while dear ok? But I don't think that's a good idea honey. Said Deborah. They'll be fine love, the door's open, and we're right across the hall ok? She looks at him staring at Lisa. Deborah felt compassion for Yosef at that moment. She didn't have the heart to say no at that point. Look honey, he was raised in this house with her. If he was gonna try anything, he would've done it a long time ago. They both laughed. He's a good boy, he won't do anything to betray our trust in him. Come on, lets go to bed now. Frankly I feel a lot safer knowing he's here with her. He said to her. His words comforting her. She smiles at him. Oh Ben. Whatever you say dear. Alright honey. Deborah goes back in Lisa's room. Jo? Yes ma'mam.
If she needs me for anything, you come and wake me ok? I promise mom. Alright now, behave yourself.
She said smiling, kissing him on his forehead. And do something about this hair! She said mussing it on his head. Mom....? She leaves them. He pulls the rocker closer to Lisa's bedside. He looks at her, his heart couldn't take it any more, he just had to feel her in his arms. He gets out of the chair and sits down next to her stroking her cheek his hair falling into his face. Oh Lisa! He sighed. He slides off the bed onto the floor, his hand still across her stomach. He cries silently, his eyes closed tight. She stirs a little. Uhhhh. The weak voice sighed. Yosef. She whispered. He jumps up off the floor back onto her bed

I'm right here baby. She opens her eyes, smiling big at him. Even with her bruises, she still looked beautiful to him. My

242

Beloved. She reaches up to him playing with his hair as it hung in his face. She stroked his cheek. I love you so much Yosef,so much I love you! She said in a breathy tone. Oh God Lisa! He gathers her up into his arms. I love you too baby! I love you too! I'm so sorry Lisa, Please forgive me! I'll never leave you again! Never! Shhh. Beloved, there's nothing to forgive. He looks at her. God! You're beautiful! He said in a breathy tone. Are you gonna stay with me tonight? I'll stay with you as long as you want me to. He smiles at her. She brushes the tears from his eyes. Yosef? Yes.

Will you kiss me? Tears flowing from her eyes. Anything you say baby, anything you say. They kiss tenderly. Here is your champagne sir. The waiter's voice sounded. Snapping Yosef back into the now.
He wiped the tears from his eyes. Johnathan was a little misty eyed himself as he listened to Yosef reminiscening about the "Incident" as everyone called it back then. The waiter sat the champagne glasses down on the table, then the ice bucket with the champagne bottle inside. He popped the cork, then poured each glass. Here's to love. Said Johnathan. To love. Said Yosef, his voice trembling a little, his thoughts were now heavy on Lisa. They drink the cold beverage. Ahh! Good stuff! Said Johnathan. Yosef nodded his head. Here, have another my man. Yosef holds out his glass. Pour on mine host. They both laughed.

Yosef drank, and drank, and drank. Johnathan knew that he would end up driving them back home. So he just let Yosef drink himself out cold. Two hours later, Yosef could hardly sit up at the table. Lisaaaahhhh! He cried out loud. Shhh! Be quiet man. I can't help it man, I miss my girl. I didn't mean it John, you believe me don't you Big bro. His voice slurred. Yes, I believe you Jo, now come on with me. I have to go and get the check ok? Here, sit down until I come back. He takes Yosef over by the lounge area near the entrance into the club, and sits him in one of the big lounge chairs. Yosef's head falls back, his hair falling in his face again. Yosef opens his eyes and yells out loud. Ahhh! What's the matter Jo? I can't see! I can't see man! Johnathan comes over to him and pushes his hair out of his face. Yosef turned to look at Johnathan and screams again. Ahh! Now what's the matter? Oh, it's just you. Jo, stay here ok? I'll be right back. He leaves to pay the check. He comes back over to him, and helps him out of the soft chair.

I'm so sorrryyyyy Lisaaaahhhh! Cried Yosef. He stumbled into Johnathan's arms. Oops there. He said. Helping Yosef out the front door. Johnathan walks him outside, the warm summer air felt good to him.

Yosef then begins to feel a little nauseated, he rubs his stomach. Oh, oh. Said Yosef. What's the matter man? I don't feel so good John. I need to lay down for a while. Yeah, maybe you'll feel better tomorrow.

Oh wait a minute, it's already tomorrow. He said laughing. Yosef grabs mouth, and staggers out of Johnathan's arms, back behind the building, and heaves up the champagne. Maybe not. He said. Yosef staggers back to the car, Johnathan helps him inside, they leave to go home.

The Colour Of Love
Anne Hemingway
Chap 25.

Johnathan and Yosef arrive home. Johnathan turns the car off, and looks at the house. The lights are all off. Good the folks are in bed. Now maybe I can sneak you inside, and get you to bed. Johnahtan puts his keys in his pants pocket, and gets out to let Yosef out on the other side. He helps him up the porch steps. They get to the front door, Johnathan fumbles around in his pocket for his house keys, but Yosef keeps slipping from his arms. Lisaaaahhhh! He shouts. Shhhh! Put a sock in it man! You trying to wake up everybody? I want my baby! I miss her! I know you miss her, but be quiet about it! Said Johnathan finding his keys. Lise.....! said Yosef as he was trying to call out her name again. Johnathan puts his hand over his mouth to quiet him. They walk inside, he shuts the front door, and starts walking him up the stairs.

You'll have to sleep in our old room, we still have our bunk beds in there. I just have to get you upstairs that's all. Come on now. Good boy. Yosef misses the first stair. They both stumble nearly falling down.

Shhh! Careful man! If you wake mom and dad, we're in deep....
The hall light comes on in the stairway.
Johnathan turns around carrying Yosef with him. It was his
father. Doo,doo. Rev. Anderson began to breathe heavy. He
walked up to them, Yosef was still crying over Lisa, tears running
down his face.
Hi dad. Breathed Yosef. Rev. Anderson flinches at his
champagne breath. And uh, what have we here?
He said smiling at Johnathan. Johnathan looks around smiling
too. They both laugh. Rev. Anderson stops laughing abruptly,
smacking Johnathan on the back of his head. Ow! Dad! He
said. What do you mean going out and getting him drunk like
this? I thought you said that you were going to stop off, then
you'd be back home. We did stop off. Rev. Anderson takes a
deep breath in frustration at Johnathan. So we're a little late. A
little late! It's 3:00 in the morning boy! Ben! Deborah calls out.
Lisaaahhh! Yelled Yosef.
He bagan to slip from Johnathan's arms again. Look dad, can we
talk in my room, he's heavy. Come on, I'll help you. He said,
taking Yosef by his other arm. They take him into their old
bedroom, and gently lay him down on the soft bed. Oh, Lisa! I'm
sorry! I didn't mean it, I didn't mean to hurt you. He cried. Dad.
He reached up to hug Rev. Anderson by the neck. Jo, lay down
son. But I didn't meant to hurt her

I swear it! You gotta believe me! His voice trembling. I believe
you son, I believe you. Rev,. Anderson assured him. He lays
back down on the pillow. She'll never marry me now dad, I know
it. Now I wouldn't say that. He said comforting him again.
Johnathan help will you help me with his coat son?
Johnathan nods his head, and helps his father take off Yosef's
suit coat and his shoes. Johnathan goes over to his dresser
drawer and pulls out a pair of pajama bottoms. Here, put these
on. He flings them over to Yosef, they landed on his face.
Johnathan comes over to try to help him take his slacks off. I
can do the rest man. He said from underneath the pj's. he pulls
them off his face, and sits up in bed. he felt a little woozy at first,
but he manages to stand to his feet. He lifts one leg, and
attempts to put his foot in. He misses and falls face forward to
the floor. Rev. Anderson tries to keep a dignified face, even
though he knew he wanted to bust up laughing. Johnathan was
already doing that. Rev. Anderson looks down at him on the

floor. Are you alright son? He laughed. I'm fine dad, I'm fine.
His face still smashed to the floor.
Rev. Anderson looks up at Johnathan, who was still laughing at
him Rev. Anderson clears his throat.   Help him! He said, trying
to be serious, even though he was still laughing himself.   They
both pick him up off the floor,and help him get dressed for bed.
He lays back again on the soft bed. he looks up at the ceiling.

He sits up in bed, still wobbly. He reaches out to grab Rev.
Anderson. Dad, can you do me a favor? What is it son? Stop
this room from spinning! It's hot in here! He said wiping his face.
Rev. Anderson puts his hand on Yosef's forehead. Johnathan,
could you go and get me a cold towel? He nods his head, and
goes into the bathroom. Rev. Anderson looks at him he felt him
for the moment. All Yosef's hurt, his fears, his uncertainties as
whether Lisa would marry him or not. Or if Rev. Anderson would
even let him marry her now. He knew that he had to tell him
about Lisa at that moment. Yosef? He never answered him.
Yosef?
Look at me son. Yosef opens his eyes to look at him. I have
something to tell you. Is it about my girl?
Yes, it's about Lisa. Yosef raises up in bed slightly He looks at
Rev. Anderson, he too felt a connection of some sort. He knew
what Rev. Anderson was about to tell him. You know where Lisa
is don't you? Yes, I know where she is. I've always known where
she was. Yosef smiled a little, at least that put him closer to her
than he was before. He felt a tremendous burden lift from his
shoulders, as well as his heart. Why
Didn't you tell me dad?   He takes a deep breath. Because I
wanted you to prove yourself that's all. Prove myself? To who?
To you? No, not to me, my wife, or even to Lisa. But to yourself.
I don't know what you mean. Well for starters. If you didn't
really love my daughter, you never wouldn've gone out and done
this. Done what? Well look at you. You went out and got
yourself into a fight, arrested, and drunk

All in one night. To me, that's the sign of a man very deeply in
love. You reminded me of myself there when me and Deborah
broke up. Yosef gasped. You and mom broke up once dad? Yes,
we did. I can't picture that about you not being with her. He

246

said. Well, it's true. I told her this earlier this evening, now I'll tell you. When she left me, I thought that I would die. Just like you. Son, it was the closest thing to death that I've ever experienced in my life. As far as I was concerned being without my woman I was already dead. It was like death to me. I've never experienced a heartbreak like that before. How long was she gone for dad? Three months. Three months! Lisa's been gone for three days, and it feels like an eternity to me dad. I feel like a part of me is missing. He said with his head down. I know son, believe me I know. What did you do that brought her back? I couldn't stand it any longer, so I went to her, and apologized for the way that I behaved. And I never saw that girl again. What girl? Someone that I used to date before I met Deborah. I met her after me and this girl broke up. I instantly fell in love with Deborah.

I still had not resolved all my feelings for Nina yet. I felt sorry for her one night, she and her new boyfriend were having some problems, and she came to me. She knew that I was in love with Deborah, but she didn't care. She wanted revenge. I didn't know this at the time, and one thing led to another. Deborah caught us in the midst of this leading. We were kissing, and Deborah walked in on us. I'll never forget the look on her face as long as I live. You would've that that she had died right there on the spot.
Just like Lisa. Said Yosef. My father saw how heartbroken I was over her leaving, and he decided that he would put me out of my misery. He had a long talk with me about what happened between us. He shared something with me that I've never forgotten. Now I'll share it with you. He told me that many a man has lost his dignity, self respect, even the love of a good woman over his lust for that of another. He asked me. How do you feel now? Now that your one and only has left you? I told him, I felt like hell! He then said this to me. Son, there is no need for any man to chase after a piece of hell, when God has given you a slice of Heaven. You see some men measure their manliness by how many women they've had. But he said no Ben, that's not true. For the true manliness of a man is not measured by how well he keeps many women of the world. But by how well he keeps the one and only woman that God gave him. You see Jo, I lost Deborah all for nothing. I let my lust for another get in the way with what I had with my one and only love. And when I saw that I had been "played". I then quickly began to re-evaluate my life and my relationship with God and with Deborah. I knew that a choice had to be made. I then let all of

247

my feelings go for Nina, and when I did that. All of my love for Deborah blossomed like a rose in the springtime. It took some doing, but by the grace of God she came back to me. We've never been apart since. And I've never allowed anything or anybody to ever come between us again. Remember this son, it'll help you in your relationship with Lisa. I will dad, believe me, I will. I have something more to tell you. What is it?

Well I spoke to Lisa. You did? I mean what did she say, is she alright? Where is she? He interrupted him. Hold it, hold on there! He smiled. Dad, please, I have to know if my girl is alright. He pleaded, tears forming in his eyes again. She is alright son, and she has a message for you. Wha, what is it? He stammered. She said that she still wants to marry you. Yosef's face lit up like the fourth of July. She does? Yes, she does. She told you this herself? Yes she did, she called me early Friday morning. She said that she was miserable without you, but she only stayed away because she thinks that you hate her!
Hate her! How could she even conceive a thought like that dad? It's easy when you've been treated as unfairly as you treated her. Remember what I told you about that moment, how long would it last? Yosef lowers his head. He did remember. She thinks that you don't love her anymore,and she has to prove herself to you before you'll love her again. What! He breathed. Oh Jesus Lisa! How could I ever stop loving her dad? I can't even think like that about her. She doesn't have to prove a thing to me, not one thing dad. I love her I always have and I always will. I never stopped loving her, I never stopped. And I never will. He takes a deep breath. The news of Lisa made his heart sink deep within him. I'll do whatever it takes to make this right with her dad, anything. He said. Rev. Anderson nodded his head. I

Know son, but I'm not the one you need to convince, you now need to convince her. You can tell her that for yourself tomorrow. Well, today. Yosef looks at him surprised. What do you mean? I'm gonna take you to her son. Rev. Anderson had gotten off the bed and was standing in the middle of the bedroom waiting for Johnathan. Yosef staggers out of bed over to his adopted father. He throws his arms around him hugging him hard. I have no words to thank you dad. Rev. Anderson patting him on his back. I know son. Look get some rest now. She'll be

expecting you this afternoon. Clean, and dressed. And uh, about this hair...... he said mussing it all over his head. Dad....? He turns to get back in the bed. Oh, Yosef? Yeah dad. Here. He walks up to him, Rev. Anderson reaches into his robe pocket and pulls out Lisa's engagement ring. Yosef looks at him gasping. Ohhh! He shakes his head, tears flowing from his eyes.
She left it in her room before she left, I thought that you might want to take this with you when you see her and all. He embraces Rev. Anderson again crying harder this time. There, there now Jo-Jo. He pauses.
I love you son, I love you just like I love my own child. By the way where is that boy with that towel?
Never mind dad, he's playing in the water again. They both laugh a little. I love you dad, I love you and mom so much, Thank you all for putting up with me. Jo? That's what families are for. Get to bed now.
Yes sir. He said, He walks over to the bed looking at the ring sparkling like a small star in his hand.
He remembers the story that Rev. Anderson had told him about what Mr. Wawsczyk said about their first

Shipment of rings. He could still hear his voice echoing in his mind. *"It's like Heaven has come down to us in many colours."* He sets it down on the nightstand, he seemed to be mesmerized by it's shimmer. He lays down in bed, he never took his eyes off it. Johnathan then comes out with the towel. But by then Yosef had quickly fallen into a deep restful sleep. His thoughts all on Lisa. They heard a gentle snoring sound coming from him. I think he won't be needing this now son. Said Rev. Anderson softly. Maybe not now, but he will tomorrow when he sees Lisa. Give me that! Said Rev. Anderson snatching the towel from him. Get to bed! Yes sir! He said laughing. They both laugh together. Goodnight son, night dad.

Saturday came in early and hot, as this happens in the
Summertime. Everyone was awake and busy around the house.
Everyone except Yosef. They let him sleep in for a while. He was
beginning to stir a little, then he woke up abruptly. "Lisa!" he
said out loud. He rubs his head a little, then he attempted to get
out of bed. He fell right back again. His head spinning slightly.
There was evidence of a slight hangover present. Oh man! What
did I do last night? Dad! He yells. Rev. Anderson and Deborah
and Johnathan were all at the kitchen table having their coffee.
Looks like somebody's up. She said. I'll go dad. Said Johnathan.
He rushes upstairs to him. Morning bro. Good morning John.
Ready for the big day? Yosef looked at him. What did I do last
night? Johnathan looks at him smiling a very michevious smile.
Man you were wicked last night! Yosef's eyes widen, his mouth
hanging open. He was trying to talk, but surprise had taken his
words away from him. I thought you were gonna get arrested
again. Yosef stood up from the bed, his eyes still wide, his mouth
hung open even more. Finally his voice returns to him. What do
you mean? That blonde, man! Ooooooh weee! What! What
blonde? Boy if Lisa finds that out! Johnathan pauses laughing
at him. Yosef could then tell that Johanthan was messing with
him. You jerking me man! He said charging at him. His
hangover still not gone yet, reminds him that it's still present. He
staggers into Johanthan's arms. Hey! I cradled you last night.
Today, it's Lisa's turn. He said helping him to stand to his feet.
The mention of her name sobered him a little. He smiles, as he
feels a slight arousal coming on him. Oh, oh! What's that!
Teased Johnathan. Well there's one part of you that's up even if
the rest of you aint yet. Yosef covers himself with his hands.
Leave me alone man, I can't help it. And besides, haven't you
ever had a girl turn you on just thinking about her? He said
going back over to sit on the bed. He puts his pillow over his
slightly swollen groin.

Johnathan thinks a minute, he walks over to sit down beside him. Yeah, I have several. He said. John, don't you have that one special woman in your life, that one that you just can't live without? I mean what about Deneice? Johanthan thought about her, he did really love her,but he was afraid to admit it to her, to Yosef, and even more to himself. Yosef could see it in his expression, he smiles at him. You do love her don't you? Johanthan holds his head down. I'm gonna tell you something man. Just between brothers ok?
He said holding his hand out shaking it in brotherly fashion. Just between brothers man. You're right, I mean I just can't hide it anymore. I love Deneice. Just like you, I've never felt this way about a woman before. For the first time in my life Jo. I'm in love. And I'll tell you this. It feels darn good! Everytime I think about her. I, His feelings for her overwhelm him taking his words away from him. I know the feeling John, Believe me I know the feeling. He said looking underneath his pillow. His arousal was still present. Johanthan pauses a little, he looks at Yosef, curiosity speaking to him about her. He had always

Wondered what made him love Lisa so much, when there were so many other girls? What is it John? You want to ask me something, what is it? Johnathan chuckles a little. Why Lisa man? Why her? Yosef looks out the window. You'll have to ask God that one my man. I could've gone with just about anybody. But when I saw Lisa, something happened to me. I can't explain what it was. I just know that I can't live without her man. I can't! It's like God branded her in my heart forever. I mean, she's it for me. I can never let her go John. Never I'd rather die than loose her again. Johanthan nods his head. You love her that much man? Said Johanthan. And some, Said Yosef. Johnathan smiles at him. I didn't mean to tease you man. Yes you did man, you just couldn't resist a good tease couldn't you? Yosef interrupted him. You my blood. I 'm happy for you man, really. I'm happy for you. And I. He paused. I love you Jo-jo. He said tears in his eyes. I love you too big bro. They both embrace. They wipe their eyes of tears.
Johnathan looks at Yosef's pillow. You alright now? Yosef takes a peek underneath. Yeah, everything's calmed down now. I think I'll go take a shower. You do that, hope the water's cold. Said Johanthan. They both bust up laughing. Yosef dresses to go home. There he gets showered, and dressed. His mother even

cut and trimmed his hair! He has a brief talk with her of how he and his father had mended their ways, and that he gave he and Lisa his blessings on their pending marriage. He kissed her,, and left to go back over to the Anderson's home. Sarah called it his home away from home. Yosef goes inside calling out to anyone there. Hello! I'm back! We're in the kitchen! Deborah yells back. He walks inside, everyone was sitting at the kitchen table. Rev. Anderson was sipping on his cappuccino, and Johanthan on his coffee, as was Deborah. Mamie had left to go into town with one of her friends from the Entertainment hall. Everyone had plans for that Saturday evening. Johanathan was taking Deneice to Dinner, then to the movies, then to the beach. Rev. Anderson and Deborah had some plans of their own to go to prayer meeting then out to supper with Rev. Mathews and his wife Irene. As Yosef walked into the kitchen, Johnathan stops driking his coffee to whistle at him. Dad, don't get too close. He may cut cha he's so `sharp. Yosef, you look very handsome in that suit son. Said Deborah. He was dressed in his usual

Casual wear. Dark navy blue slacks with matching shirt, and outer coat. And Black shoes. He was beaming with joy, as he was nearing the time that he would be reunited with Lisa. How do you feel son?
Asked Rev. Anderson walking over to shake his hand. I feel better now. My mother gave me some homade broth and some ginger ale. I feel 100 % better. I trust this won't happen again tonight when you and Lisa celebrate getting back together. You can trust me dad. No way will I ever do that again. Where's
Your get up and go little bro. Teased Johnathan. Thanks to you, it got up and went. Said Rev. Anderson.
Deborah laughed at them. A little pick me up, and he can't handle it. Said Johnathan still teasing. Your
Little pick me up, laid him down last night boy. Said his father. Johnathan laughed, he and Deborah. Well, that's all over now now. I called Lisa about twenty minutes ago, and she can't wait to see you son.
Really? Said Yosef. Yeah, she said so herself. Said Deborah.

Getting up coming over to him. Now you two boys had better get going. You don't want to keep her waiting now do you? He looks at his adopted mother, seeing Lisa in every expression on her face. He smiles no ma'mam. I wouldn't want to do that. She

252

kisses him on the cheek. What was that for? Oh, just to say I love you son. You're just like my own child Yosef. You've been a part of our lives for so long, I can't see my daughter with anyone else but you. You may not be the son of our bodies, but you are the son of our hearts to me and my husband. And we love you so very deeply Yosef. We always have. Yosef becomes teary eyed. So did Rev Anderson and Johnathan. A pause between them. I'll never forget what you have done for me. Thanks for being my family. You're welcome honey, so welcome. My dearest. I love you jo-jo. We love you so much.

She said, tears streaming down her soft brown face. Oh, Sarah buzzed your hair for you! It looks great honey. She said mussing it on his head. Mom.....? What you give me mouth now, I do this all your life, nothing. Now you speak. And this I need eh? Eh. Said Rev. Anderson and Johnthan together.

Yosef looks at them all laughing. Oh, Jesus! My mother's contagious. They all bust up laughing.

Rev. Anderson looks at his watch. It was 12:30p.m. You ready son? Said Rev. Anderson. Yes sir, I'm ready. He said smiling. He was touched to belong to such a loving and caring family. They loved him, and he knew it, and he loved them the same. Rev. Anderson kissed his wife. See you this afternoon honey, wear something pretty for me tonight. He said, speaking about their outing with Rev. Mathews. I will baby. Stay out of trouble you. He said to Johnthan. Yes, sir! He said saluting him. Come on Jo, let's go and get my child. I'm with you dad. They both leave to go to South Haven, Michigan to get Lisa. They

Went in Rev. Anderson's car, since Lisa had the family van. They talked all the way up there about many things. From the break up to babies. It was a meaningful time for the two of them. The trip took two and a half hours as they drove up I-94. they get to Bangor, Michigan and stop at a hot chicken spot there for a quick drink of tea. They finally get into to town. South Haven was beautiful this time of year. It is high season there now. So there were tourists from all over the Country visiting. It is a most beautiful resort city. One of the most top rated in the Country. It was early June now, and Harborfest was to kick off soon.

The city was buzzing with excitement waiting for this wonderful event to take place. Rev. Anderson and Yosef drove all up and down Northshore Dr. and looked at all the nice homes in the area. Yosef gasped as he beheld the sights. It was simply breathtaking! On they drove until they came to the Harborside of Northshore Dr. Look, out there son. Yosef looks at the harbor, seeing all the incredible sailboats, and yachts there. Whoa! He breathed. Dad, this is awesome! He turned the car around and headed back to the Northshore Beach. He pulls into the beach parking lot, driving slowly. Look over there Yosef. Rev. Anderson points to a large beach home with hanging flower pots. Geez! This is beautiful! Yes, it is. My wife and I bought this place when Lisa was just a baby. We always brought her here, Johanathan loves it here too. But Lisa was especially attracted to this little place. As she grew, her love for this place grew with her. Yosef pauses a moment. Dad. May I ask you a question? Yes, of course. How did you know Lisa was here? Never underestimate the bond between a father and his daughter. At first I didn't, but when I missed her the night that she left. She was so deeply hurt over the break up and all. I guess she couldn't stand being around the house knowing that you wouldn't be back, or so she thought that you wouldn't. Well, anyway. I began to miss her terribly. I couldn't sleep, Deborah kept me up most of the night anyway pacing the floor worrying about her. Which of course you can understand. Yosef nodded his

Head. Since I was already up, and knew I wouldn't sleep, I got up and went into her room, and turned on the light. When she wasn't there in bed. Something happened to me. I don't know what. It's like I felt her hurt in a way that's inexpressible to me. I went over to her bed, and sat down. I never felt so empty in all my life. Yosef nodded his head in agreement, he had felt the same way himself. Then I looked on her nightstand and discovered that she had left her engagement ring there. But I also noticed something that unfortunately my wife missed. A clue that she left me. What was that? Yosef asked. Well I noticed that not only had she left her ring, but that she had taken her favorite lighthouse with her. Her favorite lighthouse? Asked Yosef. Yeah, it's a long story, I won't go into all that right now. But whenever she wanted to come to South Haven, she would bring it to me and her mother and say. Let's go see the little lighthouse daddy! We never said no to her. It's kinda hard to say no to Lisa. There's something about her that has always had me and her mother baffled. And what's that? Well, it's her purity of spirit, a certain kind of tenderness of heart quality that she has. We don't know where she gets that from. But because of it, we've always been very guarded over her. That's why we were concerned when the two of you found

Interest in each other. Why dad, because I'm a Jew? No, no son. Not because of that. It's kind of hard to explain. See Lisa has the kind of soul, that finds it even more difficult to say no, than it is for you or me to say no to her. She's so giving and caring. She really knows what it means to give of yourself to others without asking for anything in return. I know that like everyone else, she has her little ways about her. She can be quite the spoiled one at times. But I've always admired this about my daughter, She never let our spoiling of her, ruin her. She's maintained a kind of wisdom in our giving to her. I'll always appreciate that quality in her. I'm sure you will too. I already do dad. Lisa, if she can will do just about anything for anybody. She simply loves to love. She's in love with loving. I don't know if that makes any sense or not, but she is. No matter who they are or aren't, she loves people. She will even try to find some

Good in everybody, even those who mistreat her. She'll still find something good to say about that person, or go out of her way to love them. That's what concerned me and her mother. People often take qualities like hers for weaknesses. When they are in fact strengths to her. Lisa finds her strength in love. I'm so proud of her son. She has made me and her mother very proud. So you see Yosef, I couldn't just let any one marry my daughter. I felt that the man who married her had darn well be established in God, have a relationship with Jesus Christ. Someone with morals, and with the means to take care of her. Not some Don juan wanna be out there sleeping with every Tilly, Tally, and Ally that comes around. Laying up around the house doing nothing but vegging out being non-productive. While she's out working herself to death trying to take care of him and everything else. I would never do her like that dad! He interrupted. I know you wouldn't Jo, I was just saying, that's pretty much the thinking of some men these days. Not all men, but some. You have proven to me and my wife, that you meet all the qualities that would make you a good husband to Lisa. We know that you really love her, and we trust her in your care. Thank you dad,

255

you don't know what that means to me to hear you say that.
Well, I was a little skeptical there for a while.
What do you mean? Well when you hurt Lisa the way that you
did. I mean that was a rather drastic move to call off your
engagement over a misunderstanding. Son, you don't know how
much you broke our hearts when you did that. But even more
how deep you hurt Lisa. Yosef held his head down. He did know.
The wounds that it caused him were reopened again. The pain of
them was as fresh now as it was then when she left. I'm so sorry
dad. I didn't mean to overreact like that. All I know, is that I'll
never do this again ever! There was a pause between them. Is
that why you didn't tell me where Lisa was? Yes, it was Jo, yes it
was. I felt that you needed to be taught a lesson. And maybe
this will cool that temper of yours. Believe me dad, it has. I've
learned my lesson. Believe me I have. Yosef paused. Dad? Yes
son. I'm sorry for hurting the family like I did. I really didn't
mean for any of this to happen. Jo, I don't hurt my child, and I
won't stand for anyone else doing that to her either. Yes sir. I
hope you can forgive me dad. There's nothing to forgive son.
Your apology means a lot to me, I feel that I can rest now. And So
can you. We're here. They pull in behind the family van. Yosef
looks at the cottage. This is beautiful dad! Yes it is son. Now
remember the past is past. Yes, sir. Ok, you're on your own now
boy. Go

In there and get engaged again, and stay that way this time! He
said laughing. Aren't you coming in with me? No, I'm not. This
is between you and her now. And besides, I have a long drive
back home, and me and Deborah have some pretty hot plans of
our own tonight. Yosef smiles. I hear that dad. He said,
slapping fives with him. And uh, by the way. I know how you
young kids are these days. You haven't seen her in a while. So
keep yourself cool if you know what I mean. I do dad, but tell
that to my harmones. They laugh. Get outta here boy! Hey!
Yosef turns around. If she's in there. Go down the hall to the
right first room! Yosef gives him a thumbs up. Rev. Anderson
pulls off. Yosef scales all the stairs.
He didn't even knock on the door, or ring the doorbell. He just
turned the knob, and opened the door.
Geez! They don't lock their doors around here! He goes inside.
The house was bright warm and welcoming. The Summer Sun
was streaming in through the windows. He takes a deep breath,
the smell of

Nostalgia in the air. It was about 2:30p.m. He remembers what Rev.Anderson told him. He went down the hall to the first room. It's a soft pink and white pastel room, there were pictures on the wall from when she was a little girl. Next to it was a picute of the little red lighthouse that she loved. Tucked inside was a family picture of her and her parents, and him after his Bar Mitzvah. I haven't seen this picture in years.

He whispered. His heart fills with longing for her at that moment. Just then he hears a gentle sigh. He looked over to the right of him, stretched out on the white laced bed, dressed in a soft powder pink sun dress was Lisa. He takes a deep breath, and begins to walk slowly over towards her almost like in a trance like state. The Sun shining off her hitting her just right, she looked like a bronze angel. Whoa! He breathed. He sat down next to her, unable to take his eyes off her. She was still sleeping, but not restfully, she seemed disturbed about something. He moved in closer to her, her soft breast were rising up nd down Like two tender melons. Yosef bent closer to kiss her gently on the lips. She sighed again. His arousal was excruciating. She moans sensuously at his kiss. Yosef looks down, his manhood is like stone. Jesus! He said at the sight of himself. He takes his outer coat off and lays it across his lap. Behave yourself! He said to it. Lisa's heartbeat began to speed up more, she knew that it was him, her beloved he had come for her! She slowly opened her eyes and saw him there struggling to keep himself concealed from her. He was trying to hide his arousal, but she knew better. Yosef. She breathed to him. He stopped his struggling, and looked up at her. Her smile was one like he never seen before. He was so taken by it at that moment, he could not speak. He just sat there batting his eyes at her, as they welled up with tears. Oh God! He breathed. LISA! YOSEF! They both said she reaches up to him, he pulls her up onto his lap.

They embrace hard, crying into each others arms. Beloved! She cries to him. It is you, isn't it? It's really you Yosef? Yes, it's me baby, it's me. He said kissing her all over her face and neck, she kissing him the same. I'm so glad that you're here! Me too Lisa, me too! I thought you had left me forever he said to her.

Shhh! Not now beloved, just let me enjoy you, I've missed you so. She said tears flowing down her soft brown face. Ahhh! She sighs as she feels the hardness of his manhood underneath her. She stops and looks at him. I, I. She stuttered. I thought that you hated me, that's why I stayed away. She cried. No, no. Lisa. I can't even think like that about you. She attempted to speak again. He puts his index finger on her lips. I'm here now baby, that's all that matters now. Lisa opens her mouth, and swallows his finger sucking it gently. Ooh! He moans out softly. She leans down to kiss him, opening his mouth with her tongue. She slides it slowly into his mouth. They deep kiss tenderly. Lisa raises up on his lap, straddling him . she unbottons her dress slowly her large breast bouncing up and down with her every movement.

Yosef had already thrown his outer coat off his lap, Here. He said moving her hand over to his manhood again. She smiled at him. Ahh! She moaned, louder this time. Oh yes beloved. Her body felt like an inferno of passion for him. He looks at her breast inviting him to touch and caress them. Whoa! He breathed. His eyes big and staring at them. Oh God Lisa! He looks up at her, her eyes begging him to make love to her now! She slides her hands around the back of his neck, massaging him gently. Pulling him into her bosom.

He slow grinds her soft bottom harder now. Oh Lisa, I love you! I love you! He kisses her breast tenderly.

I love you too my Beloved! Oh! Lisa! Ooooh! What's happening to me! Aahhhhhhh! He screamed. He pulled her body close to his tightly. He cried into her arms. Oh God! He screamed, his body convulsing as his flow spilled into his clothing. Lisa looked down at him her body following his in like passion, as she too released into her clothing as well. They both smiled at each other for a moment. Unsure as to what had just happened to them. But they knew what had just taken place. She smiled at him sweetly as her arousal

Returned to her, she feels a surge of passion flow through her body again. She moans sensuously in his ear.

Oh Yosef, I want you, I need you so bad. But we promised. She said stroking his hair. She kissed him deeply again. Yosef's arousal returns to him more intensely than before. He looked at her, the longing in her experession excited him even more. He knew that she wanted him to make love to her. But he too remembered their vow. His senses were screaming for her body to pleasure him in everyway imaginable to him. He wanted her! Lisa I can't stand it! I've dreamed of you every night since you've been gone! I can't stop thinking of how I want to make love to you! She kisses his neck, he moaned out loud again.

Oh God! He said softly, as he pulls her down onto the bed mounting her. Ahhh! She moans Jesus! Lisa! He tries to unzip hi slacks, fumbling as he tries. She pulls him down to her kissing him deeply. I want you Lisa! I can't take it anymore! Don't you know that I want you too Beloved? But we promised, we can't, not yet! Yosef still slow grinding her soft bottom. Lisa please, just once, nobody has to know. He pleaded. We'll know. Yosef Please! Don't make this any harder for us than it already is! I have to say no! Please try to understand that, just for now. And in a short while, when I am all yours. We'll make love in ways that we've only dreamed of. I'll love you in ways unimaginable! You'll experience the totality of all my love. He listens to her, stopping to kiss her.   He mounted her again. I want you now Lisa! He moaned, tears streaming down his face. She throws her arms around him, kissing him uncontrollably. It was nearly impossible to resist his strong body. Oh Yosef! Please don't make me do this! She tears at her dress, he tore his suit shirt off himself. I can't wait any longer! I don't want to wait! Make love to me Lisa! Make love to me now! Oh God I love you Lisa! He said, nearly pulling all his clothes of himself and her. They wrap each other in the bed linens. Lisa at that moment was torn between her convictions and her harmones. She knew that something had to be done now! Or they would violate their vow to stay chase until they married. And what had taken place between them already, they were just about there on the verge of doing just that. She moans as he rubs the stonelikeness of his manhood against her soft tummy. Oh God! Yosef! Please! No!no! Please! She pleaded. Just one time Lisa, just one time

Please! She begins to cry as guilt overwhelms her.   He tries to enter her womanhood, but she had not taken off her under panties. I'd give anything to make love to you Beloved. But....Shhhhh! he kisses her into silence. She begins to cry as he kissed her. She felt that all that she had lived for and believed, and waited for and promised was about to be broken. Baby don't cry, please Lisa don't cry. He knew what she was crying about. But as he so often said. He couldn't help it at that moment. His love, his passion for her had overpowered him! It seemed there was no stopping him! Oh God! Please help us! Don't let us do this! She sobbed painfully in his arms. Just then, a blinding radiance filled the room. Yosef looked over in the corner. It was the Warrior Angel that had appeared to him before. A look of disappointment in his expression. Yosef saw the Being, but Lisa did not. She for the moment had fallen into a deep sleep. Yosef unmounted her, and began to dress himself. The Angel then spoke to him. *" Your time is drawing near son. And you must ready yourself for the Willl of God in you life. Cleanse yourself of all manner of* Sin, *draw near unto Him, and He will draw near to you. It is at the prayers of your Beloved Lisa, that I was sent again unto you. To keep you both from sinning in His Presence."* Yosef held his head down. He knew that the Angel spoke the truth. If he had not come, he would've forced Lisa into violating their vow. He felt a deep remorse at that moment. *"Hear and know this son, that His Presence is with you always, and that you will see me again, and I will give you instructions as to what you must do. Until then, Keep your heart pure before Him, for your greates hour is about to come, and He will use you to work His Will. Keep her close to you, for there will be a great disturbance soon, and she'll be taken. But if you'll only believe, you'll see the Glory of God! Believe son, believe.....Only Believe....."* The Angel again vanished out of sight. But his words lingered longer with Yosef this time. What! Who's gonna take her? He said pulling Lisa close to him embracing her hard. Fear welled up inside of him. No one will ever take you from me. Not even death! He kissed her forehead. Ummmm. She sighed, her sleep was leaving her now.

She looked at Yosef, he was fully dressesd now. Honey, you're dressed so quickly. She smiled at him. He looked at her, his heart still disturbed at the Angel's words. He tried to hide his feelings from her, but his expression gave him away to her. She saw that he was troubled about something. Beloved, are you alright? He wipes his eyes of tears. Yes, I'm fine baby. I'm just fine. I just love you so much Lisa. She smiles at him again. His arousal starts to return to him again. Jesus Lisa! Don't smile at

me like that. You know what that does to me. He said pulling
her close to him. She was still undressed. She kisses him
Tenderly. Make love to me Beloved. Oh God! Lisa! She pulls
his coat off him again, he starts to undress again, they embreace
hard, kissing deeply. He then remembers what the Angel said to
him. He stopped kissing her, looking at her. His arousal leaves
him quickly. What's the matter? Did I do something wrong? She
said her voice trembling. He looks at her smiling, stroking her
soft brown cheek. No baby, you didn't do anything wrong. You
were right, we made a promise. And as long as we stick to that
promise. Our Wedding night will be one of the most blessed
nights of our lives. I believe He'll see to that personally.
He said pointing up to the ceiling. Ok? She smiles at him. Ok
Beloved. Now get dressed before I forget everthing I just said and
attack you again. They both bust up laughing. He goes over to
the window to look out at the beach and the lighthouse. It was a
gorgeous Saturday afternoon.   His thoughts on everything that
had just happened between the two of them. From their
passionate reunion, to their nearly violating their vow, to the
Angel's visitation. All flooded through his mind. Yosef, I'm ready
now. Her sweet voice snapping him out of his moment with his
thoughts. He smiles at the sound of her. She was fully dressed,
and looked sweet and beautiful to him. She walks up to him,
putting her hands around his

Waist. She looks up at him, her thoughts too spoke to her about
how close they came to nearly breaking their vow.   He looks at
her too. What's the matter?   He shakes his head at her. You
seem to get prettier everytime I look at you. She smiles a little
What am I gonna do with you? She reaches up on her tippy toes
to rub her nose with his. Just love me Lisa, never stop loving me.
Not a problem Beloved, not a problem. They both look ourside,
the Summer Sun shining brightly in the late afternoon sky. He
holds her close to him. Honey? He didn't answer her. Yosef? He
seemed a little distant. He looks at her. I can't believe how close
we came to blowing it today. He caresses her again. She thought
on that again too. Yes we did. I'm sorry in some ways, but at the
same time I'm not. I know that doesn't make any sense, I don't
even know how to explain that. She said. Don't even try baby.
Are you ready to go now? Yes, and no. What is it? He said to
her. Can we go to the beach after supper and watch the Sunset
before we go home?

He looks at his watch, it was 3:45p.m. I don't see why not. I'd love to. He said to her. We can come back here after supper and pack me in later. Yosef thought about their episode of passion. Sweetheart, I think it'll be safer for us if we don't come back here, we should head home after supper ok? She knew what he was thinking about. Ok Beloved. He helps her get packed in the van, then takes her to one of the local restaurants there. They then go to the beach to wait for the Sunset, There they talked over many things.

From what happened at the hospital, to their moment of passion. To their wedding. They had a chance to resolve many problems between them, calling upon the counseling that Rev.Anderson had given them over the Spring and early Summer. The time seemed to just fly by. It's now nearing 9:00p.m. they sit in the family van together watching the tourists and the lovers and families on the pier by the lighthouse. As the Sunsets, it lights up the sky in the most brilliant, spectacular display of colours. Each one more and more beautiful as the huge red orange ball makes it's way down the Lake Michigan horizon. There were gasps of awe as God blessed the spectators with the most incredible Sunset in the history of South Haven. People were taking pictures, and video taping it. Wanting to capture the Master Architect Himself at work. Painting an awesome picture in the evening sky. The reds, and oranges, and the blues of the sky hitting the

Clouds just right. All blending together in perfect atmospheric harmony. Yosef and Lisa could not believe their eyes, it was the most breathtaking thing they had ever seen in their lives. When the display was over, just like they said, instead of going back to the cottage, they headed back to Chicago. It was now nearly 10:30p.m.

Yosef and Lisa pull up in front of her parents home. They got out
of the van. He walks over to her taking her by the hand. Lisa? I
have something to tell you, that I didn't get a chance to tell you
back at the cottage. What is it honey? Well, it's the way that I
treated you at the hospital. I lost my head over nothing
And I took it out on you. That wasn't fair at all, and I'm so sorry
that I. He paused. My behavior, I have no words to tell you how
truly sorry I am about hurting you. Can you ever forgive me?
Please Lisa forgive me. Lisa looks at him, her heart filled with
compassion for him. There's nothing to forgive Beloved. I
understand, believe me. I understand. You were under a lot of
pressure from home, and with Rabbi, then the Land Deal at work.
I mean so many things were weighing down on your mind. Don't
worry your handsome face about it any more ok? She reached up
and kisses gently on the lips. He looks at her stunned.
He then smiles at her. How do you do that? He said shaking his
head. Yosef, If we don't forgive one another, He won't forgive us.
She said pointing to upward. You'll have to teach me how you do
that one day. Oh, Beloved. We'll have the rest of our lives to live
and learn from each other. That's how it should be with
husbands, and wives. If they spend their time growing together,
learning from each other. Then

There will never be this growing out of love, or out growing one
another. Things in the divorce courts will begin to get a little
scarce around here. Yosef chuckles. She looks up at the night
sky. The stars are so close, you could almost reach up and pick
which ever one you wanted. She said, the soft porch light bathing
her in it's light. She then feels an overwhelming sense of love
welling up in her heart for him.
He loves you Yosef, you know that? He nods his head. Yeah, I
know that. She kisses him tenderly.

She feels the stiffness of him again. Oh, what's that! She said stepping back a little. Lisa......? He said playfully. They both look down at his slight arousal. He stares at her, love filling him to overflowing for
Her. I love you more than my own life. His thoughts said to her. Lisa's heart heard them. His expression echoed those words as well. She reads them back to him. And I love you more than my own life too. He looks at her stunned again. How'd you know that? I saw it in your expression, and I heard your thoughts Beloved. Can you also see that I want you to marry me more than anything in this world
Lisa? This time she was the stunned one, her words leaving her. Yosef gets down on one knee, taking her hand. He pulls out her diamond engagement ring slipping it on her finger. Lisa begins to cry uncontrollably. Oh Yosef! Lisa, will you marry me? Will you be my wife? His voice trembling, tears streaming down his face, the porch light was now bathing him in it's glow. He looked hansome to her. More beautiful than anything that her eyes had ever beheld at that moment. Yes! Yes! My Beloved! Yes! I will! I will! He stands up and embraces her hard, they kiss the same. Oh God! Lisa! I love you so much! I love you too my Beloved! Would you have any objections to having the engagement party over at my parents house? I want to do this according to our Jewish Tradition. Just like I told you a long time ago. Remember that? I believe I do. It's called a, a uh....Hum.... Help me Yosef. She struggled to remember what the ceremony is called. "simkha" He said to her. That's it! She said out loud. I've only been to two of them that I can remember. It's really a lot of fun. He said, excitement surfacing now.

I'll explain it to you further later. Ok? Ok. I'm sure it'll be wonderful. Yeah, it will be. Well what do you say, will you? Oh Yosef, I would be honored to have your simkah at your parents home. She said, her tone more serious now. You mean, our Simkha. He said. He kisses her again. He hugs her tenderly. I'd better go now, I have to get up early tomorrow. He said. It is tomorrow, she said. He looks at his watch,
It was 3:00am. They had stopped off and talked much more before coming home. I have to meet the band for rehearsal. Pastors day is next Saturday. Lisa nods her head, she held onto his hand. She didn't want to let him go. What's the matter? He said to her. I wish you could stay with me tonight. He laughs. Well, I won't sleep tonight anyway. He said to her, looking at his

manhood, which was still slightly swollen from her playing. Sorry about honey, but I can't help it. I love you so much. She said, his words coming back to him. You're amazing Lisa! I'm tired she said to him. He pulls her to him one last time before going home. You go on now and get some rest, and I'll see you after I get out of Church ok? Yes ma'mam. He

Said to her smiling. He kisses her again. They each part to go home, their hearts filled with excitement, and many other things. They were soon to be husband and wife. Their thoughts said to them. Yosef goes inside to find his mother asleep at the dinning room table again. She was waiting for him. He kissed her on the cheek. She stirs a little. Yosef? It's me mom. Yosef! Oh my boy! You're home! She seemed more excited than he. She stands up and hugs him hard. You feel good to me mom. There's nothing like a mother's touch son. I must've fallen asleep, I was waiting for you. She said. She sat back down at the table. He goes over on the other side smiling big at her, he thought that he would burst at any moment.
She looks at him smiling. Now what is that smile about there? He held his head down. I gather things went well for you and Lisa eh? Eh. He said. Yes, they did. She claps her hands together. She stands back up again, going over to him, fixing his lapel on his outer suit coat. So, will she be my daughter in law or what? Yes! She said yes! Mom! They embrace. I can't believe it mom, I just can't believe it! She still

Loves me. And after all that's happened between us, she still loves me! I just don't know what to say about that at all. She's the most amazing girl I've ever known in my life! He said picking her up and spinning her around. Yosef! Put me down, I'm getting dizzy. Oops, sorry mom. But I can't help it. I've never seen anything like that before, she so beautiful. He pauses, his expression serious. She forgave me mom. I mean she forgave me of everything that I did to her. How does she do that? That is one of many of God's greatest mysteries. The heart of a woman. Especially one that has a heart that is more full of forgiveness, than bitterness when she is wronged. Lisa has learned to not only forgive, when she is hurt. She has learned to live forgiveness son. And that my dear child is not an easy life to live. And It is also like I told you. If you treat her right, she'll not only give her life to you, but for you. Yes, this is true. She said. Now off to bed with you now. Your friend terry called here for you. But it is late, call him in the morning.

I will mom. Goodnight son. Night. I love you! He kisses her cheek, then scales the stairs to go to bed. Sarah sits down at the dinning room table, a tremendous burden is lifted off her shoulders as she rejoices about the news of her son, and Lisa. She holds her hands together, and prays a prayer of blessing and Protection around them.

Father, God of Abraham, Issac, and Jacob. I thank You
For how you have worked Your Perfect Will in bringing
Our children together again. And Dear Father, I pray and
Ask a blessing of favour and protection around them. Shield
Them in Your hedge of Protection, and fire, let it surround them
Totally. In the Name of Yeshua Ha Mashiach. Amen.

Tears streaming down her sweet face. She then turns the light off, and goes to bed. Sunday morning comes in like all the rest of the Summer days. Hot and muggy. It was a serene Sunday morning. Yosef is

Awakened by the aroma of freshly brewed coffee. He gets up and goes over to his bedroom window, his thoughts all on Lisa. He wondered what she was doing about now. But he already knew. She was getting ready for Church it was 10:00a.m. They had left at 9:00a.m. for Sunday School, Lisa had to teach that morning. Her lesson was on the Forgiveness of God. What a lesson that would be for everyone! He gets showered and dressed to go meet his bandmates for rehearsal. He had written a new song that Lisa had inspired in him. He comes down to see his mother busy looking at a wedding magazine. She would make Lisa's wedding gown and veil for her. She also was thumbing through another magazine full of beautiful

Wedding decorations. Yosef, come here look at this one son. Tell me what do you think about this? Do you think that Lisa would like that? He looks at the pretty laced gown design. Mom, I think Lisa would love anything you pick out for her. I think so too dear, she's not a hard one to please that one. No she's not. Me and Deborah are going downtown shopping after we come from seeing your father today.

She looked in her purse, she only had $20.00 dollars left. Yosef saw that it was breaking her heart. She wanted to buy everything that she needed to make Lisa's dress for her. He reaches into his pocket and pulls out his wallet, and hands her a huge wad of money. Here mom, take this. She takes it into her hands. She could hardly hold it all. But there's so much here. How will you get around today yourself son? Mom I have plenty ok. Now you go and enjoy yourself with my other mother ok? But....No but me mom. I'm

Still your son, you listen to me,go buy my wife to be something pretty for me alright? I have to go now to meet Terry and the guys. But I can't if I stand here talking with you all morning eh? Eh she said laughing. When will dad get out of the hospital? He asked picking his bass off the floor. This week sometime the Dr. said. Well, we'll go up to see him later too when Lisa gets back home. Alright son. She smiles. Kiss Lisa for me today. I will. He said, leaving. Bye now. She nods. She counts the money that he gave her. Whoa! She breathed. He had given her $300.00 cash! Lisa and her parents arrive home, it' s now about 12:30p.m. They had a wonderful time at Church, as eight people came forward to make a decision to receive Christ into their lives. They came home to have their Sunday supper, Johnathan and his girlfriend Deneice stopped by also. He had given his father the news that he would resume his position as Head Deacon for Pastors Day coming up next Saturday. All were overjoyed! They discuss many things about the Conference, Even Mamie herself had some good news. She would rejoin the Usher board for the Conference too! More rejoicing in the Anderson home that Sunday afternoon. Deborah had now changed her clothes, as well as Lisa, she would stay at home to wait for him to come to pick her up to go the hospital to see Rabbi with Yosef.

Yosef pulls in front of Terry's garage, taking his bass inside. My man Jo! Said James. He sets his bass on the floor, Give me some bro. Said James hitting fives with him. They all shake hands and embrace each other. So tell us man, you know we have to know what happened with Lisa. Said Brad. Yosef smiles big at them. It's on! Is it on bro? Said James. All the way drummer man! Said Yosef. James laughs out loud, picking Yosef off the floor! I'll be so glad when you and this girl get married Jo, you're both driving me crazy! Said Brad. Just then, there was a

knock at the garage door. It was Billy. They all looked at him. Yosef was so overjoyed with Lisa being back in his life, not even Billy's presence could touch his happiness. Joseph, Billy. They said to each other. May I come in? Terry looked at Yosef. He nodded to him. Come in Billy, but please for your sake don't start anything man. Said Terry. I give you my word, I
Come in peace. He said sarcastically. If he starts any thing, he'll leave in pieces. Said Terry. He
 comes in and sits down in his usual corner. I Just wanted to say that I'm sorry about what happened, and no hard feelings? Forget it man. Said Yosef, stepping over to the amplifier hooking up his bass. They tune up for play again. Billy Listens to them play. Yosef steps up to the mike. To sing the song that he wrote for Lisa. This is the one that I told you guys about. You have your sheet music? Got em. Said Terry. Terry starts off the Introduction to the song. Yosef closes his eyes, and sings the first verse.

I knew not where my life would go, as I walked this lonely road To nowhere, I was lost. Dispair and sadness were my friends. To Last until the end. But then I saw the Cross. You said my child Come to me, and let Me set you free. From darkness, and from sin Just leave your burdens at My Feet. And let Me give you life complete
In Me, I'll be your Friend.

You came, and turned my life around, put my feet on solid Ground. You filled my life with song. And as I looked into Your face, I had never known such grace. Until you came Along.

Billy Listens as Yosef sings for his Beloved Lisa. His heart filling up with anger, and jealousy. He Looks at him, Yosef had tears

streaming down his face. Wow! Man! That is beautiful! Said
Terry. Just like Lisa. Said Yosef. Hugging his bass close.
Bet. Said James. Has Lisa heard this yet? Said Brad. Uh, no
she hasn't. he said clearing his throat, he had choked up a little.
As they all did, except Billy. He sat over in his corner glaring at
Yosef. He never felt such hatred in his life for a person as he did
for Yosef at that moment. I'm sure Lisa will just love it man.
After all in a little while, my man here will be a husband. They all
cheer him on. Billy sat up abruptly when he heard that. He
could tell that from what James had said. Yosef and Lisa were
definitely engaged again, and soon to be married. He thought
back to when Yosef beat him down for attacking Lisa.
He remembered all too well what Yosef told him He would do to
him if her ever came near her again. His anger began to surface,
but he remained silent for some strange reason. Not like Billy at
all. Terry noticed his every move. So when's the engagement
party? Said Terry. No sooner my father get's out of the hospital.
And when is that? Said Brad. I don't know. Dr. K hasn't given
my mother any definite date yet. But when he does, I'll let you
guys know. But I get the feeling it'll be just in time for Pastors
Day.
Has he changed his mind towards Lisa at all? Said James.
Changed his mind? He's had more than just a change of mind
my man. My father's had a change of heart all together. He's
accepted her. And he gave us his blessing on our marriage. Look
at that! Said James. You said he would Jo. Never understimate
the power of Faith James! He said. Billy couldn't take it
anymore. He gets up and storms out of the garage.

Yosef caught a glimpse of Billy as he passed by him. He gives
Yosef a evil glare. Yosef shakes his head giving him a look that
said to Billy. You don't even want to go there with me today man.
Billy walks outside, then leaves all together. Yosef stares at him
as he leaves. James comes over to him. You alright man? Yeah,
I'm fine.. I just can't wait to see my girl that's all. He puts his
bass back into the case, and prepares to leave. Don't forget Jo,
last rehearsal is this Thursday ok? I'll be here. He gets into
Lisa's car and leaves to go pick her up to go to the hospital to see
his father.

The Colour Of Love
Anne Hemingway
Chap 28.

Sarah was busy fixing her hair when the phone rings. It was Dr. Kaplan. Sarah? Yes. This is Dr. Kaplan. Yes Dr. There was a slight pause on the line. Sarah I have some news for you. Yes of course Dr. What is it? It 's about Yacov. Yes Alton, is it his heart again? Her heart felt as though it would burst. No it's not his heart at all. As a matter of fact. His heart is doing pretty well considering all that he's been through. It's not his heart that troubles me. Then, please Dr. Tell me what is it, before my own heart stops! She said frustration rising. Well something developed this morning after he had his breakfast. The nurse came back to report to me that he was having a series of mini strokes. T I A's we call them. He later suffered a massive stroke that paralyzed his entire left side, he then slipped into a coma. He's resting at this moment,
But I don't know how this one will turn out for him. There's a 50/50 chance that he'll come out of it. But I can't say right now. It's still too early to tell. I just feel that whatever you had planned for today, needs to be put on hold. And come down to see him. I feel there's not much time left. But we'll do all that we can for him Sarah, he's a strong man, you have my on word that. All that we can. His voice even though it was comforting and reassuring did not keep her heart from breaking , and fear from seizing it like a vice. She lets her comb drop from her hands to the floor. The phone droped from her other hand. "Hello, Hello! Sarah, Hello! Said Dr. Kaplan. As Sarah sat down in her chair, she was stunned at his news about her husband. Fear had taken her words away from her. A single tear makes it's way down her soft cheek.

I wonder what's keeping Sarah? Said Deborah, as she goes over to look out the picture window. In her spirit she felt that something was wrong over there. Ben? Hum? I'm going over to see Sarah. I think something's wrong. Deborah you and your intutions. He breathes laughing a little. Ben I feel her, she 's hurt. He gets up and walks over to her. I tell you honey, she's hurting. Me and Sarah have been prayer warriors for years, and we can both tell when something isn't right. I know it, I feel it in here! She said, patting her chest. Lisa came down stairs, when she stopped right in her tracks gasping like she was out of breath. They both look at her. Lisa? Her mother called. She never answered her, she walked over to the picture window, placing her hand on the glass. I can see you Ms. Sarah, and I see him. She whispered. She saw rabbi in her heart, he was lying in a deep sleep from which he would never awaken if God didn't intervene. Then her body began to shake a little. Her parents stepped back some. They knew that God was dealing with her about him in prayer. He would use her to complete His work in Rabbi The front

Door opens, it was Yosef. Rev. Anderson puts his index finger to his mouth, pointing over to Lisa. He walks in to see what was happening. She began to mumble under her breath. She was interceding in prayer for him. What's called warfare praying. Lisa then began to wail out loud, tears flowing from her eyes. Yosef stood there staring at her. What's going on with her dad? I'm not sure what's happened, but she's fighting for him. For who? He looks at Yosef. Your father. Yosef didn't quite understand this type of praying, they mostly prayed out of a prayer book. But these people prayed out of their hearts. I've never seen anything like this in Temple before. He said. Lisa's wailing got louder, as something else began to overwhelm her right before their eyes. A bright light started to shine forth from within her. It
Got brighter, and brighter, until she shone all over almost like the Sun! It was the very Presence of God
That had come on her bathing her in His Glory! The Light had filled the whole room, they could not only see it, but they could feel it all over them! It was unexplainable! And It was all over Lisa. She then gasped, and fell to the floor in a heap. Lisa! Yelled Yosef. Yosef Nooo! Yelled Rev. Anderson trying to stop him. He ran over to Lisa, then he stops in his tracks as His Presence had now come upon him! He felt it get stronger, and sstronger! What's happening to me dad! He reaches out his hand to Rev. Anderson, but he refused to take it. He smiled at him, he had seen this phenomenon before many times
In his Church as well as his Father's campmeetings. It's what's called the "Slaying Power of the Holy Spirit." Lisa was already struck, now he was about to experience the same thing. Yosef

don't fight Him son, just relax, and flow with Him. No harm will come to you. Yosef's legs turn to jelly, he falls to the floor in a heap of helplessness like Lisa. He looks over at her, she was still out. Mom! Dad! We're right here son. Said Deborah. Rev. Anderson walks over to him, helping him off the floor. He walks him over to the living room sitting him down on the couch. What about Lisa? She'll be fine, let's just sit you down right here for a moment. What happened to me? That my dear boy is called the Power of God. Or the Anointing. The what? The Anointing. It is the Spiritual Presence of God that comes upon a person to carry out a specific Work that God has call a per son to do for Him. He nods his head over in Lisa's direction. She's called into the Healing Ministry. He uses her in ways that I've never seen anybody used before. Lisa stirred a little, they look over at her. Yosef gets up to go over to pick her up from the floor. When he feels God's Presence come back on him again. But this time it knocks him off his feet back up under a small table that sat in front of the window. Whoa! What was that! The same thing, but stronger this time. It feels different than the first time. How so? Well the first time, I felt numb all over, I could

Smell a sweet fragrance that I can't explain, sometimes dad, Lisa's breath smells like that when I kiss her.
Almost like a sweet crème. What do you feel now? My whole body's tingling all over, like currents of electricity flowing through me, but it doesn't hurt or anything. He gets up and walks back over to the couch sitting down. He shakes his head trying to clear it. What do you think about what just happened to you? Would you like to experience it again? He looks at Rev. Anderson smiling. God Yes! I've never felt anything like this in my life! Is this what happens to those people that I see on television, when they're touched, they fall down? Yes, yes it is son. It's pretty much laughed at and mocked now. But that doesn't mean that it's not real. You've just seen for yourself how real His Presence is. I use to think that all that
Was fake too dad. But, I'm a believer now. He said. Is this in the Bible anywhere? Thank you for asking that. Yes it is. Remember the time that I told you about the story of when the Roman Soldiers came to

272

Arrest Jesus? Yosef thought back to that time. It was about seven or eight months ago that we talked.
Yosef nodded his head. Well, when they asked Him Who He was, and He told them, the same Power that knocked you to the floor, is the same Power that knocked them to the ground. The Bible says that they fell
Over as "dead men." That's where the term the "Slaying Power." Of the Holy Spirit comes from. Because the men fell over as though they were dead. Let's see, that's in....? John 18:1-8.
Yosef interrupted. Very good son. My daughter has taught you well. Lisa began to stir more this time. Is it safe to go near her now? He asked. Yes, I believe it is son. They both go over to help her. She's still a little weak. Yosef, and her father stood there holding her to her feet. You alright angel? Her father asked. Yes, I'm ok daddy.

Just then the phone rings. Here son, hold her. Yosef takes Lisa into his arms cradling her. He answers the phone. It's Deborah, she tells him about Rabbi, and that they need to get to the hospital quickly. He hangs up the phone. A look of sorrow, and hurt fills his expression. He goes back over to Yosef. Dad, what's wrong? He breathes deeply. That was my wife, she's with your mother. It's you father son. He's suffered a massive stroke. He's paralyzed on his left side, he pauses. He's in a coma. He said choking up a little.
Yosef's heart broke deeply within him. No, no! dad! Not now! Lisa begins to cry. Yosef looks at her
He caressed her close comforting her. Son, listen to me. Don't you see? Now I know what she was praying for. Lisa walks away from them and goes back over to the window. She stopped crying and began to smile, as she felt the warmth of God's Presence come back on her, as His Light began to shine forth again. Rev. Anderson and Yosef both gasped amazement taking them over. Look at her face dad!
She was shining like lightening all over, His Presence was stronger this time on her. Yosef could not believe his eyes as she stood bathed in the glow of His Presence. Is that the same thing like before?
He asked. Yes it is son. That is the Spirit of the Living God all over her. Will she be alright? Believe
She's never been more alright than she is right now. Go, go over there and get her. He said, nudging him a little. Yosef was somewhat hesitant as he remembered what happened to him the

last time that he got too close to her. Rev. Anderson assured him
that it was alright for him to go near to her. He walks over to her
taking her by the hand. He didn't quite know what to say about
what he was witnessing, but if filled him with a closeness to God
that he's never experienced before. He also felt even closer to Lisa
than before as well. He started to walk her to the front door,
when she stops. Lisa what is it? She looks at him, tears filling
her eyes. Your father will live and not die beloved. I heard from
Him. He will heal him totally. Rev. Anderson looks at Yosef.
What's she talking about dad? Son, let's just listen to her ok?
Let's go get your mother and my wife. We have to go now! They
leave, Yosef and lisa get inside the family van. Rev. Anderson goes
over to get Deborah and Sarah. Yosef looks over at Lisa, the light
had left her for the moment. He cradles her in his arms kissing
her gently on the forehead. I don't know about things like this,
but I'm willing to learn if you'll teach me. He said to her. Just
then, Lisa sits up and takes his hand. He felt a strong surge of
power flow from her into him. It went all over his body. He began
to shake all over. He saw in his heart a man, this man glowed all
over just like he saw Lisa glowing. This man was fearless, and
covered in God's Glory! The man that he saw was himself! He
didn't understand what that meant either. But the Warrior Angel
told him that it was nearing the time for him to be used of God.
The vision that he just saw, was only a reminder of what the
Angel told him. Rev. Anderson and Deborah walked out with
Sarah. She was still in shock over Rabbi. They sit her in the
back of the van, and buckle her in. Yosef tried to comfort his
mother, by telling her what Lisa had told him about Rabbi not

Dying. It was difficult for her to receive words of comfort at the
moment, her thoughts only spoke of death to her about her
husband. She was quiet, and tearful. Yosef held her hand, she
prayed under her breath all the way to the hospital.

Hey guys! May I come in? Said Billy. James looked back at him.
You back here again? What do you want man? He said to him. I
just want to come hang out for a while, Helen will be back to
pick me up in a few, I just wanted a place to go, this is as good a
place as any. He said walking into the garage. Terry offers him a
seat. He sits down over by the door leading into the house. So
tell me boys, any of you seen Yosef around lately? They all look

at each other, then back at him. What business is that of yours, and why do you ask? Said Brad. Just curious that's all. There was no answer from any of them. Well have any of you seen Lisa? I mean did she and Jo work things out? I know how pretty tore up he was over her leaving him and all. Hold it right there man, you came over here to see if you could put the hit on Lisa? What makes you think that it's over between them? You were here earlier. You heard what Jo said. It's on! Ok like in they're getting married on. Am I coming in loud and clear Jethro? I don't believe this! He said. I'm surprised you can walk homes. That took a lot of testosterone for you to come over here and do something like that. Said James. Brad stands up looking at him, disgust in his expression. Lisa was right about you Billy, you're nothing but slime. What makes you think that she would want you man huh? Said Brad, his anger rising up at him. Well, you might as well find yourself another target, because this one's out of your range son. Said Brad. She has never liked you, and she never will like you! Hey so it takes a little getting to know me. I kinda grow on people. So do warts, but you don't see her out romancing one of them do you? Said Terry. Has it escaped your memory what you did to her? You still remember that night don't you man? Said Terry. Hey! I was a little drunk! I wasn't gonna hurt her, I was just gonna

Season her a little that's all. He said patting his groin. James tried to charge at him, Terry stops him.
And besides, I was p.o'd at Helen. Wanted to make her jealous. You lied about her. You told Jo that you slept with her! Fired James. The closest that you'll ever get to a prize like Lisa, is in your dreams man.
Lisa is it for Yosef, she always has been and she always will be. Billy looked stunned to hear those words
They tore into his being savagely tearing at his heart. No man is that damn faithful, no man! He said, his anger now surfacing. What are you getting at? Just believe what I say, no man is that faithful. He said cracking an all too familiar smile of mischief. Not all men cheat Billy, there are some men who would rather die, than cheat on their woman. And uh, Jo is one of those men. So give it up Billy, said Terry.
Never! He fired back. I nearly had her that night, until he came back and took her from me again. Again? Said Terry. Has it escaped your memory what Yosef told you he would do to you if you ever went near her again? Don't you remember that? Said

Brad. Boy, you're playing with fire, and Yosef will burn your behind! Said Terry. I kicked his Jew butt once before, I can do it again, no problem. He said in a concited tone snapping his finger in the air. No you didn't take my boy down. Said James. Yeah, I did, if you don't believe me you can ask Helen. She was there! She'll tell you! If it's anything, he let you get to him, because he was all messed up over loosing Lisa. But you know you can't take him Billy. He beat cha down once before, he'll take you out this time man. Said Terry. Billy's ego couldn't take much more of their support for Yosef and Lisa. He just exploded on them. LOOK YOU STOOGE! SHE WAS MINE! YOU HEAR ME! SHE WAS MINE! AND THAT JEW BOY TOOK HER FROM ME!! He was out of breath from his outburst. He quiets down some. And I'm gonna get her back, so help me I will. I'll get her back , you'll see, she'll loves me and only me. You're crazy Billy! Said James. What about Helen? Said Terry. What about her? I just have her along for a little relief if you know what I mean. He said patting his groin again. They all shook their heads at him. Reason is speaking to you Billy, you should listen to it. It'll save your life! Said Terry. You know how he feels about her, you've seen it. If you so much as even raise an eyebrow at her. He'll freaking kill you man! Said James, his anger returning to him. I have a score to settle, and so does Helen. And we're gonna settle it! It's between us, you stay out of it! He said. His tone nasty and arrogant just like his father. Who covered up the whole attempted rape and assault incident to spare billy from going to jail. He now gets up to leave. You're crazy man! You're crazy! Shouted James at him. Yeah, yeah. BILLY! Shouted James. Let him go J. this thing's too deep in him

Not even God can help a person like that. He doesn't want His help or anyone's for that matter. Said Terry comforting James. You ok Bro? Yeah, I'm ok . Nice knowin ya Billy, we'll miss you around here! Said Brad. He looks over at James and Terry. NOT!!! He said. They all laugh. Billy walks outside looking at his watch, he was waiting for Helen to come and get him. He lites up a cigarette while he waits for her. The garage door was opened, they all came over to watch him. Just then Helen pulls up right on time, he gets in the car, they pull off. Terry watches them. He's up to something. What? Said James. Billy, I get the feeling he's up to something. Yeah, something very dangerous. Said Brad. I know one thing, he's gonna get himself killed if he messes with that girl. I know my boy Jo. He'll kill him man. What's wrong with his head anyway. Said James. Can't you see what's wrong with his head James? Did you see the look on his face when you told him that Jo and Lisa were getting married. What you getting at man? He's in love with Lisa. Brad and James gasp. What! They both said together. Read my lips, he's in love with Lisa. The man reads like a book, it's all over him. The way he looks at her when she's around, I mean he drools all over himself. I've seen it. Why didn't you say anything Terry? Said James. I had to be sure. And today after all that, I'm as sure he's in love with her, as I'm sure today is Sunday. Brad and james look at each other. Well lets not jump the gun yet. Said Brad. I just pray that he comes to his senses before he gets himself wacked. What senses? He's never had any. Said James. They laugh.

Well do we tell Yosef or not? Said Brad. I don't know, I'm debating on that. Said Terry. Let's not say anything for now ok guys? Bet. Said James.

The Colour Of Love
Anne Hemingway
Chap 29.

Hello Mrs. Epstien right this way. The orderly walks them down the hall to the front desk. Your husband is resting at the moment. Dr. Kaplan will be with you shortly. Thank you much my dear boy. Said Sarah.
They all walk Sarah down to the waiting area, where Rabbi's room is only two doors away. All of a sudden, Rev. Anderson feels a strong urge to pray. Lisa notices it as well, she feels the same thing in her heart too. Dr. Kaplan comes over to them informing them of his prognosis. There has been no change. It's just like I told you over the phone. There's a 50/50 chance that he'll make it out of this Sarah. We've done all that we can for him. He is in God's Hands now. I can't think of better Hands for my Yacov to be in about now Alton. He takes her hand kissing it gently. Stay prayerful, he needs your prayers about now. And I need yours Alton. She said. I can only give you just a few minutes at a time ok Sarah?
I understand. I will be brief. He turns to walk away. Alton! He comes back over to her. Is there a chance that he could, that he could. She stammers. She found it difficult to even say the word.

She never pictured herself facing a trial such as this. Is there a chance that he could, die? Yosef goes over to her comforting her. Lisa overhearing her silently weeps to herself. Then she hears His voice in her heart again. *"He will live and not die, For I will heal him."* She goes over to them. No Ms. Sarah, he will not die. Death will have no chance to take him ma'mam. They all looked at her. They could see faith in her expression, and it was building and getting stronger. Dr. Kaplan nodded in agreement with her. Listen to her, she is a wise one. He said smiling. Yosef looked at Lisa. I Love You. He mouthed to her. She mouthed the same to him. She then leaves to go and pray for Rabbi more. Father, I know he's not been what You would have him to be, and yes, he's suffered much. But he needs a chance to really know life, his family, Your Love.

I need a chance to know him. Whatever it is that You want me to do. Then Father do it quickly. I'm ready now. Use me, use me for Your Glory, and for his good. Turn it all around , that Rabbi may see Your Glory! I ask in the Name of Jesus My Lord and Savior. Thank you Abba Father. Amen. Yosef heard her, tears streaming down his face. Rev. Anderson at that time came over to Sarah. I need to see him first, it's imperative that I go in first Sarah. He pleaded with her. Yes, of course Benjamin. Deborah came over to

Walk her over to sit down in the waiting area. Rev. Anderson takes Lisa by the arm. I'm going to go in first. Ok daddy. But I feel like you should come in with me. I don't know what's going to take place on the other side of that door, but I feel that whatever does happen. You are to be a major part of it. What about Yosef? He looks at him standing over by himself. He looked as though he would break at any moment. Jo! Yes sir. Come over here son. We have to get in there to see your father right away. I believe that you need to be in there with us ok? Yes sir. They all go in together. Yosef takes Lisa by the hand, following behind Rev. Anderson. Rev. Anderson stands beside his friend's bedside, Yosef and Lisa stand at the foot of his bed. Tears began to stream down all their faces as Rabbi lay before them helpless, and worn. He looked as though he would take his last breath at any moment. The stroke had left his entire Left side sagging like melted clay. Death had come, and was hovering over him like a thick black cloud.

Rev. Anderson lifted his hands towards Heaven, and began to pray in a thunderous voice! He felt as though all of Heaven Itself was surging through him.

Father, hear my cry! I stand in the gap for this Your Servant
I bind the spirit of death from him! You will not take him!
For we have already heard from You Father, that he will Live
And not die! And it is for this time that Your Servant was raised
Up so that all might see Your Glory! Fill her now with Your Power
Fill her with Your Faith. Let Thy Glory come down!

Yosef and Lisa stand there watching Rev. Anderson pray for Rabbi. The room was suddenly filled with a soft light. It was coming from Rev. Anderson. He began to shine just like Lisa did earlier. Whoa! Breathed Yosef. Look at that! He said. I see that! Breathed Lisa. He looked at Lisa. Come child, do what He has called you to do. She stepped away from Yosef and stood next to Rabbi's bedside. Rev. Anderson stepped back to give her room. Lisa looked at Rabbi, his breath coming in short gasps now. She looked up towards Heaven herself. Fill me Father! She breathed. She then began to glow just like she did earlier, her face glowing as a surge of Power rose up from with in her! She then laid her hands on Rabbi's mid section. His body jerked like he had been electrocuted. Lisa closed her eyes smiling as the warmth of healing flowed into his body. Just then, she looked at him, compassion overwhelming her for him.

No more hurt dad, no more pain. Let it all go now
It's all over. Take it out of him Father God, take all
Hurt and the pain from his past away from him, he'll never
From this day forward ever hurt again. Fill him with Your
Love, Your Grace, Your Compassion. And Have Mercy upon
Him. Forgive him of all wrong towards his wife and son. Let
Forgiveness reign in his life now. I forgive you Rabbi. I love
You! Bless him with Long life, and show him Your Salvation
I call you back to us now! Rabbi come home! We Love you!
You've suffered for too long Healing has come unto you. Do it
Father! Do it Now!

Yosef broke to hear his Beloved Lisa pray for his father. He could not stop his tears, Rev. Anderson
Weeping the same. Her sweet voice sounded good to him. He laid there underneath her soft hands, as the healing flowed into him. Tears began to flow from his eyes, as he listened to her prayer. It was the most beautiful thing he had ever seen. Just then Lisa opened her eyes. She stopped abruptly as she stared at the huge hideous creature standing over in the corner of the bedroom. The spirit that had held Rabbi captive all his life was standing there glaring at her. Lisa felt fear come on her. Yosef could not believe his eyes, as he looked at the spirit glaring at Lisa. Tell it to leave Lisa, you know how! Tell it to leave him now! It's alright I'm right here. It can't hurt you! I'M NEVER LEAVING! THIS IS MY HOME! It shouted at her. Rev. Anderson stepped up behind her, laying his hand on her back. Tell it to leave angel. In the Name of Yeshua, Leave Him! Leave him now! Death leave the Man! NOOOOOOO! The demon wailed as he faded out of the room. Rev. Anderson took out a small vial that contained blessed Anointing Oil. He bent over Rabbi crossing his forehead with it. Quickly now Lisa! Yosef came over to stand beside Rev. Anderson. Then right before their eyes a Miracle happened. Lisa then took the covers all the way off Rabbi's body. She looked up towards Heaven once more. Praying.

Life flow! Fill me with more of You Father! More of You! In the Name of Yeshua. Raise Him!

Tears streaming down her soft face. She laid her hands on him again. Rabbi's face began to change, as it took it's normal shape again. The face that had once drooped like melted clay began to take on it's orginal apperance! His face started to glow like Lisa's. she moved her hand down to his limb that had fallen inward, and was distored. It too began to give way to the Power of God that was flowing through Lisa's hands. An even stronger surge of Power flowed through her as God healed his body right before Rev. Anderson and Yosef. They looked at each other amazement overwhelming them. Look! Dad! Look at that! Said Yosef. Rabbi's leg began to straighen up, then grow out to it's normal length! His arm followed the same, as it too straightened out to it's original form! Colour came back to Rabbi's face!

Then before their eyes. His body slowly sat up in bed as an unseen Power raised his body from death's door! Yosef and Rev. Anderson's eyes were wide and staring as they watched a Miracle in action! Ahhhhhh! Yelled Lisa as her slender body crumpled onto the bed then to the floor. Lisa! Yelled Yosef.

No! son, not yet. Rev. Anderson snatched him back. They both then looked at Rabbi. He slowly opened his eyes, his body totally well! He looked at himself, he could hardly believe it! He looked towards Heaven. Thank You! Oh my Dear Lord! Thank You! He cried. He then noticed Lisa lying down on the floor beside his bed still under the Power that had healed him. Oh! My dear child God Bless you! God Bless you! He buried his head in his hands and wept in gratitude for what God had done for him. Rev. Anderson and Yosef were crying and laughing at the same time, embracing each other. Rabbi notices the

Both of them standing over behind Lisa rejoicing with him. Yosef come here! Come quick! Look at me! God has done this thing in me! Yosef goes over to him hugging him hard. Oh my son! My son! Look at me I am alright now! I am alright! This is incredible! Look at you dad! If I hadn't seen it with my own eyes. I wouldn've believed it. You're well dad, I mean look at you! Rev. Anderson wiping the tears from his eyes. Rabbi notices him. Ben! You old geezer! Yosef laughs out loud. Jacob you old buzzard! He goes over to him, they shake hands. Hey! That's quite a grip you got there old man! Uhhhhh! The weak voice sounded from the floor. It was Lisa, she was trying to get up. Yosef, would you help me son? Yosef couldn't for the moment take his eyes off his father. Who watched them take her over and sit her down in the soft chair. They leave her there then go back over to talk with Rabbi. Yosef looked back at her, she was out deeply. Rabbi looks at his son and friend. I have something to say. He said to them. They give him their attention. For many years, I have been unfair to my wife and son. And your child Ben. I was wrong for the way that I mistreated all of you. And I want to say that I'm so sorry. Can you please find it in your hearts to forgive me? Rev. Anderson looked at him. There's nothing to forgive Jacob. He looks at Yosef. Amen. Dad. How do you feel Jacob? Rabbi pauses a moment. I feel like a brand new man Ben.

He claps his hands rubbing them together. Where's my wife? Get her in here! Rev. Anderson and Yosef bust up laughing. Ummmm. Lisa sounded again. They go over to her. Yosef sat next to her cradling her to him. He felt his heart for her at that moment. So full of love, and adoration for her. Thank you. He whispered to her. Kissing her forehead gently. Will she be alright dad? His concern rising for her. He'd never seen her like that before. Yes son, she'll be just fine. She's never experienced Power like that before. He really pulled it out of her. She may take a while longer this time. No problem dad. I'm gonna go back over to talk with him ok? Sure, I want to stay with her anyway. He brushes her hair out of her

Face. Ben I really do owe you and Deborah and Lisa an apology. As well as my son. I have treated his girl unfairly, and I must make this right with them both. When she is better, I will make this up to her.
Thank you Jacob, I appreciate that, and I'm sure my wife will too. Oh by the way speaking of wives.
There is a young lady out there who hasn't seen you lately. I think I'll go out there and get her for you.
Rev. Anderson walks over to open the door, but it opens before he could touch the doorknob. It was
Dr. Kaplan. What is all this noise I hear? He looks at Rabbi sitting up in bed totally well! He takes his glasses off his face slowly walking towards him. He is stunned by what he sees. The patient that was near death, is now awake and full of life. He even looked a little younger! Merciful God in Heavan! Is the dead raised before my eyes! He breathed. He looks around the room. Who is this man! Who stole my patient! They all laughed. Yacov....? Is it really you? Yes, it is I my friend. He said nodding his head.

A calm resolve filled his voice. I'm going to get Sarah. Said Rev. Anderson. Yosef nodded his head. Lisa then begins to stir again. Yosef.. She breathed. I'm right here Lisa. I can get up now. She said, her voice still weak. She holds up her hand. Yosef stands her up to her feet, but she stumbles backward into his arms. He laughed a little. Sweetheart, that's not going to work. Lets just stay here alright? She nods, as he sits her back down, cuddling her close to him. Rabbi and Dr Kaplan talk a little more, then

Lisa tries to get up once more, her strength had returned to her so she could stand to her feet this time. She was still a little weak, but she held up well. Dr. Kaplan looked at them. Yosef? My God! Son. I haven't seen you since you were just a little one. Now look at you! Hello Dr. Kaplan. And who may I ask is this lovely young lady? That is my future daughter in law. Lisa, Lisa Anderson. Dr. Kaplan reaches out his hand to shake Yosef's hand. I'm please to meet you Lisa. He said grabbing her hand. Ouch! Her hands are like

Coals of fire! She has fever yes? No, she doesn't sir. Like fire they feel to me! He said rubbing them.

Maybe you should take her home to rest now. She's tired eh? Eh. Said Yosef. Come on baby, I'd better get you home now. He looked at his watch it was 3:15pm. They walked towards the door. Nice to see you again Yosef, and meeting your fiancé . Thank you Dr. Kaplan. I'll come see you tomorrow after work alright dad? Alright son. Take care of her. I will. Goodbye Lisa. Said Rabbi. Lisa looked at him, she felt
A new sense of love overwhelm her for him at that time. She runs over to him hugging him hard. Tears streaming down her face. I love you Rabbi. She kissed him on the cheek. Yosef smiling at them, it touched his heart in ways that he couldn't describe. He wiped the tears from his face,as quickly as he could wipe them away, more would come streaming down after them. Lisa runs back over to him he takes her by the hand. Bye Dad. She said to Rabbi. He looked at her in surprise, it felt good to him for her to call him that. His heart was now overwhelmed with love for her this time. Good bye my child. He said as he like his son wiped tear after tear from his face. She's quite a girl, that one eh? Said Dr. Kaplan. Eh, she is, she is. Said Rabbi nodding his head. He felt his cheek where she had kissed him. More tears flooded his eyes. Yosef and Lisa leave the room. What's the matter with Lisa? Said Sarah coming up to them. She grabs Lisa by the hand, and like Dr. Kaplan gets the same thing. Dear Lord Yeshua! She blows her hands frantically trying to cool them from the heat that was still flowing from her hands. Her hands, Yosef, like coals of fire! She said. I've never felt anything like it. I can't understand it myself mom, but I believe in time that I will soon. He paused a little. Mom, there's a young man in there asking for you. You should get in there to see him. He's asking for you! Go on! Cookie, come on dear. Said Rev. Anderson taking her by the arm, Deborah taking her by the other arm, they escort her

inside.   There were many shouts of surprise, and laughter
coming from in there. Sarah couldn't believe her eyes! Her
husband once at death's door, now awake and full of life! Lisa
was still a little wobbly, so he takes her over to one of the lobby
chairs and gently sits her down. He sits next to her. He couldn't
take his eyes off her. She still had a slight glow about her. Whoa!
He breathed. He takes her hand into his, but instead of feeling
the heat of them, he felt a strong surge of power flow from her
into him. It knocked him backwards into the chair. He closed
his eyes tightly. He saw her in trouble, she was being dragged off
to some unknown place. She had been beaten by someone. He
snapped out of it abruptly. Tears in his eyes. He didn't have a
clue as to what the

Vision meant. He pondered it for a moment. Then all of a
sudden, he felt a stronger surge of power flow from her into him
again.   It was a boldness a strength that came from deep within
him. Now the same glow that was coming from Lisa was
emanating from him too! He could hear this Scripture verse come
from inside of him. Lisa would often quote it to him, when he was
depressed or fearful. *"I can do all things through Him [Christ, Who
infuses inner strength into me. I am equal to anything,and
everything*
I am self sufficient in His sufficiency] Phil 4:13 Amp Bible. He
knew within himself, that whatever the vision meant, that God
would give him the faith to see he and Lisa through it. Lisa then
began to stir, he looked at her, he was glowing slightly just like
she was earlier. He looked strong and handsome to her.
She felt safe at that moment. I Love you. She whispered to him.
He stood up, picking her up in his arms.
I love you too Lisa. He kissed her forehead, as he carried her out
of the hospital.   He felt stronger, and powerful than he had ever
felt in his life! He didn't know what had just happened to him.
But he would come to know it soon. As both their faith would be
challenged in a way that would cause it to rise to a new level that
they've never known before.

Rev. Anderson and Deborah, and Sarah finish their visit with
Rabbi, all still amazed at his Miraculous
Healing. Yosef took Lisa out to dinner at their favorite
restaurant, Bernies. He then dropped her off at home. He was
concerned about leaving her there alone, until Mamie came home
from the area Hospice center. She had been working for the last
two months now. And she was trying to give up her gambling.
And doing very well. Yosef and Lisa told Mamie everything that
happened at the hospital with Rabbi, she was stunned to hear the
news.   I can't believe it! I mean I can't get over it! So when will
he get out of the hospital? Well it's still too early for Dr. Kaplan to
say. But I'm sure it won't be long at all now. He said.
Lisa began to yawn. I'm so sorry guys, I'm very sleepy all of a
sudden. She said in a soft tone. She's had a pretty long day Mae
mae. Said Yosef. He kissed her good night night Beloved. She
said yawning again. Mamie laughs at her. Night baby, I'll see
you tomorrow ok? Ok she said.   Mamie begins to yawn now.
Stop it girl! You're making me sleepy now. And You know what a
night owl I am. It's too early for the kid to go to bed. she and
Yosef laughing. Well alright Ms. Owl face, you stay up, I'm going
to bed.   I love you Lisa. Said Yosef. I love you too honey. She
yawned her way up the stairs.   Mamie yawned again, and went
and laid down on the couch. A slight snoring sound was coming
from her. She had fallen asleep quickly. Yosef felt a yawn coming
on him as well at the moment. He looked at his watch. It was
just a few minutes after 7:00pm. I'm getting out of here! He said.
He leaves to go over to Terry's.   He wanted to talk with him, but
not about rehersal. He wanted to talk with him about what
happened at the hospital.   He pulls in front of the garage, going
inside. Yo! Anyone home! Hey! Bass man! Said Terry
He was wiping his hands with a dish towel, he had finished
helping his wife Susanne finish the dishes.

Yosef told him everything that happened that day. Terry was
totally amazed at the news too! Are you serious man! He said.
Serious as my love for my girl. He said. Now that's serious! Said

Terry.   I'm happy for you and Ms. Sarah man. Do you know
when he'll get out of the hospital? No not yet. But I'll keep you
guys posted when me and my mom know alright? Sure, sure.
Terry paused a little. Yosef could see that something was on his
mind. Is there something wrong man? Terry looks at him. You
remembered what you said about your love for Lisa being
serious? Yosef smiled at him. That's because it is man. I'm
seriously in love with my girl! Terry nods his head, he knew the
seriousness of that love as well, he had lived around their love for
each other all their lives, every since they all were kids growing
up together.   What about that man? Said Yosef. He takes Yosef
by the arm bringing him further inside the garage.   He goes up to
shut the side door that lead into the house. He then comes back
to him. Yosef sit down I need to tell you something that
happened today over here too, I mean after you left to go see
Rabbi.

He told him why Billy had been such a problem to him about Lisa
over the years. Yosef was in for the shock of his life.   Billy was
here again this afternoon. He was asking a bunch of questions
about you and Lisa. What! Don't worry man, we didn't tell him
anything, but it's not what he asked that bothered me. It's what
he said. What did he say? I know why he's been such a butt
head about Lisa all this long time.
And Why is that? He said, curiosity speaking to him.   He's in
love with her! What! It's true man. He's in love with Lisa, I saw it
today, it may or may not make any sense to you. But it's the
truth. He loves her man. He always has I think. Yosef stood up,
putting his hands in his pocket, he brushed his hair back. How
do you know this? Well it's what he said today that really gave
him away. And what was that?
He said something about her being his, and that jew boy took her
away from me or something.   All of us heard him say it. Brad,
James. You should've seen him, I mean the boy went totally
postal up in here man!   Does Lisa know? Terry walks up to him
putting his hand on his shoulder comforting him. I don't believe
she does. No, she doesn't man.   Look Jo. Lisa has always been
in love with you, you truly don't believe that he can just come into
her life and yours after all this time, and suddenly sweep her off
her feet, and out of your life forever do you?   Yosef breathes a
sigh of relief. No, of course not. He chuckled.
She loves you man. You know that Jo, I mean, you're it for her.
Lisa never talks of anyone else but you

When she's not talking about the Bible, or Church. Or even her music. She's talking about you. Really? Come on man, you've known her all your life. Lisa is the closest thing to Heaven that you'll ever have in this life man. She could care less about Billy. And you're sure that she doesn't know how he feels about her. I'm certain of it. Good, you won't say anything to her will you? You know me better than that. Thanks man. Yosef was relieved to hear that. But there's something else I need to tell you about him as well. What's that? He said that he would get her away from you. He's planning to take her back or something. I'm really afraid for her Yosef, he may try to hurt her you know? Yosef looked at him. Terry saw Yosef's expression full of rage at that moment. If he touches her, if he comes anywhere near my girl at all. So help me Terry. I'll kill him! I mean it! I'll kill him! Terry for that moment shook with fear, he never seen him like that before. He's seen Yosef angry before. But this time it was different. He felt the heat of his anger. And it burned! I hear you man. Loud and clear. He breathed. On a more brighter note, have you and Lisa setteled on a date for the Engagement party? Terry's question cooled Yosef's anger. He began to smile a little. That'll be the same Saturday as Pastors Day that night at 7:00 p.m. Where? At My Parents house. And Lisa's ok with that? Why wouldn't she be? Lisa would do just about anything I ask her. That scares me for her sometimes man. Why? Asked Terry. I mean she's so caring, she gives 100% of herself to anything and anyone. She amazes me man. Seems like you've asked her to do everything for you already, except die for you. Said Terry laughing. Don't say things like that man. Said Yosef walking away from him over to the window. Well think about it. I'd never ask her to do anything like that for me. Terry stops a moment and thinks about what Yosef just said. Jo? Yeah. I believe that she would. Would what? Die for you. Come on man, not the D word ok? Jo, Lisa loves you just that much, she's even said it a few times. Yosef looks at him. She did? Yes, she did. Well I'd never ask her to do a thing like that for me. There was a pause between them. Jo. He looks at Terry. With her you wouldn't have to. Yosef thought on his words. He then quickly vanished them out of his mind.

Billy and Helen were sitting in his car talking about Yosef and
Lisa. What did you find out about the party? Asked Helen. Well
I heard it through the grapevine that it's gonna be on the same
day as their Conference that Saturday night at around 7:00.
Yosef's old man will be getting out of the hospital soon, so let's
see what we can do to make the festivities a little more.
Heh,heh,heh. Festive. He leans over towards her, pulling out
from the back of his jeans a medium sized pistol. He takes his
hankerchief from his jacket pocket and begins to polish it. Ohhh!
Helen gasped. What are you gonna do with that thing? Now, now
sweet cheeks, just keep your bloomers on. It's just a little hill
BILLY justice that's all. He kissed the pistol, and slipped it back
into the back of his jeans. Shhh, Ok? She felt somewhat
hesitant as to what she had gotten herself into. She flings the
cigarette butt out of the car window. A cloud of smoke fumed out
of her mouth. Billy you're really not gonna use that thing are
you? I mean I don't want to see him get hurt. WHAT! You
wimpin out on me now huh! You forgot how he left you high and
dry at that bar that night! Huh! You remember that! He
screamed at her. Yeah, but. He interrupts her. NOW YOU
LISTEN TO ME HELEN. YOU'RE GONNA DO THIS
UNDERSTAND! AND IF YOU SO MUCH AS EVEN WINK IN HIS
OR LISA'S DIRECTION. LET'S SAY I'M GONNA HAVE MYSELF A
LITTLE PIG ROAST! He shouted at her grabbing her chin so tight
that he left his nailprints in her face. Ohh! She gasped. Am I
makin myself clear? He said in a softer tone. Yes Billy, yes. She
whispered. She was crying hard. That's my little sweet cheeks.
He said kissing her hard. He lays her down on the seat of the
car, they engage in a brief encounter. When they finish, Helen
was still crying over her delema. Shut your mouth, and clean up
your face! Now remember, I'm doing this for you as well as for
me. I just want to scare them that's all Nobody's gonna get hurt
ok? Ok Billy. She said. He reached down and fondled himself a
little. I still have something that I owe her from that night. No
girl turns down Billy Bravens, no girl at all. He starts the car and
drives off.

Monday comes in unseasonably hot for early June. Yosef
returned to work smiling happy, glowing all over. His life had
turned around completely. He had his girl back into his life, and
they would be husband and wife soon. All he could do was
whistle his happiness that morning.   He walked into Mr. Dennis'

office still whistling. Mr. Dennis was on his desk phone to Michele. They were going out that night themselves. It was to be a very special occasion for them. He's about to ask her to marry him. He had already bought the ring. Baby, I'll call you back in a few ok? I love you too. Bye. He hangs up the phone. Well what's this? Yosef grabs him by the waist and starts dancing with him. Don't tell me. It's on? Yosef nods his head still whistling and dancing. Ha,ha,ha! That's wonderful boy! See I told you
Everything would work out. He said patting him on the back. Yosef, he said in a funny kind of tone. Would you let me go, and stop dancing with me. I'm beginning to get excited. They both laugh. Sorry Mr. Dennis, I can't help it. I've never been this happy in my life. I'm finally getting married! Cut it out with that Mr. Stuff. You're practically my partner now. Call me Adam. Adam? But your first name is William. Yeah, I know, but I've always liked my Middle name better than my first. William Adam Dennis. You have three first names. Laughed Yosef. Mr. Dennis parroted his laughing at him. My parents were very confused prople. They didn't know what the hell to name me. Yosef laughs again.

So tell me man, what happened? Well for starters, her father took me to where she was. And where was that? South Haven, Michigan. Ahhh. South Haven. I know it well. I've been there several times. Beautiful place! Just beautiful! I'm going to take Michele there for Harborfest in June. Lisa's father was telling me about that. Ahh man it rules! Said Mr. Dennis. I mean it kicks some serious butt man! Hey, maybe you and your band could play there one summer. The people there would eat it up! I can pull a few strings and get your guys booked in up there. He said. I'll keep that in mind. You do that. Anyway back to you and Lisa. Yeah, her father took me to their vacation home there. And sure enough. I got inside of the cottage, walked into Lisa's bedroom, and there she was!
I mean she was lying on the bed looking like something that had just stepped out of Heaven Itself! When I saw her man, my hormones went ballistic! I mean I couldn't help myself! I nearly blew everything.
I never wanted sex so bad in my life as I did at that moment. And her? Well she was a bit more controlled than I was. She reminded me of our promise. We prayed a little, then we got dressed and left. I brought her home, and proposed to her all

over again. She accepted, again. So now we're making our wedding plans for the big day. Which is man? In 1 month. He said holding up one finger. Can you last that long?
What other choice do I have? We made a vow, and it's been the most torturous vow that we've ever made in our lives. I wanted her so bad I could taste her man. He said brushing his hair back. I'm really happy for you Jo. I'm serious. Not only am I happy for you, but I'm proud of you as well. Because you uh, had me worried there for a while there. Yosef smiles a little. Thanks for helping me Adam, I was pretty messed up over loosing her. Now that I have her back in my life, I'll never let her go again. See to

It that you don't. And besides, that's what I'm here for. Hey, after all. You helped me didn't you? Yosef gives him a puzzled look. I don't know what you mean. Me and Michele. Ohhhh. How are things with you and Michele these days? I'm so glad you asked my man. I can't explain it Jo, I mean, she's great! I've never known a woman like her before. I feel about her like you do for Lisa. I've never felt love like this before. She's about as down to earth of a woman that I've ever met in my life. Her insight, her love for life and adventure. I mean, Michele is everything that I could ever dream of in a woman. Yosef looked at him his every word about Michele reminded him of Lisa. He knew what he meant. He was now speaking to him about Michele the same way that he often times had spoken to him about Lisa. He nodded his head in agreement. There was a pause between them. Mr. Dennis wiping the tears from his eyes. Jo, can I show you something? Sure, what is it? Mr. Dennis reaches into his pocket and pulls out a medium sized ring box. He opens it. Yosef gasped when he saw the huge diamond engagement ring. Whoa! He breathed. That is beautiful! He said. Yes it is just like my Michele. I'm gonna ask her to marry me Jo.
Tonight. I'm taking her to dinner at Chae's place. Yosef was mesmerized by the shimmer of the ring. It's

Sparkle reminded him of Lisa's ring. Which to him was even more beautiful than Michele's. Well what do you think? You think she'll say yes? Yosef looked up at him. I know she will. He hands the box back to him. I can hardly believe it man, for the first time really since Pat's death. I can truly say. I'm in love!

I love Michele! And she loves me, I mean really loves me. For me, not for my bank account, or my home, or anything superficial. She's truly in love with me. Do you know what I'm saying here? I didn't think that loving someone this way could be possible, but since she came into my life. I'm a firm believer that true love doesn't see any colour man, no colour at all. I saw that with you and Lisa. He pauses, he was nearly our of breath from excitement. He sits back down near to Yosef. Thanks man. For helping me to see what true love really is. Thanks for sharing with me about love at true sight. I saw her heart, and she saw mine. I'll never forget this as long as I live. God in Heaven Bless you and Lisa. Oh, by the way, how is she? She's her usual beautiful self. She was a little down today. Oh and why is that? What's the matter? She's had a lot on her mind lately. Like what? Well you know her aunt has a bit of a gambling problem. No, I didn't know that. Well she does. Then when her and Mamie moved back up here, and Lisa started working at her old job. Her boss assaulted and tried to rape her. Then he fired her. Then our break up happened. I mean one thing after another. And with the wedding only a month away. Everything is really beginning to take it's toll on her. I just want to get her away for a while. And do what then Jo? He smiled at him. And just totally spoil her man,. I mean she's been through hell since she's been back home.

Her aunt's gambling was the first thing, I mean she completely blew all my girl's savings on her gambling, then all that other stuff that happened to her. I mean that's quite a lot for a woman to handle. She wants to work again. To help out she says. But I make enough to take care of her. I have plenty saved. Mr. Dennis paused. Jo, I want to do something for you and Lisa. As a matter of fact, I have something for the two of you anyway. Think of it as sort of a pre-wedding present. When will you see her again? Today, she's coming here to pick me for lunch this afternoon. Cool! I want to talk to you both. Have you set a date yet? Yes, she said she always wanted our wedding to have fireworks. So, we've decided on the fourth of July. Outstanding! Said Mr. Dennis. Uh, would youand Michele like to come to the wedding? Really?
Yes, really. We'll be there! Solid! They shake hands. Oh, uh Jo. Yes. When does your father get out of the hospital? Sometime this week from what from what my mother told me. But Dr. K

still hasn't made a definite decision yet. We should know for sure today or tomorrow. Keep me informed. So my young friend, are you having a bachelor's party or what? It's more like an or what thing for me. What do you mean? I thought that I would break the traditional norm and do something completely different. We are going to meet at my parents home this Friday, and talk about men's issues, the things that make a good marriage, and a good home and all that kinda stuff. Lisa's father will speak to us that night. And what

About the women, they'll be doing the same thing in another part of the house as well. Lisa's mom will be speaking to them as well. It's really for me and her. A kind of sharing thing between us all. No strippers?
No. No drinking? No. No making your wildest fantansies come true before the big day? No sir none of that. He thought on the idea a little smiling. I like it! I really like it! Sounds like a cool thing to do, a little out of the ordinary, but cool! Would you like to come too? Really Jo? Yes really. I wouldn't miss it for the world. Maybe they can teach me somethings too huh? Whatever you say sir. Whose idea was this anyway? My girl's Lisa? Yeah, Lisa. He breathed. I'll be there! Solid! Said Yosef. Well, I have to go son, I have to get ready for a meeting with a few of our client's associates. I think we're getting close to landing this thing. I should be back around 11:00 or so ok? Ok. Tell Lisa to wait if I'm not back before you guys are ready to leave. I have to speak with you both. He looks at his watch. It was 9:45a.m. Once again, congratulations son. Same to you and Michele. Mr. Dennis leaves for his meeting. Yosef goes back into his small office to finish up some work on his forms,and makes a few phone calls for Mr. Dennis.

Yosef was sitting at his desk filing some forms away when his cell rings. Hello Beloved. The sweet voice sounded. Yosef smiled a smiled that went from one corner of his face to the other. He had been thinking of her all morning. How's my girl? Your girl is fine. That you are baby, that you are. So tell me, are we still on for our date this afternoon? Yes we are. Mr. Dennis wants to talk to us both before we go, is that alright with you? Sure it is. What time do I need to be there? How about 11:30? You got it! I'll be there ok? Ok. I have to go help my mother and Ms. Sarah in the kitchen, I'll see you then. I love you sweetie.

I love you too baby. Bye. They hang up. It seemed like only a few mintues past by after Mr. Dennis had left for his meeting. It was now 11:15a.m. and Mr. Dennis returns to the office smiling big. Yosef knew that from his smile, that the meeting went better than expected, and that it was definitely good news. They talk briefly about it. When there was a knock at the door. Come in, they both said at the same time. It was Lisa. She stepped inside. Yosef walks up to her kissing her forehead. Hi baby. Hi Beloved. He brings her inside the office. Mr. Dennis walks up to her taking her hand kissing it gently. How are you my dear?

I'm fine this morning, and how are you? Great! Just great! Jo, keep her here ok? I'll be right back. He leaves them for a few minutes, then returns carrying a long envelope. He hands it to Yosef, he then hands it

To Lisa. Why don't you open it Lisa. Mr. Dennis said to her. She does. To her and Yosef's surprise. It was check for $5,000! It was a pre-wedding present. It's for your honeymoon, or whatever you guys want to use it for. Lisa threw her arms around Mr. Dennis's neck hugging him hard. He and Yosef embrace. Thanks Sir, you don't know what this means to us. Oh yes I do son, yes I do. If you don't mind my asking. Where were you two going for lunch? Downtown to Bernies. He paused. What do you mean were going? Yosef asked. There's been a slight change in plans. I know how you've always wanted to take Lisa to Chae's Place. But I already made plans. Cancelled! Interrupted Mr. Dennis. You need

Reservations just to park at Chae's. Reserved! He interrupted again. Yosef took out his wallet. No, son. Your money's no good there. It's already been arranged for you. Just go and use my name, they know me from way back. Believe me they'll know who you are. Go, go, go now. Get going. I'll expect you back here at 1:00p.m. More work to do on the deal. You got sir! He sees them off to lunch. He had planed to give him the rest of the day off that Monday. He wanted to get an early start on his own evening with Michele. He called her promptly after they left. Yosef came back to work at 12:55pm. He looked almost like he was in a daze of some sort. He had, had a wonderful time with Lisa. He told Mr. Dennis all about it. They finished up the last of their work in the office getting prepared for when Mr. Walden was to return from overseas. He was in Europe with his wife on a brief vacation.

And would return next week to meet with him and a few business associates. Mr. Dennis let's Yosef off at 2:30p.m. Lisa picked him up from work. When he got home. His mother told him the good news about Rabbi. Dr. Kaplan has agreed to release him from the hospital this Friday. He had ran all of the tests that he needed, he was still in shock over his Miraculous healing. That Friday, Dr. Kaplan signed the papers to release him from the Hospital.

To his family, friends, colleagues, and to a new life!

The Colour Of Love
Anne Hemingway
Chap 31.

When they arrived at home with Rabbi, they were met with the shouts of all their friends and family! There was a surprise homecoming party for him! Lisa and Deborah planned the whole thing. They didn't even tell Yosef and Sarah. Everyone was there! Rabbi Marcus, and Connie, all of the other Rabbi's from Temple. Yosef's band Daystar were there too. All welcomed him home. He was the guest of honor that day. He shared with them, all that God had done in his life. He had time to pause and reflect back on his life after the heart attack. What had brought him to that point in his life that nearly killed him. The bitterness, the hurt, resentment. The pain of loosing his beloved family. He felt that God had done him an injustice in letting him see them murdered before him, and then leaving him alive to bear the scars that it left him with. He felt that there would never be any healing for him for surviving such an ordeal. How wrong he was! When he had the stroke, and how he saw death itself hovering over him. He saw his life flash before him in a matter of minutes. And when God so used the very person that he had held a disliking for, for so many years. So graciously lay her hands upon me for Yeshua to heal me. I knew then that I did not want to die! I wanted to live, I wanted to love! I wanted to experience everything that had been taken away from me. The togetherness of a family that loves me. Friends that accept me. Colleagues that look up to me and respect me. And God Himself that gave Himself for me! And healed me! To you my dear. I owe the deepest thanks. He

said walking up to Lisa. Thank you dear child. Thank you for helping me to see beyond the colour of skin, and seeing the true Colour Of Love. He kisses her forehead.
Yosef my son. Take her and love her! Be all that Yeshua can make you to be to her. You belong together.

My dearest Sarah. My wife. My deepest applogies to you my love. You have stayed with a man who made stubbornness, and bitterness his mistresses. Yet you still loved me. An age to age, eternity to eternity combined would not be long enough to tell you how grateful that I will always be to you for staying by my side, when most women would have left me along time ago. I pray that God will flow the life of love itself back into your heart for me, as He has in my heart for you. Sarah walks up to him. The flow of that love never ran dry for youYacov. In all this time. It never has. I love you my dearest. She kisses him deeply. There were cheers and shouts from everyone there! Johnathan steps into the middle of the living room. Let's party! Everyone there bursted with laughter. John my boy how are you! Said Rabbi grabbing his cheeks and rubbing his bald head. I hate it when he does that! Everyone laughs out loud. Rabbi had truly been changed by his near death experiences. He was given a second chance at life. He was truly a changed man! As the party went on, the men wanted to have their get together now since they were all there. All agreed. Rev. Anderson spoke with Deborah. She agreed as well. I have an announcement to make. Said Rev. Anderson. Tonight is the night that my soon to be son in law will have myself and some of the other brothers here speak to him on his pending marriage to my daughter Lisa. While it is traditional for a man to have a bachelors party. My daughter and I thought it would be better to get away from Tradition and settle for something less risqué. She wanted to give her husband to be something to look forward to. We are going to share with him our hearts and experiences of what true married life is to be for him. And the same for Lisa. Son, would you come up here to me. Yosef walks up to him. I've loved this young man just like he's my own child. He may not be the son of my loins. But he is the son of my heart. I love you Jo,Jo. They embrace. Thank you dad, I love you too. Johnathan, come here. He walks up to them. This is my first born child. They were both raised together. Not one time while my wife and I was rearing them right over there across the street was there ever any jealousy between them.

They've loved each other like brothers every since they were young lads. And I'm proud of them both! He then looks over at Lisa standing next to Deborah. Come here baby girl. Lisa walks over to him. This is my angel, my pride and joy. He kisses her cheek. He gives her over to Yosef, who took her into his arms embracing her gently. They're the reason we're gathered here tonight. My wife will be speaking to Lisa in the other family room. I along with Elder Mathews will be speaking tonight as well. Let's make this a night for him to remember as long as he lives. Then he too can pass this new tradition along to his own sons. Jo-Jo, Johnathan. Shall we gentlemen. They all left the living room to the family room near his

Study. Lisa and Deborah and the other female guests went into the den the opposite side of the house.

Rev. Anderson opened up his message with Scripture taken from Genesis the second chapter. *"It is not good for man to be alone, I will make a helper, or companion suitable. Especially for him."* Gentlemen, when God spoke these words, the instiution of marriage began. It started out as being an union between a man and a woman unlike any other union on the earth. The uniqueness of it is something so precious, so holy in the sight of God. So precious is the union between a husband and his wife that the only separater between them would be death itself. How tragic that marriage now days has become something that two people do just because they can, or it's the right thing to do when a child has been conceived out of wedlock. Or they've lived together for so long, they might as well make it legal. How many would really be honest enough to say that they married their spouse out of a deep and abiding love, and a total comittment to their wife or husband? I ask you brothers. How many men would be honest to say. I love my wife so much, that to me one moment without her in my life would be like death to me?   This is not only the way that I love my wife. But the way that I live my life with Deborah. We've lived this way the entire time of our union together. In the New Testament Paul said to the Church at Ephesus, that the husband is to love his wife even as Christ loves the Church. How many men really do love their wives this way? Why are we so afraid to love the way that God has instructed us to love? We're so afraid that we

In someways end up sabotaging our own marriages, instead of making them the safe haven that it was intended to be for us in the beginning. We refer to marriage not as something that will unify us with the one that we have betrothed not only our hearts to, but our very lives to. It now has become something like "getting hitched", "Taking the plunge" Some people have the vows in the reverse. Instead of forsaking all others saving only her or him to themselves. They've become martially dyslexic and thought that it means forsaking him or her, and saving everybody for themselves. The divorce rate has hit an all time high in these last few years. More and more people are getting "unhitched" or divorced as adultery hits an even bigger all time high. Yet the Scriptures still say the same thing it's said all this time, and will continue to do so. Adulterers and Adulteresess God will Judge. Because of infidelity of heart, we have allowed it to make a home in our marriages. They go out and have their affairs, and come home and lay next to their spouse, and behave as though they've done no wrong. How will we answer in the day of Judgement? Yosef and all the others listened attentively as Rev. Anderson shared with them his heart on what marriage was intended to be for all. They never took their eyes off him as he spoke very candidly about sensitive issues regarding sex, and marriage. There were many there that asked him questions about those things, he gave them the answers that he knew would challenge them to reevaluate themselves and husbands and fathers. Lisa listened as attentively as Yosef as her mother shared deep insights with her and the other guests, touching on some of the same issues as her husband. She shared with her how some women just like some men, make similar mistakes when it comes to love and marriage. She shared the same Scriptures with them. The Bible tells the women to love YOUR OWN HUSBANDS." I cannot stress this enough when he have marriage seminars at Church. I mean ladies. I get woman after woman come to me after Service crying their little eyes out , about how brother so and so broke my heart. I thought that he was gonna leave his wife and be with me. But he lied to me. I mean you've heard the sob stories haven't you?

My advice to them is this. If he's unfaithful to the one that he made a vow before God and man to. What's to stop him from being unfaithful to you? Just as he's lied to his wife to be with you, he'll lie to you too just to be with someone else. I say that a choice has to be made here. And sadly many women go on to

make that one choice that will keep them in bondage to a relationship that God never intended for them.
They wait and they wait and they wait. Until they've wasted their entire life away on a person that they can see for themselves is not God's best for them. What hurts me even more than this, are the ones who become pregnant in these relationships thinking that having a child with this person will make him love her more, or that she can somehow hang on to him for the rest of his life because she has a baby by him now.

Nothing could be farther from the truth! It's time for women to wake up to themselves, and realize that an affair with another woman's husband doesn't make you special. It makes you stupid! Hey, reality check here. It does. I would say to you that. Making the choice not to engage in such activity as that makes you special, and more appealing to that one special man that God is preparing to send to you, or send you to him. Understand what it is a man really wants in his life. You'll be surprised what you'll find. She spoke further to them. It was humorus at times, and at other times very serious for them all. Yosef and Lisa were about to be married soon, and the older men wanted to share their insights with him. And they did. He soaked up every word. He wanted to make sure himself that he would not fall into the many subtle traps that snare, and entrap a man or woman into making decisions that would be detrimental to their Marriage. Lisa was doing the same thing. Soon Yosef felt his love for his girl speaking to him again. He looked out into the hall and excused himself. He left to go find her. He saw Mamie out in the hall coming from the bathroom. He asked her to have Lisa come out and meet him on the front porch. He leaves to go out and wait for her. She comes out to meet him a few minutes later. It was quiet and private. They embraced and kissed and loved on each other. I so missed you Beloved. I missed you too baby. He said softly kissing her forehead. He kissed her deeply. Moaning out her name. *"Oh God Lisa."* Are you better now honey? She asked. He was silent. No? she asked again. He looked down at his manhood.

Oh, honey. Again? They laughed. I can't help it Lisa, it just happens. You know how much I love you?
Yes, I do. I do. She kisses him again. Whoa! He breathed. The kiss made him lightheaded. Are you alright? I think so. You're

not gonna faint out on me again like you did at dance class a few days ago are you? No, I'm not gonna faint out you. I'm fine now. You sure? Yeah, I'm sure. They both laughed. They remembered that day. Yosef and the boys were in the garage, they had just finished up with rehearsal. They were talking with him about the little place that Terry's father loaned them for their wedding night. It was a cute little cottage right down town on the Lakeshore. They were talking about how they were to fix it up as a surprise for Lisa that night. So tell me man did you get all the supplies that we need for the house? Asked James. Me and my father went down to the hardward store to get most of the stuff man, my mother picked out everything else. Your mother! Said Brad and James together. I had to go with her man, she made me do it. They both laughed at him. Yosef held his head down chuckling to himself. You don't know what it does to a man, to walk into a fabric store surrounded by all that lace, and ruffles and stuff man. I couldn't wait to get outta there! They bust up laughing again. Yosef was sitting on the stool in the midst of them laughing. I know what you mean Terry. My mother tried to get me to come with her too. She's making Lisa's wedding dress. And the dress for our engagment party.
She's nearly done with them both now. I can't wait to see her in them. Yeah, she'll be a vision and half won't she man? Said James. Who was wearing an ice pack on his eye. He had hurt himself playing
Football with some of his other partners that morning. He had ran out to catch a field kick or something, he looked up at the sun just briefly, which impaired his vision. He misjudged his distance, and ran into
The goal post and knocked himself out cold. He was left with a very sore black eye. Yeah, she will. Hey I have to get going guys, I have to pick her up from dance class at three. Wait a minute man. Said James.
We got a little time. Me and the guys just want to take a little time to tell you that we're very happy for man. I mean to be married to a treasure like Lisa. I mean, it's like a dream come true. All that soft little body wrapped up in your arms on that night, hugging her close to you, kissing her like there's no tomorrow. Yosef begins to fantasize James' words. He was teasing him really. Oh, Jesus Lisa! He said.
Oh, oh. I would say we have his full attention now right guys? Laughed James. They all burst out laughing at him. Thanks a lot guys, I'm sure I needed this. And what am I suppose to do now? Well, let's go get Lisa. Said James patting him on the

shoulder. What! I can't go out there like this man! They all laughed again. This aint funny to me at all guys. Said Yosef, trying to ease his stiffness. Here my man! You need this more than I do. Said James, taking his ice pack off his eye and putting it on Yosef's very swollen groin. There ya are. That ought to calm you down some. It's almost 2:30, I really need to get going, she's waiting for me. He gives James back his ice pack, as they were leaving. James stayed behind to put the pack back on his eye again. Hey! Jo! You melted my ice man! Yosef runs back in there after him snatching him by the arm. Will you come on! They hurry out to the dance center. Lisa had just come out wearing a long black silky outer coat that clowed with her every movement. Underneat it she was wearing a black matching body all with low v-neck. It hugged every curve of her slender body. She walks up to him. Well honey, what do you think? I bought it last night. She took the coat off and bent down and touched the floor. She stood back up facing him. It fits a little snug, but I can still move around pretty well in it. Yosef stood there looking at her, his eyes fixed on her. Honey? She said. Lisaaaaah......? He moaned out, his eyes rolled backwards in his head. He then collapses to the floor . James and Brad were stupidified as well. Terry then spoke up. Look what you did! Go, go get something on now! What's the matter with him! Please Lisa go now! Can I help? Nooooo! If he wakes up and sees you like that, it's

Lights out again. Now get going! Ok, ok! She runs back into the dressing room to change. Brad and James were still fixed in their place unable to move. Come on man, snap out of it! Said Terry lighly tapping Yosef on his cheeks. He wakes up, his head swimming. There you go big guy, let's get you over here ok? He walks him over to one of the benches and sits down with him. Is it alright to come out now!
Yelled Lisa from the dressing room. Yeah, it's ok now Lise. Why is she yelling like that? Said Yosef rubbing his head, he shook himself trying to clear it. What happened? You fainted, that's what happened. I did? Yeah, I mean like bam! Down you went bro. Yosef looks over at Brad and James still in their stupor. What's up with them? He said trying to stand up. They reacted a little like you when they saw Lisa, but you lost it, they didn't. Yosef shook his head smiling at them. Lisa walks up to them. You alright honey? Yeah, I'm fine. What happened to you? You happened to me, he said. What? All I did

Was show you my new body all, and you loose it on me. Uh,huh.
He said snatching her into his arms
Deep kissing her. He lets her go. She looks at him stupidifed.
Uhhhhhh! She moaned, collapsing to the floor in a heap. Will
you two stop that! Shouted Terry. Well she started it! Said
Yosef. Oh, get her!
He said his frustration rising in a playful sort of way. Pow!pow!
snap out of it! He said to Brad and james smacking them
playfully on the back of their heads. Come on let's go! Yosef
picks up Lisa's
Limp body, she moans as he carries her out to the car. Looks like
you'll have to drive man. Said Yosef to

Terry. Yeah looks like. He said. Their laughter brings them
back into the now. I remember that, that was funny. Said Lisa.
I think that we should be getting back in there now. They'll miss
us. She said. No they won't. Said Yosef softly to her, kissing her
gently on the lips. Whooooo! They turn around to see that
everyone in the house had become their audience. Wolf whistles,
and shouting, and cheering was coming from them all, as all eyes
were on them. They looked at each other and laughed. Lets give
them something to really whistle about. He takes her into his
arms and kisses her deeply again before them all. So in love.
Said Mamie. Her and Deborah hold hands smiling at the couple.
They then leave, giving them their privacy. I Love you Lisa. I
Love you too, my Beloved. Hold me, hold me close. She said
softly.
They kiss again tenderly.

Saturday was as hot as any other day that Summer. As this happens this time of year. It was sweltering that day. But no one complained about the heat at all. For many the day had come, it was finally here! Pastors Day International Conference! That was the biggest day for many. But also it was a very special day for two special people as well. It was also Yosef's and Lisa's engagement party that day too!

Everything was set for both. The Church workers worked feverishly to prepare the Church with decorations of flags and banners from every Country, and Church that would be represented there that day.

The parking lot attendants were dressed in their attendants uniforms, the Deacons in their best suits, the Ushers in their white uniforms as well. One of which was Mamie. She had agreed to resume her position as Head Usher for the Conference. Rev. Anderson and Deborah were overjoyed to hear that she would usher in Church again. Yosef and his band Daystar,and Lisa were as vocally prepared as they were spiritually to Minister that day. Yosef had completed the song that he would sing not only to Yeshua, but also to his beloved Lisa. His heart swelling with gratitude for Him bringing her back to him. It was nearing 9:00a.m. Everyone that would speak, or sing were already present at the Church and awaiting the

Next step before the Service was to begin. Rabbi and Sarah were there seated in the Reserved section in the very front row. Yosef went over some last minute details with his band before Service was to start which would be promptly at 9:00. All the speakers were in place in the Pulpit along with their reperesenatives and Missionaries that they sponsored from other Countries from Germany, to Jerusalem, from South America to China! The parking lot was jammed packed with vans, buses, trucks as many came from all walks of life and Cultures and Denominations, and from other far away Nations! Excitement filled the air, everyone could feel it! Nearly every Denomination was there, from Catholics, Baptists, Pentecostal, Charismatic, Lutheran, Wesleyan, AME, CME, and Jewish. I mean everyone attended. And all were welcome. Yosef's boss Mr. Dennis and his fiancé

Michele were there too seated in the Reserved section on the opposite side of the Church. Rabbi Marcus and his wife Connie. And Rabbi Horowitz, and his wife Anna were there also in the Reserved section. Rabbi Epstein invited the Shofar players from his

Temple there to bring a festive air to the Service. One of them also let him play the instrument. After hitting many sour notes, he finally decided it's just best to let the professionals do it. All enjoyed his jovial mood that day. He seemed to anticipate something in that day, he just didn't know what. He seated himself back next to Sarah who couldn't believe herself the incrediable change that had taken place in

Her husband. As did everyone that knew and loved him. Rabbi, after he seated himself looked all around him in awe as he beheld the beauty of the vast array of the colours of people. Black people, White people, native American, Eastern Indian, Jewish, German, Chinese, Japanese. The entire colour spectrum of man Surrounded him! He watched and listened as they fellowshipped with each other as though they had known each other all their lives. There was absolutely complete harmony there! All were there for one common purpose in mind, and that was to bridge the gap that keeps us as people a Nation, and Community apart, and to see the wall of Race hatred broken down! Sarah could hardly contain herself as she attened Pastors Day every year. There were to be three Dignitaries that would speak briefly giving updates as to what God is doing in their part of the World. The Service would open up with Prayer, then announcements After that. Praise and Worship lead by Yosef, and Daystar,and Lisa. Rabbi was dressed in his Vestments with matching Yamika. Sarah was dressed in a beautiful white laced dressed that she made for her and Deborah. Lisa was dressed in an all white v-necked dress, with pointed long sleeves. She looked beautiful! Yosef found it difficult to take his eyes off her as usual. Rev. Anderson was still in his office kneeling in intense prayer. His desire was to see the dream that his father had instilled in him come to pass.

The time is now 9:00a.m. Time for the Service to begin. The Master of Ceremony, Bishop Elden Henry Sr. steps up to the microphone. There were cheers and shouts as he stood in front of them. "Praise God!"

I'm so glad to be here in your beautiful city of Chicago, Illinois. The windy city. And she's still got it going on! Amen! Amen!

Shouted the Congregation all were standing, the air was charged
with excitement! Glory! I just want to say that I'm deeply
honored that your Pastor Rev. Benjamin Anderson
Asked me to do the honors of being your Emcee for this years
Pastors Day International Conference, and I do believe that this is
the day that we will in this Church here today see many Miracles
in our midst! The crowd roared with applause and shouts!
When I recived the phone call from Rev. Anderson to come here
to be with all of you on this momentious occasion. I just couldn't
miss the opportunity nor could I turn down the offer. I telll you
this years program will be the best yet. I'm so excited that I can
hardly contain myself up here! How about you out there! The
Congregation roars again. I know how anxious that all of you as
well as myself are ready to get started, so without further adieu, if
you have your programs in front of you. I want to introduce to
you all the way from Orlando Florida. Minister Dale Jacobs, who
will open us up in prayer. Please remain standing if you will.
Minister Jacobs. Just then a tall slender distinguished looking
white man steps up to the mike. He is dressed in his Ministerial
robes. Black in colour trimmed in gold. His hair a salt and
pepper colour. His voice soft at first. Then it escalates as his
prayer deepens with emotion. Tears streaming down his face.

*"Father in the Name of Jesus, we come before Your Awesome
Presence. Father we give You thanks and we give You the Praise
And the adoration that is due Your Holy Precious Name. Oh,
Father
God as we look to You to come into our midst here today, and to
have
Your way in this place, to move amongst us by Your Holy Spirit,
and to
Let thy Glory fall upon us. Lord we ask that You, would bring much
Healing, and much togetherness between us as we depend on You
to
Touch each and every heart that is here today, those from far
away
Lands, and Nations, as we Gloryify Thy Great Name here on the
Earth
Father God, we ask that you would Anoint our speakers, anoint
our
Singers, Father anoint our musicians as they minister under the
direction*

Of thy Spirit. Father and mostly we would ask that You would Anoint our

Pastor Rev. Benjamin Anderson as he brings the message that You laid

Upon his heart. Fill him with Thy Spirit, and let Thy Glory fall upon him

As he speaks to us this day. We ask for a Mighty move of Thy Spirit in this

Place today. We agree that it is done Father, and we give You the Glory

For this Confererence is not for the glory of man, but for the Glory of God!"

In Jesus Great and Wonderful Name. Do signs and Wonders and great

Miracles. Praise God! And Let all of God's people say.......Amen."

Bishop Henry steps back up to the microphone wiping his eyes of tears, he himself is a very distinguished black man, of medium height. His hair nearly all gray. His solemn features tell the story of a man who has seen and done much in his near fourty years of Ministry. Yosef pulls Lisa close to him embracing her. I Love you. He whispered in her ear. She turns to look at him. I Love you too my Beloved. She whispers back to him, winking at him. He squirmed a little. Behave yourself girl. We're in Church. Anything you say Beloved, anything you say. Bishop Henry then called for Deborah to come to the mike to make any Church announcements, which she did very quick like. She was then escorted back to her seat. All the Congregation had seated themselves after prayer. Bishop Henry then makes the next introduction. The childrens choir were then assembled down in front of the Church just below the Pulpit. They were lead In song by their director. Mrs. Juanita Vazquez, an older Hispanic Church member who was in charge of The childrens Ministry there. The children sang the song "Jesus Loves the Little Children." Everyone watched them made up of just as many colours as the Congregation. Yosef looked at Lisa. She was holding his hand. Caressing it gently. He thought to himself, that soon their children would be standing down there singing to the Church eventually. It filled him with an even deeper love for Lisa. He kissed her cheek. He hugged her close to him. When the children were finished with their selection. Bishop Henry calls for the Ushers to prepare for the offering to be taken. The offering was to be placed into special Ministries that

Sent food, clothing, medical supplies, and to the building of Churches in other Countries. After the offering had been taken, Bishop then Introduced the Dignitaries and speakers from other Countries. They told of the happenings in Jerusalem, Indonesia, and etc. The time was now 10:20a.m. Bishop then introduced the praise team, and band. Now I want to introduce to you at this time. The Praise team, who will bless us with a special selection. I tell you I just love this group of people right here. He said pointing to Yosef and the band. They have a sound that just ushers in the Presence of God. They will now Minister to us in song. Give a warm welcome to Daystar! The crowd cheered thunderously.   Yosef steps up to the mike adjusting his bass. He and the band were all dressed in black suits, with matching Yamikas.   Lisa and Rita, who was now showing her three month old pregnancy, stood in place in front of the mikes waiting for Yosef to give them the cue to start the selection.   This is one of my favorite songs from the Homeland of Yerushalim Let Us Go Into The House Of the Lord. He begins to count off. 1,2. 1 2 3 4. They start to play and sing gloriously.

Let us go into the House of the Lord.
Let us go into the House of the Lord.

Let us enter His Presence with thanksgiving
And with Praise. Let us go into the House of the

Lord.   Oh Let us go into His Courts with a song
Let us go into His Courts with a song. Let us Worship

The Lord our God Oh Magnify His Name. Let us go into the
House of the Lord.   Oh Let us go into His House with our
Praise, let us go in His House with our Praise. Let us Bow

Down before Him, with our holy hands we raise. Let us go into
The House, let us go into the House let us go into House of the
Lord.....................................!

Written By   Anne Hemingway

The entire Congregation gives them a cheering standing ovation! Hallelujah's ring out from the people. Bishop Henry then steps back up to the Pulpit clapping his hands. Rabbi and Sarah still clapping along with the rest of the people as they had totally enjoyed the selection. It reminded Rabbi of happier times when he immigrated from Germany here to the United States. He was brought over along with another

Holocaust survivor. He was an older gentleman, who too had lost his wife and son. He befriended young Jacob, and allowed him to travel with him to the New World. When they reached New York, they could not believe their eyes! There she was standing tall, and beautiful, and welcoming. Her torch seemed to reach into the Heavens! They watched her reverently as their boat sailed by her. The Statue of Liberty. Home of the Free, and Home of the Brave! Rabbi thought that he would never know happiness again until he saw her standing there. A single tear makes it's way down his small cheek. Come now my little one. We are here. Upon arriving at the docks. They were met with the Security, and little Jacob watched them checking the people for numbers on their arms. Some of them even wore a golden star. He didn't know what it all meant at that time. They were then taken to the Registration Department for processing. The older gentleman that had befriended him all this time had been registered, and taken away.

Where are your parents? The young woman asked him. Jacob looked up at her, his tears now flowed for a different reason this time. His fear had once again taken his words from him. She bent down to him. Is there no one with you child? Her voice soft and comforting to him. Her heart breaking for him. She knew then that his parents were either dead or he had lost contact from them. It was more the former than the latter The young clerk took him by the hand over to the front desk. She spoke briefly with one of the head people there. They checked into a large book for a phone number. The clerk then makes the call. The Security guard comes and takes little Jacob by the hand away from the young clerk. He takes him over into a small section where there were many children, they too like him had no parents. There was the tooting of a horn outside, it was a large bus. It had come for them, they were to be taken to the Orphangage. It was there that little Jacob finished out the rest of his years until he became an adult. He then left to attend the nearest Yeshiva college and finish out his studies. He had left briefly one day for a walk to the park. There under a shade tree sat a very beautiful young woman. Her long flowing brown hair hung down her back. She stood up and looked him for a moment. And it was that moment in time that was etched in his heart forever. For the young woman that held his heart captive, was his beloved Sarah Berkovitz. He hadn't known what it was like to feel what he was feeling before. It was new to him, as well as a little strange. But it also felt GOOD! I am Sarah. she said in a thick Yiddish accent. Mm, my uh. He stammered over his words trying to find the ones to properly introduce himself to her. Pardon me ma' mam, but I've never seen anyone like you before. For the first time since he was ten years old he was feeling something that he never thought it possible for him to ever feel again. Love! Jacob was falling in love! What is your name? She asked him. Her voice soft like the ripples of a gentle stream it seemed to wash all over him. Her eyes soft like doves eyes, they were inviting him to look deeper into her heart, there was quietness about her that held him spellbound. She laughs a little at his stammering.

My name? He stares at her the same way that Yosef stared at Lisa when they first met. Yes your name what is it? She asked again, chucking a little louder. What is it? He asked himself. He stammered even worse than before. Finally his senses allowed him to speak to her. His voice returns to him. Jacob! Jacob Epstien! Whew! He said rubbing his forehead. I am pleased to meet you Jacob Epstein. The honor as well as the pleasure is mine. He said, he was unable to take his eyes off her. Would you like to walk with me Jacob? He smiled at her. That I would, ma'mam, that I would. He takes her by the hand, they walk through the park. It was the beginning of a love relationship that would last as far as they were concerned
For eternity. I told you these kids are as they say today. Off the hanger. Everyone in the Congreation erupts in laughter. Yosef nearly falls off his seat. Lisa wipes the tears from her eyes she was laughing so hard. Their laughter snaps Rabbi back into the now. His eyes fixed on Sarah. To him she had become that same ravishing beauty that God had branded inside his heart forever. He puts his arm around her hugging her close to him. His heart

was filling with love for her all over again. What's the matter?
Asked Bishop.

You got it wrong Bishop. It's off the hook! Said the childrens
choir laughing hysterically at him. Oh,oh! That's right. Well
ya'lls slang changes so much, there ain't no telling what yall
might come up with next!
The Church laughs again. I'm so glad that we can all laugh like
this together, do you know what this does
To the Heart of God when his people gather together in harmony
without letting the slightest difference in us make a difference at
all? The Church applauds his words. Here Look at our Banner
up here. Everyone looked upward towards the ceiling at the
beautiful banner stretched out across the platform. It read....

"UNITY THROUGH LOVE."

*"And He has made from ONE BLOOD EVERY NATION
Of Men to dwell on all the face of the Earth....Acts 17:26*

Let's all quote this passage of Scripture together. The whole
Church stands to their feet and quote together.
After they had finished quoting the Scripture, there was a
thunderous applause of praise that went forth.
Time ticked on and on. Speaker after speaker brought forth
report after report. Yosef and Lisa and the band played and sung
most of the day. The time finally came for all to break for lunch.
It was now 11:30a.m. The Conference resumed again promptly at
1:00p.m. again there where more selections, and preaching and
testimonials. Rev. Anderson stayed in Prayer the entire day. He
chose to only speak at the afternoon portion of the program. He
felt that it was necessary for him to stay in study and prayer to
deliver his message that he calls the Message of the New
Millenium. A timely message dealing with the wall of racisim
coming down. He had seen it in a vision after Lisa and Mamie
had come back home. He never spoke about it to anyone. He felt
that it would be better to study the vision out for himself and let
God deal with the rest. Little did he and the rest of the Church
know that He would do just that, that afternoon. When
Conference resumed, Yosef and the band played another selection
one that he and Lisa wrote together. Their voices blended

309

beautifully as they sang their duet together, 1,2. 1 2 3 4. He counted down again. Let's Rock this Church people! He said!

"Deep to deep oh hear the Master calling.
(echo, calling)
Can't you hear His gentle Spirit calling you?
(echo, calling out to you.)
Deep to deep oh hear the Master Calling.
(echo calling).
Hear His gentle Spirit calling out to you.

Lord I will Praise You, Lord I will Praise You.

In my heart I know that I must follow.
(echo follow.)
Like the deer, I long and thirst just for You.
(echo, Long just for You.)
In my heart I know that I must follow.
(echo follow.)
Like the deer, I long and thirst just for You.

Chorus.
Lord I will Praise You, Lord I will Praise You (For Your Love)
(repeat three times.)

Come and sit beside the peaceful waters.
(echo waters.)
come and let My Words of rest joy Comfort you.
(echo. Let Me Comfort you.)
Come and sit beside the peaceful waters.
(echo waters)
Come and let My Words of rest and joy Comfort you.
(repeat Chorus ad lib to fade).

Deep to deep oh hear the Master calling. (echo Calling)...........
In my heart I know that I must follow. (echo Follow).........
Come and sit beside the peaceful waters. (echo waters)........

Written by Anne Hemingway.
Copyright c 2002 Annie's Songs Music

Wow! That was awesome! Said Bishop Henry. I never heard the two of you sing together before. Outstanding kids. Just Beautiful! Said Bishop. That a boy Yosef! Said one of his partners in the
Congregation. Everyone laughs. The time was now here for Rev. Anderson to give his Message.
Now I want to take this time out to prepare you for the moment that you all have been waiting for. I know I've been so excited about what my dear friend is about to share with you. That I can hardly contain myself up here! I already know what's gonna happen in here when he steps to the Pulpit. He's gonna kick the slats out from under the enemy! The whole Church stands to their feet in a roar of praise! Whistles coming from all over the people! Race hatred has gone on for too long, and it's been a long time coming for it to stop not only in America, but all over the World! Come on Bishop! Cheered Johnathan. He felt the Spirit of God coming on him as Bishop felt a preach coming on himself at that moment. You see as far as the Mind of God is concerned there is no distinction between Jew or Greek, Black man or White man. Baptist, or Catholic. Male or Female. For our God is no re-spec-tor of Persons! Can somebody say Hallelujah!

HALLELUJAH! Shouted the people! Cheers rang out from all over the Church! As excitement had started to build again. The atmospere was charged with the Love of God all over everyone! Go head and help yourself sir! Said one of the older Deacons. I had better quit now, I'm not the one who will speak to you tonight, but my heart can't imagine how prejudice must grieve the very heart of God Himself, as he watches in total sorrow as His masterpiece Creation, the Race of Mankind squabble, fuss and fight, and even kill one another and all for what? What is it that we hope to gain from all this nonsense? People let me tell you one thing. There is only one God, and you, and me are not HIM! Go head Preacher! Said
One of the Ushers standing in the middle eisle. Bishop Henry looks at his watch, it was now 3:35p.m. Now I want to take the time to introduce to you all our Speaker for tonight. A man that I've known in

Ministry for many, many years. I've never known a time that his Ministry didn't touch my heart and bless me in some way or another. And people, God truly work Miracles in his Services. I've seen them! And I believe that we'll see them again tonight in a way that I just can't describe! Would you please stand to your feet and give your warmest welcome to Reverand Benjamin Anderson! The people thundered in applause as Rev. Anderson is escorted down the eisle by his Deacons, Johnathan being one of them. Rev. Anderson was dressed in his white gold trimmed Vestments. He looked stunning! And ready to Preach!

Yosef and the band stood to their feet Lisa could not hold back her tears as her Father walked down the eisle to the platform. A soft glow seemed to emanate from him as he had been in prayer all day long, and away from any human contact. He took no chances in allowing anything or anybody to break his concentration. He wanted to hear directly from God. This was his way of doing so. There were gasps of awe coming from the people as he stepped up to the Pulpit. He raised his hands toward Heaven his eyes closed. The people still standing and applauding. Whoa! Breathed Yosef. This man is awesome! You may be seated people, Thank you for standing, God bless you all. Before we get started with our message
I have an announcement to make to all of you. But I can't do this one alone. My dear friend. Rabbi Jacob
Epstien, and his lovely wife cookie, I mean Sarah. Would you please come up to the platform and help with our announcement? Everyone applauded, The Ushers help them out of their seats escorting them up
To Rev. Anderson, and Deborah. Yosef hands Brad his Bass, and takes Lisa by her hand as they walk together. Rev. Anderson , looks at them both, mist begins to fill his eyes for them. He clears his throat. Many of you here know my baby girl Lisa. She's been our pride and joy all of our lives. And this young man many of you know him as well, he and my daughter were raised in the same house together. The people laugh a little nodding their heads. Never one time did he ever disrespect us,or mistreat our daughter
Or was he ever jealous of our son Johnathan. They have all loved each other as family all this time. I mean a Jewish boy raised in an Afro-American home, you don't hear talk of such things like that these days. But to us he's one of us, he is blood to us. And

we love him just as dearly as we do our own children. The people applaud. Jacob would you come over here Sir? Rabbi steps over to him, they shake hands, embracing in brother fashion. Sarah and Deborah hold each other waiting for Rev. Anderson to give the news. We are happy, overjoyed, and thrilled beyond words to announce to you the engagement of our Children Mr. Daniel Joseph Epstien, and Elizabeth Marie Anderson. Yosef and Lisa. The entire Church stands to their feet cheering! Whistling and calling out their names. You rule Jo!. Go Lisa! The couple embrace as the people applauded them. Rabbi, Bishop Henry, and Cardinal Jakes would you all please come up here to the platform. I want to pronounce a blessing on these kids before we go on. They too are escorted to the platform, and stand around the couple. Now I want everyone of you out there to stretch your hands towards them and repeat this Blessing after me over them.....

"Father God of Abraham, Issac, and Jacob.
Look upon these two Your children, and make
Thy Face to shine upon them, them and their
Children. I pray that Your love will fill their
Hearts, and their home. Crown their heads
With Wisdom O Lord we pray. And Have Thine
Own way in their lives. Let peace and comfort
And joy. Harmony and goodness fill their home
From the day that they pledge themselves to You
And before man. In the Name of Yeshua we pray
Amen."

Amen. Said the people. Rev. Anderson and Deborah. Rabbi and Sarah kissed and embraced the couple. When all had ended, the Ushers escorted the others back to their seats. Now I want my future son in law to bless us with a song. He wrote this one for his Beloved Yeshua, as well as Lisa. I bring to you Daystar. Make them welcome. Yosef. He steps up to the mike adjusting his guitar strap on his shoulder. I wrote this song for my girl Lisa a few weeks ago. I had had the music in my heart for a while, but I had no words. When we broke up and for those three days. I felt like my whole world as I knew it had come to an end. So I asked Yeshua to help me. I prayed that if He would bring her back to me. I would not only serve Him. But that when we marry. I would be the best husband that I could be to her. I

313

never knew that love like this existed until He as well as she came along. That is the name of this song. And I dedicate it to my Lord and Savior Yeshua my Messiah. And to the most beautiful woman in the world to me. My Beloved Lisa.   A beautiful piano introduction plays as Yosef began to sing like he's never sang and played before.

I knew not where my life would go, as I walked this lonely road
To no where, I was lost. Despair and sadness were my friends.
To
Last until the end. But then I saw the Cross.

You said My child come to me, let Me set you free. From darkness
And from sin. Just leave your burdens at My Feet, and Let Me give
You Life complete in Me, I'll be your Friend.

You came, and turned my life around, put my feet on solid
Ground. You filled my life with song. And as I looked into
Your Face. I had never known such Grace. Until You came
Along.. (Chorus).

Now I'm not lonely anymore, for my sorrow's turned to joy. You've
given
Me such hope. My eyes are opened and I see. What Your Life has
done for me.
You've given me such peace. The old man had nothing to gain, you
washed away
My every stain. The old became the new. To leave the old life's
hurts and pain.
I had to die to live again. I found my place in You. (Repeat
Chorus).

The old man had nothing to gain. You washed away my every
stain. The old
Became the new..................To leave the old life's hurts and pain.
I had to
Die to live again. I found my place in You......

How Great a Love You've shown to me. For Your Mercy was the
Key.
You gave me Liberty. Now I'm not lonely anymore. I never knew
such

*Joy before. Until You came along...........Until You came.........Until
you
Came along.............uuuummmmmmm................*

Yosef raised his hands towards Heaven. Tears straming down his face. I Love you Yeshua. Thank you for saving me, and bringing my girl back home to me. He looks over at Lisa who had seated herself next to her parents on the platform. I love you Lisa. He cried to her. Her tears flowed gently down her soft brown face. Her father nudges her to go over to him. She gets up and runs over to Yosef, He caught her into his arms embracing her hard. They kiss briefly. The Church stands to their feet giving him a standing ovation! They applauded thunderously! He escorts Lisa back over to her seat next to him. Rev. Anderson Steps back up to the mike, shaking his head, a look of seriousness in his expression. The song had touched him deeply. He wipes the tears from his eyes, as did Deborah. Rabbi could not believe his ears as he listened to his son seranade his Beloved Yeshua, and Lisa. He never felt more proud of him as he did at that moment. Sarah too could not stop her tears from flowing as well. Tissues were being passed from pew to pew as he Ministered his song. Wow! That was awesome son. I didn't know you could write and sing like that boy. Yosef smiling at Lisa. I didn't know I could love like that Sir. He said looking at Lisa.

The people laugh. Now my angel will bless us with a song that she too wrote for this occasion. Make her welcome will you? The Church applaud, Yosef kisses her forehead as she steps to the mike.
How many of you out there know that He is Almighty? Come on Lisa! Cheered Johanthan. And that there is nothing too hard for Him, I tell you if you are in need of Salvation, healing for your

body. To just have your life totally turned around as my Beloved just finished singing to us. Just believe that He is Almighty, Lord of All. The band played as her beautiful soprano voice filled the Church with the very Presence of God!

You are the Most Holy, You are the Mighty God.
You're all I desire, You're a Consuming Fire!
For trials great and small. You're my All in All!
You are Almighty, Lord of All to me.

You are the Mel-o-dy. In every song I sing. You
Are my Mercy Seat. The Lord Who Healeth me.
For every need I have, You are my Great I AM!
You are Almighty, Lord of All to me.

You are Almighty, You are Almighty, You are Almighty
Lord of All to me.

Nothing's to hard for You. Father I Worship You.
Through valleys high and low. Wherever You lead
I'll go. To Heaven I proclaim. The Glories Of Your
Name...! You are Almighty, Lord of All to me. You
You are Almighty Lord of All to me. You are Almighty
Lord of All to me......

Written by Anne Hemingway.
Copyright c 2002 Annie's songs Music.
Adm. By I AM Ministries.
International Copyrights Secured.
All Rights Reserved.
Used By Permission.

As Lisa sang a very beautiful thing began to happen. It was like ripples of glory started to flow from within her! Her face began to glow in that all too familiar way again. The band gasped at what they saw, as did all the Church! What's happening with her man? Asked James. It's what the Bible calls the Anointing! Look at her face Sarah! She's so beautiful! Breathed Rabbi. He had never heard her sing before. Sarah
Had heard her many times. But this time it was different. A strong surge of power flowed from her out to the people! A man that had been diagnosed with a mental disorder ran up towards the platform. Yosef saw the man as he charged at Lisa. I'll Kill You! Stop it ! I can't stand it! I'll Kill you! He shouted at her. Yosef took off his bass and shoved it into Brad's arms. James and Terry hold him back. Let me go man! He struggled. Joseph! Yelled Rev. Anderson. Watch son, just watch. The man approached the platform. I hate you! I hate your kind of singing! Lisa slowly opened her eyes, she looked down at the man writhing on the floor in agony. She walks down the steps to him. He backed away from her.

Don't you touch me! I'm never coming out! Oh yes you will! She said to the spirit that had held the man captive. I know why you're here. She said to the man. Your wife hurt you a long time ago and left you for another. You've never forgiven her for what she did to you. She took your only son that you haven't seen in over twenty years. It has left you bitter, and resentful towards her and God. But sir if you'll only open your heart to Him, He'll take all that bitterness, and hurt away from you. And fill you with such love, and forgiveness. After all, He forgave you didn't He? The man looked at Lisa, tears streaming down his face. Yes! He did! I didn't do anything to hurt her, or my boy and she left me, and took Jason with her! Oh God help me!!! The man cried out. Yosef then began to calm down as he felt an overwhelming compassion for the troubled man. I'm alright now. He said softly. Come here. She called to him.

He walks up to her, his arms outstretched to her. With tears in her eyes, she placed her hands on both sides of his cheeks, the spirit wailed out an earpiercing scream through the man's voice. He collapes to the floor in a heap. He then opened his eyes batting them rapidly. Lisa extends out her hand to help him off the floor. The people watching waiting what will happen next. He gets up and looks around him. Smiling faces met his everywhere he turned. He then looked Lisa directly in her eyes. His eyes blood shot from his alcholism, met her eyes full of God's Purity. She touched him again, he wobbled and fell back to the floor, Sir, you'll never touch alcohol again! The Church roared with Praise as God right before their eyes delivered a very troubled man from a hopeless crisis! Lisa went back to the platform glory flowing from her! She steps up to the mike. No one here has a right to judge the man for what his life has gone through.

God's love belongs to the hopeless, as well as to the hopeful. Bishop Henry said it already. God is no respector of persons! Amen! Amen! Shouted the people. They applauded, as she walked back to her
Seat. Amen baby. Said Yosef. He takes her into his arms kissing her on the cheek. Are you alright baby? I'm fine Beloved. That you are girl, that you are. He smiled. They seated themselves. Rev. Anderson steps up to the mike. Ahhh! He breathed. The atmosphere is just right for preachin now. He said. Everyone laughs. If you have your Bibles would you please turn with me to Psalms 133. and we will begin reading from the first verse. The people stand to their feet. And read the verse along with him Yosef and Lisa share his Bible. *"Behold how good and how pleasant it is for brethren to dwell together, in UNITY."* My title to this Sermon is called "Unity through Love." I want to start my message off tonight with the prayer that when I leave from up here, and you leave to go your separate ways back home,
That you'll leave with a new sense of Love, comradery and respect for your fellowman. Let's pray.

Father in the Name of Thy Precious Child Jesus.
Let me speak to this Your people, let the Glory of
Your Spirit fill this place. Touch each and every heart
Here tonight. Touch and anoint my lips that I may speak
Thy Word rightly, and accurately. Change hearts, and

Transform lives. And whole Nations with Your Love.
Every Nation, that is represented here tonight. In the Name
Of our Precious Lord and Savior Jesus Christ. Amen.

Amen responded the Congregation. All seated themselves. As
Rev. Anderson began his message. Many
There took out note pads and began to take notes as he spoke.
Writing down Scripture after Scripture for their references as they
followed along with him. I remember when I was a young lad
growing up in
Southern Mississippi, I recall the stories that my father Rev.
Hezekiah Anderson would tell me. Back when he was a young
boy, How when the older black men of his day would walk the
streets, if they saw a white man coming on the same side of the
street as they. That they themselves had to cross over to the
other side of the street. Black men were not allowed to walk on
the same side of the street as white men. If you even looked a
white man in the face. It meant your death, and death back then
for black men was very brutal.
This anacdote from the history of black people as Rev. Anderson
relayed on and on. Made some of the white people a little
uncomfortable. Many of them were already sitting next to black
people, and vice versa. The Jews suffered in a way that is to me
the most inhuman tradgety that I have ever seen in my life!
I can remember reading about the death marches, the Gas
chambers, the starving of men women and children, as a so called
method of exterminating pests as they were called back then off
the face of the Earth. How will we answer to God in the day of
Judgement for the inhumane, cruelty that we have inflicted on
another? What is suppose to be the purpose of this so called
doing away with other Cultures

As being inferior to that of another with their idea that they are
superior to everyone else? Did all of you
Notice the Scripture on our Banner up here? Everyone looks up
at the Banner again.   What does that Verse say people. Read it
out loud for me.

And He has made from ONE BLOOD EVERY NATION of MEN
To dwell on all the face of the Earth... Acts 17:26

319

Does that sound like God has a problem with Colour or Culture, or Nationality? It says here that He has made from one Blood not the blood of many, but one blood every Nation of men to dwell on all the face of the Earth. Well if God made us for this Earth, then why is there such a problem between the Nations?
Why is there so much fighting? And what is so unfortunate is that it's even crept into our Churches.
That's right Rev. Said one of the people. I mean look, the Bible doesn't even call us the races of man.
He never divides us up into little groups of this bunch over here, or this group over here. Man did that.
Now look at us. Now it's as though either this bunch wants to be superior over this bunch or vice versa.
And none of them realize that in all of their efforts to be the "Superior Race" that Hell as well as Heaven is just as full of their kind as it is my kind and everybody elses! The Church stands applauding, and cheering.
Come on people, it's time for this filth to stop! Racisim doesn't belong in our Neighborhoods, it doesn't belong in our Schools, it doesn't belong in our Churches! Hello! The Church cheers louder. It doesn't belong in our Governments, it doesn't belong in our Nations! Do you think that there is segregation in Hell? No! everyone there is miserable! Do you think God has Heaven sectioned off as well? No! Everyone there is blissfully happy beyond description!   We can see just from this little bit that I've shared with you already, that racisim is just a waste of everybody's time. I've never seen people waste such time

And energy into promoting something that makes absolutely no sense whatsoever to anyone, and profits them nothing as well.
When in God's eyes. He has made every man in His Image, and in His Likeness.
I would say that that puts us all on an equality there doesn't it?
Amen! Shouted the Congregation.   I mean
Frankly can't we see the beauty of what God has done here? As I look out there amongst all of you. I see a vast array of colours. A sea of colour. I see my Black brothers, my White brothers, my Native American Indian, Eastern Indian brothers. I see my Jewish brothers, my Catholic brothers. Lutheran, Episcopalian. I mean from where I stand I see nothing but beauty out there!
Seeing all of you out there fills me with such

An overwhelming sense of Love, and Compassion for you as well as my fellow Americans, of which I myself am very proud to be! I say Let God arise in our Churches, In our schools, our Communities. Our Nations! For in the day of Judgement, how will we answer to Him for the vile and cruel way in which we have treated his most precious of all Creation! The Creation of Mankind! I say to all of you, Let Freedom

Ring! And Tear down that wall that has kept us so far apart from one another! Tear it down! Tear down that wall of race hatred, intolorance, indifference, and strife! And Let's together build bridges, that will link us arm in arm, hand in hand. Nation to nation! Let's build the Bridge of togetherness, harmony, and Brotherly Love. And let it continue from Generation to Generation! GLORY! GLORY! Let our Cultures learn from one another instead of shutting out! Let us Oh God in Heaven let us practice acceptance, instead of rejection! Embracing all of Mankind! We can do it if we'll band together! Oh stand to your feet Church and give God praise in this place! The Church was already standing and thundering in praise for the message. Yosef and his band and Lisa were standing to their feet tears streaming down their faces.

Deborah as well as Sarah seemed to flow back in time to when they were having their Intercessory Prayer Warriors Meeting, They were all gathered around the Altar praying for what Rev. Anderson had just finished preaching about! It was taking place right before their eyes! For there in their midst, people from all Cultures, and Nationalities were running up to the Altar asking for forgiveness of what their ancestors had done to theirs. Black men were embracing White men. Jews embracing Germans, Native Americans, embracing White men. If the Denominations were opening up and accepting those of Denominations that differed from theirs! It was like a wave of Love and forgiveness had swept across the Church! Yosef stood with Lisa and the band holding Lisa close to him. He took her hand into his. When all of a sudden he felt a little wobbly. He saw in his spirit the same vision that he had seen in the hospital. Lisa thought that he had felt God's Spirit come on him at that moment, in which he did. But for a completely different reason. He was showing him what was to happen. Lisa smiled at him and left him to his moment. There were shouts from among the people, as many that day were set free from prejudice, and racisim. Rev.

Anderson and Deborah walked out and laid hands on those who wanted to receive blessings from God and to be finally released from the bondage of racisim.   I didn't know that I was like that Pastor Anderson said one a White Southern Baptist Pastor. I didn't know it's as thought it was so subtle and unnoticeable. But yet it was there all the time.   I remember the Civil Rights Movement, believe me I do. I was one of those who felt that Blacks belong with their own kind, as well as Whites with theirs. But now in today's time, I thought that I had put all that away from me and out of my Church. Looks like I hadn't. Now look at all

Of us here. We're fellowshipping like we've known each other all of our lives. He takes a deep breath.
And you know Rev. Anderson. That's the way that we should be. Sir , I have no words to say how grateful that I am for the way that you opened up our eyes here today.   Can you ever forgive me? I'm so sorry, I've had my share of racism, and that share was one share too many for me. I can't live like that and still claim to be a man of God. What a slap in the face that is to Him. Yes sir it is.   Said Rev. Anderson. I'm truly sorry, will you please forgive me for the unfair way that I have treated your people? My dear Brother, there is nothing to forgive. Said Rev. Anderson. Blessings be upon you and your Church! He said to him, laying his hands upon his head. The man fell backwards, one of the altar workers catching him.   Rev. Anderson and Deborah then went back to the Platform. Yosef would you and the band sing Psalms 133 for me? Come on people let's join my future son in law as they sing Psalm 133! They played and sang To Dwell in Unity! The people rejoiced and danced as they Ministered to them. When the song had ended.

Lisa stepped up to the mike, she had a song in her heart herself. She stood there in front of them, tears gently streaming down her soft cheeks. Ma To vu. She mouthed to Yosef. He nodded his head. They softly played as she sang like she never sang before! More tissues were being passed from pew to pew again.   As she sang, Rabbi broke down in tears as her sweet soprano voice filled the Sanctuary.   Oh my!
She so beautiful Sarah! Sarah nodded as she wiped her tears again.   As her song ended. She stood there silent, it was like the

322

whole Church was hushed, there was total stillness that had overtaken them. Yosef and his band stood there themselves a look of intensity filled their expressions as they as well as the Church Itself gave Reverance as Lisa had sung God's Presence into the Place! Just then a Native American Chief stood to his feet with his hands raised, a flow of tears falling from his eyes. He then began to Praise God in His native American language. Soon the entire Church was standing to their feet Worshipping and Praising God with him. There was weeping and wailing before the altar. Just then with his eyes lifted towards Heaven. He remembered the prayer that his father prayed when he was a little boy. He began to pray.

Father God in Heaven, Hear my prayer. Move amongst the people And Melt them! Melt them Father! Melt away all the hardness of Heart, all the indifference, all the hatred, all the intolorance, and the
Strife. It's gone on for far too long Father for too long. Fill them with
Your Love, Yor Kindness, Your Compassion. Oh Dear Father, Destroy the
Yoke of racial bondage, and remove from them the burden of prejudice!
Melt them Father! Melt them! Give them a new heart, one that knows
Your Will for all Mankind, a heart that is receptive to receive Your Word,
Your Plan and Purpose for them. Do it Father Do in now! In the Name of
Jesus our Lord and Savior! Amen..

When he had finished praying. He heard the Voice of God in his heart speak to him He had answered his
Prayer....

"Tell my people I want them to cleanse their Churches of Racial
prejudice, and pride. For this rises as a stench in My nostrils. If

323

they will hear My Voice, I will hear their cry, and I will Manifest
Myself unto them. Tell them son! Now see My Glory come down!"

Lisa then began to speak in a language that sounded like perfect Hebrew. Yosef understood every word she said. As did Rabbi and Sarah. Terry comes over to him. I thought that you said that Lisa couldn't speak Hebrew. She can't, I mean I've taught her some things, But this is amazing man. It's like the words are flowing out of her like water! But that's impossible! How can she do that! Yosef looked upwards as did Terry. Ohhhh. When Lisa had finished her speaking. Rev. Anderson spoke out the message that God had given him to give to the people. When he had finished giving them the message, all cheered and applauded! Just then all the people heard a loud rumble of thunder. Brad stepped over to Yosef. Sounds like thunder outside hey Jo? That didn't come from outside Brad. It came from in here. What! Said Brad. Look. Said Yosef. Brad looked up at the skylight in the ceiling of the Church. Not one cloud in the sky! Lisa was still standing in the same place, she never moved a muscle in the whole time since she stepped up ther to sing. What's happening in here man, I'm getting a little nervous. Said Brad. Have you ever asked God the question, God, if You're real, then prove Yourself? Asked Yosef. Well.....yeah. I have. Well, He's about to do just that. And that is Jo? Yosef looks at him smiling a little. Prove Himself!

The thunder that Brad and the rest of the people heard had truly come from inside of the Church! Lisa then opened her eyes, and walked back over to Yosef and the band. He takes her into his arms holding her tightly. Are you alright? Yes, Beloved. I'm ok. He held her next to him. Just then, Yosef looked at the back of the Church, there coming from the back was a Huge Luminous White Cloud! It shone with an indescribable radiance! Ohhhh! Gasped Yosef. Baby look! He whispered to Lisa. She looked at the sight she too gasping in awe. Oh my God! She breathed. Rev. Anderson saw the Cloud making it's way towards the front of the Church. He had seen this phenomenon before. He saw it several times in his father's Campmeetings. It is what's called the Shekinah Glory, or the Manifested Presence of God!

He had come down to them to move in their midst! He was aware of what God could do when His Power moved in this manner. Deborah all of a sudden pitched forward falling out of her seat! One of the ushers ran up to the platform to help her up. Leave her! Rev. Anderson commanded. Step back man, and watch God work in this place! The usher stepped back, Yosef held Lisa even closer to him. All the band members stand to their feet their eyes wide and staring. As the Cloud approached further in, a very common occurance began to happen. People started to fall! A few in this pew, then a few in the next.

The Dignitaries on the Platform had stood their feet as well, and began to step back when they saw the strange happening. Cardinal Jakes dropped his staff to the floor! Bishop Henry whispered to Rev. Jeffries

Didn't I tell you? Miracles! Just then a Catholic Nun stood to her feet, and started to laugh in the Spirit!

A Holy laughter began to spread all throughout the Church! Others sat quietly as God Ministered to them. Others cried as they felt the brokenness lift from their hearts as delieverance had come! Many others ran to the Altar to receive Christ into their hearts. Rev. Anderson, I want to be saved! They shouted. He prayed the sinners prayer with them, they then left the altar changed from the inside out! As Christ had filled them with Himself. God's Glory had begun to fill the people, as wave after glorious wave of His Presence washed all over them. Lisa then felt an urge to lay hands on people for healing. How many of you know that the Healer is in the House tonight! The people roared with praise! If you need a healing in your body, come on up here. I feel a wave of healing flowing through me! The people nearly ran over each other

To get there first! Many of them had heard of God's dealings with Lisa when it came to Ministering healing to the sick. The people flooded the Altar. People again began to fall like dominoes! Some fell before she could even touch them! One man who had just had surgery and was still in discomfort came forth. Beloved would you help me please? He gave Terry his bass, and went down to her. She took his hand and placed it on the area that had been operated on. Then she placed her hand on top of his. It was his stomach. He had, had tumors removed. She then felt a strong surge of power jump out of her and into Yosef's hand. Ahhh! Yosef and the man cried out together. Both men jerking at the same time. The man fell backwards into the hands of an altar worker standing behind him. The surge was so powerful that not only did it knock the man into the hands of the altar worker, but it knocked them both to the floor! Yosef nearly lost his footing himself. Whoa! He breathed. I've never felt anything like that before! Would you like to feel that again? She asked. God yes! Just yield to Him Beloved. It's all His touch, not ours. We're just vessels that He's working through. Ok. He said nodding his head. They went down the line as grandmothers and grandfathers brought their grandchildren up for blessing and healing. Yosef and Lisa laid hands on them, and God blessed them. Rabbi could hardly believe what he was seeing. There was Complete harmony and unity amongst the people. He was speechless as he watched A God that he had never given himself a chance to know move right in front of him! The Cloud neared his pew, he didn't see

It coming. Sarah then suddenly fell forward onto the floor! She was completely overcome with His Presence. She glowed all over. He looked up at Yosef and Lisa. They had gone back to the platform. They raised their hands praising God for His Love and Mercy on the people. He then noticed something

That was happening with Yosef. Right above his head was a whitish gold looking flame coming down upon him. It settled itself on him then disappeared inside of him. Yosef then threw up his hands and began to speak in a language that he didn't recognize. God had filled him with His Spirit! Then the both of them

Started to shine like lightening all over. Their faces had changed They looked like two angels! As God's Glory had covered them. Oh my God Sarah! Look at them! Look see there! He pointed at them.

There was no answer, Sarah was still down on the floor. Rev. Anderson could hardly take it all in as

He watched the God that he loved and served all his life move in a most spectacular way! He looked upward

With his hands raised. Heal them Father, cleanse them! Let Your Fire fall! There was another loud rumble of thunder inside of the Church again. Just then, a glowing whiter than white Light appeared.

Oooooohs, and ahhhhhs filled the Sanctuary. It first resembled a beautiful Dove with huge flapping wings of Fire. Then it separated Itself like small flames until it had filled the entire building. Then it rained down on the whole Church! The people roared with more shouts of praise as God had rained His Glory down

Upon them! The rumble of thunder returned hushing the people. All were stunned as to what happened next. As they were hushed. They heard the very Voice of God Himself speaking to them....

"Remember the Word that I the Lord Your God has spoken to you this day
and Heed my commands. Or the next fire that you see will be the Fire of
My Judgement! Cleanse yourselves and your Churches, Your Nations, that I
May bless thee!"

All that had been opposed to the blending of the Cultures of Man, and the fellowshipping of the Denominations, were changed when they heard His voice and His commands. They started to weep And wail all embracing each other. Rabbi wept before God as he repented of his hatred of Blacks, and Germans, his unfair treatment of his wife and son. And Lisa. He wept uncontrollably his face buried in his hands. Oh my dear Lord Yeshua forgive me! I've been so wrong! So wrong! Please cleanse me of this filth forever, and ever! Never again will I ever mistreat my wife, my son or his girl. Or any man because of his colour, or any difference, that differs from mine. For I know now that You really do see not as man sees. For you Lord. Look at the heart of man. He looked at Yosef and Lisa on the platform. They were lost in each others embrace. True love sees no colour, no colour at all....

Service had ended a little later than planned which was to be at
5:00p.m. It was now 6:45p.m. It was only fifteen minutes till
Yosef and Lisa's Engagment party.   But nothing mattered to
anyone that night. As all left the Service changed in such a way
that it was sure to make a difference when they got back to their
own Churches, and Nations! Never would they forget what God
had done for them that day.   Many people had jammed into the
parking lot making their way to their cars, Buses, vans etc.   The
Police had to direct the traffic as the streets were full filled with
the cars and other vehicles pulled out to go their separate ways.
Yosef and Lisa and the band and their parents all rode in the
Limo that had been called for them. Maurice Sumner and Tim
Johnson broke down all the band's equipment to take to Terry's
home.
All except Yosef's Bass. He placed all his equpment in the trunk
of the Limo. They talked about the Service each sharing how God
had touched them in a way that was precious and personal to
them. Yosef and Lisa couldn't take their eyes off each other.
There he goes again staring her face off. Said Sarah. Everyone
breaks up laughing.   Yosef! Stop that! She said to him
playfully. I can't help it mom
She's so beautiful to me. He said in a trance like voice. And you
the same to me Beloved. Said Lisa like wise. The Limo pulls up
in front of the Epstiens home. All get out and go inside. Rev.
Anderson and Rabbi linger outside for a brief moment discussing
the nights events at Church.Well Jacob, how did you like your
first Pastors Day Conference? Rabbi thought on his question a
little. Ben, I have no words to
Tell you how I'm feeling right now. I've never seen such things
like this in Temple. In all my years of college, I've never come face
to face with... He stammered trying to find the words to explain.
Rev. Anderson watching him knowing what he was trying to say
to him. Face to face with uh...Rabbi looks up at him. With God!
He breathed. I must hear more of these things and learn of and
from them. Would you teach me Ben? I would be honored my
friend. Come, lets go now. Our children are waiting for us. They
escort each other inside the house, which was decorated in all
Jewish décor. It was beautiful! The Menorah was prepared and
would be lit when the time came. Yosef and Lisa were staring

lovingly into each others eyes, they kiss briefly. He became so overwhelmcd with love for her at that moment, that he

Became lightheaded from kissing her. I love you Lisa, I love you too Beloved. Oh, cut it out you two! Said Terry breaking through the both of them. He took Yosef by the arm, Yosef thought that he would
Die to be separated from her. The guy's so gooey, you could slurp him through a straw. Said one of the male guests. Lisa stood there watching Terry take him away from her, she too thought that even just for that brief moment, that it felt like an eternity without him. John, come and help me with this guy will ya? I don't want to have to scrape him off the floor again. Come on big guy. Said Terry. Johnathan takes his other arm, they both escort him upstairs. Come on baby girl, lets get you dressed and ready ok? Said Mamie. I love him so much Aunt Mamie. I know you do sweetheart, it shows. Boy! Does it show! She brushed Lisa's cheek with her hand. Come on now ok? Ok. She said taking her to the downstairs guest room where her clothes were laid out for her. Rabbi and Sarah were still dressed in their attire from the
Conference. So were Rev. Anderson and Deborah. He had removed his Vestments, revealing his black
Suit. Soon Yosef was escorted down the stairs to the large living room. Johnathan had come over to do

A last miniute adjustment on his clothes before the Ceremony. Just then the door opens to the guest room .
Mamie escorts Lisa out them. She looked breathtaking! Sarah had made for her a stunning white and gold trimmed Ceremoial gown with matching shawl that covered the bottom half of her face. Tears made their way down Yosef's masculine cheeks. All were silent as Mamie escorted her to her parents. She stood in between them. Rabbi then began the Ceremony by reciting a Benediction from the Siddur. He then nods to Sarah for her to light the Menorah. As she finishes lighting the last candle. Rabbi begins to Chant a Jewish Prayer over Yosef in Hebrew. He then kisses him on both cheeks. He then goes over to Lisa, and does the same. He then returns to his starting place of the Ceremony still chanting. When his prayer had ended. He looks at Yosef

and nods to him. Yosef steps forward speaking to her parents.
As I have already made known to your daughter my undying love
for her, I make known to you. I've asked her to be my lifemate,
my wife. And she's accepted. Now I ask you. Do you accept Sir?
He asked Rev. Anderson,
I do son. Do you accept Ma'mam? He asked Deborah. I do. She
said tears streaming down her face.

Start here

They each take Lisa by her arms and escort her over to him.
Rabbi comes over to take Yosef's hand, Rev. Anderson and
Deborah take Lisa's hand placing them in each others.   Yosef
and Lisa stare deeply into each others eyes.   I tell you, she'll have
no face left when he finishes with her. Sarah whispered to
James.
He places his hand over his mouth to shield his laughter. As long
as Yeshua lives, so will my love for you Lisa. He said to her in
Hebrew, kissing her forehead.   As Long as God Himself is
Eternal, so is my Love for you my Beloved.   She said to him also
in Hebrew. A look of surprise filled his expression. Lisa couldn't
speak fluent Hebrew.   But she spoke those words to him as
though it was her native language.
Yosef then begins to quote from Isaiah 62:5, and John 14:2 over
her.

For as a young man marries a virgin, so shall your sons
Marry you. And as the Bridegroom rejoices over the Bride.
So shall God rejoice over you. I go to prepare a place for
You, and if I go and prepare a place for you, I will come
Again to receive you to myself. That where I am, there
You will be also. I love you Lisa.

Lisa quotes from the Song of Soloman 8:6 and Rev. 21:2

I will wait for your return my Beloved. That when we are joined
as one. We'll be together always.

Lord set me as a seal upon His heart, and upon his arm
For our love is stronger than death. And I saw the Holy City
The New Jereusalem coming down out of Heaven from God

Prepared as a Bride adorned for her husband. I Love you Yosef.

Yosef then removes her vail from her face, and kisses her deeply.
Rabbi ends the Ceremony with a
Chant of praise over the couple. He pronounces peace and
blessing over them and their future home
Shalom! He shouts! SHALOM! Shouted the rest.   They
embrace warmly. L'Chaim! Everyone shouts together. Yosef and
Lisa are escorted over to the drink table to drink the ceremonial
toast to their new
Betrothal. He drinks from one side of the chalice, she from the
other.   After their toast, all began to loosen up and mingle and
help themselves to dinner. Which was very lovely. Afro American
and Jewish dishes prepared by Sarah, Deborah and Lisa for the
occasion. Rev. Anderson and Rabbi talked more about Church,
Lisa and Yosef talked with each other, and the band. Deborah
and Sarah busied themselves around the house serving the
guests. I never thought that I would see this day come to pass.
Said Rabbi
Well Jacob, what's important now is that it finally has, and their
happiness is all that should matter to us now. You are right
again as usual my friend. Where is that wife of mine? Asked
Rabbi looking around for her. She had just brought out a very
lovely serving tray of lemon pound cake that Lisa made. It was
Rev. Anderson, and Yosef's favorite. Uh, excuse me. I need to see
Sarah. Said Rev. Anderson. Oh, Cookie!
He called to her. Deborah stood next to her laughing as he
approached them.   Yosef and Lisa watched as their families
celebrated together enjoying one another's fellowship. Johnathan
told more of his corney
Jokes that had everyone laughing more because of their corniness
instead of humor.   Yosef took Lisa by

The hand out into the hall, leaving their families to their
celebrating. They embrace again. He looks at her.
You want to tell me something don't you? She asked him. How
do you do that? Do what? You know that. You know what I'm
about to say before I say it. Oh, that's easy. I could see it in your
eyes, that's all.
Well since you've managed to find me out, I do have something to
tell you.   He took a deep breath. I have to leave for a little while

331

ok? Leave now? Yes, but I'll be right back alright? I have to finish something.

And what might that be? She asked, sadness had come on her. He smiles a little, but he could see the sadness in her expression as well. It's a surprise! He said trying to lift her spirits, it wasn't working good for him. She smiles for a moment, then an overwhelming sense of fear comes on her. She begins to tremble all over. Yosef frowns at her. Lisa what is it? I don't know, I feel a little strange. She said shaking herself. Don't let it bother you now ok? You go and finish whatever it is you're working on. I'll be ok. She said to him, holding her head down. Lisa are you sure you're alright? I'm ok honey, I just miss

You when you're gone that's all. He looked out into the hall, the band was out there waiting for him. Baby look, I'll be back before you've even had a chance to miss me ok? Ok. She said. He holds her close to him. He then feels her trembling in his arms. Lisa, you're shaking like a leaf. What's the matter? I,I. She stammered. I just had a cold chill that's all. But I'm fine now. Really, I'm better. That's what she said, but Yosef could see something in her eyes telling him differently. He saw a deep fear there. But he chose to say nothing about it. When I get back, I won't leave your side for the rest of the night. I promise ok? I'll hold you to that. He kissed her forehead again. And ran upstairs to get changed. He returns wearing a pair of black jeans with matching crew necked shirt. Lisa had changed as well, into a long calf length v- neck dress with long sleeves. It flowed with her every movement. Yosef spotted her in the hall, she looked Even sadder than before. I'll be right back guys. Hey! He called to her. He takes her into his arms. You look beautiful! He whispered. I do? Yes you do. So do you Beloved. She looks at him briefly wishing that this moment with him could be frozen in time forever. You're so precious to me Yosef. I can't imagine my life withour you. I never want to live without you. She pauses. I'd give my life for you, and never even question God about my death. For you, I'm willing to die, just to show you how much I really and truly love you. Because I know in my heart that you won't let death hold me for long. Baby what are you talking about? I know how much you love me. I've always known that. Why are you talking like this? I've never seen you like this before. He didn't know what to make out of her words. I have felt this way about you all my life Yosef, and I always will. You're not going anywhere accept right back in there with our family and friends, And wait for me ok? Ok. And no more of this talk about death you hear me? Yes, I hear Beloved. She said softly. He kisses her tenderly ' She looks down, he had risen again.

Honey.....? I can't help it Lisa. You make it happen. Well like my brother always says. It be like that sometime. She said in a sassy home girl tone. Yosef laughs out loud. Jo, come on man! Shouted James.
You amaze me girl. I love you. He said to her. I love you too my Beloved. Jo! I have to go now ok?
I'll try not to be long I promise. He said to her. He runs out to them in the hall, he stops and takes one
Last look at her. I love you. He mouthed to her, she the same to him, blowing a kiss to him. He and the
Band leave. Lisa goes back into the dinning room with her family. She felt a little thirsty, and gets a cup to help herself to some punch. She looks around on the table for the ladle, not finding it. Mom! Where's the punch ladle? Deborah comes into the dinning room from the kitchen. What is it baby girl? The punch ladle, I can't find it. Oh, it's right here. She looks around for it, not finding it as well. Lisa felt the fear returning to her again. She began to shake all over. She drops her cup to the floor. Deborah noticed her
Behavior. Lisa...? Baby....? Look at momma. Are you alright dear? She said to her. Concern filled her voice for Lisa. Oh mom, I'm fine, just a little nervous that's all. I'm gonna be married soon! She said trying to cheer up her mother. It wasn't working . Deborah has always had a deep insight into things, and

When she had an impression in her spirit, it was usually accurate as a bullseye. She could tell that something else was wrong. I just need to wet my tast buds that's all. She said trying to laugh, but her fear wouldn't let her. She began to shake terrible all over. Oh, Mom. What's wrong with me? I can't seem to get a grip on myself tonight? Shhh. There, there now. Momma's here. Ok? Ok. She said.
Is it because Jo Jo left for a little bit? Somewhat. But not entirely. I can't explain. She said. Don't try sweetie. Don't try.

Said Deborah comforting her holding her close to her. Come on honey, let's get you something to drink Lisa tried to laugh again, but laughter was far from her, I asked Mamie to bring that thing with her. Where is she anyway? Mamie! Mamie! Yeah! Yeah! What is it girlfriend? Where is the punch ladle that you were supposed to bring over? I did bring it, it's right over here. Right next to the punch bowl. She went over to get it. It wasn't there. Oh child I'm dangerous tonight. I must've left it on the kitchen counter at home. I'll go get it. No, no. Let me go get it aunt Mamie. I need some fresh air anyway. I'll be right back girls she said. They watch her leave. What's the matter Debbie? There was no answer. Look , I said I was sorry about that thing. You know my mind. My memory is about as long as dust on a bottle. That's not what's bothering me sissy. Well what is it then? It's Lisa. She's not herself tonight. What do you mean not herself? Well, Yosef left for a while, but he'll be back in a few. You know he's not gonna be away from her for too long. Especially tonight, their engagement night.

Said Mamie trying to comfort her. Mamie, did you notice anything strange in Lisa's behavior at all tonight? No, other than I've never seen her so happy. She's about to get married girl. She's probably got a case of pre-marital jitters. We all go through that, you were a basket case if I remember correctly.

She said. No, she was scared about something tonight. Come on child, she's just a little nervous that's all.

Look, I know my child, Mamie. I've never known Lisa to be too afraid of anything. But tonight she acted as though she was scared to death or something. I mean she trembled all over, she dropped things. I believe Yosef even saw it. He said to me before he left. Watch my girl for me. She seems a little frightned about something. Now do you see? He saw it too. It's not like her. I tell you she feels something, but she would tell me what it was or is that she feels. I'm afraid for her Mamie. Debbie, stop talking like that! You're scaring me now! Mamie saw the fear in Deborah's expression, then something took her over, a strength that she was envious of Deborah and Sarah. Debbie, I've known you most of my life. And I've never known a time that when something went wrong. You we're quick to take to you knees in prayer about it. I don't know what it is that you or Lisa feel tonight, this impending doom or something. But child, let me tell you. If anyone can move the Hand of God when it comes to prayer. I know you can.

Why should this time be different from all the other times that He's answered your prayers. Think about that for a moment.

But in the mean time. I want you to come into the kitchen and have yourself a nice hot cup of cappuccino. Sarah just made some fresh. You'll see honey. Yosef will come back home to her in a few short minutes, and she'll light up just like a little firefly like she always does. Ok? Oh, Mamie! Thank you so much! I needed to hear that. She embraced her. Now you come with me. She'll be just fine. Said Mamie taking her by the arm into the kitchen. Deborah looks back at the large picture window. Hurry Yosef! She whispered.

The Colour Love
Anne Hemingway
Chap 35.

Lisa leaves her party her thoughts all on her Beloved. Oh! How she missed him! She ached for his return.
And to feel his strong arms holding her close to him where she felt her safest. Hurry back Beloved, hurry!
She whispered. She walks outside onto the front lawn. She then hears a rusling in the bushes behind her.
She stops and turns around. There was no one in sight. She turns to walk on across the street to her parents house. She reaches the porch fumbling in her dress pocket for her house keys. "Hello brown sugar." The voice said from behind her. It was Billy,he had Helen with him. A slight fear rose up in her. She quickly fought against it. What do you want? She said, he rbreathing became a little heavy. We have some unfinished business to settle. And what business is that? She said in a defiant tone. Let's just call it a matter of unrequited love. Lisa laughs at him. What in the world do you know about love little man?
He glared at her. Where's Yosef? Asked Helen. None of your business, and why do you wish to know where he is anyway? I have a score to settle myself, he knows what it's all about. Yeah, sure he does. Said Lisa. Now don't worry honey. I won't take him from you, I just need to talk to him about some issues that's all. She said in an arrogant tone. Take him from me! Laughed Lisa. As If. Helen, he's Jewish, he's not into pork! Billy lowers

his head laughing. Shut up Billy! Said Helen pushing him away from her. Enough of this crap, come on lets go before he gets back. Said Billy reaching up to take Lisa by the arm. Go? Go where? She said pulling back from him. You're coming with us! He said jerking her away from the front door. Helen blows a cloud of smoke out of her mouth, flinging the cigarette butt in the air. She then blows the rest of the smoke in Lisa's face. You don't even want to go there with me Lady. She said to her, her breathing becoming heavy. Girls, girls. Said Billy stepping in front of

Helen. Come on now, lets not fight amongst ourselves. He said stroking Lisa's curls. Get your hands off me! She said jerking away from him. Don't be like that baby. He said in a whinny tone. I'm not your baby! I'm not going anywhere with you! She started to walk around him, when he pushes her hard back up to the front door. Oh yes you are! He said stepping back, he reaches into the back of his jeans pulling out his pistol. Lisa stares down the gun barrel gasping. Heh,heh,heh. He laughs. Now come on, that's right. Nice and slow. That's a good girl. He pushes her past Helen. Like I said we have some unfinished business to take care of. He said, taking her behind her parents house, Helen following close behind them.

Your boy is not the man that I thought he was, getting engaged then leaving his girl on a night like tonight. Silly boy. Seems like he had me fooled too. Said Helen. Let me tell you and your girl something Billy.
Yosef is more man than you'll ever be, and more man than you've ever seen Helen. She said confidently.
Oh, is that right? He said, anger beginning to surface now. He spins her around slapping her face. She stumbles off balance. Can your boy hit like that! Huh? Come on! He shouts at her. He marches her around to the same spot in the backyard of her parents home where the incident took place two years ago.
You remember this Lise? Huh? Yeah, you do remember don't you? Billy, why are you doing this? Shut up! He slaps her again. Does this all look familiar to you? It should, I was raised here fool! Helen looks away chuckling to herself a little. Wrong memory! This is where it all began. Where all what began? You know what I'm talking about! YOU WERE MINE! I LOVED YOU LISA! AND YOU LET HIM TAKE YOU FROM MEEEE!! He

336

screamed. Now he's gonna pay. But not before I make you pay
first. I still owe you from that night. Come over here sweet
cheeks. He calls to Helen. Hold this on her, if she even looks like
she wants to run. Helen nods at him taking the pistol shakily
into her hands. Oh God, I need a cigarette! She said, her voice
trembling nervousness had come on her. He steps up to Lisa.
Come on brown sugar, lets make this a night to remember. Lisa
steps back from him. No Billy. She said shaking her head at
him. He walks up to her, her backing away from him, Helen
following them with his gun still pointed at Lisa. He takes her
into his arms, Lisa struggles to get away from him. He may get
you Lise, But I can say I had you first. His eyes staring big like
something had come on him driving him all of a sudden. He felt
an overwhelming arousal take him over. Steady boy. He said
softly patting his groin.

She's ours now. He tries to take Lisa into his arms to kiss her.
She runs her hands over his shoulder's trying to pull him closer
to her. He grabs her throat tight. Try that again, and I'll kill you!
He slaps her to the ground. I was never yours Billy! Never! You
hear me! NEVER! His fury got the better of him, he reaches
down snatching her up to him. He hits her with his fist knocking
her to the ground again. Lisa grunted in pain as her slender body
fell hard to the soft ground. Helen winced in pain turning her
head away, as her nervousness had become full fledged fear!
Ohhhh! This boy has tripped! She said under her breath. She
turned to look again, watching as Lisa's body took blow after
brutal blow of Billy's savage abuse. He kicked her over into the
grass, Lisa falling over onto her side. Uhhh! Lisa grunted again,
he had
Nearly kicked the breath out of her. She fell into the grass
squirming in pain. Plea,pleaseeee he,.....Help Mmm,meeeee
Helen! Don't let him do this! Pleassssse Help Meeeeee! Get
somebody to help me! She pleaded with her. She won't listen to
you! Fired Billy. Helen was listening, but fear gripped her tighter
than she gripped Billy's pistol. She had never seen him like this
before. Ahhhhhh! Billy pleaseeeeee! Screamed Lisa. Shut up!
Helen listened to Lisa's screams for help. She looked at the pistol
then at Billy then at Lisa. She was aiming the gun first at Lisa,
then she felt her hand shift her aim from her to him, her finger
tightning up on the trigger. She shakes her head trying to clear
it. She felt a myriad of emotions

Overwhelm her at that moment. She finally screams out in desperation at him, her hands shaking violently

At him. NOOOOOO! BILLY, YOU'RE GONNA KILL HER! He stops his assault of Lisa, to look at Helen. He didn't even notice that she was no longer aiming the gun at Lisa, but at him! So what! If she dies, she dies! After all, that's wanted wasn't it? Her outta the way so you can jew boy for yourself? And besides, I told you, I'm doing this for you as well as for me. She lowered her head as well as his pistol. She felt a strange feeling come over her. She had no reason to like Lisa, there was no fondness between them at all. Yet she came within inches of killing Billy to save her life! I need a double shot of vodka!
She breathed under her breath. Billy looks back at Lisa, his arousal had left him now. He had grown tired of beating her. She had slipped into unconciousness now. He walks back to Helen, trying to take the pistol from her. But she was still holding onto it tight. Relax, sweet cheeks. It's ok. Pappa's here now. That's right. Let daddy have his toy back. He said in a sarcastic tone. Not even realizing how close he himself came to loosing his own life just a few seconds ago. She releases the gun back to him. He takes it putting it back into his jeans. Come and help me! He snapped at her. They pick Lisa up out of the grass, carrying her over to his car putting her in the back seat. Billy stood up after they had gotten her all in. He begins to yawn a bit. Helen looks at him. Disgust filling her for him at that moment. She then begins to feel something that she's never felt before. Courage! I'm tired. He breathed. Taking out his cell phone. Helen looks in the car at Lisa, she was still out, and very bruised. I can see how you would be. Beating a person nearly to death is bound to be tiresome for someone like you Billy. That took a lot of energy to practically kill someone. She said in a confident tone. Billy put his phone back into his pocket, grabbing her by her throat very tight, nearly cutting off her air! He put his nose close to her sniffing her like a dog
In heat. Looks like you've been smelling your bloomers a bit too much! Don't you ever, I mean EVER! GET PISSY WITH ME AGAIN! He shouted at her, slamming her hard against the car. I'll hurt you Helen, You hear me! I'll kill ya dead! And never even bat an eye about it! Now get in the car! Helen's brief encounter with courage did not last long. It felt good to her for the moment. But Billy's arrogance cut that moment very short. Yes Billy. She said lowering her head, tears welling up in her eyes. I should've

338

killed you when I had the chance. She said under her breath.
Billy heard her mumbling something to herself. He turns to look
at her. What was that you said? Nothing Billy, nothing! Don't
mess with me tonight Helen, now do what I told you! He pushes
her into the car. Stay back there with her, in case she

Wakes up. Helen gets in the car, her thoughts flash before her
now like a scroll revealing scene after scene of her loveless
relationship with him. Hardship after hardship flashed across
her mind, from the time that they were young, up till now. Even
just a few short moments ago, when she nearly came so close to
pulling the trigger on his pistol to save the life of a person whom
she envied with an unquenchable
Passion! She detested Lisa! But yet she was very confused as to
why she was willing to kill Billy to save her? She pondered over
her thoughts questions, and feelings. Uhhhh. Sighed Lisa,
snapping Helen out of her moment with herself. She's coming
around I think. She said in a quiet tone. Shut up, or I'll give you
something to moan about! He yelled at Lisa. She's out again.
Said Helen. Good, now I don't have to listen to her mouth. He
gets on his cell phone, he was setting his next plan in order.
Yeah,yeah, I'll see you all there in a few. Later. He said putting
his phone back in his pocket. You know what to do next?
Yeah, I know. She said, hesitation filled her voice, and Billy
detected it there. He turns around and sees it in her expression
as well. Try anything, anything at all. I'll bury you! Got it! He
reaches back grabbing her face like he did the other night. Go get
the rest of the gang, and tell them to meet us over at the old
gravel pit on fourth and El Dr. Now get going! He shouted at her,
pushing her face from him. Helen left to do what Billy ordered.
He drives off burning rubber behind him.

339

The Colour Of Love
Anne Hemingway
Chap 36.

Come on man hurry up with that. Said James to Brad who was
carrying an arm load of plush assorted pillows of different colours
and sizes. I'm coming boss. Said Brad, as he walked up to
James taking some of the pillows from him. They arranged them
neatly on the bed. Yosef was standing near the open window
looking out into the darkness. His mind was on Lisa very heavily.
He flashed back to where saw the fear in her eyes, her trembling
in his arms. He rubs his hands up and down his arms. Oh, how
he wished they felt her soft body in them about now. *Lisa.* He
sighed. Jo,Jo. Called James. Come on man
Take a look it's finished. He said snapping him out of his
moment. Yosef followed him into the little bedroom. It was
gorgeous! The band had redecorated the entire bedroom just for
he and Lisa for their wedding night. The little cottage was loaned
to them for their night's stay by Terry's Father. It was a little get
away cottage that he bought for his wife over twenty years ago. It
was his wedding present to Yosef and Lisa. Yosef gasped at the
sight! The scented candles, of all colours, shapes, and sizes
scattered Throughout the room. The white laced curtains, the
satin bed linens. And who says that men can't decorate! Said
Brad. Whoa! He breathed. This is amazing guys! Lisa will flip
when she sees this!
Yosef had helped in the purchasing of the materials needed for
the makeover. But the band did mostly all the decorating
themselves. I can't believe you guys did this! He felt a
tenderness for them all at that moment. It touched him deeply.
Hey Jo, we're all in this together right man? Said Brad. I don't
know what to say. Said Yosef, he was choking up a little. Don't
say anything bass man. We Love you and Lisa.
We love all of you too. Thanks! He said they walked up to him
patting him on the shoulder. Let's get you back to your girl now.
Said Terry. Yosef smiles to hear that. Yeah, my baby's waiting
for me, I can't wait to see her. Well what're we waiting for? Let's
go bass man, let's go! Said James. They all turn to leave, when
Yosef stops dead in his tracks. In his spirit he sees the vision
that he saw at the hospital returns to him. He sees Lisa being
brutalized, she was being taken away. But he couldn't see by
whom. His breathing becomes heavy. What's wrong man?
Asked Terry. It's Lisa, she's in trouble! What! They all said
together. What do you mean in trouble? Said James. Look, I

can't explain, something's happened to her. I have get to her, let's go now! He said. Brad shook his head, he was skeptical of her being in any serious danger. But we're not finished yet. He whinned, carrying a small bag of decorations. LEAVE IT! Yosef yelled at him. He drops the bag, He starteled him. They all left rushing back to his parents house.

I wondered what's taking Lisa so long to find that ladle? Said Deborah to herself. Her spirit was even more uneasy now. She knew like Yosef, that something had happened to her, but what? Was the question.
Ben and Rabbi were standing over by the fireplace talking. Sarah was still busying herself around the house serving guests. It's the most company their home had seen in many years! She was enjoying herself tremendously. Deborah unable to ease her impressions any longer, calls for her husband. Ben....She beckons for him to come over. Excuse me Jacob. He walks over to her. Yes love. He said sipping on his cappuccino that Sarah had made. You look as though you've seen a ghost. Ben, I sent Lisa home to get the punch ladle. Yes...So what's wrong? Honey, that was fourty five miniutes ago, I haven't seen her since!
She talked in a quiet tone, so as not to attract attention to them. Now, now dear don't worry about her, she's a big girl now. I'm sure she's ok. He said stroking her soft face. I'm sorry Ben, but I know I'm right
Something's happened to her, please listen to me! She's in trouble, I know it! Something has happened to
My baby Ben. Rev. Anderson heard the desperation in his wife's voice, and saw it in her expression. Fear had come on her, and he saw it, it could not be ignored this time. He saw how deeply troubled she was about Lisa, and decided to listen to her. He takes her arm and steps ove to the large picture window. He sets his coffee cup down on the little table. They look out over across the street together. The porch was dark, there were no lights on inside the house. Not a sign of her anywhere. Ohhh! Gasped Deborah.

What's happened to her Ben? Lets's home, if she's not there, we'll call the police. They leave to go home, they go up the steps to the front porch. Ohhh! Yelled Deborah. She had stepped on something that made her stumble back into her husband's arms. Careful love. He said catching her. They both looked down. Fear rising up in them both as they notice the silver clustered object. Deborah bends down to pick it up. It was Lisa's house and car keys, she had dropped them when Billy and Helen took her. Ohh! She sighed, as she clutches the keys to her chest, her eyes closed tight. Oh, Ben! What's happened to her?

What's happened to our baby! Rev. Anderson, more than ever now is convinced of his wife's intuition. Fear began to grip him, his mind filled with questions, and no answers as to who could have done this

To his daughter. It was near impossible to stay in character as fear spoke to him. "She's dead, she's dead!"

He quickly regains himself, he takes Deborah by the arm, walking her back over to the Epstiens home. He walks her through the front door, Deborah can hardly stand to her feet, as an overwhelming fear had nearly caused her to loose consciousness. He sits her down in Rabbi's recliner. Stay here love. Jacob! Jacob! Come quick! Everyone in the house stopped what they were doing, wondering what was going on. Yes, my friend I'm coming. What is wrong? Sarah was at that moment carrying a serving tray full of coffee and desserts when she heard the dreadful news. It's my daughter, it's Lisa. Yes, yes! What is it? He takes a

Deep breath, tears falling heavy from his large brown eyes. She's been kidnapped! Gasps come from all over the room! Sarah stunned, dropped the serving tray to the floor! An expression of horror on her face.

Dear Lord Yeshua no! She shouted. Ben! Call the police! Call them quickly! He cried to Rabbi. Yes, Yes, of course right away! He said as he hurries over to the phone to make the call. Just then Deborah stood up, horror returning to her again. Oh God! She shouts, putting her hands on both sides of her face.

Rev. Anderson walks over to her. What is love? She looks up at him. Yosef! She breathed. It seemed as thought all time had stood still when she mentioned his name. Rev. Anderson looks over at Rabbi, who had paused while making his call. He looked at Sarah, who was still in shock. At that moment, everyone Heard the sound of a car, screeching to a halt outside. It was Yosef and the band. They rush inside to find everyone in silence.

He walks inside looking at them all, they didn't know what to say to him. What's happened? He looked around the living room for her, not finding her in sight. Where's Lisa? He said walking up to Rev. Anderson. He looked over at Deborah, she was in tears still, her expression called to him. He went over to her. Mom, where's Lisa? His voice trembling, he too knew that something had happened to her. An eruption of tears burst forth. Oh Yosef, I sent her home to get the punch ladle son. She never came back, She Never Came Back! Her voice escalating more and her tension with it.

SHE NEVER CAME BACK!!! She collapses into his arms. He sits her back down in the chair. Sarah comes over to her. His heart beating faster than his thoughts were racing. He looks at Rev. Anderson.

She's been kidnapped son. He said to him. Saddness filled his voice, as did helplessness his expression.

The band gasps in horror as did everyone earlier. No dad! NO! NO!!!!! Tears streaming down his face.

LISSAAHH!!!!!! He screamed. Please no, no! Rev. Anderson comes over to him. Yosef, get a hold of yourself son. Come on now. That's it. He said in a comforting tone, shaking him a little. Yosef'senses return to him. Who? Who did this to her ? I don't know, I don't know son. "I know." The voice said

From behind them. It was Helen. She had come inside the house, they had left the front door opened.

Sarah looked at Deborah, she was cradling her in her arms. She rubbed Deborah's hands trying to comfort

Her. There, there dear. Shhh, quiet now. She said rocking her in her arms. They took my child Sarah. She said in a quiet tone. We will find her dear. It will be alright. Quiet now. Come in here Helen. Rev. Anderson calls to her. She steps further in the house. Yosef quickly flashed to his conversation with her earlier before he left. He walked over to Rabbi. This is all my fault dad. Rabbi had finished calling the Police, they were on their way to his home. He hangs up the phone. What are you talking about, this being all your fault? You had nothing to do with this son! I never should've left her, she was trying to tell me she didn't want me to leave her alone tonight. She was so scared, I've never seen Lisa so scared in all my life. She trembled in my arms, I felt her! I felt her fear, it was all over us both! I never should've left

Her dad! If anything happens to her because of me.... He broke
down in his father's arms. Yosef, we'll find her son. Believe me
we will. She will be alright! He turns to look at Helen, calling to
her. Helen,
You know who is responsible for this taking, yes? She looked at
everyone, afraid to speak because of Billy, but even more afraid
not to because of Lisa's family and friends. Rev. Anderson walks
up to her.

A look of intense fury in his eyes. They for the moment seem to
glow a firey red colour. Answer him.
He said to her. His voice sounded like it came from a deep cave.
Where is my daughter? He asked her.
She stood there motionless, her eyes about to pop out of her
head. Rev. Anderson voice sent shivers up her spine. She
swallowed hard. Trying to answer him. His anger began to
surface more, his breathing became hard and heavy. His voice
was more authorative and commanding now. WHERE IS MY
DAUGHTER!!
He roard at her. Helen jumped like someone had lit a match to
her bottom. Whoa! Breathed Yosef. He walked even closer to her.
What happened to Lisa Helen, don't make me keep asking you?
Finally her
Voice returns to her, her words jumping out of her mouth. Billy
took her! More gasps sound all throughout the room. Yosef's
body began to swell up with rage. His mind flowed back two
years ago to the incident.
What he promised he'd do to Billy if he ever went near Lisa again.
His face, and fists tighten as rage fills his being. Everyone
looking at each other. Billy took her? Asked Rev. Anderson.
What for? She was silent. I think I know why Dad. Said Yosef.
He stepped up to Helen. Does this have anything to do with what
happened between us two years ago? Yes, yes it does. She said
nodding her head. He's determined to get his revenge or
something like that. I saw her being hurt Helen, did he touch
her? Asked Yosef. She held her head down. She remembered
the savage and cruel way that he beat Lisa. Yes, he uh. He beat
her
I mean really bad. It's like he went totally out of his mind! She
looked around at everyone, they were all looking back at her in
disgust. Oh, Jesus! Breathed Yosef. He made me do it! He was
gonna kill me if I didn't help him. I swear I'm not lying! He had a
gun! What! Shouted Rev. Anderson. Yosef grabs his stomach,

fear had seized the pit of his belly. He felt a slight nausea come on him He walks away from her. You mean to tell me you stood there with a gun in your hands and you did nothing to help her! Fired Rev. Anderson. You watched that animal beat my daughter and you didn't do anything to stop him! I was scared ok! I was scared! She remembered how she nearly came close to killing Billy, she could still feel the anger, the coldness of the trigger in her fingers as she tried to squeeze it just a little bit more, thus bringing an end to Billy Bravens. She could still hear Lisa's screams and cries for her to help her. Remorse began to come on her. This was the only way that she knew of to redeem herself for her part in Lisa's kidnapping. Since she didn't have the courage to kill him, at lease she had just enough of it left over in her own hardened heart to turn him in. She thought about how he put her down telling her about being

"pissy" with him. This was her way also of having her own revenge. It felt good to her. Why did you do this? Rev. Anderson's voice snapping her back into the now. I didn't know he was gonna go this far with

her. He's crazy! Where are they now? Asked Rev. Anderson. At the old gravel pit on fouth and El Dr. I know where that is. Said Yosef. It's where that old steel Mill used to be, the one that closed about four years ago dad, across from the El tracks. I remember now. Said Rev. Anderson. Let's go now. I believe I still know the way there. Wait! Shouted Helen. I think there's something else you should know. They stop to listen to her. He won't be alone. He has his gang there, they'll be waiting for you. He really means to kill her. Her and you Yosef. Everyone looks at each other. Well we'll just see about that. Fired Brad.

In a huffy tone. Yosef looked at him smiling a little. That boy has been nothing but an anal discomfort

To this Community as long as I can remember. I think that it's time that God gave this neighborhood an enema. Billy and his people have been stinking up this place for too long. I think a little flushing is in order here. Can I get an Amen? Amen! Shouted everyone. Amen dad. Said Yosef. Helen's courage, left her suddenly fear coming on her again. But if Billy gets in trouble, his father will have my head on a platter. She whinned. Yosef looked at her, disgust filling him. That would be an improvement for the rest of your body Helen. Said Yosef, walking towards the front door. I'll be back. He said. Where are you going? I'm going to get my girl dad. Wait a minute! Didn't you

345

hear what she said? His gang will be there waiting for you, armed I'm sure. This is between me and Billy dad! And us! Said Rev. Anderson.

Look, she's not your wife yet young man. She's still my little girl. I won't let you go out and risk your life and Lisa's . But... Yosef interrupted him. No but's here son. We all go together understood? Yosef calms down. Yes Sir. Now uh...let's go and get my child. They all leave in Rev. Anderson's family van. What about me? Whinned Helen. I'll tell you what about you. You're gonna stay right here with me until

The Police come. Now get in here and sit down. Don't even make me go off up in here. Helen went over to the sofa and sits down, left with her fears. I wish I were dead. She cried softly. The night's still young

Helen. Said Mamie in a cutting tone. Helen drops her head in her hands and weeps painfully.

The Colour Of Love
Anne Hemingway
Chap 37.

Yosef was silent as they drove over to the Old Steel Mill. His thoughts were constantly on Lisa. A myriad of feelings would speak to him. Fear at the top of the list, doubt right behind it. The uncertainy of her still being alive haunted him viciously. Then suddenly from down within him. He hears Lisa's voice speaking to him.   *"I can do all things through Christ Who strengthens me."* He begins to smile. Yeshua, If ever I needed that strength, it's now. He prayed. He began to squeeze a handgrip that Lisa gave him for Christmas last year. His smile gave way to his rage, nothing consoled him from this point on. His bandmates tried, but all to no avail. All he wanted was Lisa back in his arms, and Billy in the ground.

They finally tuen off of fourth street onto El Dr. They pull into the yard following the road around to the

346

Gravel pit. All looked at the surroundings. This place gives me the creeps. Said Brad. Rev. Anderson shuts of the motor. Everyone began emerging from the van together. The abandoned building looked

Dark and forboding, some of the windows boarded up, some broken. It resembled something out of an old horror classic movie. Casper wouldn't haunt this thing man. Said James. Tell me about it J. Said Terry.

Yosef looked around him. Not a sign of life anywhere. There was a streak of lightening that flashed across the sky. The wind beginning to pick up a little. The heavens were disturbed that night, not because of the weather, but because God was about to pay a little Judgement call on Billy and his friends. And let me tell you. That's not gonna be pretty! So I see you made it didn't you jew boy! The voice sounded out of the darkness. Yosef and everyone there knew whose voice it was, they all turned in several different directions

Looking for him. Hell, you even brought a little company. That's ok, I brought a little company of my own. He whistled into the air. From all around them, the figures started to emerge from out of the building and from out of the parked cars in the back of them. They completely surrounded them in the

Center of the pit. The clouds began to form over them slowly. The lightening flashed again causing a beautiful display of skyworks above them. Where is she Billy? Yelled Yosef, walking towards his voice.

That's right jew boy come to me. I've wanted to take you down for a long time. I want to see her right now! Demanded Yosef. All the gang members laugh at him. You're in no position to make demands here

Jew boy. Come on out where I can see Billy. You want a piece of me? Huh? I took you once before, I'll take ya again! Heh,heh,heh! He laughed in a sadistic tone. You know I still owe you from that night. His attitude was cocky and arrogant in a James Dean sort of way. Billy, this is Rev. Anderson. I want you to release my daughter this instant! His voice boomed louder than thunder! Well if it isn't my future father in law. Keep your cross on Pops, I'm just having a little fun! You know I would never hurt my little brown sugaaahhh! Oh, my. This boy has totally wigged out! Said Terry shaking his head at him. I'm

347

gonna take her back Billy, and there's nothing that you or your little friends can do to stop me. You're outta your
Freaking mind jew boy! Look around you, you're outnumbered! His gang had completely surrounded them, and were starting to close in on them. There was no place for them to go, above the pit as well as in the center of it. Yosef remember a Bible story that Rev. Anderson told him when he was in his teens about

In the book of II Kings the 6th chapter. And How the Syrian Army had come for them. They too just like Billy and his gang had surrounded Yosef and his family. Gehazi had become fearful when he saw the entire army all around them. Elisha said to him. *Do not fear, for those who are with us are More than those who are with them.* He then prayed that God would open the young man's eyes. God did as he had requested. The story went on that when He had opened his eyes. He beheld the mountains was full of horses and chariots of fire all around them! He really didn't know why that came to him all of a sudden
But how like the Lord to remind us of His past dealings with our enemies, would He not do the same for us today. After all He is the same Yesterday, today and forever! She doesn't love you Billy, now let her go!
Yelled Yosef, his anger rising more and more. She was mine! I saw her first! Then you came along and swept her away from me! Well, I've got her back now. You'll see for yourself, she really does love me.
Want to hear for yourself? He whistles, and from out of one of the parked cars over by the building. A very large black man dressed in a black leather suit and silver chains gets out of the car with Lisa. Her hands were tied behind her back. The man was practically dragging her. He throws her at Billy, he catches
Her into his arms Yosef! She screamed. Yosef makes a run for them. His anger driving him fearlessly
At Billy. Stay back jew boy! Billy pulls out his pistol aiming right at Yosef. He freezes in place! Rev. Anderson and the rest gasp when they saw the gun. He choke holds Lisa close, she was squirming in his grip. Beautiful isn't she? He kisses her on the cheek. Billy please! Yosef begins to weaken when he hears

Her voice calling out to him. She was still very bruised, Yosef noticed that her dress had a footprint on the side of it he remembered what Helen said about him kicking her in her side.

His rage returns in a fury Yosef squinted his eyes at Billy Let her go man! He said walking towards them Billy then looks at one of his gang boys. A tall sort of man about Yosef's height,a little heavier than him. He too was dressed in black leathers and silver chains. Somewhat muscular. He was carrying a silver link chain. Billy nods at him to charge Yosef. The man then started running at him, whirling his chain in the air. Yosef saw the man coming at him, he braces himself. Rev. Anderson hoped that at that moment his teachings of Martial Arts hadn't left Yosef about now. The man charged faster now, Yosef smiled at him, a boldness filling him now. As the man approached him, he just stepped aside slightly. The man couldn't stop in time. He fell head first onto the gravel , rolling over and over finally coming to a rest on his stomach! He sat up
Spitting out rocks and gravel looking like an over grown child in a sand box. Yosef didn't even flinch at the man, he just stood there looking at him. Get up! Get him! Screamed Billy at the man. He gets up and charges at him again, yelling and twirling his chain, he looked almost like a human helicopter about to take off or something. Yahhhhhh! He screamed at Yosef, he smiled at him again, this time growing weary of his attempts. The man takes a swing at him with his chain. Yosef ducks, then as the man past him. He elbows him hard in his side. Ahhh! He yells in pain. Yosef then grabs the chain, swinging the man around to face him, punching him hard in the face with his fist! He drops the chain, Yosef then executes a beautiful spinning back kick to the man's face, crumpling him to the ground in a silver and black heap!

The gang member crawls away from Yosef staggering to his feet running away in pain like a whipped puppy! Yessss! Shouted Rev. Anderson. You gonna let that jew pig whip on you like that! James and Terry slap fives. That's my boy! Said James. The man is baaaddd! He cheered for him. Yosef smiles at him shaking his head again. He then turns around to see Billy shaking Lisa violently Lisa! He yells. let her go Billy! This isn't about her anyway, it's about you and me. So let's keep it that way No! You stay away. You just want to take her back from me again! Oh, I just don't want to take her away. I'm gonna
Take her back! Stay there! Or I'll kill her! He said pointing the gun barrel to Lisa's temple this time! Yosef's eyes became big as saucers. The rest of the gang members close in on them more.

The Heavens becoming more and more violent as Judgement makes it's way to the Earth! Rev. Anderson and his wife, and the rest circle themselves together holding hands praying intensely. Yosef moves closer to them. Let her go! His voice roared at Billy. Just them fed up with him, Lisa decides to make a move all her own.

She steps on Billy's foot hard! Ow! You little bit...! He slaps her to the ground. LISA! Shouted Yosef.

Back off jew boy! Or she gets it! Lisa stands dizzily to her feet. Get over here now! She stands there defiying his commands. No Billy she said in a weary voice. She was still weaked from his beating of her, as well in discomfort. Lisa what are you doing! Said Yosef. I'm tired of all this fighting, this has to stop somewhere. I've had enough of this! She said breaking down in tears. No Lisa, stay out of it baby alright
I can't take it anymore Beloved, I can't! she said. He could hear the sound of desperation in her voice.
Billy now aims the gun at Yosef. This is all very touching, but my patience is running out. He said in a sarcastic tone. Now get over here, or I'll kill him! Lisa's eyes now are wide and staring. Fear filling her expression. Ok! Ok! Just don't hurt him! Please! Oh, God! I love to hear a woman beg! He said, his arrogance getting the best of him. She stepsback over to him, he snatches her by the arm back into his choke hold again. Now that's more like it! My sweet brown sugaahhhh! He said kissing her on the cheek again. Lisa becomes nauseated. Lisa I'm sorry, this was not to involve you. Shut up! She's always been involved! You're not so big now are you jew boy?   Billy for the last time, let her go! You don't have to do this man! The past is past! Let it go! Billy thought a moment on Yosef words about leaving the past behind. He knew that he was right. He looks at Lisa, then back at him. Just then, anger rose up in Billy, his eyes staring big at Yosef. You're right Joseph, the past is past. I'll let it go, but you're going with it!

Start walking away from me right now, walk now! Yosef backs away from him, he turns to walk away. Billy then throws Lisa to the ground. He aims the gun at Yosef's back, and fires a single shot at him. NOOOO!!!! Screams Lisa. She gets to her feet and runs up behind Yosef, He turns to see her running up to him. The bullet coming like a streak of fire at him. Just as the bullet

approaches Yosef, shaking his head at Lisa, she jumps in front of him sticking out her chest taking the bullet into her body! LISA!!!!
Screamed Yosef. Oh, my God! My God! Yelled Deborah. No, No, NOOOOO!!!!!! Shouted Rev. Anderson. Not my angel! Not my angel! Johnathan and all the rest could not believe their eyes. As Lisa's words had come to past. *"I would give my life for you Beloved."* That was the reason for her unusal behavior, her fear. She knew somehow that her words would be fulfilled that night. Her body fell limp in Yosef's arms as he catches her lowering her to the ground. Billy looks at the gun then at Lisa. No, no not her! I wanted him dead not her! No, No! baby please no! cried Yosef, shaking his head. It's as thought all of time had stood still, as all had watched Billy take away from them the one ray of sunshine that had blessed their lives. She listened herself as her own words echoed in her ears. She would give her life for him. Yosef cried uncontrollably holding her close to him. All froze in horror as she lay helpless in her Beloved's arms, blood oozing out the corner of her mouth. Rev. Anderson remembered the prophecy that his father had pronounced over his daughter about her making an ultimate decision. So that many would be changed by her sacrifice. He was now a witness of that prophecy come to pass, as his daughter, lay dying right before his eyes. Tears streaming down his face. Rabbi and Sarah were shocked beyond words, as horror had taken them from them. No one could speak. All they heard was Yosef's weeping over his Beloved Lisa as she lay dying in his arms. He too could remember what the Angel had told him When they were in the cottage. *"She shall be taken."* Lisa why did you do this baby, why! He cried more and more, his tears coming in torrents now. Suddenly Lisa begins to stir in his embrace. Yosef.

The whispered. He looked into her eyes, tears falling like soft raindrops. She was still alive! I'm right here baby. You, You. She stammered. You must believe, believe Yosef. You told me that you believed in Him, even in the impossible! He can do the impossible! You said that you have faith in Him. I need that faith now If you want me to live again, then you must believe me back, believe me back to you Beloved. Use your faith sweetheart, it's in you! I believe in you Beloved, now you believe in Him! Don't let death keep me from you! She said in a confident tone. Her faith gave rise to his. He felt at that moment a strength building in him. He looks at her parents. Mom! Dad! They both come over to them.

Here! Hold her! He said. Deborah taking Lisa into her arms. My baby! Oh Lisa! My baby! He stands up. He looks Rev. Anderson, the man who raised him, and loved him as his own child. The man that he called daddy. Looks at him, courage filling him moment by precious moment. He knew that he needed to act fast if he was to save the life of the woman who had just saved his. Rev. Anderson looks at him, a tender expression on his face for him. The Heavens were more violent now, as a loud rumble of thunder sounded. They all look up to the night sky, It was a pinkish fluorescent colour as the lightnening flashed acrossed it. Suddenly there was a huge white cloud making it's way down from the sky! Yosef was standing there with Rev. Anderson standing behind him both men praying ferverantly. Yosef's face took on an expression of intensity as his prayers penetrated the very Heavens itself! The cloud grew as it got closer and closer to the pit. Billy and his gang stood there not knowing what was happening, or what Yosef was even doing! But they would all find out now. All of the others knew what he was doing, and they

Began to stand back as they felt the power that emenated from the huge cloud. It finally reached the pit, out of it flashed streak after beautiful streak of lightening. It sizzled, and cracked in the air charging the atomosphere around them. A blinding radiance shone forth from within it. It then began to separate Itself until it completely surrounded the pit. Then as the smoke cleared, there all around them were the Mighty Hosts of Heaven! Yosef opened his eyes, and saw the same sight that the young man with the Prohet Elisha in the Bible saw. Chariots of Fire. Angels with gleaming, flaming swords! The sight was awesome! Everyone gasped when they saw. All except Billy and his gang. Just then the Warrior Angel stepped forth out of the cloud. He was even more beautiful then the first time that Yosef saw him! He gleamed with the Presesnce of God! *"WE ARE HERE AT THE REQUEST OF YOUR PRAYERS. I SAID THAT I WOULD RETURN TO YOU AGAIN FOR THE LAST TIME. SAY THE WORD, AND IT SHALL BE DONE!" LOOK, AROUND YOU SON, FOR OUR MASTER HAS SENT US, AND WE ARE READY!"*
Yosef looked around him again, smiling at them. Can they see you? He asked, looking at his family.

YES. He said nodding his head. *"THEY CAN SEE US WITH THEIR HEARTS."* He said to him. Yosef looked back at Lisa, she was struggling to stay alive, and time was ticking away from her. My girl is dying, I can't live without her, I can't I'll do anything to save her, anything. Please tell me what I have to do! *"ONLY ONE THING SON. BELIEVE!"* what about them? He said speaking about Billy and his gang. *"IT WILL BE AS YOU SAY."* Yosef smiled. Open their eyes and let them see you! He asked.

Just then the Being turned to look at Billy and his gang waving his large hand. They were still standing around looking like puppies in a rainstorm or something. As the Angel waved his hand, the eyes of Billy and all his gang boys were opened. They too saw the flaming Chariots surround them. They were speechless as they saw all the Heavenly Host looking down at them. Whose out numbered now Billy?

Said Yosef smiling big.

The Colour Of Love
Anne Hemingway
Chap 38.

Billy and his gang were stunned as they watched the beings looking at them. An expression of anger filled their faces. Oh it's on now! Said James. I believe we'd better step back now. Said Rev. Anderson. Billy's heart became even more hardened at Yosef. I hate you boy! I want you to kill them! Kill them all now!! He screamed. Just then the Angels begun to leave their chariots as the Warrior Angel gave them the signal.

They swooped from all directions, covering Yosef and his family .
Lisa.was beginning to gasp for breath.

Hold on baby! Hold on! Said Deborah holding her close to her. I'm so cold mom, I'm so cold. She said as she felt the warmth of life leaving her body. Billy gave an order himself for his gang to open fire on Yosef and his family. It was like a shoot out on a battlefield. The Angels had completely surrounded them all. They raised their huge wings, and their hands towards Heaven.

The bullets ricocheted in every other direction! There were sparks flying everywhere as the bullets were being stopped by the Angels Yosef then felt a surge of faith rise up within him. His body swelled not in anger this time, but with courage! The Warrior Angel then raised his hand and the rest of the Angels swooped down out of their chariots after the gang. Let's get outta here! Shouted one of Billy's boys they were scattering in every direction! Billy watched, his anger rising even more within him, as his boys deserted him. You bunch of sissies! You cowards! Come back here!!! The Angels flying after them! They wouldn't let them leave the pit. Billy then notices his gun lying on the ground by itself. He had dropped it after he shot Lisa.

He walks over, reaching down after it. But Just then Yosef's Warrior Angel stepped in his way. He tried to swing at the huge being, but his hand just went through him. The Angel raised his hand slightly, sending Billy flying into the air a few feet! He landed by one of his gang boys. He was just lying there looking up at the stars. He looks over at Billy. That's how I got over here, If I were you, I'd just stay right there and watch the twinkles. He said. Billy jumps to his feet. I never turn down a good fight! I ain't scared of no sheets! He fired back at the man. The gang member turned his face back up to the sky, for more twinkle watching. The Warrior Angel notices Billy walking towards him. Yosef then begins to walk towards the Angel. I want this one for myself. Said Yosef in a soft confident tone. The Angel nodded, and moved aside. Come to me Billy. He said, flexing his muscles, standing there waiting for him. This will be a piece of cake! Said Billy snapping his finger in the air. His arrogance getting the better of him. He charges at Yosef. I'm gonna kick me some more jew butt! He fumed at Yosef. Yosef smiled at him, as his faith begins to rise more and more, just like Billy's arrogance. A light begins to emanate from within him!
It shone all around him! It was the light of God's Power! He runs up to Yosef swinging at him, Yosef blocks him, then punches him in his face hard. Billy stumbles off balance. He gathers himself and charges at him again. He jumps in the air trying to execute a flying back kick, but Yosef catches his foot in mid air, and throws his body to the ground! Whoa! Breathed Terry. Good bye Billy nice knowin ya! Mocked Brad, looking at Terry and James. They all paused looking at each other. NOT!!! They all said together

Billy jumps to his feet again. That's all you got jew boy? I'm not even warmed up yet! You're gonna die tonight, you hear me boy! You're gonna die tonight, just like your girl! Billy's words fueled Yosef's anger. He squinted his eyes tight at him. Yosef felt strength surging to every muscle in his body. He clenched his teeth together. Come and get some. He said, his voice calm and confident. Yahhhhhh!

Billy screamed at him. He swings hard at Yosef, he blocks his fist one last time, then he executes a beautiful roundhouse kick to Billy's face. One after another. It was like a repeat beating that he took two years ago. Yosef, then kicks him hard in his stomach. Billy wheezes, as he gasps for breath. Go Head Boy! Cheered Rev. Anderson. Yosef's parents could not believe their eyes as they watch him beat Billy to a pulp. Yosef's memory begins to remind him of the beating that he gave Lisa two years ago, and tonight. His anger then turns to fury, bringing rage with it. He knocks Billy back to the ground again.

He then sat on him and savagely beat him. He remembered what he told Billy that he would do to him if he ever touched her again. And tonight, he was about to keep that promise. Oh, no! said Rev. Anderson. No son! No! screamed Rev. Anderson. But Yosef did not hear his cries, he heard nothing but his own anger speaking to him to kill Billy. The other Angels were still holding the gang members at bay, not letting them leave. Just then out of the darkness, stepped forth a tall hooded figure. It was the spirit of death. He had come for Lisa. She held up her hand, her mother taking it into hers. Come on baby, you can do it. Hold on! She cried, she felt Lisa's body growing cold in her arms. Tears streaming down her face.

Yosef's continued to pound on Billy, as flash after flash of the way that he beat Lisa that night flooded his mind. His face became tighter, his expression more and more savage. Yosef raised his fist once more, hoping that the final blow would kill Billy. Just then the Angel steps up to him. He could feel Yosef's anger. He looked at him, raising one finger shaking his head "No." At him. " He belongs to Him now."

Yosef, began to shake all over, as his rage wanted satisfaction. It screamed out to kill him! Noooo! He screams Jumping off Billy. He stood to his feet, his breathing heavy. The Angel looked at Yosef, his heart filled with compassion for him. Yosef looks at the huge being, the Angel reached out and touched Yosef's

Cheek. He smiled at him. Yosef begins to calm down, as his anger starts to leave him now. He turns and slowly walks away from him. Billy tries to stand to his feet, but he kept falling back over on the ground.

He notices that his pistol is still laying on the ground, and starts to crawl over to it. Lisa looked at the spirit that haad come for her. She looked over in Yosef's direction, he never saw her looking at him. With tears in her eyes, she breathed her last to him. I Love You, My Beloved. Ahhhhhhhh. She breathed. Her hand drops slowly back to the ground. Yosef had stopped to look back at the Angel. He nodded for him to go on his way. He saw Billy struggling to get to his feet, He smiled a little. Yosef!!!!! Screamed Deborah. He turns around abruptly. And starts walking towards her voice. Billy reaches his pistol, and stands very shakily to his feet, Blood hanging out of the corner of his mouth. He aims the gun at Yosef's back. Goodbye jew boy! Heh,heh,heh! He laughs. Yosef never even turned to look at him, he could feel Billy, he raised his hand behind him. And just like the Angel. An unseen force came out of his hand! It hit Billy, knocking him again several feet into the air! He landed right back over beside the same gang member where he had landed before. The man looked over at Billy. Weren't you just over here a few minutes ago? He lets out a deep breath turning his eyes back towards the sky again. You should've stayed here to watch the twinkles. He said in a southern drawl. Billy then collapses to the ground unconscious.

Yosef ran over to Deborah, when he reached her. He found to his horror that his beloved Lisa was dead.

His eyes wide and staring. NOOOOOOOOO!!!!!!!! He screamed. His voice echoed all throughout the pit.

It's not her time! It's not her time! He cried. You promised me! YOU PROMISED MEEEEEE!!!!!

He screamed. Just then the heavens begin to part, like a scroll opening revealing the most spectacular

Display that human eyes have ever seen! The very Glory of Heaven Itself was revealed to them! They looked at each other unable to take in It's indescrible beauty! Every Angel on the Earth bowed themselves down as they watched the Tall Man in the Middle stand from His Throne! His Presence was beyond words! There were thunderings and Lightenings flashing and booming from all around Him! His Presence was like Fire! There were no words to describe His Beauty! He stood to His Feet. All could see the Nail prints in His Hands, and His feet, Glory streaming forth from them! His voice was unlike anything they had ever heard! It was like the roaring of many oceans! There was a compassion that flowed like gentle streams, they could feel His Love! It absolutely radiated from Him! Tears flowed from all their eyes.

"HE WHO BELIEVES IN ME, THOUGH HE WERE DEAD, YET SHALL HE LIVE. FOR I AM THE GREAT RESURRECTION. MY SON, DID I NOT SAY IN MY WORD THAT IF THOU SHALL BELIEVE, THAT THOU WOULD SEE THE GLORY OF GOD! FOR WITH GOD ALL THINGS ARE POSSIBLE! AND NOTHING IS TOO HARD FOR ME!" Yosef looked at the spirit that was still waiting for Lisa. NOT EVEN DEATH CAN TAKE HER FROM ME! IN THE NAME OF YESHUA, LET HER GO! The spirit began to back away from Lisa's body. He walks over kneeling down taking her into his arms. Deborah gets up and goes back over to Rev. Anderson. He stands to his feet with her limp body. He looks up towards Heaven, with tears in his eyes. He could hear the Choirs of Heaven singing. Father You said that if I believed in You, that You would give me the desires of my heart. He looks down into Lisa's face. I Love her Father, give her back to me. In the Name of Your Son Yeshua.

Give my girl back to me. I believe in You! I believe in You! He cried. He kneeled back to the ground with her. *"THEN SON, SEE THE GLORY OF GOD! I SAY UNTO YOU DAUGHTER, ARISE!"*

At His words, there was a calmness all around them. The was a gentle rumbling of thunder. Yosef's body began to glow again as the Spirit of God's Power began to flow from within him. A single tear makes it's way down his cheek falling into Lisa's face. The spirit of death was still standing waiting to claim her totally. Come on Lisa breathe! Open your eyes baby. Please! Breathe! I know you can hear my voice.

I won't let death take you from me! Come back to me Lisa. I Love you. He kisses her gently on her lips.

Ummmmm. Yeshua was still standing from His throne. He had raised one hand at His command. Lisa then began to stir in Yosef's arms, as the body that life had left behind began to squirm. Her face glowed as her colour returned bringing warmth with it. Ahhhhh! She breathed as life had flowed back into her body! Her eyes slowly opened, looking right into the eyes of her Beloved! She smiled a radiant smile at him. Yosef! She said, still

weak. Lisa! Lisa! You came back to me!   Oh God! Thank You!
Thank You! He looked up at Him, He was still standing. He
nodded His Head at Yosef.   He looked at the spirit

Still standing waiting. Back off! She's mine! He said pointing his
finger at him. The spirit then lowered his head, and faded away
into the darkness. He then looks at Terry. Call an ambulance.
On it! Said Terry, as he jumped into the van to use the car
phone. Honey... She tried to speak. No Lisa, don't try to talk
now. Yeahhhh! Said Rev. Anderson hugging Deborah close.
Sarah and Rabbi Kiss each other as they rejoice with them.
Whoooo! Shouted all Yosef's band members. As God had
returned Lisa to all that loved and adored her. Just then they all
hear the sound of police sirens wailing down the dusty road to the
gravel pit. The Police and an amulance had arrived on the scene.
The policemen flooded out of the paddy wagons after Billy and his
gang boys. They couldn't see the Angels present. They tried to
tell them that they were the ones who held them there and
wouldn't let them leave. The Policemen laugh at them all.
Listen to me! Shouted Billy. There's one of em' now! He's over
there! Look! The policeman looked over to where Billy pointed.
All that they saw was a dirty old raggety sheet blowing from out of
the old building. That's just a sheet sir. He said wanting to
laugh again.   You ain't scared of no sheets are you son? Said
one of his boys as the policeman walked him by Billy. He then
himself was cuffed and marched away and put into the paddy
wagon along with his boys. Yosef and the rest of the family
laughed
Together as they watched them being filed into the wagons.
Yosef then looked back at Lisa, she was looking up at him, her
heart beating faster then her lips could speak. Lisa, you came
back to me. He said his tears returning to him. I told you that I
would give my life for you Beloved. Yes you did baby. Yes you
did, I knew that you wouldn't let death hold me for long, And
most of all Yosef. I told you. Not even

Death can keep me from you. She blinks her eyes slowly. I love
you, my Beloved. Yosef gasped at her words. It's like he hears
them for the first time with his heart. I love you so much Lisa. If
you only knew how much I do. I really love you! He kisses her

tenderly. What happned to Billy? He laughs a little looking at them still being driven off to jail. Well lets just say he and his boys saw the light. She looks funny at him smiling. The EMT'S emerge from the ambulance. Sir we need to take her now. Said one of the techs. Yosef hands her over to them carefully. He watches tearfully as they strap her to the gurney. The Warrior Angel stepped back up to Yosef. They hadn't left yet. The police and the Emt's never saw them. *"Well done son."* I don't understand, He gave her back to me. Why? If it was due for her to die, then why did He spare her life? *"Son, hear the words that I say to you this night." Many a sacrifice has been made on the behalf of others. So that by their giving of themselves others might benefit from their sacrifice. She gave her life for you so that you might know the true meaning of Love. God's Love. Our Master and Creator God Himself gave the Ultimate, the Supreme Sacrifice, the Life of His only Son Yeshua. So that by His Sacrifice now all Mankind may have free access to Him, by the simple act of faith. If they would only come to Him like a little child. He said that He would in no way cast him out!" Believe this son. For it is a faithful and true Word of the Living God for the entire Human Race." IF only they would believe. For a person to die without Christ in their lives, is for that person to die without never knowing how much they were truly loved." You have done well, and for this you will be rewarded.*

There was a pause between them. Yosef thought heavily on his words. I understand everything you said except one thing. I know I asked before, But I'll ask again. Why, please tell my why He gave her back to me. *"Because you asked Him, and because He loves her, and you." "God loves all, He Himself is Absolute Love!" Go now she waits for you. She will live, and bear you three children. Two sons, and a daughter." As it is spoken, so shall it be done."* He said as he and the rest of the Angels were slowly starting to ascend upward. Yosef looked back at Lisa, as they were putting her into the ambulance. Just then the Cloud appeared again. It had overshadowed the Angels. Yosef and all the rest watched in silent wonder as the Heavens received them out of their sight. The light slowly fading away into the darkness once more. The sky was now calm, calmer than it had ever been. There were no words that any spoke at that moment. All that could be heard from them was the silence of their joy, for it was unspeakable! Their eyes had beheld the Glory of God, and now they all would live to tell about it. Their testimony of God's

Miraculous intervention would live on long after their deaths blessing the lives, and touching the hearts of all who would hear and dare to believe!

The Colour Of Love
Anne Hemingway
Chap 39.

Billy and his gang are taken to court, and found guilty of various other crimes. Including attempted murder and assault and kidnapping. The assault and attempted rape case that was washed over two years ago was reopened. His father Police Commissioner William Bravens Sr. was tried and convicted of hiding the evidence, as well as other charges of drugs, and racketeering . He was fired from his office. And Terry's father, Walter Copeland that was elected to Commissioner in his place. Helen was given a light sentence because of the information that she gave that not only sent Billy and his father to prison, but that helped them locate Lisa.   She was sentenced to 90 days in jail with five years probation. Lisa was admitted to Saints Of Mercy Hospital with a bullet wound to the chest. The Dr. that performed her surgery told of a very strange happening in the operating room. According to him and several witnesses there, Lisa should've died instantly when she was shot. The bullet entered her body directly in from of her heart. But somehow it took a detour, and lodged itself behind her heart. I believe we all know Who was responsible for that bit of fancy manevering! Now the tricky part was how to remove it from her chest without any heart damage? When the incicion was made, the Head Surgeon looked at her x-ray to see the bullet's location. When looked back at her opened chest, they saw a shiny object peeking from behind her heart.

There it is! Said one of the other surgeons. I see it! I see it! How can I get this thing out of her? Oh Jesus Help me!   He said. Just then, Lisa's chest began to fill with fluid! The bullet was then dislodged from it's place, and seem to just float up all by itself! They all looked in unbelief at what they had just seen. Ask and ye shall receive. Said the surgical nurse. Somebody up there really likes this girl! He said. Amen. Said the rest. The surgeon then took his instrument and removed the bullet. Suction! He shouted.

They began to suction out her chest immediately. Alright, people let's call it a night, and close her. God's already done the hard part. He said. At that, the other surgeon closed up Lisa's chest cavity. Which left a medium sized scar that resembled a jagged cross in the middle of her chest. After the Surgery, he spoke with Lisa's parents, and Yosef. He told them of what happened in there. He stated that it was the most unusual operation that he had ever performed in his entire Medical Career. He walked away still baffled, but now a firm believer in the God of Miracles! Lisa was released three weeks later.

The Day!

Ohhh! Lisa you look stunning! Said her Deborah, she was still fussing over her. Lisa's wedding gown was made in Old Victorian style of pearls and lace. The dress was a beautiful sheer white with golden trimming with off shoulders and long puffed sleeves which pointed at the wrists. The dress had tear drop pearls in the bodice, with an intricate embroidered swirl design. Her vail was a beautiful silver and gold Tiara stuffed with veil material in a puff design that was absolutely gorgeous! It covered her from her face down to her bare shoulders. The train was nearly seven feet in length which had embroidered on the center of it. The Star of David. Her Bridal bouqet was a lovely array of pink and white carnations, with baby's breath. It had a single Lilly in the center. There was a knock at the door. Who is it? Said Mamie. I want to speak with my daughter. Said Rev. Anderson. Mamie opens the door. Where's my angel? Back there with her mother and Sarah. He steps inside the dressing room to see her. He gasps when he sees her. Lisa looks herself over. Well Daddy. How do I look? Just like you mother. He breathed. Honey, may I speak with her alone please? Sure dear, but it's almost time. I'll be brief. He

361

said. She, and Sarah leave them alone. Look at you. He said
his emotions pulling him all different directions. His fathers pride
coming on him. His smile big and proud. I'm so nervous daddy.
Ahh! He breathed, fanning his hand. This is a piece of cake. He
said snapping his finger in the air. What's a father to say?
Except I'm so darn proud of you girl I could bust! Well control
yourself ok dad. We have enough to clean up around here
already. They

Laugh. I'll try to keep a lid on myself just for you. He said
touching her nose with his index finger. She holds her head
down smiling a little. What's the matter child? To know that
you and mom are proud of me. What that makes me feel like
today. I have no words to tell you dad. I have you and my
mother to thank for that. She sniffled. Daddy? Yes love. I want
to tell you how much I love you and mom, and how much I thank
you for all that you've done for me. Me and Yosef. I couldn't've
gotten through this without the both of you. Aren't you
forgetting Someone? He said looking upward. Yeah, mainly Him.
You've taught me so much, I'll be grateful for the rest of my life.
She pauses. I'm so glad that you're my father.
Thank you daddy for being my father. They embrace hard. She
begins to weep. I love you Daddy! I love you too angel. Now, now
what's all the tears for? You can't go out there like this. His
falsetto voice returning. I can't help it dad. I love you and mom,
Ms. Sarah and Rabbi so much. Here now lets dry those tears
now. He takes a tissue and dries them for her. How's Yosef? Oh
that boy's a mess! Shoes on the wrong feet, shirt inside out,
pants on backwards I mean he's messed up!! Dad... Huh? You
aint got no luggage why you trippin on me? They both bust up
laughing. Better now angel? Yeah, much better now Daddy. He
Kisses her forehead, then lets her veil down over her face.

There was a knock at the door of Yosef's dressing room. Come in.
He said. It was Terry. Less then ten minutes to go. He said
shutting the door behind him. You don't think she's changed her
mind do you John? He said. His nervousness getting the better
of him. Boy chill out! Jo! What! It's ok little bro. Just breathe.
He said trying to calm him down. I'm sorry but I'm too nervous to
breathe man. Here, just this one more thing, and you're good to
go. He finishes adjusting his tie. There. Perfect. He said to him.

362

Johnathan looks at him. His thoughts flow back in time a little to when he and Yosef were younger.
How they played together, laughed, and cried together. Never one time were they ever jealous of one another. They had loved each other like brothers all their lives. Now they were about to become officially united as family! What's wrong John? He holds his head down. I was just uh,.... Thinking about all that we've been through together man. What we've shared, did. I don't know, just our lives together period.
I just want to say that I love ya man. You're my little bro. Yosef was near tears himself this time. Thanks for standing with me man. I couldn't get through this without you. No sweat Jo. They embrace again. And now for the finishing touch. Said Johnathan. He takes from out of a small box a white Yamika, and places it on Yosef's head. Now it's your turn. He said to Johnathan. He placed one on his bald head too.
Yosef is dressed in a Formal Tuxedo. So was Johnathan, All of the groomsmen were his band mates. They too were dressed in tuxes and matching Yamika's for the event. They looked at each other for a moment. Both remembering their lives together as young kids. Yosef following Johnathan everywhere he went. Johnathan more than willing to take him. Both men choke up a little. They were snapped out of their moment as the Shofar blowers sounded their horns. There was another knock at the door. Come in.
Said Yosef. It was Terry. It's time. He said, he was a little nervous himself. His wife Suzanne was Lisa's Maid of Honor. They looked at each other as Terry shut the door behind him. You ready little bro. Yosef takes a deep breath. Yes sir! He said saluting him. Then come on boy! Let's go get you married!

Johnathan escorts him out into the Sanctuary. All stand in place, the Shofar blowers sound their horns again as the Ceremony begins, as both Fathers would officiate the Service. The Church was decorated in
Beautiful Jewish and traditional African American décor. The canopy that Yosef and Lisa would stand under was decorated in an assortment of white baby mums, and Lillies that streamed down its tresses. Rabbi Epstein began the Ceremony with a Ceremonial Hebrew Chant from His Siddur. When he had finished his chant. The music begins to play. It was a song that Lisa had especially written for their wedding day. Yosef looked at

Johnathan as he hears his Beloved Lisa's sweet voice serenading him this time. A single tear makes it's way down his masculine cheek. Down came the Bridesmaids, each escorted by their Groomsmen. Next came the flowergirls, all four of them dressed in pretty pink and white pastel gowns. Throwing their flower petals in front of them. Next came the Ring bearer, Brandon. Terry's son. When all were in place. The whole Church stood to their feet as Rev. Anderson Marched his daughter Lisa Anderson down the aisle. There were gasps from everyone there as they beheld her beauty. She was breathtaking! Whoa! Breathed Yosef. His knees wobbled a little. He nearly fainted into Johnathan's arms

The Church gasped at him. Steady boy. Said Johnahtan as he steadied him back on his feet again. Oh God! Is she ever beautiful! She looks like a dream to me. He whispered to Johnathan. He nods in agreement with him. Lisa could hardly take her eyes off her Beloved. He too looked like a dream to her!

Oh Jesus! He's so beautiful to me! She closes and opens her eyes slowly. Her heart thumping faster than she could keep up with. As they approached the Canopy, he stands there with Lisa, as Rabbi begins the Ceremony with the giving of Lisa to Yosef. Who gives this woman to this man? Asked Rabbi. I do Said

Rev. Anderson. He then gives Lisa's hand over to Yosef. He takes her hand into his. They stand together underneath the Canopy. They had written their own vows for themselves, to go along with the Tradtional Wedding vows as well. What is it that you vow to your Beloved son? Asked Rabbi. Yosef turned to Lisa Tears in his eyes.

"My Dearest Lisa, I take you to be my Lawfully Wedded Wife.
May I fulfill all God's plans and His purposes as your Covering
Your protector, and as your Lover, and Friend. May I be to you
what
He would have me to be as your Lifemate. To Love and to Cherish
you,
To be the Husband that your life needs. I forsake all others saving
only

You for myself, and to myself alone. For you have been my strength, my
Comfort In times of trouble. As Well as the Joy of my life. God as truly
Blessed my life with you. For you are my Treasure, my lover, and now my
Wife. May I follow God's Perfect Will in our Marriage, and in our Lives
So that we may live a quiet and peaceable life in Christ Our Lord. Both
Now and forever. Until the serapation of death, or until the Coming of
Our Lord Yeshua. I love you Lisa. In the Name of Yeshua Our Messiah.
Amen.

That is so beautiful! Said one of the attendants there. He takes his wife by the hand staring deeply into her eyes. I feel the same way about you that he feels about her. He kisses her gently on the cheek. They then turn to listen to Lisa say her vows. What is it that you say unto this Man daughter? Said Rev. Anderson. She looks deeply into Yosef's eyes. Tears gently falling from her soft brown eyes.

My Dearest Yosef, I receive you unto myself to be my Lawfully Wedded
Husband. May I too fulfill all that God would have me to be as your
Wife, That I may Love, and Cherish and submit unto you, as you Stay submissive unto Him, and His plans and Purposes for our lives.
May you Love me evan as Christ Loves the Church, that I may bring
Honor to the name that you now give to me. The Word says that a man's
Glory is his wife. May your head always be crowned with the glory that
I bring you, as well as the Wisdom that He gives you. That I may respect

365

And and be obedient to you, as you obey the will of our Heavenly Father.
For I too forsake all others saving only you to myself, and to myself alone.
I love you my Beloved. As God is Eternal, so is my love for you. Until the
End of my very life, or until the Return of our Lord Yeshua. In the Name
Of Jesus our Lord and Savior. Amen.

Rev. Anderson and Rabbi and both their wives, as well as the whole Church wiping the tears from their eyes. There were sniffles and soft sighs coming from all over the people. As their love had begun to flow all over the people. They could feel it coming from them! They then repeated the Traditonal Vows of Marriage before God, and Man, after Rev. Anderson. The Rings please. He said. They again recited the Traditonal Vows of Marriage as they exchanged rings. Yosef's wedding band, a beautiful solid gold, with three small diamonds across it. It matched the solid gold Bridal set that he bought Lisa. If there be anyone present who feels that these two should not be joined together in Holy Matrimony, let him or her speak now, or forever hold your peace. Just then a tall Black man stands to his feet and spoke. Would you please, please marry these kids now before this boy explodes! He said in a Bill Cosby sounding voice. Everyone in the Church bust up in laughter. Rabbi chuckles out loud. Rev. Anderson could hardly keep a straight face! Levi, you always were a fool! Said Mamie shaking her head at him. Deborah and Sarah covering their mouths laughing. Good ole uncle Levi. Said James. Yosef and Lisa laugh with all the rest. Rev. Anderson then with his hands raise over Yosef and Lisa, still chuckling some. Performs the finality of their Ceremony. Now by the power vested in me by the State of Illinois, I now pronouce that they are HUSBAND AND WIFE! Terry takes the empty decorated Bottle and lays it down in front of Yosef. He steps on it breaking it. POW! It sounded off. The Church cheers roariously! Mazaltov! Everyone shouted. Deborah and Mamie then lay a decorative laced Broom down in front of them. Jump over the Broom! They all shouted again. Yosef and Lisa jump over it. The Church cheered again. They turn to face Rabbi and Rev. Anderson. You may Salute the Bride. They both said together. Yosef then turns to

Look at Lisa, lifting her veil. With tears in both his and her eyes. He deep kisses his new Bride. Whoooo! Said everyone there. Wolf whistles and thunderous applause came from all over the place! Go head boy! Shouted Rev. Anderson. They embrace warmly. I now Present to you Mr. And Mrs. Daniel Joseph, and Elizabeth Marie Epstien. More cheers and shouts from the people. I now invite you to follow the wedding party into the Fellowship Hall for the Wedding Banquet. Please allow our Bride and Groom to leave first. The flower girls run to get in front of Yosef and Lisa, for more petal throwing. The rest of the wedding party march out behind them. The rest of the people follow. Yosef and Lisa could not believe their eyes As they stared at the sight before them. The Followship hall was decorated in the same Jewish and Traditonal Afro American décor as the Sancutary. Over the Bride and Groom Table there was a Beautiful Banner that read.

YOSEF AND LISA.

True Love Sees No Colour......No Colour At All......

The Colour of Love
Anne Hemingway
Chap 40.

The photographer is escorted in to take the pictures for the Wedding Album, then the Bride and Groom were taken over to a huge table table draped in a White and Gold laced tablecloth. It had both their names embroidered on it. It was their Gift table. There were gifts from all their family, and friends . The table was as long as it was wide. And Loaded down with gifts galore for the Couple. They looked over to the right of them, and there was the most beautiful Wedding cake they had ever seen! It stood at least five feet in height! It had double colummed pillars, flowers, and vines that decorated it's four layers! On the top was the

Bride and Groom standing underneath the White Canopy with white baby mums and Lillies flowering down it's tresses. It was gorgeous! It was made by one of the most famous Bakeries in Chicago.

As for the Banquet Dinner itself. All of the people from the surrounding neighborhood where Yosef and Lisa lived banned together to make the dinner themselves. As well as with a little help from some of Mr. Dennis' catering friends. The Mother's on the Mother's board at Rev. Anderson's Church through in some of their delicaies as well. I mean these old women threw down! Every kind of dish that you could name was there. Jewish, American, Afro-American, Native American. Polish, German, Greek cuisines. Ohh! It was and outstanding Kings feast spread out for them. Everyone was so excited there, that they forgot that Yosef and Lisa were to leave to be alone after the Wedding according to Jewish Coustom. But in their excitement they were obilivious to that coustom. They either took him from her, or her from him. So to ease his frustration, Yosef helps himself to a glass of red wine. One of Helen's friends, Judy was there, she was not invited, she just made an apperance. She said something to Lisa that upset her. James saw

The two of them talking. Oh,oh. He said. What is it J? Said Terry. Over there. He said nodding in their direction. "I just want you to know that White men usually go back to their own kind after a while. He's just gonna use you that's all. And when he finishes, he 'll just go on to the next conquest. Lisa remained silent as she rambled on. Her thoughts were not on her ramblings. Just on her new Husband. And when he comes to his senses, he'll see that White is always right." Ha,ha,ha! She mocked at her. Sorry to put a damper on things for you, this being your wedding day and all. But......That's enough! The voice interrupted. It was Deborah. She grabbed the young woman by the shoulder and marched her away from Lisa. I thought I smelled something disgusting! She said to the girl. Why I got half a mind to...the girl started. You better ask the other half to see if that's a wise desiciion or not! Deborah interrupted, as she walked right passed everyone. There were gasps as she took the woman outside into the hall, she then had one of the Ushers to escort her outside the Church! She came up to one of the greeters at the side door. Where is Blake? I don't know Mother Anderson. He told me to stay here until he got back. He didn't say where he was going. Here! Take this outside for me

368

will you? She said shoving the woman into his arms. Let me
know when he gets back will you? Yes ma'mam. He said.
Deborah walks back inside the Fellowship hall. This way
ma'mam. He said letting her outside. He looks down both halls
to see if Blake would turn up. No sign of him anywhere. Ooooh!
Black folks! He sighed, frustrated. Mamie and Terry were
standing by the Wedding Table the whole time watching the whole
incident that took place between Lisa and Judy. Yosef steps up
to them still sipping on his wine. A look of sadness filled his
expression. He wanted to be alone with his Beloved.   They saw
it, they felt it. Yosef? Yeah, Mamie. He looked at her
Still sipping. Can you tell me why your new wife is standing over
there all by herself, when you should've taken her out of here long
ago to take care of business. And you know what I'm talking
about. Yosef looked over at Lisa. She was standing over by one
of the guest tables, she had been crying. Judy's words
Echoing in her ears. But more than that. She too wanted her
Beloved. His heart filled with longing for her. He drops his glass
to the floor, splashing it's contents all over Mamie's purple gown.
Lisa looked up at him. Her eyes giving him that come and take
me expression. He walks over to her, stopping momentarily to
look at her.   Their eyes filled with an overwhelming desire for
each other. He takes her

By the hand, and walks out with her in a trance like state of some
kind. James and Terry smile. Oh it's on now! Said James. Go
head Jo! Cheered Terry. Go Lisa! Cheered Brad. Go head girl!
Cheered Mamie
Smiling big at her. Whoooo! They all shouted at them. Rev.
Anderson and Deborah spotted the couple leaving. They smile
big, they knew what they were leaving for. You got my ear plugs
honey? He whispered to her. Yes. She stopped to think about
what he said to her. Teasing her. Oh, Ben! She said smacking
him playfully on the shoulder.   They both embrace each other
laughing. Yosef and Lisa get inside the Limo that was waiting
outside for them. They leave to go to Terry's father's little cottage.
They pull up in front. Yosef gets out, then he takes his new Bride
by the hand escorting her from the vehicle. We'll be out in a few
or? Very good sir. The middle aged chauffer said to him. They
walk away from them. Umm,umm,umm! She's gonna make that
boy hollaaaaahhhhh! He said to his co-driver. They both laugh

hitting fives. Yosef opens the door, taking Lisa inside. They walk together to the bedroom that was especially decorated for them. Lisa gasped when she saw it! It was beautiful! The aroma of the scented candles filled the air. Yosef picked her up into his arms, and carried her inside, kicking the door shut behind him. He puts her down, they both stare deep into each others eyes tenderly. They kiss deeply.

Tonight they could be free to love as they had wanted to love all their lives. Tonight, there would be no Angel visitation to interrupt them, to remind them of their vows, for they had fulfilled them. Tonight, they would share, and know love in a way that they've never known it before! Her soft body next to his, his strong body next to hers,caressing, and feeling each other this one special way that they've waited their whole lives for! It had come at last!   Yosef takes her veil off letting it fall gently to the floor. He unzips her dress in the back, it slides off her shoulders a little, revealing them more. He runs his hands over them Savoring their softness underneath them. He trembles a little as a strong surge of ecstacy comes on him,
Lisa closes her eyes she too savoring every touch of his hands on her body.   She sighs softly to him.
Yosef looks down at her chest, peeking from under the lace was Lisa's Cross wound. He could see it rising up and down beating in time with her heart. He flashed back to where he called her selfish in the hospital, then on the night of her kidnapping, her jumping in front of him taking the bullet, giving her life to save his.   He remembers cradling her cold lifeless body in his arms. He is snapped back into the now, as he feels the warmth and life of her body in his hands. He closes his eyes tight embracing her hard to him.
Oh Lisa! I Love you! He cried to her. I Love you so much! I Love you too! My Beloved! She cried to him. She slides his outer coat off, it falls gently to the floor, joining it's place near her veil. She removes his tie, and unbuttons his shirt. He cups her face in his hands kissing her more passionately now.

He takes her hand and moves it over to his Manhood, which had risen up to meet her. They rub it gently together. He smiles at her, she smiles the same at him. He removes her dress off her shoulders, it falls to the floor in a heap. He picks her up out of it.

She wraps her legs around his body as he takes her over to the bed that was prepared for them.   They remove the remainder of their clothing, he gently lays her down, wrapping each other up in the bed linens. Yosef mounts her, she positions herself to receive him. The music plays softly behind them as they consummate their Marriage. He enters her gently. His eyes close as he feels passion flowing through his body. Lisa moans sweetly as she feels her Beloved's Manhood going deeper and deeper inside of her. She begins to speak to him in his native Hebrew tongue.

Anyi, anyi Yosef! (I Love you, I Love you!).   He stops and looks down at her, her soft brown face flushed, sweat beginning to form on her brow. He speaks back to her in his Native Hebrew language.
This is the Night that I've waited all my life for, now it is here! I will Love you tonight, and Forever
My Love, My Lisa! Yosef strokes her deeper and harder this time. Oooh! Lisa! He moans. Make Love to me! MAKE LOVE TO MEEEE! My Life's dream was the Night that I would Love you this way Yosef. She said again to him in Hebrew. Now Yeshua has made my Dreams come true! Oh! Love me Yosef!
LOVE MEEE!   She said her voice like his escalating more as they feel Love's flow overtaking them both.
Lisa arches her back as Yosef fills her with the fullness of his Manhood. Ohhhhhh! YOSEF!!!!! Her moans sounding like sweet music to his ears. He smiles down at her. Her breath coming in short pants now, she brings her body up to him, he pulls her close to him. She yells out an earpiercing high note as her Womanhood releases it's ecstacy! Yosef closes his eyes tightly as his flow explodes powerfully inside his Bride! Oooooooh! Ohhhhhhhhhh! Lisa! LISA!!!!! LISAAAAAHHHHHHHH!!!!!!!! He screams! He folds her up in his arms, his body still jerking spasmodically from his orgasm! Ahhhhhhh!!!!! He yells again.. OH! GOD! LISSSAAAAHHHHH! I LOVE YOUUUOOOOO! He cried out to her. As his Manhood pulsated uncontrollably inside her. She felt the pulse of his love for her. He too felt her love griping him not wanting to let him go. Oh! Their Lovemaking was beautiful! Their voices raised together in a symphony of love and praise, that had been blessed by the Hand of God Himself! They look at each other for a moment. Whoa! They both breathed together, smiling. He rubs his nose with hers. Yosef

nearly loss conciousness, as his orgasam was as blinding as it was explosive!   Are you alright Beloved?

She asked him. Still out of breath herself. I don't know. I've never felt anything like that before. He shakes his head trying to clear it. How about you? Are you ok baby? I don't know either, I can't feel my body. I mean it feels so light to me. Do you tingle all over? He asked her. Yes, yes I do. She said. Like electricity or something. Me too. He said. He looks at her briefly. He kisses her gently. Ummm. She sighed. Your kisses taste like more to me. More? Yeah, as in I want more. He smiles. Anything you say ma'mam. Anything you say. He kisses her tenderly. They make love deeply again.   Once more the air was filled with their voices as they loved again and again.   They looked at each other as they finished their lovemaking. They cried in each others arms.   Oh God Lisa! I pray it's like this forever and ever. You know Beloved?   What baby? I pray that each time will be better than the time before it forever and ever, and ever. She said stroking the back of his head.   He looks down at her smiling big at her. Yeah. He breathed, as he rolled off her, and pulled her close to his chest. A soft glow emanated from them, the glow of love. They fell asleep in each others arms smiling.

The Colour Of Love
Anne Hemingway
Chap 41.

Now just come with me here dear, I want to talk with you. Said Rabbi to Sarah. He takes her outside to their family van, and seats her inside. Are you comfortable dear? He asked her. Yes, of course Yacov.

What is all this? I need to talk to you about somethings. What things? I don't understand. Well to start, over the years, I've not been the husband and father to you and to Yosef that you both deserve. He looks down at the floor a little. I have no words to express my deepest apology to you both. Thank God that you gave him to Ben and Deborah when you did. My behavior would've only ruined him. She looks at him, her heart filling with compassion for him. He looks at her aged face, the lines in her expression speaking to him of a love that she once knew, but has long since passed from her. He could see the longing her face for it's return! He saw it all in her sweet face. He flashes briefly to the night that they too consummated their Marriage. Sarah somehow made that same connection with him at that very moment. Oh! My dear Sarah!
I'm so sorry! I never meant to hurt you or Yosef, so help me I didn't! Sarah's expression turn to one of surprise! As Rabbi told her everything that he had done, and why. From his unfair treatment of Yosef and Lisa, to his affair with the prostitute. She listened attentively as he poured out his heart to her, bearing to her his very soul. They stare tenderly into each other's eyes. As they flash back to their wedding night

The same passion that filled them that night, begin to fill them at that very moment. Rabbi pulls Sarah close to her, kissing her affectionately! Oh Yacov! She breathed, weeping into his arms. How I've waited for this moment to return! Oh! How I've waited for you to come back to me! She cried. I Love you my dearest Sarah! I love you! He said to her, as their passion began to mount feverishly! Can you ever forgive me my Love? He said to her with tears in his eyes. There's nothing to forgive my dearest, there's nothing to forgive! She cried to him. He lays her back on the small soft bed. It felt good to her body.
Love had turned her into that ravishing beauty that she once was on their wedding night. She glowed all over as God had answered her prayers! They make love! For the first time in five years they make love deeply! Now she would know that love again, that sweet communion between a husband and wife. Rabbi was now that handsome young bridegroom that Sarah once knew, as Love had taken age away from them, making them young and vibrant as a long awaited passion filled them!

The Limo drivers look at their watches, their frustration building a little. They change CD's in the player, and play another game of cards. Let me help you with that honey. Said Yosef. He walks up behind Lisa

Zipping up her dress. He slides his hands around her slender waist pulling her close to him. He had stiffened quickly again. Ohhhh! Lisa! He breathed. *"Yosef."* She whispered in a sensous tone. She had ran her hands around the back of his neck massaging him gently. Her moans begging him to love her again. Honey, we'll make love again if we don't stop. We have to get back now. He bends down kissing the side of ner neck. Ahhhh! She moaned again, as he cupped her soft breast in his hands. He turns her around to face him. We're married now. He said smiling at her. Yeah. She breathed to him. He looks down at her chest and notices the Cross wound again. He touches it with his finger. He could feel her heart beating through it. His eyes fill with tears. He pulls her to him kissing her tenderly. I love you baby. He said to her. I'll never forget what you did for me that night. Never Lisa. He said softly. Oh God ! thank you for giving her to me! It is I who thank God also for you my Beloved. You gave me the will to not only die for you, but to live for you as well with you. Which I will do for the rest of my life. She said tears streaming down her soft brown face. She reaches up and kisses him deeply. Your kisses taste like more, as in I want. He said to her. She smiles as he echo's her words back to her. He unzips her dress again, she reaches up to kiss him opening his mouth with her tongue. He moans at it's warmth and softness. Oh God Lisa! He breathed. He moves her hand over to his Manhood again, she felt the hardness of him even more than before. She strokes it gently, he puts his hand on top of hers. He moans softly at her. Tonight Beloved, you'll experience the full weight of all my Love. Now and forever. He stares at her briefly not knowing what to make out of her words. They ooze all over him like warm honey.

He smiles at her kissing her deeply. He picks her up taking her back over to the bed. They make love again deeply.

The Epstiens emerge from the the van smiling and hugging each
other close. They fixed, and fussed over each other's clothes as
they walk back inside to the fellowship hall. Rev. Anderson and
Deborah noticed them as they came in. They were glowing all
over. Rev. Anderson and Deborah looked at each other. They
knew what had taken place between them. They cover their
mouths chuckling together. Look at that! He breathed as he
watched him escort Sarah over to the Banquet table.   The
beautiful array of food made him gasp. Where do I start? He
asked the young server. A handsome young black man about
early to mid 20's. Anywhere you want Rabbi. He said, handing
him a fresh plate.   Go for it man! He said.   Rabbi and Sarah
chuckle as they prepare to help themselves.   Just then Yosef and
Lisa return to the Hall. They glowed like the Sun as they walked
in, Lisa cradled in his arms. He was still kissing her on her
forehead.
They were totally oblivious to everyone staring at them as they
entered the Hall, as Lisa had forgotten her veil, she left it at the
little cottage, as Yosef did his bow tie. His shirt was still open a
little ways, his tux coat
Not buttoned. None of these things mattered to them at all. All
their thoughts were still on their lovemaking, and how they would
make love more that night, before leaving for their honeymoon
Sunday morning to South Haven, Michigan. He brings his new
Bride over to the Bride and Groom Table, where their parents
were waiting for them. One of the female guest there leaned over
to Mamie. Where did they go?   Everyone has been waiting for
nearly two hours for them to get back. After all this is for them,
they're supposed to be here. I mean like isn't that like
inconsiderate or something? Mamie and Terry look at each other
then at her. Look Ms. Hoochic doochie, they've been waiting to
be together all their lives, and maybe it's escaped your attention,
but this is their Wedding Night! And since you don't have one of
your own, just try to find an imagination then use it Duh? Said
Terry rapidly at her. Mamie busted up laughing at her. Boy you
crazy! She said. He then takes Mamie in his arms and waltzes
away from her.

Yosef and Lisa walked up to their parents who were waiting for them. They smiled at the couple as they still shimmered from their lovemaking. They welcomed them back to the banquet. Yosef and Lisa noticed that Rabbi and Sarah were glowing all over. They look at each other in surprise! They knew what made them look like that. They chuckled to themselves. Mr. Dennis and Michele walk up to them congratulating them on their Marriage. Embraces,and hugs and kisses, and handshakes from both he and Michele. Rev. Anderson stands up taking his Champagne glass hitting with his spoon. May I have your attention please. Yosef escorts Lisa over to the two white decorated chairs for himself and Lisa. He stands with her still cradled next to him. All give their attention to Rev. Anderson. I want you all to know that this has been a day unlike any other for me and my wife. This is the day that I gave my daughter, my angel
Lisa's hand in Marriage to this fine young man here. He's been like a son to us since the day that he came to live with us when he was just a little boy. As far as Deborah and I are concerned he is our son, our blood. And we love him with all our hearts. The people cheered loudly. I want to extend our offical welcome to him to our family. He turns to Yosef, who was still ravishing Lisa as his love began to come on him again for her.
Yosef.....Yosef.....? Jo Jo! He yelled. Everyone busting up in laughter. Oh, uh, I'm sorry dad. Rev. Anderson extends his hand out to him. They shake hands. He leans over to Deborah Kissing her on the cheek. Welcome son. I love you dear. I Love you too mom. Hey, what about me! Said Johanathan.
Johanthan walks over to Yosef, hugging him so hard he lifts him off the floor! Welcome
Little bro. They hug, hitting fists with each other. He rubs Johanthan's bald head. Rabbi then comes over to them. I too want to extend our official welcome as well. My dearest Lisa, welcome child to our

Family. You are not only welcome in our home, but in our hearts forever. We love you deeply Lisa. I mean this from my heart. The people cheered again. As there were more hugs, and kisses, and handshakes amongst them. It is I who thank you for accepting me Rabbi, I will do my best to be the best wife that I can be to my husband. I hope to learn from you and Ms. Sarah as we all learn from each other.

Thank you child, thank you. Said Sarah. Rabbi hands her back over to Yosef. And now I want to propose a toast to the happy couple, and I do mean happy! Said Rev. Anderson. Everyone held up their glasses as he pronounced a brief blessing over them. Yosef and Lisa share a glass of Sparkling fruit juice together since neither of them drank. Salute! Shouted the people. More cheers and shouts fill the hall. Now for the first dance. The music plays. It's Yosef and Lisa favorite song. "If only you knew."

They walk to the floor together, he takes her in his arms, and slow dances with his new Bride. Then the maid of honor and Johanthan. Soon the bridesmaids, and groomsmen take to the floor, as everyone joined Yosef and Lisa on the dance floor. Yosef stares deeply into her eyes. Both their thoughts back on their lovemaking again. Lisa could soon feel the results of their thinking as she felt her husband's arousal against her tummy. Oh God Lisa! I Love you! I love you too Beloved. She whispered softly in his ear.

The dance ended, everyone enjoyed each other's fellowshipping, the food was fantastic! Yosef and Lisa shared the wedding cake, more pictures were taken. Their example was being followed by many of the youth there. They were making pacts of remaining abstinate from sex until marriage. Like Yosef and Lisa Did. Many parents were overjoyed to hear that news! With the growing numbers of STD's in America today. Before the banquet ended. Johanthan stood up for one final announcement. Yosef, had already thrown Lisa's garter, which just so happened Johanthan caught. Lisa had thrown her Bridal bouquet as well which Deniece had caught. I want you all to know, that my little sister, and little brother in law have taught me a very valuable lesson. They taught me that when God puts His Love in your heart for that

Special someone, it stays forever and ever. I've seen that with him and Lisa. And I want you all to know, that we'll all soon be gathered here to do this again. As I've asked the girl of my dreams to to marry me!

Rev. Anderson and Deborah. Yosef and Lisa all gasp when they hear his news. He had asked Deniece to marry him, and she accepted! It was no accident that we caught these items once belonging to my sister, and Jo,Jo. It was meant to be. Deniece with tears in her eyes looks at Lisa's bouquet, then at Lisa winking at her. Lisa winking back. They all embrace warmly, as the people cheered again and again. So much love had fill the Hall, that the people seem to float on air! Yosef and Lisa held each other close in each other's arms again kissing tenderly. So in Love. Said Mamie.

The Colour Of Love
Anne Hemingway
Chap 43.

Four months pass by. Lisa is standing in the her new home looking out the window at the Lake. Pondering her thoughts. She was four months into being a new wife. It was something new and exciting to her. She smiles a little as she flowed back in time to when she first met Yosef, their lives together, as they grew up in the same house together. And now she was his wife! Yosef walks up behind her hugging her waist. He slides his hands around to rub her belly swollen with his seed. He kisses her on the cheek. She pats his hands they both rub her belly together. A single tear makes it's way down her soft brown face.

Yosef too had been pondering his thoughts about his life with Lisa, and how God had miraculously brought the two of them together. Now they were about to become parents. He turns her around to face him. He sees her tears falling gently from her eyes. He somehow knew her thoughts, and felt her fears. He smiled at her, hugging her close to him, kissing her again. He rubs his nose with hers. His embrace made her feel safe and protected, as this is the way it should be between husband and wife. He felt her assurance when she embraced him as well, they

felt the trust and the bond that would hold them together for the rest of their lives. He looks at her once more. He could see that, that was all she needed at that moment, was to feel his arms around her to strenghthen her, to reassure her of his love. He takes her by the hand into the nursery that they had decorated together, with the help of his mother, and Deborah. They were thinking about some last minute details for it before the baby's born. We need to get going now ok? She nodded, she was still quiet about something, and a little anxious. Lisa? Are you alright? Oh Yosef, I don't know how to be a mother. She bursts out crying. Come here. He laughs a little pulling her close to him. You'll be just fine, I promise. What do you know about being a mother? You're a father remember? Yosef thought a moment. Look both of us are new at this, but we have lots of help around us. It'll be fine ok? He said stroking her soft cheek. Ok. She whispers. I love you. I love you too Beloved. She said smiling. He puts his suit coat on as they leave to go for Sunday supper at her parents house. Another four and half months past by. And Lisa is nearly ready to give birth. Yosef phoned his boss today. He would be in later that morning as he had to take Lisa for a Dr, appointment. They were given pictures of the baby after the sonogram was done. A fine healthy boy just like the Angel spoke to him. He takes Lisa back home, and he goes off to work. He is seated at his desk looking at the pictures. His eyes fill up a little. My father was not the father that I needed when I was coming up. I pray that I can be all that you need me to be to you, and more. His phone rings snapping him out of his moment. Hello Dennis and Lake Real Estate. Is this
Joseph, Joseph Epstien? Yes it is. Yeah, this is Mitchell Walden. Yes Mr. Walden. How can I help you sir? I have some news for you and Adam. Is there a way that I can talk to the both of you on the line?

Yes, sir. Hold please. Yosef calls in the next office to his boss. He then ,makes the connection so that they can all talk by three-way. It was about the Land Deal. It was close, very close. All I need is for you to set it up boys. I'll be back from California on Monday. What do you say Men are we in agreement or what? You got yourself a deal Mr. Walden. Said Mr. Dennis. Alright then. I'll see you both when I get back. And I expect some good news from the both of you, I'm really looking forward to your Company pulling this deal through for me. It means more to me and my Company than you know. We're your boys sir. Said Mr.

Dennis. Good! Good! How about we set the meeting for this Monday at 9:00 a.m sharp?

You got it! Said Yosef. Solid! I'll be there. They all hang up. Mr. Dennis runs into Yosef's outer office

Grinning from ear to ear. We're nearly there boy! Shouted Mr. Dennis. All we need is the agreement forms prepared and checked over by our Attorney, which I will take care of myself. If you can draw up the forms for me Jo, I can take care of the rest when Michele and I get back on Sunday. You're leaving now? Asked Yosef. He wondering why Mr. Dennis was leaving so early on a Friday morning. I have to, I can't leave my new wife waiting can I? Oh, I guess not. He said as he turned to walk out. He thought about what he said, then turned and came back in again. Say that again. Say what again? I'll be back On Sunday? No, no that part. Then which part? He said as he was putting on his suit coat. The part about your new wife. Mr. Dennis smiled big at him. He sat Yosef down on the corner of his desk. Well, while you and Lisa were away on your vacation for that two weeks in South Haven. Michele and I made it offical. Yosef looked at him in surprise. I'm sorry that you and Lisa weren't there for the wedding. It was a small thing, we didn't want anything elaborate. Just something small and simple. Yosef smiled. He held out his hand to him. Congratulations sir? Thank you son. I never thought in a million years that I could be this happy. He pauses a little. I don't know what I would've done without your help. My help? Said Yosef. Yeah, you and Lisa. Yosef smiles again. Oh, by the way how is she? She's incredible! And the baby? We're due anytime now he said. I have pictures of the sonogram. Would you like to see them?

I sure would. They go into Yosef's small office, he looks at the pictures. Yeah, that's a boy alright. He said laughing. Now how do you know that? Did you see the size of that thing? Just like his ole man.

He said pointing to the baby's genitals. They both laugh. Let's go see if our secretary has the agreement forms ready that we need for the deal. There was still much paper work that needed to be ironed out before all would be ready for the meeting on Monday. They go out into the outer office over to the new secretary's desk. Julie Henderson was now on maternity leave, and her husband had already informed them that she would not be returning to work. They looked around but Helen was not there. Her desk was a mess! All of the work that was supposed to have been processed two weeks ago was still sitting on her desk, it hadn't even been touched! There were papers all over the place. Amongst them was the buy sell agreement forms that Mr.Dennis and Yosef needed to review before Mr. Walden was to sign them for the Deal. Oh my God! Yosef what is all this? This looks like one of the most biggest Deals that our Company has ever seen just sitting here being ruined! Where the hell is this new secretary you hired? Yosef could feel his temper rising along with Mr. Dennis'. I don't know sir. I'm sorry about all this. Jo, you know I trust you. I trust you like my own son. But look at this! We have to get this work done, and done fast! His anxiety was surfacing. Mr. Dennis, I'll take all this home to review myself, to see what needs to

Be done ok? Then I'll bust my butt to get all that we need in order for the Meeting on Monday. I promise
It'll be be alright. I won't let you down sir. Please, just give me a chance to do this ok? Mr. Dennis calms down at Yosef's words. Ok Jo, but if we don't have this ready for Mr. Walden, we can kiss all of our dreams goodbye. It'll never happen. Mr. Dennis looks at the mess of paperwork on Helen's desk. I hope you believe in Miracles son, because it's gonna take one for this. He said picking up some of the forms
Letting them drop back on the desk. I have to leave now. But call me by cell when you have something good to tell me. He said, his confidence in Yosef returns to him. I'm counting on you for this Jo. I believe in you. If any man can do this, you can. He said patting him on his shoulder. Like I said, I won't let you down. Mr. Walden is counting on us, and like I said, I'm counting on you. I know sir, I know.
I want you to go and have a good weekend, and leave this to me. I'll take care of it. Mr. Dennis nods his head. He leaves Yosef alone with Helen's mess. But the thing is. How was he going to make up for two weeks of back logged work in three days?He was now beginning to regret that he let Lisa talk him into hiring Helen. She was only hired because she needed to show her probation officer that she could hold down a steady job. And they agreed to give her a chance and help her since she helped them locate Lisa

When she was kidnapped. Mr. Dennis had now left for the rest of the day to start his weekend with his new wife Michele. Yosef gathers up all the paper work and takes it back into his office to look through. He throws all the papers down on his desk in frustration. He brushes his hair back. What have I done? He breathed. He hears the outer office door open. It was Helen. She had just come back from a smoke break with Jim, and three other co-workers. He picks up the work and takes it out there to her. Oh Hi Yosef.

Mr. Epstein to you. What? You heard me. He said. She could see that he was not in the mood for any

Of her games. He was very, very angry at her. Look at this! He holds the forms in her face. Oh yeah, well I ws gonna get to those, I needed some time to check into how the processing procedure works here. Different Companies have different ways of doing things ya know. She chuckles. Yosef stood there looking at her. She stops laughing. Clearing her throat. You told me that you had experience in Real Estate Processing did you lie to me just to keep me and Lisa from sending you to prison? No, I didn't!

I didn't lie! It's been a while that's all! I forgot how. Look, it was a small Real Estate Company, nothing big like this. That was five years ago Yosef. I mean Mr. Epstien. Why didn't you say something to me, or to one of the other secretaries if your little brain needed some refreshing? She never said anything. Do you know how long it's going to take to process all this work that you left sitting here? Huh? She shakes her head. We have to have all this in order, and ready to sign on Monday. This is a Multi Million Dollar Deal I'm holding here! Do you know what you've done to this Company? No sir, she said in a fake whinny voice. Yosef still not convinced of her sincerity, but decided to go a little easy on her. Look Lisa and I

Forgave you for the kidnapping thing, she wanted me to hire you only as a gesture of forgiveness on her part. Frankly myself, I still don't trust you as far as I can throw you. But I agreed because she asked me to. Now I'm beginning to regret that descision. Ok, ok. I'm sorry. Maybe I can get Annette and some of the other girls to help me. No! You don't understand, it's too late for all that now! This has to be completed by Monday! That's three days away! Any of this coming through up there! He said pointing at her head. I have to take this home with me tonight, and figure out a way to do two weeks worth of processing done before Monday! Got it! Yes, Yosef. He gives her that look. I mean Mr. Epstein. He looks at his watch. It was still early, nearly noon now. I have to take the rest of the day off now. You might as well go home yourself. There's nothing for you to do here. Just leave Helen. Will you be needing me for the Meeting on Monday. He turns around to glare at her. For what? So you can be of no use to me then as you are to me now? Think about it a while. He leaves to go back into his office shutting the door. He sits at his desk, his mind burning up with what to do next about the land Deal. He looks over at his Wedding picture of he and Lisa. He smiles, it was the most he had smiled since that morning. Sitting next to it was a glass object shaped like a heart. He picks it up into his hands holding it up a little. The Sun shinning off the small metal object in the center of if. The object that once took the life of his beloved Lisa.

He could still hear the gunshot. He looks at it bursting into tears. It was the bullet that the Dr's. took out of Lisa's chest. The same bullet that was meant for him, she took that night of her kidnapping. She had asked the Dr. to save it for her before she slipped into unconciousness. She had made it into a paper weight. The inscription read..... *"Not even death can take me from you!"* My Love Eternal, Lisa. The phone rings snapping him out of his moment. He wipes the tears from his eyes. Hello Beloved. She said, her voice
It's usual sweetness. Lisa! Hi baby! He was glad to hear from her. How's my girl? Your girl's fine.
The baby's really moving around a lot now. He chuckles a little. Is he? He said smiling. Yeah the Dr. said that he's coming along just fine. And so am I. That's my girl. He said. There was a slight pause. Honey are you alright? She asked him. He was still looking at the paperweight. She had given it to him on their wedding night. He flashed to that moment quickly. They had just finish making love for the first time. Jesus Lisa! How do you put words around something like that? I don't know Beloved. I'm just as wordless as you are. They sat up in bed. She reaches down underneath the bed and pulls up a beautifully wrapped gift box. I have something for you Beloved. For me? Yes for you. Now don't say no to me. I want you to open it right now. He takes the box and sits on his lap. I think we should open this together.

He said. Really? Asked Lisa. Yeah Really. He stares deeply into
her eyes. He kisses her. Honey? Honey? Hum? The box, the
box. Oh, oh. He said. They open it up together. Yosef lifts the
glass object out of the box. It was beautiful! Oh Lisa! He
becomes misty eyed. I don't know what to say. Say nothing
Beloved. He places it back into the box, setting on the floor on
the other side of the bed. He looks at the Cross wound again,
running his finger up and down, and across it. You're sealed in
there forever and ever my Beloved. She looks at him, tears in her
soft brown eyes. I Love you. She whispered. Yosef takes her into
his arms again both of them crying into each others arms. They
make love again passionately.
Yosef! Honey you're scaring me! She said. Her voice bringing
him back into the now. He could hear the fear in her voice.
What's the matter? Is everything alright there? I'm alright ok? I
was just thinking that's all. About what? She asked. About you
and me. And the baby? He smiles. Yes, and the baby too.
I love you so much Lisa I love you too Beloved. And you're sure
everything's alright? I'm fine, you have
Nothing to be afraid of ok? Ok Beloved. Just then his other line
rings. Baby I have to take another call now ok? I'll be home
soon. He hangs up and takes the call. Is this the Northshore
Downs race Track?
The voice said. No, no it isn't. he said hanging up the phone.
Helen's laziness was taking it's toll on him.
Yosef looks the papers over one last time, rubbing his hair back
on his head. He takes out his cell phone, and calls Mr. Dennis, to
get the rest of the day off. He gathers up all the unfinished work
putting it into his briefcase, and leaves to go home.

Yosef began to worry more than ever now as he drives home. And
with the baby due anytime now, only added to his anxiety. He
pulls his Cherrokee into the driveway, taking his worries with him
into the house.
He gets inside, Lisa wasn't anywhere in sight. Lisa! He calls out
to her. There was no answer. Lisa, I'm home! He said. His voice
sounded tired as well as frustrated. He walked into the kitchen,
and smiles a little. Lisa was up on her tippy toes trying to get a
bowl down from the top shelf in the cupboard. She never heard
him come in, or calling for her. He puts his hand on thesmall of

384

her back, and reaches up to get the bowl down. He gives it to her kissing her on the cheek. Honey! She said. She was glad to see him, as well as he was to see her. She puts the bowl on the counter, kissing him affectionately.   I didn't hear you come in. I'm so glad you're home. She said hugging him close to her. I'm glad to be home too baby. How's my girl? Fine. She said in a soft tone.   He loosens his tie and sits down at the kitchen table. He brushes his face in his hands. He looked worried about something to her. Would you like some tea honey? No I don't want anything right now. I'm just tired that's all. How was your day? He said taking her by the hand kissing it gently. It was fine. She said.   Still not convinced that all was the same for him. I made your favorite dinner tonight! She said, she was very excited about many things that day that she wanted to share with him. But all would come crashing in on her as it already had for him. Smells good, but I'm not hungry at the moment. He sat up to the table, frustration getting the best of him. He kept rubbing his face, and brushing his hair back. He looked as though he was about to burst into tears at any moment. As all that he and his boss had hoped for in the Land Deal was sitting in his briefcase wasting away. What's the matter Yosef? Nothing's wrong Lisa. He snapped at her. She looked over his snapping at her. Did something happen at work today? I'm just trying to help that's all. He thought briefly about Helen not being there at her desk when he and Mr. Dennis came out to see if all was in order for the sale

Her desk in a mess, the blank forms that should've been processed and signed two weeks ago still sitting there just as blank as they were when she first took them out of her desk at that time. Mr. Dennis' anxiety
His fears all savagely spoke to Yosef at the same time. It's finished! It's over! You've lost the deal, and it's all her fault for talking you into hiring her! Yosef, do you hear me? I'm just trying to help. Well maybe I don't need your help! He said jumping up out of the chair. Yosef! She gasped. Honey, please don't do this! Let me help you! What's the matter with you! Is there some part of no you don't understand!! He shouted at her. He ran past her into the living room upstairs slamming their bedroom door.   Lisa stood there helpless, she didn't have a clue what upset him so. She went into the living room drying her eyes

of tears. Ohh! She said stumbling. What the ...? It was Yosef's
briefcase. He dropped it
When he came inside. Some of the papers had fallen out. She
stoops down to gather up everything. It was all the forms that
Yosef had told her about two weeks ago. Ohhhh! She gasped,
now she knew what had upset him. The Company was in
trouble, and she felt that it was her fault because she talked
Yosef into hiring Helen. Oh my God Yosef. I'm so sorry, I'm so
sorry. She looked up thet stairs, she didn't see him, but she
heard the shower running. She goes back into the kitchen to the
wall phone just inside there to call her father. Hello, Anderson
Residence. Daddy, It's Lisa. Hi angel. How's my baby? I'm ok
dad, but I need your help. What's the matter? He said, in a
serious tone. It's Yosef, he's in trouble at work. The Company's
in trouble dad. I need you help, and I need it fast! I can't explain
over the phone. Can I come over and show you? Of course angel.
I'll be there in about 45 minutes. I'll be here love. He said. They
hang up. She goes upstairs to their bedroom. Yosef was out of
the shower and dressed in sweat pants. He didn't even bother to
put on a shirt, it was so hot that Friday afternoon. He would
usually meet Johanthan for a game of one on one. But he
cancelled out for obvious reasons. He was lying in bed on his
back looking up at the ceiling thinking. His thoughts all on the
deal. What was he going to do, and how?

Lisa felt for her husband at that moment. She would do anything
to help him. And she would too. She just needed a little help
from some experienced professionals in the field of Real Estate.
And her father was at the top of that list. She begins to cry for
him. He hears her crying out in the hallway. He sits up in bed.
Guilt fills him, for he was the source of her tears. Come here
Lisa. He calls to her. She walks inside to him. He spreads his
legs open so she could sit between them.   He hugs her close to
her, rubbing her belly now eight and half months pregnant. I'm
sorry I yelled at you. I'm so sorry baby. I didn't mean to hurt
you. You know that. Please believe me. I didn't. I have a rought
day at work and I come home and take it
Out on you. You're the reason I came home early in the first
place.   Forgive me? He said kissing her cheek patting her round
tummy.   Just then, he felt something kicking underneath his
hand. It was his baby. Whoa! He breathed. Did you feel that?

She smiles, they both look at the baby kicking in all directions. Whoa! They both said together. Yes, I felt that. She said. Honey, I want you to know that No matter what circumstances we face, you can always sit me down and talk to me about it. I don't care How bad it is. We can overcome it together. Please don't shut me out. I need to hear from you. I'm your wife, and I can help you in more ways than you know. She said stroking his cheek. He palms her head close to him kissing her on her temple. She paused, staring deeply into his eyes. I believe in you Beloved.

I trust you with my very life. She paused again. I Love you. He chokes up a little. He kisses her again.
What would I do without you in my life Lisa? I love you so much, I can't explain it sometimes. They kiss tenderly. He lays her down on the bed kissing her more. She strokes his chest playing with his nipples with her finger. Oh God Lisa! I Love You! He moans. His arousal getting the best of him. They make love carefully, but passionately.

The Colour Of Love
Anne Hemingway
Chap. 44

Yosef is wrapped in the bed linens sleep coming on him. Lisa this time is staring up at the ceiling thinking about how to help her husband. Oh Lord, what can I do to help my husband? She gets up and goes into the nursery. She looks at the books on the bookcase. She pulls out one book in particular, but another one falls out accidently. The title clicks something in her spirit. *"The Elves and the Shoemaker."* She remembers the story and smiles to herself. She picks it up hugging it to her chest. Lord, You're something else. Thank You. She breathed. She quietly goes back into her bedroom, Yosef still in a love zone from their

lovemaking. He was smiling to himself about her, moaning out
her name softly. She shakes her head smiling at him as well.
She gathers up her clothes and goes into the bathroom to get
dressed. She emerges from the bathroom fully dressed in a
powder blue maternity dress, and white sandals. She feels the
baby moving slightly, he gives her a slight discomfort. She
smiles, and rubs her tummy. There, there now. It won't be long.
So until then little guy behave yourself. Yosef....? He moans a
little, his ecstacy still hasn't left him yet. Honey..? She walks
over to the bed sitting down next to him. Honey? Hum....?
I'm going over to see my father for a while, I won't be long ok?
He opens his eyes slightly to look at her.

She looked beautiful to him. He smiles sleepily at her. Alright
baby, drive carefully ok? I will, I 'll call you if I need anything. I'll
be here. She starts to get up off the bed, when he takes her by
the hand. Where's my kiss? Sorry. She said. She kissed him
slightly on the lips. He still wouldn't let her leave.
Taste like more. Honey? I can't help it. You're spoiled that's all.
She laughed. She kisses him again.
Now go to sleep ok? That won't be a problem at all. I love you
Lisa. I love you Beloved. They trade winks at each other. He
moans out again before a restful sleep took him over. Lisa arrives
at her parents home. She informs her father of the whole mess
that Helen left the company in. Let's see what we have here. Uh,
huh. He reviews the forms and other documents over. Ohhhhh!
He breathes. I think I know what needs to be done. I'm a little
rusty at this but I think I can help. He gets up and goes over to
the phone. I have a few phone calls to make. He makes them
three of them. To reputable Real Estate Companies that he was
familiar with in his day. I have some people that I know can be of
help to him.
They owe me a favor. He said smiling at her. Lisa feels the baby
moving around again. She felt a slight dizziness come on her.
Daddy! What's the matter love? I think I need to sit down. Come
here. Sit right here. Better now? Yes, thank you. There, You
mother went through the same thing with you and Johnathan.
You'll be just fine. I know, thanks daddy. He rubs her head, she
calms down under his touch.
You just wait right here. Daddy will be right back. He goes back
over to the phone to make one last call. To a friend of his, also
retired from the Real Estate business. He makes the call. Hello.
Tim? Ben. Benjamin Anderson? Yes the same. I'm fine, my

wife's fine. All's fine up here. Look I need you to help me with something. My son in law is in a bind. I need you to help him. He informs him of the mess. All that was needed was some lightspeed processing for the forms that was backlogged by two weeks. But what can I do? He said on the other line. There is plenty you can do for them. Them? Yes, his wife is my daughter. Lisa? Yes, Lisa. Their expecting their first child. And this could mean a big promotion for him. As in Partnership in the Company. Wow! Wow! Is right. Ben, Idon't know. Rev. Anderson's frustration rise a little at him. Look, I've already gone over all the details with you. All you need to do is A little on-line processing for me. Send a few E-mails, and so forth. Lisa's head begins to clear now , she sits up in the chair. You can do this for me right? Ben...? He said dragging out his word. I still remember what you did the night of our Christmas party and who you did it with. Uh, huh. Ellen still thinks what I told her for you that night, but I still arrange otherwise. I don't care how old she is. If it's one thing a faithful wife never forgets is an unfaithful husband. And boy you tipped with Florence that night. I thought so, I'll expect it no less. This has to be completed before Monday morning. What!! The voice

Shouted on the other line. What do you mean you're not God? I never said you were. Lisa sat up in her chair smiling. How am I supposed to do this before Monday? He asked. That's what computers are for.
Now will you help me or not? Ellen.....remember? Ok,Ok! I know somebody who's an expert at this stuff. Good, good. Said Rev. Anderson smiling. I'll just give you the name of my boy's Company. He's at Dennis and Lake Real Estate. Yes, Downtown on Wacker Dr. Send any faxes to his home. He lives right here in Chicago. Area code 312 639-5555. He gave them their e-mail address as well. As well as the Company's E-mail address. Thanks my friend., it's a real favor for these kids. You, bet. Bye now. He walks back over to Lisa smiling big at her. She gets up walking up to him. Daddy Blackmailing people.
Yes, wonderful isn't it? Ohh! She gasps again. Rev. Anderson looks at Lisa's belly jumping in all directions. The baby's really kicking up a fuss these days. Yes, he is. The little guy. That's what his father calls him too. She said smiling. Rev. Anderson puts his hand on her tummy, the baby relaxes under his touch. Here you go sweetheart, all you have to do is a few last minute

touches on these,and get Yosef and his boss to sign them. The rest you will have to do on your own, as far as filling them out, and as I said their signatures and the Company's Attorney's as well. It should be smoothe sailing for him after that.

I hope so daddy, I feel just awful about all this. I feel like it's mostly my fault for talking him into hiring Helen in the first place. Well, I wouldn't fret over all that now. It'll be just fine. You'll see. And you tell that husband of your's when he's promoted to partner, I want dinner out at the most expensive restaurant in Chicago! You got it Daddy, and thanks! I'll get on these right a way. He kissed her on the forehead. He watches her leave. Deborah comes inside. Who was that honey? Oh, just my angel that's all. Lisa! She was here! And you didn't tell me! Now dear. Don't you now dear me Benjamin. What was the matter? Is she and the baby alright? Oh, their just fine. She just needed a little help from her daddy that's all. Oh, well. She said sounding neglected, she was a little disappointed. Honey, she didn't even come into say hello to me or anything. Deborah, she had a lot on her mind, it's quite serious. But she should be ok now. And besides, there'll be plenty of time for you to spoil her when the baby's born. Come, I'll tell you all about it over a cup of cappuccino. Alright, and don't leave anything out. She said. He hugs her close, kissing her on the cheek. Lisa arrives back at home, she goes upstairs to find that her husband is still asleep. He never even heard her come in. she walked over to him, he had taken the light coverings off him, it was still very warm that night. He looked peaceful, and hansome to her. She kisses him gently on

His forehead, and lets him sleep. She looked at her watch, it was 9:00p.m. I'd better get started, I have a long night ahead of me. She said to herself. She went downstairs to Yosef's study and began to catch up on two weeks of for him and his Company. She sat down at his computer and did exactly what her father told her to do. She sent e-mails, faxes, the whole works, the processing had begun. She felt her tiredness coming on her bringing sleep with it. But she had to keep going, her husband's future, as well as the future of his Company was riding on this deal. She then felt the baby move more and more. Ow! Take it easy in there! She said. She worked long and hard at his computer getting all the forms in order. She smiled as responses from her e-mails were ansered with positive answers. Just then the fax machine rings out loud.

Shhhh! Quiet! She whispered. She went over to get the papers, it was the papers that she needed from her father's friend. He had managed to come through for them. He pulled quite a few strings, which costed him more than just her father's silence about his indescresion. But he had managed to get her what she needed for Yosef and his Boss to cinch this deal with Mr. Walden. She smiles big looking up at the ceiling.

I love you sweetheart. She went back to the computer for more writing, more filling out, e-mailing, fax-sending. On and on she worked until at last all was through! Everything that Yosef and Mr. Dennis needed for their big Meeting on Monday was finally completed! The alarm on the coffee maker sounded off early that Saturday morning. It was muggy that morning and it wasn't even 8:00a.m. yet. Yosef is awakened by the aroma of fresh coffee brewing downstairs. He was to meet Johanthan for a game of one on one today since they missed yesterday's game. He rolls over to hug his wife, but she wasn't there. He

Sits up in bed. Lisa! He yells out for her. There was no answer. Lisa! He gets out of bed and goes into the bathroom, he felt the urge to empty his bladder. He then washes his face and hands. He comes out into the hallway a little more awake this time. Lisa! Still no answer. There was no sign of her anywhere. He inhales deeply, following the aroma of the coffee downstairs to the kitchen. Lisa! He yelled louder. No response. He was beginning to worry about her. Where is that girl? He hears a gently sighing coming from out of his study. He walks inside to find her with her head down at his computer sound asleep. He hadn't a clue why she slept down here at all. Maybe she was still hurt over yesterday's events when he came home and took his anger out on her. He could still hear his voice raised at her. The sadness in her expression. Oh baby. I'm sorry, he walks over to his desk, bending down to kiss her. She stirred a little.

He rubs her tummy, which seemed like it had swollen more than before. Just then he felt something kicking underneath his hand again. It was his baby! Whoa! He breathed. Hey there little guy. He said softly kissing her tummy, I love you. He said rubbing her navel, which had popped out during her pregnancy. He stood up

smiling at her. His love growing more for her and their son. He looks over
To the right of her and sees a large folder. He picks it up and stares at it, couriosity speaking to him.
It read. *"The Elves and the Shoemaker."* Everything in it was all neatly filed, and in order by dates and times. Very professional looking. What the...? He said. He opened it up and was nearly floored at it's contents. It was all the unfinished work that Helen left him and Mr, Dennis with. But the thing about it

Now is that it was finished. Ummm. Lisa sighed. He looked over at her thinking that she was waking up. He goes over to the little sofa on the other side of the room and sits down to review the work. Oh Lisa no you didn't! he flipped through some more of the forms, all was completed in order and ready for signing from him and Mr. Dennis. His face lit up like the fourth of July! Oh baby yes you did! He jumped up off the couch dancing and leaping up in the air! He nearly hit his head on the ceiling light. Yessssss! He shouted. Oh. He said catching himself. He didn't want to wake Lisa. Oh God thank you! Thank you!
He looked down on the floor, a note had dropped out of the folder. *All things are possible to those who*
Believe." Now go Land this thing! Love Lisa. He stops his rejoicing for the moment. Seriousness coming on him.
Ummmmm. Sighed Lisa in discomfort. Yosef puts the folder down gently. Don't go anywhere. He said. He goes over to her picking her up in his arms. He kisses her gently on her soft face.

He hugs her close to him as he takes her into the living room. He lays her down on the sofa covering her with a beautiful afghan that Lisa's mother made for him. She stretched out and curled back up again smiling in her sleep. I love you. He said to her in Hebrew. He went back into the study to get his folder.
Still unable to believe that all the work that he fretted about, and hurt his wife's feelings over was now all finished. It's finished! I can't believe it's finished! He carried it back out into the living room, he looked at Lisa again. He smiled at her. He then went up stairs to shower and change into his sweats. He makes a call to his Boss to inform him of the good news. Mr. Dennis is overjoyed at what Yosef told him. He didn't tell him that it was Lisa who had come to their rescue. He himself didn't even know who else were the other "elves" that had a part in saving their

Company. He for now just kept the news to himself it would later come in handy for him as well as Lisa. he comes back down stairs. Johanthan was just coming in through the front door. You ready to get your head whipped on man? Said Johnathan spinning the ball on his index finger. Yosef smiled His confidence had returned to him. He felt as though he could walk on water after what Lisa had done for him and his Company. I smell a challenge coming on. Let's go bro.

They leave for the community center basketball court in town. Lisa is still sleeping, unaware of what she had done for her husband as well as their future. Yosef had left her a note on the coffee table that he was with Johanthan for their game. His phone call to Mr. Dennis had gone very well. They had arranged by teleconference call to set a date for the Meeting. It was definitely to take place on Monday morning at 9:00am. Sharp. Yosef and Johanthan are out on the court playing their game. It was Yosef's best game in a long time. He never played like that before! He hit nearly every basket. Showed Johanthan a few new moves. Very pretty ones. His tall lean muscular body moved like it defied the laws of gravity out there on the court. He seemed to float through the air! Johanthan finally called it quits after a while. You just too much for me today boy! What happened to you? You skunked me out there! What's up? Yosef spins the ball on his index finger this time. My wife! That incredibly beautiful girl I married. What about her?

Man do I have a story to tell you! They go into the locker room to get their things, Yosef telling him about all that had been done. Whoa! Johanthan breathed. That's what I said man. She's amazing! I mean she stayed up all night long to help me and my boss. I don't know what to say about her sometimes man. Jo, there are somethings that just don't need words. I think this is one of them. Come on let's get you home, she'll be worried about you. Yeah, she's been having a lot of discomfort lately. I really think she'll have the baby anytime now. Dr. Osborne said he's already in position. So now it's just a matter of waiting. And with that promotion coming, he couldn't come at a better time. Said johanthan patting him on the back.
Johanthan arrives back at his home with Yosef letting him off. I'll see you next Friday? You know it man.

Kiss my sister for me. I'll do that. Take care man. Later.
Johanthan drives off. Yosef gets inside the house. Lisa had
showered herself, and changed clothes. She had prepared dinner
for them. He comes inside the living room. Lisa! I'm here honey
in the kitchen! He goes inside, she was looking and feeling better
after she had, had most of the morning to sleep. You look
incredible. He said to her. Pulling her to him. Which was a little
difficult because her belly was in the way. How's my girl? Fine.
How's my beloved? Awesome! I kicked johnathan's butt on the
court! He said dancing around the kitchen. Oh, by the way, this
is for you. He kissed her on the cheek. That's from your brother.
He tells her more about their game over dinner. He helped Lisa
finish the last of the dinner dishes. They have a very enjoyable
weekend. He was overjoyed that things were looking better for
them. Now the only thing was would
California accept their Proposal? He would soon find out on
Monday.

The Colour Of Love
Anne Hemingway
Chap 45.

(1).
Monday comes in a little cooler today. Only a muggy 85 degrees.
Yosef was a little tired this morning. He was up most of the night
with Lisa. She was in discomfort all night. But that didn't put a
damper on things for him. He was too excited to notice his
tiredness. His spirits are high from his weekend with Lisa and
johanthan. And that the Land Deal was just about in the bag for
them. He was up early that morning
And especially dressed for the occasion. Today he is dressed in
his beige business suit, everything matching his personality.
Bold confident, and very professional looking. Lisa had chosen it
for him last night. He left her sleeping since she didn't sleep well
last night. I Love you baby. He said kissing her forehead, He
leaves for the office. He reaches the office, His boss and their

Client and many other representatives from Mr. Walden's Company were present. Here he is! Our boy! They all greet each other shaking hands cordially. I've heard a lot of great things about you son. You keep this kind of work up and you'll be at the top in no time flat! Thank you for your confidence in me sir. I'll do the best that I can.

Ahh! That's the spirit! A man who knows where he's going, and not afraid of the trip there! Said Mr. Walden. He himself was a very tall distinguished white man. Silver haired, a very experienced, and well revered man in his field. He has a kind heart, but a short fuse at times. Well shall we get started? Said Mr. Dennis. Let's. Said Mr. Walden. They all sit down to discuss the Deal. Everything went smoothly, as Yosef made his presentation, as well as their proposal. Looks good! Said Mr. Walden. Well I think we should make contact with our Land Contractors in California, and see what happens. Yosef and Mr. Dennis look at each other. Hoping that Lisa and her father's friends made the right connections with the right people at the right time. Yosef goes over to the computer, to begin the processing. He pulls up the
Proposal on line. It showed that all that they needed was in order, and ready. Mr. Dennis and Yosef both let out a sigh of relief as they watched Mr. Walden review the computer screen. He was a very meticulous man, everything had to be done just right. If one thing was not in order, he would drop it like a bad habit.
He absoulutely hated delays. He reviews the paperwork that Lisa had finished. Very nicely done, very professional. Good work men, good work. I'm liking this already. He smiled at them. More sighs of

Relief from Yosef and Mr. Dennis. Ok, gentlemen, one last thing and we're in business. Said Yosef confidently. He hits one of the buttons on the computer. It makes it's usual computer noises letting them know it's processing through. Then the words. RECEIVED DATA. Flashed across the screen. Then the word. PROCESSING. Flashes. They all wait with anxiety for the final word. Then it comes from
California. The word. ACCEPTED! Flashed accrossed the screen! The screen did a little more flashing as they saw a Bald Eagle soaring into the blue of the sky. It landed majestically on a

395

snowcapped mountaintop. The words   THE DEAL HAS
LANDED!   CONGRATULATIONS !!!   Flashed across! They all
jumped out of their seats, hugging and shaking hands with each
other. The Deal has landed! Shouted Mr. Dennis.   They look
back at the screen. The Eagle sqwaking it's victory! Yosef had
tears in his eyes, as did Mr. Dennis.   Thank you Yeshua for my
wife. He said under his breath.

(2).

Helen was seated at her desk when the phone rings. Dennis and
Lake Real Estate. Hello, Helen? This is Lisa. Helen's expression
changed to one of disgust for her.   Oh, uh. Hi Lisa. What is it?
Is my husband available? It's an emergency! She pauses a
moment. He's not here right now. Can I take a message? Helen,
I need to speak with him immediately. I'm in labor! The baby's
coming! Please I need him to call me please! Ok, I'll see what I
can do to track him down for you. She said, jealously filling her
tone.
Nearly ½ hour goes by. Yosef and his boss and their new client
are still making plans for the new structure that will go up soon
out in California. Yosef takes out a rough draft of the building
that he had drawn up himself. He shows the drawings to them.
Both boss and client are impressed with his work.   More phone
calls are made to Major Architech Companies for planning on the
New Building. Helen's phone rings again. It was Lisa. Her
contractions were coming a little faster and harder now. Helen, Is
Yosef back yet?
She said. Somewhat out of breath.   Anxiety coming on her. She
stuttered a little. Yeah, Yes he is, but he's in a very important
meeting, I can't disturb him right now Lisa, This is a very
important deal for him and Mr. Dennis.   Helen, I'm aware of the
deal, but our baby is a priority! Please! Call him for me! Lisa,
calm down! I'll go tell him right now ok? That's what she said.
But her heart was far from telling Yosef
Anything about Lisa being in labor. Helen hangs up the phone.
She was still very envious of Lisa and Yosef. Not only was she
married to him, but she was about to give birth to his baby. That
should be me not you! She fumed. And to think I was gonna
save your life for you. I should've let him kill you! She fired. She

sat at her desk her thoughts on hurting Lisa.   My Billy's in
prison because of you! And you're gonna pay! She said in a very
nasty tone. She knew that she would be calling back again if she
didn't hear from Yosef soon. So to keep her from getting through.
She puts the phone on voice mail. Then she purposely tied up
the other line. Another hour goes by. The phone rings and rings
off the hook. Helen looks over to see the phone recording the
message. She knew it was Lisa. She rolls her eyes at the phone.

She smiles a little, then continues her conversation with Judy,
who was telling her about Yosef and Lisa's wedding. Well what
do you say gentlemen, shall we break out the Champagne, and
toast to our little Venture? Said Mr. Walden. Yosef Looks at Mr.
Dennis. You're the boss! He said. Boy you rule! He said to him.
Yosef laughs out loud. Jo, I'm darn proud of you boy. We never
could've pulled this off
Without you! Well I can't take all the credit for this sir.   What do
you mean? I have the love and the prayers and the support of a
good wife who loves me and supports the work that I do.   I
couldn'tve gotten through this without her. If it haden't been for
her, we never would've landed this thing. What did she do son?
Asked Mr. Walden.   Well, let's just say that I'm grateful that she
has experience in this area when she used to work for her father.
Who is her father? He asked again. Rev. Anderson. Benjamin
Anderson?
Yes sir, you know him? Yes I do, I've known him for years, we've
been collegues forever. Great man, and friend he's been to a lot of
people, and other respective Real Estate Companies.   Well
Joseph, I must say that this was by far the finest piece of work
that I've ever seen in all my career.   Your wife is quite a girl eh?
He and Mr. Dennis look at each other. Eh. They both said.
Yosef thought on what Lisa had done for them again. The Elves
and the Shoemaker. He whispered. What was that Jo?   Asked
Mr. Dennis. Oh, I was just thinking about a childrens's story
that's all. He smiled. I Love You Lisa. He whispered again. How
about lunch, I'm starved? I could eat a horse and his shoes.
They all laugh together.   Mr. Walden pours another glass of
champagne.   Joseph, you're not having any? Uh, no thanks
none for me sir. I don't like Champage. He remembers when he
got drunk and sick that night.   He looks at the time. It was
11:45 a.m. Yosef, get your things and come with me. Said Mr.
Dennis. He goes over to his desk drawer, pulling out the keys
that he showed Yosef a few months ago. Mr. Walden would you

Like to come with us? Sure, what's all this? This is for the new
Partner in our Real Estate Company. Mr. Walden looks at them
both smiling. For the man who Landed one of the biggest Deals
our Company has ever seen. I'm proud to announce Mr. Joseph
Epstein as Senior Partner in Dennis and Lake and Epstien
Real estate Company! Yosef was speechless as Mr. Dennis takes
him into his new office! Yosef choked up a little. Whoa! He
breathed. I don't know what to say sir. Say nothing, you've
earned this one.   I told you, you land this for us, and you'll have
this office right next to mine. I'm a man of my word Yosef.
Always remember that. Said Mr. Dennis. I will sir, I will. And
I'll work even harder now. I have a lot of responsibilities at home
now sir. I know you will son.   Yosef looked as though he would
burst at the seams he was so thrilled at his new promotion.   He
grabs Mr. Dennis dancing with him. Yahhhooooo!
He yelled out loud. Mr. Dennis and Mr. Walden laugh with him.
I can't wait to tell Lisa! He shouted.

Oh, how is she? No baby yet? Asked Mr. Dennis. No, not yet.
He said. Oh, you're gonna be a father? Asked Mr. Walden. Yes
sir, any day now.   How long have you been married son? Asked
Mr. Walden.
Eight and half months now.   And you're gonna have a baby
already? That's right. Boy! That must've been some honeymoon!
Said Mr. Walden laughing. Yosef thought a moment on his
wedding night. He smiles from ear to ear. That it was sir. That it
was.   They all walk back out into Mr. Dennis' office. Yosef was
about to walk out the door when his cell phone rings. It was Lisa.
Yo! He said still smiling,
Yosef! She said out of breath, I've been trying to get a hold of you
all morning! Lisa! What's the matter?
He could hear the anxiety in her voice, she had been crying. It's
the baby! He's coming! I called this morning and told Helen. She
said you were gone! Wait a minute, you called me this morning?
Yes, and she said that you had left, I tried to call back, she said
you were in a meeting and couldn't disturb you.   I told her it
was an emergency about he baby. Honey, I hurt! I hurt bad!
The contractions are coming about every few minutes now! Mr.
Dennis and Mr. Walden stand there looking at each other. Yosef
walks over to the office door and peeks out. Helen was still on the

phone! I tried to get you, but when you never returned my calls. I got worried. Honey will you be able to get a way at all today? I really need you! She cried. I'll be there as soon as I can, I'm on my way alright? Just try to calm down Lisa. I'm coming! He hangs up his cell phone. Yosef, what's happened. My wife is in labor, seems like she started this morning.

She called here to tell me, and Helen didn't put any of her calls through. What! They both said. They all march out into the outer office where Helen was still very engaged in her conversation. Yosef hangs up her line. What the! She turns around to see them all staring in disgust at her. My wife called to let me know

She's in labor and you didn't tell me! He said through his teeth. I, I. Helen stammered. Is this true Helen? Not really, she called, and asked for you. But she didn't say anything about the baby. She never said anything to me about an emergency at all. I asked her if she wanted to leave a message. She said no. that's all I swear. She was lying and they knew it. How many times did she call here? He asked her.

Just once. I was on the other line taking some inventory, and cleaning up some orders. Ysoef then noticed the red light on the message phone blinking off and on. He hits the answer button. "You have 15 new messages." The voice spoke. They were all from Lisa. All stating emergency about the baby. He glares at her. She swallowed hard. What kind of an animal are you! He said through his teeth again,his face clenched tight. His anger boiling at her. I didn't know! I was on the other line! I have to go now, I'm sorry, but I can't have lunch with you. Son go to your wife now! Said Mr. Walden. Yosef grabs his suit coat and his briefcase and starts to leave. He stops at the front door. He looks back at Helen. Oh by the way. You're fired! Mr. Walden and Mr. Dennis stare at her wanting to tear her limb from limb. Looks like your boy's gonna need a new secretary. Looks like. Said Mr. Dennis. You heard him. Get up and get out! Said Mr. Dennis. Oh, I'll be putting in a little call to your probation officer for you, they'll need to know your new position in the unemployment line. Helen drops her head fear coming on her. She knew what this meant for her. She begins to clear her desk, slamming things around. To start her new unemployed life, as well as a nice little stretch of time in jail for loosing her job. Strange how jealousy can just make the life of the one so

insensed by it plain miserable! Just look at the last five letters in the word.
LOUSY! Which is what Helen feels about now.

The Colour Of Love
Anne Hemingway
Chap. 46.

Yosef throws his things into the car leaving to go home, when his cell rings again. Yo! Beloved, it's me!
Lisa! Honey, the baby's coming faster now! Give me that phone! The voice said in the background.   Hello! The voice spoke again. Who's this? Asked Yosef. This is Mamie. He lets out a sigh of relief.
Jo talk to this girl, her contractions are coming about every three minutes now! And that's just too close for me to deal with. I don't do babies! I don't think she can hold on much longer! Mamie, can you get her to the hospital for me? And I'll just meet you there? We're trying! We, we who? Me and Johanthan. Oh thank God! You're both there with her. She's really scared Jo. Please talk to this girl before she has this baby right here on the living room floor! Let me talk back with her. He said. Lisa. Said Mamie handing the phone back to her. Hello. She was still crying. Lisa, I want you to go with Mamie and Johnathan you hear me? I can't, I'm so scared. She cried. I'm know you're scared baby, But I need you to go with them now ok? Look, I'm not gonna make it in time to take you myself. Please Lisa!   She pauses a little. Will you be there with me at the hospital? She asked softly. I promise. I never break a kiss remember? She smiles. Ok Beloved. I'll see you there we're leaving now. That's my girl. I'll be there as soon as I can. I'm on my way now alright? Ok. I love you Yosef. I love you too baby. He hangs up his cell. Relieved that her family is there to take care of her, and get her to the hospital. Johanthan and Mamie arrive with Lisa to Saints Of Mercy Hospital. They get her checked in. Yosef will take care of

all the Insurance information when he arrives. Lisa is taken immediately up to the Maternity ward. She is examined and taken to the labor room. Yosef arrives 15 minutes later, he fills out all the paperwork, and is then escorted up to the reception area on the Maternity ward Elizabeth Epstein please! Right this way sir. The Nurse takes him to her room. Lisa opens her eyes and sees him standing there talking with Mamie and Johanthan.

Yosef! He looks at her. Baby! He said to her. His excitement coming on him. He comes in to her, sitting down on the side of the bed cradling her in his arms. It hurts! She cried. Shhhh! I'm here now, try to relax ok? She holds on to him tightly. He rubs her back gently she sighs a little. He kisses her gently on the cheek. Mamie walks in the room. Boy! I'm so glad you're here! Me too! He said. Just then he feels Lisa's body relaxing in his arms. The medicine was kicking in. He laid her down gently. No, please don't leave me honey, you just got here. She said. Hugging him closer to her. Her voice sounded tired. Honey, lay down, ok. Shhhh. I'm right here, I'm not leaving you alright? He lays her back down. She slowly closed her eyes. Drifting off slightly. He smiles at her. He looks at mamie. Let's go out here. He said. What happened to you? I thought you would've been here a lot sooner. I could've been, but my former secretary didn't put any of Lisa's calls through when she called me this morning to tell me about the baby.
What! Gasped Mamie. Yeah, then she lied about me being gone most of the morning. Then to top it all off, she tied up the other line to keep her from getting through to me.   My God Yosef. Has Helen flipped?

Seems like it. What happens with her now? Like I said. My Former secretary.   I fired her right on the spot. He holds his head down looking at Lisa. If anything happens to her and the baby...? Now, Jo. Their both fine. Lisa's a strong woman.   You married a real trooper there. He smiles at her. Yeah, that she is. A sigh comes out of the room. Lisa was awakened by another contraction. Her labor was more intense this time. Nurse! Yosef yelled. They all came flying down the hall! They do a quick pelvic exam on her.   Jesus! Get Dr. Osborne in here quick! We got a 10 going on here! She's fully dialated! Come on sir! You're about to become a Father! Said the tall Black orderly. He grabs Yosef and takes him to get suited up in a pair of scrubs taking him along with Lisa to the Delivery room.   Lisa is moved onto the

delivery table, as the Nurse gets her prepared and ready. Yosef stands behind her supporting her. All are waiting for the Dr. to arrive. Which he does fast! Dr. Lonnie Osborne arrives on the scene. A fine young
40ish tall and very handsome Jewish Obsetrician. The nurse helps him get scrubbed, helping him with his rubber gloves. He goes over to Lisa to check her one last time. Oh Yosef! Sighed Lisa, as she squeezes his hand a little. I'm right here baby. He takes a small towel that was soaked in ice water laying it on her forehead. That feels good. She said to him. He smiled at her kissing her gently. Ok, let's see what we have going on here. How's Lisa today? Miserable! She said. Laughing a little. I don't know about you, but I'm hurtin! She said in a home girl tone. Yosef turns his head laughing. All bust out laughing with her. Well it'll all be over soon Lisa. Mr. Epstien how are you today sir? I'll let you know after this is all over with. He said. They all laugh again. He looks under the hospital sheets. The baby's head was crowning now. Very nice. He's coming along just fine. He sits down in position, the Nurse comes over

all the others standing by awaiting the new arrival. Yosef waits for the Dr. to signal Lisa. Ok Lisa I want you to push and push hard! Yosef helps her sit up a little. Push Lisa! He cheered. She pushes hard. Come on, one more time! Said Dr, Osborne. She pushes again. The baby's head shows Mr. Epstien look up into the Mirror. He looks up and sees his son's head coming. His eyes fill with tears. Ok Lisa push!
Said the Dr. She pushes again. This time the baby's head and neck are delivered. The Dr. turns him slightly suctioning out his little mouth. Rest a little. He said. Lisa eases off. Yosef strokes her head for her. Ok girl let's do it again! Said Dr. Osborne. Push Lisa! Yosef sits her up again. She pushes hard. The baby's shoulders and mid section emerge. Good girl! He said. Ok one more time you're almost there he said. How there are we? She said panting hard. They laughed again. This one should do it. Ok Lisa one good one! Here we go! Push hard! Come on baby you can do it! Cheered Yosef. Uhhhhh! She grunts as the baby's whole body slides out! The Dr. takes the baby sitting him on Lisa's tummy! Oh my God! Look at him! Beloved! Look at him! He kicks his little legs, his arms flying all over the place! Jesus! Lisa! He's incredible! They couldn't stop their own tears from flowing as they watched the tiny life that once kicked around

inside her, now kicking around on top of her. Ok daddy, get over here and cut this cord. I'm not gonna do everything around here! He goes over to the Dr, and his new baby, the Dr. gives him the scissors. He cuts the cord, the Dr, clamps it off. As he cut the cord, something happened inside of him. A sense of accomplishment. He had landed the biggest deal in the history of his Company, was then promoted to partner. Now he watched the birth of his first born child. All in one day! His words left him for the moment. Nurse would you please for me. Said Dr, Osborne. She comes over and takes the baby wrapping him In a blue blanket. She takes him over to the other nurses. Yosef watches as the nurses clean the infant off. He weighed in at 7lbs. 10oz. 19 inches in length. He wails as his tiny body is cleaned and dressed. They wrap him in warm blankets and bring him over to his parents. The nurse places him in Lisa's arms. He's beautiful Lisa! Said Yosef, tears streaming down his face. He had plenty of dark hair just like his father. He promptly starts to suckle at his mother's breast. Hungry little thing aint he? Said the Nurse. The Dr. Looks at Yosef. You two got a name for your new son? He looks at Lisa.

Yes we do Dr. His name is Benjamin, Jacob Epstein. She said smiling at Yosef. He smiles back at her.

Sounds like a winner to me. Said Yosef. Lisa is filled with just as much excitement as her husband as she watches her little one falling slowly asleep in her arms. She kisses him gently. Yosef. She calls to him.
He comes over to her. Here you go papa. She said smiling at him handing him his new son. He looks at her. Taking him into his arms. The baby looked like a small doll in his huge arms. Oh Lisa! He breathed.

Tears still flowing down his face. Look at him! She chuckles to herself a little. As she watched her husband and baby together. Tears streaming down her face as well. He's so beautiful! He was too overwhelmed to say anything. He couldn't take his eyes off him. The baby looked up at him, making cooing sounds. Whoa! Breathed Yosef. He let out a soft yawn, and fell asleep in his father's arms.

The man is hooked! Said the Nurse. Like a fish! Said the other nurse. They all smile together. Yosef looks at Lisa. I can't believe you did this! I mean he's awesome! I did have a little help didn't I? Yosef smiles more as he kisses his baby again cradling him close to his face. He's so soft. Yes he is. She said smiling. He comes over to her handing him back to her. He strokes her soft curls. I love you Lisa. I love you too Beloved. He kisses her gently on the lips. Now, isn't that how you two got in here in the first place! Said the older white nurse. If they don't stop it, they'll be back in here again. Yosef stops kissing Lisa looking at them. Oh we plan on it! Don't we baby? Anything you say beloved, anything you say.

Yosef goes out into the hall to tell Johanthan and Mamie the good news. It's a boy! They both are overjoyed at the news They get on the phone and call Rev. Anderson and Rabbi and Sarah. It's a Boy! It's a boy! They all shouted together. I knew my angel could do it! Laughed Rev. Anderson. Deborah could not stop her tears from flowing as she remembered the night that she gave birth to Lisa. As did Sarah the day that she gave birth to Yosef. The news of the baby's birth spread quickly through the neighborhood. Lisa is released from the hospital two days later. Yosef arrives home with his new family only to find that there was a surprise welcome home party for them! All the grand parents fuss over the little arrival to the family. Pictures were taken of them. Rabbi and Rev. Anderson both pronouce a blessing over the new parents and their firstborn child. Three weeks pass by. It's Sunday morning. It's the baby's Christening Ceremony. All gather at Rev. Anderson's Church. Both Grandfather's officiating the Service. 15 months past by quickly. Yosef and Lisa announce that they are expecting again. She later gives birth to another beautiful son. This one named after his father. Daniel Joseph Epstein. At his birth, Yosef remembered what the Angel spoke to him. *"She will bear you three children. Two sons, and a daughter."* *"As it is spoken, so shall it be."* Yosef and Lisa share much in their new life together. His promotion to Partner in his Company. The births of their two sons. They hope that as they embark on their journey through life that they can instill in their children the same morals and values that were instilled in them when they were children. They would teach their children the beauty of both their Cultures, and learn from others. They would teach them about embracing all of Humanity with the hope that they themselves have taken part in the breaking down of the colour barrier, and that through their example that helped to

Build the bridges that will bring the entire Race of Man together as One under the Hand of God So that when their children become parents themselves they too would know the true meaning of Love. As they have learned. They would see beyond the Colour of skin, and see the True Colour of Love. It is a love that is from the heart. A heart that dares to love as God Himself loves. A love that dares to dream in the impossible, and through faith hope and Love believes that with God all things are possible to those who believe.   And that He is faithful to those who are faithful to Him.   He watches over His Word to perform it in the lives of those who would reach out from their hearts and grab ahold of his Promises. As Yosef and Lisa proved. And that True Love sees no Colour....No Colour at all........ God Bless you.

Oh, by the way. Yosef and Lisa are expecting again!

Finis.

As I look back to the year 2000 when I began writing this work, I can't help but remember my thoughts being pulled in several different directions all at once! I had no idea as to how to write something like this

But all that I know is that, as you have read throughout it's pages, that you'll not see it as a story about two young lovers filled with a deep longing desire to spend the rest of their lives together. But as a story about

How God Himself desires even more than they to touch the hearts and the minds, the very lives of people all over the world with His Love. The two main characters themselves show a love that most of us have either written off, or never even believed could be possible in today's society of easy marriage, and even more easy divorce! But understand something reader. God is not so easily written off! He loves us with

A love that is unfathomable to man! And He'll do whatever it takes to win the heart of that one, that Community, that Church, That Nation! When I started to write The Colour Of Love on May 21, 2000.

I had just been newly divorced. I like Ms. Sarah had not known the true love of a man, nor was I permitted to give of that love that God had placed in my heart for my husband at that that time. Just as my love was rejected by my ex-husband. How we as a people have treated whole other Nations the same way. We have

Shut out the way I was shut out from him. We were denied a chance a right to live amongst those who differ from us the way that I was shut out in my marriage. Blacks treated unfairly, Jews nearly exterminated off the face of the Earth! And all for what? Whose trying to prove what to whom?

I saw a very startling Scripture in the Book of Malachi, it reads.....

Have we all not ONE FATHER? Has not ONE GOD CREATED US? Why do we deal treacherously with one another? Malachi 2:10

Then in Job 31:15 God says this to us. *Did not He who made me in the womb make them?*

Did not the SAME ONE fashion us in the womb? What is God saying to us through these Scriptures?

He is saying to us that I God have created all Men, I fashioned one nation in the womb, just like I fashioned another. And from them, birthed the Race of Man. What makes one Nation of people feel that they are more than another, when we all share the same commonality? We were all fashioned and Created by the very hands of God Himself! The same God that made the Black man is the same God that make the White man, the Native American man, the German man, the Jewish man. And all Men together. How foolish is is for us to think that we are superior to another Culture of people, and they inferior to us. When God is saying None of this is so! I made man in My Image and My Likeness! Have we forgotten Genesis 1:26

"Let us make man in Our Image, and Our Likeness. Let them have dominion over the fish of the sea, and the birds of the air, and over the cattle over all the earth, and over every creeping thing that creeps on the earth. It further reads that God made man, then He blessed man. As you read back through this verse notice what it didn't way. He never said let man have dominion over man. He said let them have dominion over all the other creations of God, He lists them there. Fish, birds, cattle etc. We have so left the Divine Order of God's plan for man, that we have poisoned the very esscence of His nature that once ruled within us. We have accepted prejudice and race hatred as a "normal" way of life instead of the way that He intended it to be. I've learned one thing, and that is prejudice is not inborn in the heart of any man. It is instilled there it is taught and learned. How this displeases the heart of God. What will we say to Him

when we have to stand before Him in the day of Judgement and give an account for the way in which we have so dealt with one another? How will we justify ourselves, our injustices towards our fellowman, in the face of His Pure Judgements? He and only He is the True and Just Judge. And His Judgements are always Loving and Fair. God tells us to *"if it is at all possible (and it is). As much as it depends on you, live peaceable with ALL MEN!" Rom 12:18.* Oh! How we have failed at this! How dare we brag about our "Religion." We we can't even stand in the same place and Worship the same God who made me, just as He made you! We scoff at Pentecostals, Mock the Catholics, Shun the Jews. Ridicule the rest. When

none of these actions follow the Love rule of I Cor chap 13. Go
there and read what it says. And tell me if any of the above
mention actions are found there? I assure you they are not.
This deeply troubles me in my spirit. God tells us to Let
brotherly love continue. Do we do this? Have we written God off
to do things in our Churches our Schools, our Nations the way
that we feel fit, and only call upon Him when there is a Tradegty
like the horrible one that we all witnessed on Sept 11.2001?
Instead of heeding His Commandment of Love, we have
substituted His love for hatred. Not realizing that it is the very
cancer that has eaten away the very fabric that binds and holds a
Nation, a people together. I feel that another
Scripture is in order here. Then I'll try to close this with a very
much needed prayer. Let's look at Psalms
62:9-10. It reads.

"Surely men of low degree are a vapor (a puff of wind)
and Men of high degree are a lie (or a delusion). If they
could be weighed on the scales (of God's Justice). They
all together would weigh less than a breath!"

Men in the lowest state of life, as well as Men of the highest share
that same thing. In their lowest state of ruin, as well as in their
highest state of glory. If you with all of your fullest could be
weighed in God's eyes
All of us together the low and forgotten to the high and mighty.
We all would weigh less than a Breath!
I think that should take the wind out some of our sails a bit. The
Bible further tells us not to think more of ourselves than we do
another. But to esteem one another higher than we do ourselves!
See we've had that backwards. But God can in His love and
Mercy can help us turn that thing back around again. If we'll let
Him. He's willing to help the life of that one that is willing to
receive His love, His Compassion. All of His fullness, It is
available to those who will dare ask and receive. In closing I want
to say this. I may sound abrasive to some reading this. But
Hatred is serious, Prejdice is serious. In fact it is darn right
lethal! And it must be dealt with harshly! Look at how many
lives have suffered and died because of it.

I'm pretty mild compared how God Himself will deal with the problem.   God will deal with it harshly, but with you in Love. Ahhh love that word that oozes over me like warm honey!   How I love loving.   I guess you could say that I'm in love with Loving. For if I cannot love, I am nothing! I can only but pray That this story will cause us all to re-examine ourselves and take a deep look into our hearts and allow God to bring to the surface any hidden prejudices lurking there. For if it be found and left to fester, it shall make a home there.   I want to leave you with this prayer asking God to once and for all to deliver you from the Sin of Prejudice and racisim.

A Racisist's Prayer for forgiveness.

Oh God in Heaven, I come to You, asking you to forgive me Racisim, and prejdice. I ask You to melt away from my heart All the heaviness, the hardness that has left me indifferent and Judgemental. Cleanse from me by the Precious Blood of Your Dear Son Jesus Christ, all the bitterness, and the pain, all the Hatred that I've held inside my heart against those who differ From me either racially or Spiritually. Father let me experience Love the way that You love. And compassion of heart like Yours Beautify my life with you Holiness, purify me totally, and forgive Me Lord. I yield myself to You,a nd I trust You to do a deep inner work In my heart. I'm so sorry for all that my hatred has done in Your sight. Forgive me, as I forgive those who have hated me as well.   Deliver me And bring me to that place in my life where I can live peacable with all Mankind. In the Name of Jesus. Amen.

The Sinners Prayer.

Oh God in Heaven. I come to you a sinner. I know that
Cannot save myself, I cannot deliver myself from sin. But
Now I come to you asking you to save me Father God
Save me from sin, and deliver me from the eternal punishment
Of hell itself. Wash me clean in the Blood of Jesus. I receive
You Lord Jesus, I make you the Lord of my life. I believe in my
Heart and confess with my mouth, that Jesus is Lord. I believe
That you died on the Cross for me. And that You served my
sentence
In hell for me. And that on the third day You were raised from the
dead
By the Glory of the Father. You ascended into the Heavens, where
You
Ever liveth to make Intercession for me and that You are to soon
return
For Your Church. Now according to Your Word in Romans 10:8-9-
10
That if I believe in my heart and confess with my mouth the Lord
Jesus I
Would be saved. For with the heart man believes unto
Righeousness, and with
The mouth confession is made unto Salvation. I Cor 5:17 says. If
any Man be in
Christ, he is a New Creation. Old things have passed away. And
Behold all things
Have become new! Thank you Lord for saving me. I'm now a child
of God!

For all of you having prayed the first prayer. That is the first step
to the second prayer. If you've prayed that prayer and meant it in
your heart. Then I say welcome to the Family of God. And.........

I'll see you In Heaven."

I   Love   You.....

True Love really doesn't see any Colour....No Colour at all.......

In His Love and mine

Anne Hemingway.

ISBN 1412006562

9 781412 006569